For John,

The Times of Malthus

Miles M Hudson

Miles Hudson

Ⓑ PENFOLD BOOKS

Published by Penfold Books
87 Hallgarth Street
Durham DH1 3AS
England

Author's website:
mileshudson.com

ISBN: 978-1-83812-587-5

Copyright © Miles Hudson 2023
Cover Design by Mecob

The right of Miles Hudson to be identified as the author of this work has been asserted in accordance with the Copyright Designs and Patents Act 1988.

This book is a work of fiction. Names, places, organisations and incidents are either fictitious or they are used fictitiously. Any resemblance to actual events or places or persons, living or dead, is entirely coincidental.

All rights reserved.
No part of this publication may be reproduced, stored in or introduced into a retrieval system or transmitted in any form or by any means electronic, photomechanical, photocopying, recording or otherwise without the prior written permission of the publisher. Any person who does any unauthorised act in relation to this publication may be liable to criminal prosecution.

Acknowledgements

The inspiration for the audiopt surveillance series of stories was a TV interview with Edward Snowden.

Amazing help and support in turning that inspiration into this finished book came from: Jane Hamilton for her awesome work throughout every stage of the production of this story; Kirsten Crombie's eagle eyes; all my beta readers, especially Carol Hudson; great editing work from Gary Gibson; wonderful cover design work from Mark Ecob; Jason and Janet Covell's hospitality, and long-standing support from the ever-incredible Stacy Miles.

About the Author

Miles Hudson loves words and ideas.

He's a physics teacher, surfer, author, hockey player, inventor, backpacker and idler.

Miles was born in Minneapolis but has lived in Durham in northern England for more than 30 years.

Miles M Hudson

Friday 18 May 2040
Some way into our future.

'It's our only chance – we've got to get away from this place, or we'll all be dead in a month.' Loshie's whisper sounded loud, in the dark at the back wall of their small beachfront hideout.

'Shhh. They'll hear us.' Ellie took her hand away from Clara's mouth and put it over Loshie's instead.

King Alfred continued barking intermittently.

Through the sliver of a gap, where the solid oak door met the door frame, Ellie could make out the silhouette of a figure wavering back and forth. She felt the solid wall against her shoulder and hoped he would give up searching for them.

Four women and a dog in a one-room, brick hut under Brighton's main promenade road would be easy pickings for the raiders from along the coast. So far, though, the men would only know for sure that a dog was present behind the thick door.

The summer heat was stifling, as the two women and two children crouched together. Ellie could feel sweat from Loshie's face trickling over her fingers.

Loshie pulled her head away from Ellie's hand and hissed, 'They'll kill us and probably eat us. If not today, then tomorrow, or next week.'

Ellie whispered straight into Loshie's ear. 'If you don't shut up, it *will* be today.'

The lumbering figure pressed its head right up to the gap. The women froze and clutched hands back over the mouths of their daughters. Ellie closed her eyes and held her breath.

King Alfred charged the door, now growling. The shadow jerked back, probably only able to make out a pair of red eyes hurling themselves towards the door. Angry dog pheromones were bound to have permeated the man's nose. Ellie smiled at the thought that the Essex Raider outside their beachside stronghold was probably just as grateful for the thick door as she and Loshie were in that moment. The brute moved away out of view, but they could hear little over King Alfred's ongoing barks and growls.

The Times of Malthus

'Alfie, shush.' Ellie wanted to gain as much intelligence about the raiding party as possible, without being seen, heard, or discovered.

'Lucky they left their dog locked in – sounds right vicious.' The drawling accent from a few miles away was easy for Ellie to differentiate from the more trill Brighton voices she'd grown up with. *Definitely Essex Raiders.* It wasn't a great leap of logic: the Essex Raiders were dominant on this stretch of coastline, and she and Loshie had both lost loved ones in battles between them and the Brighton Defence Force. Young Clara had discovered a dead body on the beach not 200 yards away, only ten days earlier.

'That means there'll be food in there though,' the voices outside continued.

Ellie caught her breath and felt Clara tense up. She was only ten years old but had grown up with famine and fear. The memorial cairn out front, yards from their door, was a daily reminder of the dangers of living in the Times of Malthus.

The corpse she had found, stinking on the beach, was a victim of the ever-present violence. He had been dead more than a day by then, and the women had been unable to move his body from the place he fell. May 2040 had been nearly thirty degrees all day every day. The gushing red fountain from a stomach knife wound was a solid black mass by the time Clara found him. Half the blackness had been the congealed and sun-baked blood, and half had been a swarm of flies born right there into a rich food source.

'Well, I'm not about to open the door and let that dog at us.'

On cue, King Alfred began barking again.

Another, similar male voice shouted down from the promenade above, 'Get up here! We found the motherlode in the hotel up here.'

Loshie's head turned sharply, just visible in the dim light that crept in around the door frame.

Ellie mouthed, 'Did we leave something up there?'

Loshie shrugged.

The raider at the door called up, 'Where we found the veg growing on the balconies before?'

The other voice laughed, 'Yeah, they never learn. On the roof this time. Proper manna from heaven.'

The discussion continued at an ever-decreasing volume as the men wandered away. Ellie hugged Clara's skinny body close to her and kissed the top of her daughter's head. King Alfred's barking reduced in tempo until she appeared uncertain as to whether to continue it at all, giving a yap every several seconds.

Loshie touched her Armulet, and the device glowed gently on her forearm illuminating the whole of the interior of the archway lock-up. She turned back and looked Ellie straight in the eye. 'We cannot stay here. Hereford is only a few days away. It's safe there. The girls will be able to play in the woods, and there's enough food for all their people and loads left over. They just give the food away.'

'So you keep saying, but I'm really not sure it actually exists. I mean–'

Loshie's interruption was sardonic. 'You don't think Hereford exists? The place they used to make all the cider? You know, the capital of Herefordshire.' Her voice squeaked a little at the end.

'What I'm saying is I'm not sure it's this Shangri-La safe haven you say is there.'

'I told you; I met a man who was there only two weeks ago.'

Ellie nodded. She couldn't bring herself to tell her friend that she thought she had become fixated on an idea, a hope, something that would probably destroy them.

The Times of Malthus

Miles M Hudson

Book 1

Earlier Times

The Times of Malthus

Saturday 16 July 2016

More than twelve years before the Times of Malthus.

Ellie and Loshie thought they were so outrageous. In their mid-teens, they would go down to Brighton pier and the promenade on Saturday nights and let the older boys from London chat them up and buy them drinks. The boys would be down for a weekend of carousing at the seaside, and there'd be hordes of them spilling out of the bars onto the beach.

The girls wore thin summer dresses, partly to tease them, but as much to show off to each other. Their changing hormones pushed Ellie and Loshie into contradictory behaviours. Intelligent, ardent feminists, they happily double-thinked their way around the trendy clothes shops of a Saturday afternoon. In a typical high street fashion outlet, one typical conversation might go:

'I love that dress on you. You look amazing.'

'You really think so?'

'Deffo. Those London boys won't be able to keep their hands off you.'

'Well, they'd better. Just coz a girl looks good is no excuse for getting all handsy.'

'I know. Did you read about that judge who said the woman deserved it because she wore a short skirt?'

'I know; awful. In fact, my mum wrote an article about that case.'

'Which one?'

'Roisin.'

'Your mums are so cool. I wish mine was. She just does whatever Father says.'

'Don't be so hard on them! It's obvious they love each other. Not that I'm ever going to get married.'

'Not unless Harry Styles gives me a call!'

'Ha, no! Anyway, do you think I should get this?'

'For sure. You look so good in it.'

Ellie would always remember the night in mid-July 2016. In later life, when recounting the story to her grandson, Jack, she'd often mis-remember it as being in 2015. Either way, it was not even a month after the summer solstice, and the sine curve of changing day length was still languidly rolling, unprepared for its sudden acceleration down towards the equinox. Past eleven o'clock, it was still light enough to wander the beach haunts.

They were out at a beach bar called Atlanta, two days before Loshie's birthday. A group of boys from London had been showing off all evening. The girls had chatted with them, playing some pool, and drinking too many shots. Sometimes the boys would touch them. Always as an accident, maybe having to squeeze too tightly behind them in the packed bar.

It was a game they had played week in, week out, all summer since finishing their GCSEs. Every unwanted touch was remarked upon, the volume of their comments dependent on how intrusive it had been, and how much they liked the boy in question.

When she reflected back in later life, Ellie figured that they had just been extremely lucky. The dangers that men posed were very real. In their innocence, the two friends had thought that waving red flags at these bulls was OK, because they had right on their side.

The sun had set around nine o'clock, but the summer sky never darkened completely. Ellie romantically believed it was the light from the sun still illuminating their high latitude country. At the shallow summer angles, just below the horizon all night, she imagined sunlight scattering in the upper atmosphere to keep Brighton's small hours vaguely lit. More likely, it was light pollution from the urban sprawl all around, plus the lights from the promenade bars that spilled right onto the shingle beach where they stood.

To celebrate Loshie's impending birthday, they decided that a midnight skinny-dip in the sea would be a fun thing to do. The young men they had been flirting with through the evening were wide-eyed at the suggestion, but the girls reckoned their macho bonding was too much to let them join in. A willing one-on-one was one thing, but a whole gang of drunken lads was skirting too close to the wind for safety, even for a pair that thought they knew

The Times of Malthus

it all.

Telling the boys that there was plenty more tequila to be drunk, Ellie promised they would return to the bar afterwards. It was a standard evening out for Loshie and Ellie, so they were not particularly worried if this group moved on. More boys would come along next weekend. Possibly even later that same night. They had each other.

The two skipped across the grey pebbles, hand in hand, giggling. The beach was littered with canoodling couples, and they danced past them down to the water's edge. The sea was black and brooding. They hailed from Brighton – this was their beach. Neither had a great deal of clothing on anyway, and their dresses fell easily to the floor. Loshie kept her knickers and bra on, but Ellie left everything on the shingle and slipped naked into the water. Both knew the feel of the stones under their feet, and the slope into the water that would bring the shiver up your legs and torso quickly. Even in the height of summer, it was cold, but they were warm with alcohol and high spirits.

The music from the Atlanta was loud, even with the percussion of the waves. They waved their hands overhead and wiggled to the beat, for song after song. There was enough vague light around to see the waves coming, and they braced for each one, squeezing each other's hands more tightly and giving a girlish scream as the wave crashed against them. But the light was not so bright that anyone else could see. If anyone had looked towards their shouts and laughter, at best they would have seen silhouettes against the splashes of white surf. Naked and vulnerable, they felt hidden – this fun was their secret. The two laughed together about what parents and teachers might think of their cavorting, not fifty yards from the crowd overflowing out of the pub.

Skinny-dipping lost its appeal after they discovered that CCTV covered all of Brighton's beaches. In a far distant future, the re-tellings to her young grandson, Jack, turned Ellie's face dark, and she warned, "But you know, we thought we were skinny-dipping secretly in the darkness. It wasn't true. The police had security cameras all along the promenade, and it turned out that not only could they see well in the dark, but the details they could pick out were incredible. The freckles on your nose were visible in the camera control room. You were never really conscious of the incredible depth of all the government surveillance before the Bitness Revelations. Afterwards though, you could only assume that they had photographed us swimming every time. And doing other things. It makes me shudder when I think of it. They never stopped girls getting raped in the shadows, but they could record it all." At this, Jack always nodded solemnly, but he lived in a different time. He could never totally comprehend what she was talking about.

Despite flirting and sometimes kissing the tourist boys, Ellie and Loshie knew that they were always just flings. They never ever imagined these nights out might lead anywhere. They weren't looking to find a boyfriend at the Atlanta.

Ellie had lost her virginity to one of them, under the broken, old pier. But it was intentionally no more than that. Teenage girls racing to find out what adulthood was like, and they wanted to learn about sex from experience. That first time, Loshie went to a boy's hotel room, whilst Ellie was with his friend under the pier. Sharing their experiences afterwards, the two girls had no secrets. Loshie would always say she was underwhelmed by her time in that hotel. Ellie was more generous in assessing the efforts of her young man. She wrote off his lack of tenderness as a product of drunkenness. At every stage in her life, Ellie would assume the best in everyone.

This night of skinny-dipping was so hot that, after emerging wet from the sea, they were happy enough to pull on their clothes again without any attempt to dry off. The evaporating breeze from the sea was refreshing, and they continued laughing up the beach to the little coffee truck parked beside the crazy golf course.

The shiny metal tables and chairs of the old Art Deco café were left out at night and were bolted to the ground. So, the coffee truck customers, many trying to sober up a bit, used them as if it were a daytime afternoon. The scene of little groups chatting and laughing around their coffees seemed like the everyday, if poorly illuminated. It looked as if a tremendous storm cloud had shut out the daylight. Except it was warm and dry, and the breeze was gentle. Ellie and Loshie bought very sweet and brightly coloured ice slush drinks.

''Ere they are, lads.' One of the pool players from the Atlanta pointed at Ellie's table and his mates all joined in with a variety of suggestive noises and grunts. The two girls looked over briefly and then turned back to their close conversation.

The loud boy sidled over, and his cronies bundled up behind him, all testosterone and skinny jeans – an amorphous cloud of patriarchal expectation.

'Fancy joining us up to the hotel, ladies?'

Ellie turned to look up at him. 'You had your chance. I think we're going to go and find some lads who fancy dancing. But we've got cocktails to finish.' There was no alcohol in their drinks, but Ellie held up her plastic cup. 'So, maybe we'll see you in Aqua if you lightweights can stay up any longer.'

'Lightweights? You're the ones drinking fucking slushies.' He took a step forward, and the support scrum behind him fell quiet.

Loshie stared down at her red drink, but Ellie gave a delightful smile, looking the man straight in the eye. 'We're only messing with you. Don't get het up. Like I said, once we're done here, we'll be heading up to Aqua. Be great to catch you in there. Remember, to win the race…'

Loshie perked up again, strengthened by solidarity with her friend, as the two girls said in unison, 'You gotta be in the race.'

He looked confused, but his shoulders softened a little, and he said, 'Well, maybe we'll join you here, and we can all head up there together in a few minutes. We don't really know our way around, so it'd be great if you local ladies could show us the way.' One of the others grunted. He grabbed the back of an empty chair beside Loshie and pulled to slide it back, but it wouldn't move. His friends laughed raucously, and his hackles were back up.

'Sorry, girls talk. We can't chat about you if you're sat here, can we?' She winked at him. 'Go on. It's just across the road up there.' Ellie waved vaguely up towards the railings above the café area, where Brighton's Kings Road promenade separated town from beach. 'See you in there in twenty minutes. First drinks are on you, though!'

The mass of men behind him were getting twitchy. They weren't as involved as each individual wanted to be, so they grabbed their friend and dragged him away. 'Come on, Billy, there'll be better chances to pull in the club.'

Ellie and Loshie had no intention of spending any time in Aqua nightclub. They always preferred Scorpio. When the boys had staggered up the stone steps onto the promenade, Loshie worried about whether they might see them again in Scorpio and there might be trouble.

Ellie dismissed this with a shrug. 'So what if they do? There's a ton of people in there who'll look after us.' Ellie expected to be able to deal with those boys herself. She didn't think any intervention by bystanders would be necessary, but she did recognise that she would be on stronger ground in a crowded club. 'Anyway, I doubt if they've paid to get into Aqua that they'll go anywhere else – they're way too tight for that.'

Loshie lived with her parents above her father's car repair garage on Little Preston Street. The quickest way to Scorpio would have taken them right past home, so the two girls always took the long way round, across three blocks and up Montpelier Road. They had a well-worn routine from the Atlanta, via a rehydration break, to a couple of hours of dancing in Scorpio: from drinking and laughing to sweating and dancing. The swelter of 2016 would live long with both of them; they called it "our summer". These were the halcyon days that formed that indefinable love for the carefree times of youth.

The Times of Malthus

In 2016, on the Brighton Marina harbour wall, a blue metal sign displayed the following text:

BREAKWATER FISHING

Fishing Charges
Day (6am-6pm)
1 Rod Adult £3.00
2 Rods Adult £5.00
1 Rod Junior and OAP £2.00
2 Rods Junior and OAP £3.00

Night (6pm-6am)
Rod £3.00
2 Rods £4.00

Fishing is subject to the following conditions:
- Children under 16 must be accompanied by an adult at all times
- Night fishing prohibited for under 18's unless accompanied by an adult
- Always use a line with adequate breaking strain or use a shock leader
- Make sure it is safe to cast before doing so
- Pendulum style casting is prohibited
- Under no circumstances climb on or over the walls or fences

Miles M Hudson

Sunday 17 July 2016
The day after Ellie and Loshie's skinny dipping.

Wayne Smith strode along the road from their terraced house, his brother chasing to catch up. Wayne carried the fishing rods and tackle. They were going mackerel fishing at the marina, and Luke had been tasked with organising the packed lunches. He was still trying to zip up his backpack as he scooted along behind Wayne. As soon as he drew alongside, the older brother knocked Luke's cap off his head.

'Oi,' Luke cried and had to chase back a few yards to enter the front garden where it had landed. When he caught up with Wayne a second time, the rucksack was on his back, and he held his cap tightly. Having shot up four inches in a year, Luke, at fifteen, was now as tall as his brother and, once level, could easily keep stride for stride with him.

Wayne grinned. 'Come on, slow-arse'.

'I was only behind coz I was making your lunch.'

'It better be good – what did you make us?'

Luke looked to the sky and counted the items off his fingers. 'Apples, cheese sandwiches, that corn snack stuff, a juice pot each, and a big bottle of water.'

'Is that it? We're gonna be eight hours at least. You'll be starving once I've eaten all that lot.'

'Mum gave me some money. She said for food on the way home, but we could stock up on some crisps on the way there?'

'Yeah, alright, that little shop on Eastern Road. The one in the marina's dead expensive, and Asda won't be open yet.'

The shop diversion meant that they arrived at their favourite spot on the marina's outer wall just after eight in the morning. They laid out their bags and equipment where the legs of two dolos met in an almost flat table, and they then sat on the pitted concrete legs of the ones in front. Luke's was at a slightly odd angle, but he knew they'd be moving about a bit so he wouldn't get too uncomfortable.

'Quick, back against the wall.' Wayne pulled on Luke's arm,

The Times of Malthus

and they pressed themselves against the main wall of the east arm of the marina. Right at the end of a long walk from all the shops and houses and action, they would spend the day trying to avoid the attentions of the fishing warden.

There was a charge for fishing off the marina and every Sunday they would play cat and mouse to keep from getting spotted. They had never avoided paying despite trying it on every week.

Some wardens would let them just pay the junior rate, but you were supposed to have an adult with you, so sometimes Wayne would have to pay as an adult. It was only one pound more, but a pound they could ill afford. Even when they stopped at the shop on the way to the marina, Wayne would make sure they kept enough cash so as not to be chucked off the marina. Their mum would pay for any fish they brought home for tea, so they had never made a loss. None of the Smith family were loaded, so they pressed themselves tight up against the wall.

Wayne was a good angler. He seemed to have a sixth sense about exactly where to cast the line, and when it was OK to take a break because the fish weren't around. When the mackerel were running in the summer, they would often pull out a string of eight hooks with several fish on them. They used a big bucket to keep them in, an old catering size vegetable oil bucket their dad had got from the factory canteen kitchen.

It was going to be hot enough that July day that they'd need to keep the bucket in the water to refrigerate their catch. This was a tricky procedure. Firstly, they had to make sure that every fish they put in was well and truly dead, or the thrashing about inside could knock the lid off and upset the bucket and they'd lose the lot. They had a strong string to tie up to, and it was usually easy enough to find a spot between blocks of concrete that they could jam the bucket into, so it was held in the water. However, with the changing tide, they'd have to shift its position half a dozen times during the day, and what had been solidly jammed in quickly became loose and wobbly.

The main problem, though, was that the cheap plastic handle often came loose from the metal can. The wave action could easily pull it out and drag the bucket away if they didn't watch carefully. Over the last year they had probably lost six buckets through inattention. The waves were quiet today, so unless they were really lazy, it should be easy to avoid losing what they caught.

'Hey, buddy.'

At first Luke thought the warden had caught them, but, when he looked up, a big guy stood on the wall above their position.

Wayne gave the newcomer a sort of wave-cum-salute, 'Yo.'

'You're in my spot.'

Wayne's head was slightly to the side to keep the sun from blinding him as he looked up. 'There's no spots. It's first come first served.'

The bloke must've been two or three years older than Wayne and was probably a foot taller. He wasn't squat like the brothers – he had a workout physique. Especially the biceps, they looked outsized for the rest of his body. 'Mate, don't give me any shit. I always fish here, and I'm gonna fish here today.'

Wayne scowled. He looked across at Luke briefly. 'Watch the stuff.' He clambered around past Luke and pulled himself up the wall onto the walkway. The lip was about a metre above the highest point of any dolos, which made it a scramble to get up and down each time. He stood up and faced the usurper. Luke could now see that the man's head and shoulders were above Wayne's head.

'That's the idea. Both of you though, come on, up you come.' He was looking at Luke and waving his fingers to indicate he should come up too. 'And bring your shit, I don't need any of that crap, I've got my own gear.'

Wayne sniggered a little and shook his head. 'Mate, we're not leaving. You can go down over there if you want, but we were here first, and we're staying here till this evening.'

Luke clambered up on a concrete block and heaved himself onto the walkway. He stood up behind his brother. Together, they probably had fifty per cent more overall bulk than the taller bloke, and he was alone.

The guy stepped forward. 'Look, you don't want any trouble.

The Times of Malthus

Be good kids and move off.'

'No. You know we were here first. There's no reason for us to move. Happy for you to join us; a little further along so our lines don't interfere, but there's room for everyone.'

'This is my spot. I think you know what the alternative is.' He squeezed his fists to make his biceps bulge noticeably.

At this far end of the marina wall, the nearest other people were another pair of anglers about fifty metres away at the other end of the stretch of dolos. Beyond that, the marina arm stretched for a good 500 metres in a big curve enclosing the safe harbour with all the fancy boats. But all of that section had no concrete piles to get down closer to the water, you had to fish from bays on the wall itself, a good ten metres above the water surface. It was still early, so a few people were spaced far apart but nobody near.

Luke took a step forward, so he and Wayne stood shoulder to shoulder. He backed up his brother. 'This is our spot. You move, we're staying.'

There was no more discussion: the guy launched a roundarm punch which hit Luke bang on the temple.

Luke dropped to the ground, his eyes fluttering for a moment. By the time he opened his eyes again, the big guy had doubled forward, holding his crotch. As Luke watched, Wayne let rip three really fast short punches to the guy's exposed side, pretty much like the kidney punches Luke had used playing the video game *Anarchy IV – New York Razed*. The man straightened up and Wayne finished him. A straight uppercut to the jaw, Wayne's arm ended up vertical, as if he were fist-saluting the Black Army leader in *Anarchy IV*.

The big guy dropped to his back and didn't move.

From where he had fallen, Luke asked, 'Shit, Wayne, what did you do?'

Wayne knelt and put a finger to the man's wrist, checking his pulse. 'He'll be OK, he's just out cold.'

'What are we gonna do? He'll go crazy when he wakes up.'

Wayne telephoned the marina security office. He and Luke were starting to get a little worried when a fishing warden, accompanied by a pair of security guards, arrived five minutes later, as the bully was still unconscious.

Wayne explained what had happened, and they showed off the purple mark that now extended from under Luke's chestnut hair down in front of his ear.

The two security guards woke the big guy with a slap and dragged him off. They didn't say what they'd do, but the implication seemed to be that they would just chuck him out of the marina.

The fishing warden stayed behind to collect their fees. He pointed out that this was why they should have an adult with them but let them off with just the junior day rate for two rods, given the trouble they'd had.

Wayne knew the warden from many similar ticket negotiations. The man was a salty fisherman, just like the boys. It was easy for Wayne to picture the warden fishing along the coastline in his own youth, trying to make a bit of money selling fish to the tourist restaurants later in the afternoon.

The temperature rose rapidly, and it soon turned into a muggy, languid day. The brothers lolled around on the dolos but struggled to get out of the sun when it shone. Fortunately, it was obscured by cloud for much of the morning.

'This is the life, eh? Working for a few quid by lounging around in the sunshine.'

'Not really working though, are we?' Wayne countered.

'Well, if we end up earning more than the tickets and the gear cost us, then that's the entrepreneurial spirit coming through.'

Wayne pouted. 'Think how much a person should be able to earn for actually working though. I mean this works well for us, but it isn't actual work. Dad's job is real work, the fishermen going out on that trawler –' He pointed at a dirty boat heading for the horizon. '– that's real work. That's what keeps the machine running.'

'God, you're not gonna go on about the machine again, are you?'

'These boats in here …'. He broke off and waved back over

their heads, indicating the plush yachts moored in the marina. They couldn't see back into it through the sea wall, but both knew the luxury craft he was referring to. 'That's the gold laminating the machine. Our dad is one of the millions of grafters, the cogs, that keep the machine running.'

'Right.'

Wayne could see his brother's eyes were closed, his head tipped back to soak up the sunshine. He probably hadn't even heard him. 'The gold veneer doesn't help the machine to run in any way – it just makes it look fancy.'

By three o'clock, they had twenty-seven mackerel in the tub, each about a hand span long but skinny. Luke reckoned their mother could make two meals for the five of them out of this haul. In addition, they had three sea bass, and they were worth plenty at the back doors of the restaurants along the seafront.

The oil can to carry the fish was too heavy with water in it, so they had to drain that away, without losing any of the catch. The two bickered about the process. It needed both of them to tip the bucket and hold the lid carefully to avoid fish loss. It was too heavy to lift up onto the walkway and just tip it all out on the flat concrete. They had a system though, whereby they could lift it up there once half the water was emptied, and their bickering was more caused by being brothers than by any actual errors or miscommunications in the task.

Wayne knew the head chef at Scirocco and reckoned they'd easily be able to sell the bass there. It was a little way towards the Palace Pier, and they walked along the decrepit end of the beach promenade. The rusty rails of the mini railway led them away from Asda's crumbling car park. Large graffiti murals decorated the homeless camp banked up against the eastern marina wall. Security kept the shelters and the ruffians outside the neatly landscaped marina area itself. The unwashed and unwanted hid behind the concrete crag that kept both the waves and the outside world at bay from the low rise, high rent apartment buildings.

Luke shook his head at a beggar, but Wayne gave the man a mackerel. There were a number of little firepits in the camp. If he could forage something to burn, the man would be able to eat fresh food for what looked like the first time in a while. He pulled on his beard in delight, but his speech wasn't coherent. The brothers carried on walking.

Climbing the steps from the beach to the upper promenade brought them up to the front of Scirocco. A man in his thirties took the keys for his Aston Martin from the parking valet and waved his girlfriend into the car. The man was talking loudly and spun his tyres before racing off along Kings Road.

'Gotta love an Aston,' Luke opined.

'It's only a car.'

'Come on though, Aston Martin. That DB10 in Spectre? I mean come on. You can't deny it's beautiful.'

'Yeah, but look at the prick that just drove off. That's what Aston Martin is really about. The great British values they'd have you believe from Bond movies are a fantasy.'

'Fantasies are good.'

'Only if you know they're fantasies. But most people are just suckered in by that DB10 union jack bullshit. And the rich keep ruling the world.'

'I know, the gold laminating the machine.'

'Exactly.'

They crossed the road and walked up a narrow alley. The restaurant's back door was propped open by a full can of vegetable oil, the same brand as the can they were using to transport the fish. A large Filipino kitchen porter nodded and took his vaping further up the alley so they could squeeze through into the oppressive kitchen heat. Wayne grabbed a metal oven tray from the nearest drying rack and laid their fresh sea bass on it to present to the chef.

The Times of Malthus

In 2016, the online university prospectus of King's College London, included the following text:

ENGLISH
- Rated the 6th best English department in the Guardian University Guide 2014
- The Department of English at King's was among the first institutions in the world to teach English
- Extremely diverse modules from medieval literature to modern poetry

With one of the oldest English language and literature departments, King's has strengths in creative writing, gender, American literature and performance studies. We offer a diverse range of modules and approaches from contemporary theory to close textual examination and historical scholarship. *The Arden Shakespeare* is edited here, and our wide range of international research activities is reflected at all levels of teaching.

Sunday 8 October 2017
Ellie and Loshie are in their last year of school, preparing for university.

Ellie piled up a nest of pillows on her bed, settled into it and called Loshie. Her friend's face filled the phone screen. Loshie's big, round glasses had dark brown frames. She needed them for reading and close work, which included video calling on her phone.

'Let's stop the Plastics once and for all!'

Ellie snorted, recognising the reference. *Mean Girls* was their favourite movie and they watched it at least once a month. The Plastics were the cool girls, the class snobs with perfect hair and makeup.

'The Plastics are goddesses!' Ellie quoted the movie.

Loshie replied, 'I can't wait to go to uni and leave all those losers behind.'

Ellie continued quoting, 'High School will end and then what will they have left?'

It was Loshie's turn to snort her approval.

Ellie said, 'I know what you mean. Having a whole class full of people who can actually hold a decent conversation will be sooo much better.'

Loshie nodded. 'It's incredible how everyone at Central thinks they're so cool, but all they do is slate anything that's actually clever.' She rarely had anything positive to say about their peers at Central Brighton Academy. 'I mean, it's like by bringing everything down to their level they'll somehow be better as a result.'

Ellie shrugged. 'I wouldn't be so down on people if I were you. Each to their own. We love books and words, and other people love football, or hip-hop, or whatever. None of it's better than anything else, just different.'

'That's my point. Why do they need to be so down on learning? I don't give football fans a hard time.'

'You can't stand football.'

The Times of Malthus

'Well, yeah, maybe football's a bad example.' She paused. 'Talking of books, how did you get on with *Scars Upon my Heart*?'

'I found them to be poems of despair and endurance, rather than anger.'

Loshie sniggered again. 'Ha ha, very funny. You can't just copy what it says in the exam question!'

'Yeah, I haven't tried the question yet. I mean I've thought about it a bit, but I'm not sure I even know what the question means.' They were both silent. 'Actually, I'm not really sure I agree that that's a good way to describe them. So, I'm not sure I can write an answer that explains why that's what they are.'

'Well…' she stared intently out of the screen at Ellie. 'That's as good an answer as any other. If you can explain why you don't agree, that would be a good answer I reckon.'

'Really?'

'Yes, that's what literature critique is. Explain what you think of it. For an exam question, you'll need to give a coherent argument about why you disagree, but I reckon that'd be an A grade answer.'

Ellie shrugged. 'Great. I'll see what I can come up with. Thanks.'

'You'll get an A anyway, though. Just get your mums to have a look over it and tell you what else to write and you can't lose.'

'God, I'd never let them look at my English work. They'd hang me out to dry with trailing subjunctives and split infinitives and who knows what else.'

'Well, they are kinda qualified to give you that sort of help. I wish my mother was a writer.'

'I promise you it's not as great as you think it is. There are no simple answers. They never just say, "yes, Ellie, put a comma here, and this piece will be perfect". Their review comments are always longer than what I've written in the first place. Usually, way beyond what I need for school. You're right that it's all great stuff, but it's not actually that helpful.' Loshie shrugged, and Ellie asked, 'How have you gone with it?'

'Got till Wednesday, thank God!' They laughed together

again.

'You gonna hit the Oxbridge application deadline?'

Loshie looked dismayed. 'I thought we agreed not to try for Oxbridge. I'm never good enough.'

Ellie smiled. 'We did. I'm just checking you're OK with that. I'd never make it either. What did your folks reckon to London?'

'I haven't dared tell them yet. They're insistent I go to uni whilst living at home.'

'That's so not fetch. Brighton uni and Sussex are both crap for English Lit. I mean, Kings is sixteenth in the world. What more do they want?'

'English? Father won't hear it when I say I'm not going to be a doctor. He doesn't even believe I'm not doing science A Levels.' She mimicked her father's thick Sri Lankan accent, '"Meddisins at Oxford Oooniversity. Mother and I are so proud of you, Little One." Little One? I wish I could take one of his spanners and knock some sense into him.'

Ellie grinned. 'You *are* a Mean Girl.'

'I really don't know what to do though, Ell. I can't afford to go if they won't help me, and I can't declare myself financially independent for the loans if I've been living here this year.'

'Don't talk like that, Losh. I know you don't really want to create a rift with them.'

'I know. But I just don't know what to say to them. It's like we're living in totally different worlds, and I can't get them to believe in mine. Actually, Mother gets it. Working in Boots, she sees real British people and understands what it's like to live in this country. Father's head is stuck in Sri Lanka, though. He keeps our lives just like he had it back home. And she won't even try to tell him anything that goes against what he thinks.'

'You're going to have to get them to agree to uni in London. Somehow. Do you want me to come round and give you some moral support?'

'No. That'll just make it worse. They'll just think you're influencing me. They'll be even more adamant that it's not really my choice, but just your ideas. Not that their plans are my idea in any way, but that doesn't seem to count.'

Ellie shrugged. 'That's parents for you. They love you. They just think their idea of what's best for you is the right one.'

'That's coz they don't really know me.'

Ellie's smile was beatific. After a long few seconds, she said, 'You're gonna have to tell them. The sooner you get them onside, the sooner you'll get help with the application and stuff. Plus, if they suddenly find out on results day, I think they'll go off it even more than if you tell them now. Give them a chance to get their heads around it.'

'I know, I just don't know how to approach it. Half the time Father just ignores what I say and says the opposite, like I haven't even said it. And the other half of the time, he explodes. Either way, what I've said never gets through.'

'Sorry to hear that, Losh. Like I say, let me know if I can help. But I'm sure it will work out. They do love you, and that'll win through in the end.'

'I hope you're right, Ell. He scares me sometimes.'

'He doesn't ever hit you, though, does he?'

Loshie shook her head quickly and turned to look off camera. 'Shush. No. Of course not. Can we talk about something else?'

'Sorry. Course we can.' There was a beat, and then Ellie went in a different direction. 'Did you see that new boy that's moved from Brighton College? He's fit!'

Loshie smiled. 'No, tell me more.'

'You did see him – at lunch in the sixth form common room.'

'Well, yeah, I saw him, but I thought you meant there was more gossip to tell?'

'I don't know any more. What did you find out about him?'

'Nothing.'

'Don't give me that, Loshie! I know you; you'll have been doing your research. I bet you've done no work this afternoon with all that internet stalking.'

Loshie's tan skin turned pink. 'No, really, I don't even know his name. How could I have been looking him up?'

'Get off it. This from the girl who had seen a guy's dog once and, within an hour, had found out everything about him.'

'And his girlfriend, remember! That's the trouble with that kind of search – always turns up unwanted information. I bet this new boy goes to neo-Nazi meetings on the weekend, or something.'

Ellie smiled, her head tilted to one side.

Loshie looked to the side again. 'My mum's calling. I've gotta go.'

'Good luck. We're starting writing our applications this week. Get them on board. Maybe start with one thing and build it up slowly over a few weeks. Get them to accept each small thing, one at a time, and then eventually we'll be in London, sharing a flat and reading books on the English course at King's.'

'I don't know, Ell. I'm not sure they'll ever give in. They think everything should be like it is back in Sri Lanka.'

'I tell you what: try getting them onside for studying English tonight. Still living at home, but doing English. With your A Levels, you can't do medicine anyway, so they'll have to accept you're going to study something else. You could try saying "Or maybe I shouldn't go to uni at all."'

'What? He'll go mental. I may not make it to school tomorrow if I suggest that.'

'Well, maybe tone it down a bit, but what I'm getting at is that you make them think that convincing you to study English at uni is the lesser of two evils.'

Loshie scowled, a combination of confusion and scepticism. 'You think?'

'Deffo. Make them think it's their idea and they're convincing you of it, and you can get anything you want. Just gotta sow the seeds and talk around the worse possibility and see how quickly they leap to pull you back to the outcome you want.'

'I never realised you were so devious.'

'Haha, I've been reading Asimov. Dodgy bloke, but some great political machinations in his stories. If I was willing to smoke a cigar, I reckon I could have been one of his characters.'

'Right, better go. Wish me luck.'

'Luck!'

The Times of Malthus
Sunday 8 October 2017
Times when Brexit and Trump dominate the news.

Ellie heard the back door open, and Matthias called in, 'Hello, only me.' She shook her head to herself. Their Swedish neighbour's garden adjoined Ellie's family's, but the front gate was padlocked, so it would have to be Matthias, or a very noisy burglar.

She closed her laptop and walked downstairs to the kitchen. The tall, blond man turned from the sink, shaking water off two handfuls of salad leaves. Ellie's mother, Jude, scraped a collection of chopped red peppers into a white plastic bowl, which she then held forth to their guest. 'Thanks so much for bringing salad from your garden. We had to buy the cucumber, but I made sure it's local.'

After dropping in the leaves, he picked up half a dozen shrivelled tomatoes and plopped them in too. 'Sun dried these myself.'

From the adjacent lounge, Roisin called through, without looking up from her laptop, 'That'll get easier and easier as global warming really takes hold.'

Matthias waved his hand dismissively towards her. Jude pitched in, 'It'd be even easier if you helped, too.' She blew her wife a kiss to cement the teasing.

Ellie jumped on the bandwagon. 'Leave her alone, Jude. Somebody's got to be the breadwinner in this house.' It was standard etiquette that Ellie called Roisin, "Mum", and she called Jude, "Jude". They had adopted Ellie as a baby, and this was how the mothers had ended up being greeted by their daughter; and nobody thought to change anything.

Jude asked Ellie to take the salad bowl and put it on the dining table. Ellie did a full 360-degree twirl on approach and collected the bowl. She had arrived in the kitchen at the appointed supper hour and chivvied Roisin to stop working too. 'Come on, Mum, it's after six, put your work down.'

'Yes, sorry.' Roisin was distracted by the screen and

continued typing.

Ellie walked further into the lounge and tapped her fingers on top of the laptop screen.

Roisin waved Ellie's hand away, in the same way Matthias had done to her earlier. 'Sorry, I'm close to a finish on this piece about what to look for in a yoga studio. But I've got hung up on the summary sentence. What's another word for "airy"?'

Jude spoke through the archway, 'Insouciant.'

Ellie joined in, 'Flippant.'

Without looking up, Roisin raised her middle finger to the room generally. 'You're both geebags.' She spoke with a Northern Irish twang that wouldn't leave her, despite twenty-five years living in London and Brighton. She could ham it up a bit too, when she felt isolated. 'That's feckin' minus craic.'

Matthias the peacemaker asked, 'Why don't you just say straight what you mean? Are you thinking well-ventilated, or more like it has a nice vibe?'

Roisin pointed her index finger straight up in the air, still staring at her screen. 'That's it, Matthias, thanks. I'll just tell them that if they like the vibe, it's the place for them.' Her fingers were immediately clattering the keyboard.

'Jesus.' Jude shook her head.

With a flourish, Roisin stabbed the full stop key and looked up at them all. 'What? Even Guardian readers like their horoscopes. Keep it vague and they'll read their own lives into whatever you tell them.'

Ellie was still standing over her mother. 'But they shouldn't. Try doing some proper journalism.'

They were all grinning. Roisin raised a flat hand in a sort of striking action. She parodied, 'Why if you were younger, I'd bend you over my knee, my girl.'

Everybody moved to collect a plate of food from the kitchen, and they installed themselves at the dining table. Jude opened a bottle of English white wine. 'I'd love to know what you think of this wine, Matthias. It's from the Nutbourne vineyard, just up the road.'

The Times of Malthus

The four all held up their glasses to the light and gave the pale liquid a swirl. Ellie found the wine to be pretty sour tasting, but the three adults praised it highly. She served herself some of Matthias' salad and started on the vegetable lasagne. Fresh from the oven, it was scorching hot, and she had to have another swig of the wine to soothe her upper palate from the heat.

'What have you been working on today?' Jude was looking across at her daughter.

Ellie made a show of chewing through a mouthful of salad and swallowed with an audible gulp. 'English.'

She was about to elaborate, when Jude explained to Matthias: 'A-Level is next summer, so the workload has really ramped up this term.'

Ellie gave a theatrical pause as if to see if her mother had finished and would let her speak. 'Yes, we've got to cover *Love poetry through the ages*, the crime writing genre, and World War One including *Scars Upon My Heart*.'

Jude responded, 'poems of despair and endurance, rather than anger.'

'Yes, how do you know they're described like that?'

Roisin interjected, 'Your mothers have a little knowledge of literature.' She and Jude had met at the LSE, where both studied journalism, and they both now wrote freelance, mostly for *The Guardian* newspaper.

Despite their teasing of Roisin's yoga studio lifestyle piece, Ellie was all too aware of her mothers' capabilities. Veteran protesters, she knew that their often intractable, almost predictable, views came from a great depth of knowledge. She worried that the outside world would only hear the standard refrains and write them off as "just another pair of angry lezzas". Her parents knew that slogans on protest marches alone weren't enough to effect real change in the world, and Ellie knew that they knew that she knew they knew that. She pictured Jude saying, 'A march is not the place for a reasoned argument – that goes in the paper.'

Out loud, Ellie said, 'Well, I rather like the comparison to *The Final Cut* by Pink Floyd I came up with.'

Jude nodded. 'Ooh, yes. There are some direct parallels there, nice one. What about that crime genre exercise?'

'Yeah. That Penfold mystery you gave me fits exactly. A modern whodunit. Both essays are due in on Wednesday, so I've been doing them all day.'

Matthias appeared lost and diverted the conversation. 'Any more thoughts on uni?'

Jude jumped in. 'Well, she's missed the Oxbridge deadline for her UCAS application. Probably on purpose.'

'That's next Sunday. But I'm definitely not going to Oxbridge. Loshie and I have been talking about London.'

'You mean for uni?'

She looked up at their friend. 'Yes, sorry. Probably King's, we're thinking. Anywhere but LSE, and anything but journalism! The King's course has a thing where you can work with Shakespeare's Globe theatre.'

'Is that the English course?' Matthias popped in and out regularly but didn't have too many chances to quiz Ellie about things.

She nodded. 'I've got this sort of idea about teaching English, so I'll need a degree to do that. And Loshie loves reading so much, there's no real alternative.' Ellie was bored of discussing her schoolwork. 'Can I walk Regis and Burgess after supper?'

Matthias answered about his dogs, 'It'll be dark by then. I'll walk with you.' Ellie marvelled at the way he had couched his answer placing her as the principal and him as the sidekick.

Matthias had raised generations of Akita breed dogs. He did it mostly for the dog shows, partly for the money, and third in importance was for the love of the dogs. He was vicariously flamboyant, and the chance to preen and dress his current favourite for a big show provided the old Swede with significant validation. Some people referred to them as Norwegian sheepdogs, and Matthias regularly corrected them. His were Akitas, and they were larger and more expensive than Norwegian sheepdogs.

He always named each new puppy after a nearby location, and stubbornly stuck to his choice of name regardless of the sex of the dog – Regis and Burgess were both bitches.

The Times of Malthus

Ellie ignored his pedantry as a way to tease him. She liked Matthias, liked having a male presence in her home life, and he liked Ellie.

Jude asked, 'Have you done enough work to get it all finished by Wednesday?'

'I've run out of steam for today. But yes, it's fine.'

The two red-brown balls of fur, Regis and Burgess, had loved and been loved by Ellie since they were new-born puppies. They knew each other very well and all three knew the walking routes intimately.

Matthias chose the seafront promenade for that evening's exercise. Ellie answered his questions about school and Loshie and boys with more verve and detail than she ever gave to Jude and Roisin. She loved the old bachelor like a close uncle. He'd been their landlord for the last five years, after partitioning his giant home into a semi-detached pair, but he'd been a close friend with her mothers since long before Ellie came along.

Even on a Sunday in October, the seafront bars and restaurants were busy, and they walked away from Brighton along the Hove part of the promenade. The colourful beach huts on the upper level were faded after the summer heat. All locked up for winter, they looked more like a string of garish storage sheds than hopeful, fun summer holiday venues. Ellie turned back to look at the noise and flashy scenes of the nightlife in Brighton and wondered if she were walking a timeline for the city.

Miles M Hudson

Sunday 8 October 2017
Still more than ten years before the Times of Malthus.

Loshie had been helping Mother for an hour. They had completed the preparations of various Sri Lankan dishes.

'Useless! Bloody useless!' Father was shouting at his radio in the lounge room. 'Four eighty-two, then nothing. How is this ever possible?' The women jumped as they heard his fist bang down on the coffee table. Father ran the family along very traditional lines, but he was rarely violent.

Mother soothed Loshie's hair and mumbled, 'Your father will be fine. The team will win.'

Loshie knew that the Sri Lankan cricket team were not considered as good as Pakistan and felt it unlikely that they would win the test match her father was following. One of the constants of her childhood was Sinhalese commentary of Sri Lanka's cricket matches. Whether in her father's car workshop underneath their flat, or in the lounge, it seemed like half the days in the year had the chattering drone of commentators filling their ears from halfway round the world. The commentary Father listened to was always from Colombo. And if the match was taking place in some far-flung land, Sri Lanka or elsewhere, then this white noise would often go on through the night.

At six o'clock, Father walked into the dining area at the end of the narrow kitchen and sat at his place at the table. The women served up the fish curry and rice with coconut sambol. The meal was eaten in silence, after which Loshie tried to engage her father with questions about the Sunday of cricket he had been listening to.

She asked two questions about the score and the top players and received no response. Before she could start on a third tack, Father demanded, 'What schoolwork have you completed today?'

'For English, I really don't like the crime genre work we've got to do, so I've been working on a poetry anthology called *Love poetry through the ages*. It's so good – I love it.'

Loshie's pun was lost on her father. 'How many hours?'

The Times of Malthus

Mother jumped in. 'All since breakfast. She's as devoted to her English as you are to the cricket.' He stared at his wife, but the look was unclear. Loshie could not tell if the wide fixed eyes were seething, or if he was baffled. Father's expression was stuck, and he did not speak to clarify his feelings.

Loshie's poetry study had included themes of patriarchy, and she wondered how much of the troubles it caused in the world was simply down to men's lack of communication. His only further dispatch was 'More before bedtime'. With that, Father picked up the battery powered radio and headed out of the kitchen diner and down the garage staircase.

Loshie looked at her mother. Their eyes met, and without a further word herself, Mother stood up and began to clear the supper dishes to the sink. Loshie picked up a share of the serving dishes and remembered words from *The Scrutiny*. She knew it was not what Lovelace was referring to, but imagined her mother slaving over the cooker, doing everything for Father.

Have I not lov'd thee much and long,
A tedious twelve houres space?

'Have you thought any more about uni?' Mother interrupted Loshie's reworking of the cavalier poet's hedonism into devotion. 'You should stay here. Your father will not like you in London.'

'We talked about this, Mother. Brighton Uni is rubbish. I can do better. You want the best place for me don't you?'

Mother did not immediately reply. She continued apportioning the leftovers into plastic containers for the forthcoming week's lunches. Loshie put her hands in the warm, soapy water and revelled in the heat. Their flat was always cold. The draught from the garage doors below was always forcing its way up the stairs. She often wondered how her parents, from the tropical shores of Arugam Bay, could cope with the continuous cold, when she struggled with it so much.

She continued to badger her mother. 'You'll talk to Father for me, won't you? King's is the best course, and I'll get the grades I need to get in there.'

'London is a lot of money.'

'Everywhere is a lot of money.'

'Unless you live at home.'

'Commuting would cost more than sharing a place with Ellie.'

'And what about medicine? You know Father wants you to be a doctor.'

Loshie stopped washing the dishes. Without taking her hands from the warmth of the water, she turned as much as possible to look at her mother. 'You know I'm not applying for medicine. I haven't even done the right A-Levels for it. I never wanted to be a doctor, and I've told you both that a thousand times. When are you planning on telling him that?'

Mother pointed at the washing up water, and Loshie very slowly started wiping the plate in her hands. She did not turn back though and kept her mother's eyes locked.

'He won't like it.'

'It's not his choice. It's my life.'

'Quiet, girl.'

She had not used the term 'girl' to Loshie for many years, and the very sound of it made Loshie's knees tremble slightly. She steadied herself and argued. 'No, Mother, I'm seventeen. We're talking about uni. I will be an adult then. This is my life, my choices. We need to talk to Father and show him that this is the way it's going to be.'

She could see a tear sliding down her mother's cheek. This single teardrop made Loshie's legs become jelly again. 'Where do you think the university money will come from?'

'Er, the student loans company.' Her voice was cruel with sarcasm. It was not how she wanted to be with her mother, but the words seemed to come out of their own volition.

The first tear had not been followed: it was the only one. Loshie let go of the plate and hugged her mother. 'We must speak to him. We must do it together. We can explain that I will be more successful in life if I am happy in what I do. You know I love English – I will not excel if I am made to do something else. Medicine is gone. It was never there. We can explain this to him and show him that it is a sensible and decent way forward. Let's tell him that I want to become an English teacher. That's a decent, honourable career he can accept for me, isn't it?'

The tears did now start to flood. Both women's eyes streamed, but they were not sobbing. They held each other tight, and Loshie could feel her mother's hair soft against her cheek. The hair transported her back a dozen years, snuggling tightly in her mother's embrace before bedtime.

They finished the washing-up and Loshie was sent to continue with schoolwork, so that Mother could prepare things. They planned to call Father up for a discussion after Loshie had completed another couple of hours, so that her devotion to studies could not be in question. At nine o'clock, she came out from her room and along the narrow corridor into the small lounge space.

Their home was a single floor flat above the workshop of Father's car mechanic business on Little Preston Street. Less than a hundred metres from the lively promenade, their urban street was tight and dirty. The backs of numerous tourist restaurants all opened onto it, and there were always dozens of cans of vegetable oil, and just as many smoking kitchen porters, spilling out of open back doors and onto the pavement. The rooms in the flat were arranged with the active living spaces at the top of the concrete stairway down to the garage, and then the two small bedrooms and bathroom off a corridor that extended away from the lounge area.

As Loshie entered, her parents were already seated. He had a beer in his hand and Mother sat beside him. Both stared expectantly as she moved to an armchair and sat down. She was intimidated by their seemingly unified front, having expected it to be her and Mother against her father.

Loshie knew this was a pivotal moment. She had been building up to it for weeks, months, years.

Silence filled the room. The cricket had finished for the day, the workshop below was locked up, and no traffic or pedestrian noise filtered up from the street. Loshie shuffled forward until she was sitting right on the edge of the chair and looked down at her hands. Then, inhaling deeply, she looked back up at her parents. Mother raised her eyebrows the tiniest amount, prompting Loshie to speak.

Miles M Hudson

Friday 16 June 2023
Some time after Ellie and Loshie graduated from university.

Ellie lay back on the beach pebbles and stretched her arms overhead. The blistering sun was scorching down and she felt the need to head back to the cool of home. Loshie seemed untroubled by the heat – positively revelling in it, she sat up with her sunglasses on, apparently staring up at the yellow disc.

'This is the life,' Ellie said. 'Lunch on the beach in the summer sunshine.'

Loshie looked down at her friend. 'Yes, I'm so glad we came back to Brighton. All the comforts of home, but with the same sort of diverse and positive population. The people who come into the bookshop are all so thoughtful. I absolutely love working there.'

'Well, I'm kinda lucky my parents are both freelance journos. I think I'd have struggled to get any work if they couldn't send some my way. Everyone in London just seems to be fighting tooth and nail for the merest scraps of work.'

'I think that's the case everywhere. Even here, the inequality has gone mad. Since we came back from uni, it seems like even here people are so much meaner.'

Ellie's eyes were also hidden behind sunglasses. She looked up at Loshie but did not call her out on the extreme self-contradiction from her previous comment about the bookshop customers.

Loshie continued, 'It used to be that people here would help the homeless on the streets. Now all I see is people abusing them.'

'You're right about the inequality. Tory bullshit just seems to be never-ending. They're getting to the stage where it wouldn't surprise me if they just come out and say, "We're in charge and we're going to take all the money and power and make sure you scum have nothing."'

Loshie giggled and joined in, attempting to mimic a generic male politician, 'And if you don't like it, we'll send the police to kick your head in and then put you on a dinghy and send you back across the Channel.'

The Times of Malthus

Ellie carried on, also using a comedy blustering man's voice, 'Right, that's them dealt with, bring me some more champagne, and goujons of deep-fried poor person!'

They both laughed so much that several nearby sunbathers turned to see what the commotion was.

Ellie pushed herself up to sitting. 'Trouble is, it's so true.'

Loshie nodded, muttering, 'Yeah'. She gazed across the shingle. 'I was gonna go back up to King's next week for the Bishford lecture. Did you see the alumni email about it? Tamara Al Najjar talking about her books and about how her dad was secretly in the PLO.'

'Yeah, it looked interesting, but I've never read any of her books.'

'Oh, you should, they're really good. All about what's it's like to be an outsider in your own land. But it's cancelled – the Home Office denied her a visa.'

'What? Why?'

'It's bullshit. They said she had to go for an interview about her bank statement and then she couldn't get any appointment for the interview.'

'How do you know all that?'

'It was in *The Bookseller*, but, of course, as soon as the story featured, and the socials lit up, suddenly her visa appointment was miraculously approved. Too late to get here for the Bishford though. And that's the only outlet that told the true story. *The Telegraph* website vilified her as a financer of terrorism.'

'Ha! Like an author earns enough money to sponsor terrorism.'

Loshie spoke, nodding. 'It's censorship, plain and simple. Anything that opens people's eyes is gonna threaten the elites' ability to make money.' She stopped nodding, stared towards the sand at the water's edge and spoke more quietly. 'Hopefully, there'll be a revolution.'

Ellie gazed at the water too. 'Yeah, but what would come afterwards? We've had revolutions before, and it always ends up the same. A new set of exploiting elites just replaces the old one.'

'Well, we need something. Let's stop the Plastics…'.

They completed the movie line in unison, 'Once and for all.'

Loshie's smartwatch beeped an alarm that her lunchtime was nearly over. Both women leapt up to their feet, and Ellie twirled herself right round in a complete circle. They set off up the beach towards the stairs up to the Kings Road promenade.

City Books, Loshie's workplace, was a few minutes from Jude and Roisin's house, where Ellie worked writing newspaper lifestyle articles under their pen names. The shingle beach on the boundary between Brighton and Hove was a ten-minute walk for each of them. She and Loshie would lunch together most days and the weather was pretty much guaranteed to be hot and sunny. That June had been over thirty degrees for a fortnight, and their lunches had enjoyed twenty-five degrees plus sunshine for the last three months.

Bounding up the last few steps onto the roadside pavement, Ellie stepped out right in front of a high-speed roller skater. Despite taking the sharpest evasive action he could, Wayne Smith collided with her and sent Ellie pirouetting around as she fell to the floor.

He was profusely apologetic and knelt down beside her to offer any assistance she needed. A second, bearded skater, similar in looks but slightly taller and bulkier, came to a halt beside Loshie who had paused to take in the scene.

Luke called, 'Great body check, Wayne.' He then spoke directly to Loshie, as she watched on. 'He should use that in a hockey match. Our coach has been telling him to be more aggressive!'

Loshie eyed up the man and said nothing.

'Shut up, Luke. I think I may have hurt this girl.' Wayne was in the middle of taking Ellie's hand to help her up but, at the word 'girl', she shook free of his hand and stood up on her own. 'I'm really sorry. Sometimes I lose myself in the skating and forget that other people aren't expecting how fast I might be going.'

She looked into the young man's face and felt herself sway slightly. It was as if she had been at the gym and exercised her quadriceps so hard that they felt like jelly. He caught her, and this time Ellie allowed him to take her weight and slowly he raised her back to standing. He didn't let go, hands on her torso just below the armpits. Ellie was embarrassed and looked past him along the road.

'Are you OK?' Wayne asked, moving his head to try and intercept her gaze.

Ellie nodded and mumbled, 'Yeah, fine.' She then added, 'Sorry, I should have looked where I was going.'

'No, totally my fault, I was going way too fast for the pavement.'

Loshie asked, 'Come on then, are we going to get back?'

Luke responded, 'Oh, do you two know each other? Sorry, I just thought you were a gawper.'

'A gawper? I'm not like that.'

'Sorry, that's my brother, Luke, and he's not very good with people.'

'Shut up, Wayne!'

Wayne grinned, and Luke told Loshie, 'Sorry, he can be a real arse sometimes.'

Ellie had not stopped looking at Wayne, and he was still holding her sides. She wondered, 'Wayne…' and then paused mulling the name over. 'Do I know you?' She cocked her head slightly to one side to emphasise the mystery in her mind.

'I'm Wayne Smith. We went to Central together, but I was in the year above you two. Luke would have been in the year below you. Our paths didn't really cross that much at school, but I certainly noticed you.' He added, 'Both of you.'

Loshie looked straight at Luke, and Ellie squinted slightly at Wayne, trying to imagine a younger version without the straggly brown beard.

'We had better get going,' Ellie said suddenly. 'Loshie only gets forty-five minutes for her lunch.'

'Where do you work?' Wayne asked her.

Loshie was still perusing the contours of Luke's face and answered without turning away from him. 'City Books. You know the bookshop up near Karma Koffee?'

Luke nodded vigorously, but it was Wayne who replied.

'Sure. I've never been in it, but I know where you mean.'

Luke then jumped in, 'I love it!'

Wayne gave him a confused look and turned to Ellie to impart silently, with a slight shake of his head and a sceptical expression, that he didn't believe Luke even knew where City Books was. Ellie stepped back to extricate herself from Wayne's hands that nobody had thought to remove before then.

'Are you sure you're not hurt?' he asked.

She walked over and put her arm through Loshie's. Without turning back, she said, 'I'm fine, thanks, Wayne.' And she pulled on Loshie to get them both walking back along the promenade towards Brunswick Square and the hill up from the sea, in the direction of City Books.

That evening, Ellie and Loshie spent more than two hours on the phone to each other, discussing the chance encounter with the Smith brothers. They spoke most nights but, having also spent lunch together, their conversations would usually last perhaps thirty minutes.

Although it was a Friday night, they had no plans to go out. The life of earning a living had made both women more conscious of their outgoings, as well as the need for sleep. They had also grown out of their teenage kicks phase.

The nightlife world seemed to be an even more dangerous place for women than ever. Despite all the benefits and capabilities of modern technology, it seemed like men could get away with whatever they wanted to take, just as they had for all of previous history.

Ellie and Loshie still went out sometimes, but they no longer followed the reckless path of youth. Skinny-dippers these days would likely end up videoed and posted on social media.

They knew there were decent men out there as well, and the challenge was to find the good ones amongst the wolf packs. Could Wayne and Luke be the sort of gems that only turn up rarely? After numerous retellings of the lunchtime collision from each point of view, Ellie and Loshie agreed that they would like to engineer further meetings to explore the qualities of the stocky skaters.

Internet searches offered little detailed information beyond some basics. The brothers had various social media accounts, but their posts were anodyne. Loshie found Luke's Facebook page, but he didn't seem to have much on there. It wasn't locked to strangers; he just didn't post very much. She didn't dare to make a friend request.

Then Ellie struck gold. With a background in journalistic research, she wondered how it had taken her so long to find the boys' backstory. Nearly twenty minutes was more than any decent researcher should have taken. Luke had mentioned they had a roller hockey coach. How many such teams could there be in Brighton? As far as she could tell, it seemed that the answer was one. Or at least one club – they had lots of different teams. The social media feeds included many pictures of the brothers Smith, and they were mentioned in a few of the write-ups of matchday exploits.

Loshie suggested that they should attend a beginners' session of the roller hockey club. Ellie's reply was a nod to their favourite film. 'I'll probably break something, but sure.' Each in their own bedroom, they both howled with laughter.

When they finally caught their breath again, Loshie suggested an alternative. 'OK. Maybe that isn't such a great plan. We do actually want to impress them after all. Do you think we can find out where they live and accidentally bump into them again?'

'I like the accidentally bumping into them part, but doing that outside their house is a bit creepy stalker.'

'True.' They mulled silently on the possibilities for a few moments.

Ellie suggested, 'Well, if they bumped into us –'

'Quite literally!'

'Haha, yeah. If they did that on the prom there by our lunch spot, then if we keep an eye out every lunchtime, maybe they'll often come past that spot. Maybe we should take our lunch on that bench by the sweet shop and see if they go skating by regularly.'

'Yeah, that's an idea. To win the race…'

'You gotta be in the race!'

Miles M Hudson

Friday 30 June 2023
Hot summertime in Brighton.

'He's so different from those fuckboys in the beach bars at the weekends.' Loshie was staring along the promenade towards the i360 Tower.

The giant glass elevator had been built as a tourist attraction at the point where the old West Pier had once come ashore. Ellie loved how the Art Deco ticket offices from the old pier had been revitalised and looked as beautiful as the old photo on her mothers' wall in their hallway. *Actually, more beautiful now*, she often thought. The old iron structure of the West Pier was crumbling more and more into the sea. It had become little more than a few pilings with some twisted iron struts between or hanging off them.

Ellie countered, 'How can you say that? We only just met them two weeks ago.' In her head, Ellie knew she could add the exact number of hours, minutes and seconds since their first lunchtime encounter. Since then, the two women had accidentally bumped into Wayne and Luke on several occasions. The brothers appeared as inseparable as they were, and they seemed to haunt the same stretch of Kings Road from the Palace Pier along to the edges of Hove.

Loshie turned sharply from the view along the prom. 'We were at school together.'

'Pph,' Ellie snorted. 'But you didn't know him. I'd be surprised if either of us talked to them the entire time we were at school.'

'I did. You remember we went around the classes selling poppies? Well, I distinctly remember him buying one and telling me how his grandad had been in the war.'

'What war?'

'I don't think he said.'

Ellie shook her head slightly. She tried to remember back to school encounters with Wayne but had never managed to come up with any such memories. She felt like she had met him for the first time only a fortnight before. On the half dozen occasions since, that they had coincidentally been in the same place at the same time, their conversations had been brief. Ellie had savoured every word. In between encounters, she had ached to go walking the promenade again the next day.

'You're right though. He's so different from the idiots we used to chase at the weekends. In those bars, we were totally in control. I felt confident and like I could do what I wanted with them – had them wrapped around my finger. Talking to Wayne on the promenade that first time, I literally felt sick. I could hardly find words to speak. It was weird – I've never felt anything like it.'

'Yeah, they are lovely.'

'He seemed pretty shy too. I could see he wanted to look at me, but his eyes kept moving to the sea and the beach behind me. Every so often, they skipped back to me when he thought maybe he could sneak a look and I wouldn't see. It was cute.'

They were both staring at the transparent bubble atop the i360 Tower, with its miniature tourists straining at the glass, looking like they were desperate to escape.

Two stocky guys shot past them on roller skates, the lead pair in a group of half a dozen skaters. Ellie felt a tiny wooziness and reached out a hand to the turquoise rail at the edge of the promenade. They stopped walking and watched as the skaters circled to a stop twenty yards ahead. The all-male group laughed together. They saw Luke Smith push another of the group slightly, and he rocked back before bending a knee slightly to get his skate's rubber stop to catch on the pavement and steady himself.

Hidden behind their dark glasses, Ellie and Loshie leaned silent and stationary, arm in arm, against the railing, as if to watch the world go by. Chatter, from a beachside café below them, and the noise of the waves were mostly beaten back by the laughter of the roller hockey team.

Wayne slid his sunglasses off and looked towards them. Ellie gave a little wave, and Loshie squeezed her arm invisibly. Wayne signed off from the group, and he and Luke rolled over to the lunchtime strollers.

'Back again?' Luke demanded.

'We have lunch out here pretty much every day. At least when I'm working in the shop.' Loshie separated herself from Ellie and stepped towards Luke.

Wayne spun round in an effortless pirouette to lean against the railing beside Ellie and smiled sidelong at her. 'So, what do you do at weekends?'

Luke and Loshie had already begun a quiet conversation, so Ellie was on her own navigating the possibility that Wayne might be asking her on a date. As it turned out, he was. And the reason he'd asked about the weekends was so he could invite them both to a roller hockey match he and Luke were taking part in.

He had it all planned out: they would take the girls along to the rink, set them up in the spectator area, and then afterwards the four would all go out for dinner to celebrate or commiserate. The matches all took place near Woking, an hour and a half's drive away. None of the four of them had a car, and Wayne seemed to think it an absolutely normal idea that Ellie and Loshie would join them in the team minibus for the trip.

Much as Ellie wanted to say yes for both of them, Saturday was the busiest day in City Books, so Loshie would always have to work on a Saturday. She was equally loath to go without Loshie, who might think Ellie was trying to steal a march on her. She looked over at her friend and smiled about how volatile she could be.

'Ellie?'

'Oh, sorry, zoned out a bit there.'

He smiled. 'I was asking whether Sunday might be better – some weekends our match is on a Sunday rather than Saturday.'

'Oh, um, yeah possibly. Loshie has to work some Sundays, but she does get some off.' She called over, interrupting, 'Loshie, are you working this Sunday?'

Wayne followed up, 'Not this weekend – there's no match. But we're on Sunday next weekend, it's a pre-season friendly, and then, um, when is it, Luke? The next time we play on Sunday?'

'I dunno. Why do you wanna know about Sunday hockey matches?'

The Times of Malthus

'I've invited the girls—'

Ellie punched him gently in the stomach. 'We're a bit old to be girls, don't you think?'

Wayne looked non-plussed and spoke with a nervous laugh. 'Er, sorry. I've invited Ellie and Loshie to come with us,' he explained to his brother. 'Watch a match, and then we'll all go out to dinner. But only on a Sunday,' he added. 'Loshie has to work Saturdays.'

'Smashing,' Luke replied. 'Not that you have to work, I mean. But that you'll come to watch us play.' It was Loshie's turn to look non-plussed. She stared at Ellie, clearly seeking an explanation of what they were all talking about. 'But I don't know when our next Sunday game is. The season doesn't start till September, so probably not till then.'

'Don't we have any more friendlies?' Wayne asked him.

'I don't know. And they're probably not on the BIPHA website – that's only league matches.'

'Hmm,' said Luke, visibly thinking through his options, 'maybe I spoke too soon. How about we just do the going to dinner part? Could you do a Saturday night instead?'

Loshie rocketed up to speed. 'Oh yes! How about tomorrow night? What do you think, Ellie?'

Ellie felt railroaded. She really wanted the four of them to go on a date, but this seemed to be happening too quickly for her, which was unusual and unsettling. 'Um, I guess so. But maybe these two have something else on tomorrow?'

Luke replied, 'Nope, we've got no game, so we'll be free anytime. Late afternoon might be a good time to meet.'

Wayne sounded hesitant now. 'We had planned to go fishing all day tomorrow. Remember, Luke?'

'Yeah, but we could do that Sunday – we've only got training tomorrow, and Sunday's totally free. Depending on how hungover we are after tomorrow night, right ladies?'

Luke made it sound deliberately crass, like an exaggerated television character, but Loshie ignored this and confirmed the decision for everyone regardless. 'Brilliant, that's settled. Four for dinner and drinks, tomorrow night. Where should we meet?'

Wayne looked at Ellie, who shrugged. 'What about right here?' he asked. 'Should be great weather again, and we can decide where to go then.'

'It'll need to be somewhere with good vegan and vegetarian options,' Ellie warned.

'No worries. What about fish? We're sort of experts on the fish restaurants round here.'

Loshie replied, 'We don't eat fish.'

Ellie continued, 'But a fish restaurant would be fine, as long as there's decent vegan stuff on the menu. We'll leave you experts to work out which fish restaurant fits those requirements, and you can maybe show us somewhere we've never been.' She stepped away from Wayne and hooked her arm in Loshie's to walk away.

'See you tomorrow,' Loshie called back, half stumbling as Ellie forged a path along the prom.

The Times of Malthus
Tuesday 11 July 2023
The hot drought continues.

After two nights out on consecutive weekends, Loshie started referring to Luke as "the one".

Ellie shook her head and shook her friend, who sat on her bed beside her. 'You've met him like five times, what are you on about?'

Loshie fell back onto the mattress, strewn with books and discarded clothing and stared up at her bedroom ceiling. 'You can't fight the fates, Ellie, you know that.'

Ellie laughed and collapsed next to her. 'Providence will provide. You're nuts, but I love you.'

Both stared up at the ceiling, both thinking back over their last encounter with the Smiths. After a few minutes, Loshie mumbled, 'We've both read the same rubbish romance books, and I always thought they'd made all that stuff up, about feelings and love and all the rest of it. But it's real, isn't it? I just hadn't figured it out yet.'

Ellie came back from her ceiling daydreams. 'You've only met Luke a few times. He's great, but we don't know that much about either of them yet, not really.'

'I know, but I feel like I can just tell, you know?'

'I get what you're saying, but give it a good while longer before you start doodling "Loshie Smith" in the back of your exercise books.'

Loshie elbowed Ellie in the side. 'Shut up! You're such a mean girl.' They started giggling. 'You don't need to do this with me.'

'Of course I do – that's what friends are for.'

They met the brothers again on a sweltering Tuesday afternoon in July 2023. Luke and Wayne had both come off a nightshift at the print factory; Loshie's normal day off was a Tuesday, and Ellie worked freelance from home. All agreed that the only thing the weather deserved was a day at the beach. They splashed in the sea and dried off on the little strip of sand that showed at low tide, before returning to their sunbathing towels halfway up the shingle.

They had chosen a narrow swathe of beach between two high groynes, just at the boundary between Brighton and Hove. Multi-coloured beach huts lined one side of the wide pedestrian path parallel to the water's edge. At this part of the shoreline, the road and the promenade and the beach were all at the same level, but here the beach descended into the water much more steeply than it did between the piers in Brighton.

Even in their early twenties, Wayne and Luke were deeply tanned, their ragged beards adding to their grizzled, weather-beaten appearance. Loshie referred to the crow's feet around their eyes as laughter lines. Ellie assumed they came from squinting in bright sunshine throughout their early lives, spent fishing and swimming and generally outdoors by their silver sea.

Ellie was self-conscious about being the palest amongst the group. She applied sun cream meticulously and repeatedly, whilst Loshie and the boys seemed unworried by the heat and intensity of the sun's rays. Ellie was caught: she wanted to catch the sun and tan her body, but she knew of too many Brightonians with melanomas that had to be removed surgically, and two of Jude and Roisin's friends had died from skin cancer.

Having only just pulled her red T-shirt on, over her bikini top, Ellie removed it again. *Right. To win the race, you gotta be in the race.* Even she wasn't quite sure which race she was referring to, as she heard herself coyly request, 'Could you put some sun cream on my back please, Wayne?'

Dutifully, he leapt into action, kneeling up beside her prone body and somewhat over-enthusiastically splashing a lot of sun cream onto her shoulder blades. 'Oh shit, I think I'll have to put some on your arms and legs too – I've squeezed out way too much.'

She gave a giggle. 'Alright, but make sure you let the sun get at me a bit.'

Luke waded in. 'If you squeeze some air out and then slide the nozzle in that big pile you've made, it should suck some of it back in, as the bottle pops back out into shape.'

Nobody said anything else as Wayne attempted to salvage the situation, mostly by scooping up sun cream and throwing it away across the pebbles. His hands were small and solid on her back. It felt more like a massage than a spreading of cream. The benefit of the excess he had squirted out was that the whole exercise took much longer than necessary. Wayne's fingers had to caress her back many times over, and Ellie caught herself pushing her back up to meet his gentle strokes.

Wayne wiped his hands on his own thighs and lay down. All four were prone on their fronts, foreheads resting on their hands. The heat stifled conversation and they lay sweating, enjoying the rest, for a long time.

Embarrassed about the way she had encouraged Wayne to touch her, Ellie then felt confused about feeling embarrassed. She was a strong, independent woman, equal to everyone. She thought she understood the world so well that nothing should fluster her, but lay silent, vexed by the mix of feelings. She knew the stories of hundreds of relationships from literature. The fact that they were fictional did not detract from their legitimacy. Ellie could connect any situation she came across in life to the action in a book she had read. She ought to understand every situation, and have an explanation, plan or solution in any scenario. She should be in control.

Behind her sunglasses, Ellie looked to her left. Loshie and Luke lay on their stomachs. They were not speaking, but their heads were turned towards each other, so there were perhaps two inches between their noses. The gold stud in Loshie's nostril glittered brightly. Ellie pushed up a bit with her hands in order to readjust her position and saw that Luke's hand was resting on Loshie's back, his thumb moving in a stroking arc back and forth.

What is wrong with you, Ellie? You've regressed to some teenage self. You've seen Loshie go to bed with boys before, and you've gone to bed with their friends, without a care in the world. This, this, amazing man does your sun cream, and you're nervous like a little schoolgirl. Get a grip!

Ellie turned her head towards Wayne and blurted out a

question about fishing.

He shaded his eyes with his hand, trying to look at her. 'We generally go most weekends, depending on what fits around our roller hockey sessions.'

'But what do you actually do? Fishing I mean. How does it work?'

Wayne moved his hand to try and get any sort of view of her, but the sunshine reflected from the water and the shingle and blinded him. 'Um, well.' He paused to think.

Internally, Ellie almost screamed at herself. *"How does fishing work?!" You've totally lost it. He's going to think you're a complete imbecile and never want to see you again. And you bloody deserve it! "How does fishing work?" I'm not surprised he doesn't know how to answer that. You idiot!*

'Well, we've both got our own rods, and we'll pick up some bait sometimes. Actually, we often go without bait. When we were kids we couldn't afford it, so we got used to making it work without any. We'll either scrape some guts up off the harbour wall that somebody else has left lying around, or usually go for something where you don't need bait. If it's mackerel season, they'll just go for anything shiny that moves quickly. They're bloody suicidal, mackerel – I sometimes think they take the hook just coz all the other fish won't.'

'Isn't it cruel though? I mean surely that hook is really painful, and then how do you kill them? Is there a humane way to do that?'

She could see Wayne straining his eyes behind the shade of his hand, trying to get a look at hers, hidden behind her sunglasses. *"Isn't it cruel?" Jesus, Ellie. You do want him to hate you. Just shut up before he leaves.*

'Um, well, we do the best we can.' He turned onto his side to get a better angle to shade his eyes. Alternately frowning and then pensive, Wayne kept adjusting his body position on the ground, shifting and turning slightly but never seeming to find a comfortable spot. 'Sometimes they come in dead, or to keep it quick and painless, we'll usually bash its head on the concrete.'

The Times of Malthus

She knew he wasn't squirming at the idea of the killing, but at having to tell her about it, when he knew she and Loshie were very much vegetarians. Her heart pounded against the stones under her chest.

Luke spoke without moving his body position at all. 'The best way is to grip around its belly, with your thumb and forefinger in the gills on each side of the head, and then... smack!' He banged his own head down on the stones, and Loshie laughed excessively.

Ellie saw Wayne wince at his brother's action and nervously look across to her. She gave him a little smile and asked no more questions about fishing.

Miles M Hudson

Tuesday 18 July 2023
Loshie's 23rd birthday.

'That one's courtship might happenstance to take place upon one's birthday,' Loshie said airily, affecting her best Lizzie Bennet voice, 'is surely the source of many a young lady's delight.'

'Shut up, Jane Austen,' said Ellie. They had both just seen the two brothers enter the newly refurbished Metropole Hotel, where they would have dinner to celebrate Loshie's birthday. 'Look, Luke's brought flowers.'

Luke held a bouquet of flowers, as the two men walked up to them in the hotel bar. Wayne's jacket was tight across his shoulders, and Luke's top shirt button never stood a chance of being fastened. His tie was knotted an inch below the gaping collar. Ellie smiled at the effort they had made.

'Happy Birthday!' The men chorused the greeting and one brother ordered four glasses of Prosecco whilst the other held out the flowers to Loshie. She gushed that it wasn't necessary, he shouldn't have, but also that they were beautiful. Ellie just smiled and took the offered fizz.

They clinked glasses, but after "Cheers!" and a quick swig, they fell into an awkward silence.

Wayne was first to speak. He addressed Loshie. 'Come on then, what gifts did you get? Beyond the flowers, I mean.'

'Oh, um, Ellie got me a book. The only Hardy I haven't ever read, which was a really clever present.' She smiled across at Ellie.

'A book?' Luke almost snorted, looking back and forth between the two women. 'Isn't that a bit like a busman's holiday? I mean you work in a bookshop.'

Ellie interjected, 'Because she loves books.'

Chastened, Luke blushed, crimson rising up his neck from beneath his untidy collar.

His brother stepped in to try and salvage the bad start to their date. 'That does sound thoughtful. What's the name of that book?' He was addressing Ellie.

She smiled and replied, 'Jude the Obscure.'

Luke stepped back into the conversation, but no more successfully. He looked at Loshie and asked, 'Ooh, what's it about?'

'I haven't read it yet. She only gave it to me today.'

He blushed again and mumbled, 'Of course.'

Ellie felt that this whole date needed some first aid. Jude the Obscure was not a particularly positive storyline, so she aimed to move them off that subject. And Loshie's birthday gift haul had been minimal. Her parents were not wealthy, and she had a small circle of friends. Most of them were standing at this bar.

'You two have scrubbed up pretty well,' Ellie said quickly. 'What have you lined up for us all this evening?'

'Well,' said Wayne, who had clearly got the message to change the subject, 'originally we booked a meal at Rod and Line, but we thought it would be better here.'

Ellie shook her head to show she didn't know what he meant. 'Better, why?'

'Because of the heat,' said Luke. Rod and Line only had outdoor tables left, and it's so hot tonight.'

That much, thought Ellie, was true.

'And the humidity's through the roof as well,' Wayne continued. 'At least in here we've got air conditioning.'

Luke nodded. 'Don't want the birthday girl sweating into her meal!' His joke was met with silence, and a hard stare from Wayne. He blushed again. Luke really needed just to keep quiet for a while.

Wayne tried again to keep the conversation afloat. 'Well, more than just the aircon, this place is really nice. And mum tells me that they've made a massive effort to offer a lot of vegan choices on the menu. It was Luke's idea to come here actually, because of that.'

Loshie said, 'Oh, how thoughtful, thanks, Luke.'

At last, Luke's blushes were more positive. He gave Loshie a little smile.

Ellie smiled inside at Wayne's generosity, trying to help his brother who kept putting his foot in his mouth. She still felt uncomfortable, though, and wanted to move things on. 'Shall we go and sit down then?'

They carried their glasses over to the restaurant entrance and the maître d' took them to a table with a stunning view of the beach and the sea. Even at eight o'clock, people were still sunbathing in their hundreds on the shingle. There were shade umbrellas and ice cream vans, people splashing in the waves and infants giving straight leg kicks to beach balls.

The place had an excellent reputation, and the range of vegan dishes was more than just lip service to providing vegan options on the menu. The quality of the food meant that it was incredibly popular – full, despite being a Tuesday evening.

Luke and Loshie quickly became quite drunk. Whilst waiting for the starters, they spent nearly twenty minutes engrossed in comic videos on Luke's phone, laughing too loudly.

This left Ellie and Wayne to chat over a couple of slowly sipped drinks. Each one watched the behaviour of their brother or friend out of the corner of an eye, but mostly they enjoyed getting to know each other better.

Ellie found Wayne engaging. He was both interesting and interested in her and the world in general. She loved his down to earth straightforward approach to everything. *Practical, pragmatic, thoughtful* and *considerate* all passed through Ellie's mind. She also realised that she found his barrel of a chest and untidy goatee beard really attractive. On several occasions, she caught herself studying his pectoral muscles, clearly visible beneath his shirt whenever the fabric drew taut. Each time she looked back up to his eyes, they were watching her face.

God, Ellie, eyes up. You'd give him an earful if you caught him looking at your body.

'Tell me about your family,' she asked.

'Well, there's me and Luke and mum and dad, and grannie lives with us too. That's dad's mum. She's really deaf.' Wayne seemed to trip over himself, unclear why he had emphasised his grandmother's hearing problems. 'Erm, well, you'll understand if you meet her.'

Ellie smiled. 'I'd love to meet her. And you're all in the

printing business?'

'Yeah. Well, me and Luke and dad. He's worked there for pretty much his whole career and got the two of us part-time work when we were in school. We've been working there full-time for three or four years now.'

'You like it?'

'It's easy work. I'll probably want to look for something new sometime though. A new challenge I guess.' Wayne shuffled in his seat. He had been looking at his napkin between the knives and forks of his place setting and only looked up when he asked her a question. 'How about you? You said you qualified as an English teacher, but now you work as a freelance journalist. English teaching not the dream job you'd hoped for?'

'Ha!' Ellie threw her head back, her blonde hair falling around her shoulders. 'I think all teachers would tell you the same story about the job: being in the classroom with the kids is great, but all the other bureaucratic bullshit is an annoying waste of time. I do some bits of supply cover teaching here and there, but I'm not sure I want the workload of full-time.'

Wayne smiled, looking down at his plate of food again, He seemed to just be toying with his glass, swirling the last half-inch of wine around repeatedly. He looked up and exhaled heavily, as a waiter arrived with the four starter plates.

They all had an initial bite of their little plates, and everybody commented about how delicious the food was. Loshie was particularly gushing, Ellie thought. She also slopped a little wine out of her glass on two occasions.

A peal of thunder rolled out across the ocean. The panoramic windows became streaked with rain, the sky turning dark grey, and lightning scratched the clouds out to sea. The last of the beachgoers were jogging back across Kings Road, towels around their shoulders, their beach umbrellas unwieldy in the wind that had blown up.

Ellie and Wayne were closest to the window, and they watched the weather and the rushing people unprepared for it. They pointed at the occasional person offering up a comedy moment, as they slipped in a puddle or had their sunglasses blown off their head. Much of the time, Ellie watched Wayne watching the folk outside. His eyes sparkled as they flitted back and forth across the scenes.

The main courses absorbed some of the alcohol and Loshie and Luke calmed down a bit. They were still lively and enjoying themselves immensely, but Ellie felt they were more on track for a fun night than earlier. Before the starters, she had worried they might go far too far ordering more and more drinks, and she had visions of having to carry Loshie home. Instead, when they finished the meal, everyone was excited to continue the night, and they decided to go on to a nightclub.

The Metropole was not far from Scorpio, and the four of them went dancing. They arrived at the club quite early, expecting Tuesday to be a quiet night. Summer holidays had clearly already hit Brighton though, as the club was packed by eleven o'clock. They joined the sweating masses on the dance floor and did their best to impress each other, whilst maintaining a cool detachment. Luke and Loshie let loose much more than Wayne and Ellie, and as a consequence seemed to enjoy themselves much more. Wayne was slightly stiff and it infected Ellie with a similar air of self-consciousness. She did not do so deliberately but found it hard to let herself go when he seemed to find it so difficult.

Wayne made a decent effort, but after about forty minutes, Ellie let him off the hook and took him to the bar for a break. Luke and Loshie took this as a cue to dance in a close embrace. At the bar, the two had to stand right in each other's personal space in order to be heard, but they were more than happy to have to be so close. Ellie's back tingled when Wayne put his hand to it as he leaned in to make a joke. Coloured lights flashed in time to the pounding rhythm. Ellie told herself that her heart pounding was caused by the loud music.

'Oh shit.' Wayne put his drink on the bar. 'We're gonna have to leave. Get Loshie and meet us by the door.'

Ellie followed the direction of Wayne's eyes. The dance floor had parted, and Luke was squared up to another man. Loshie stood behind Luke, watching the altercation. Wayne set off swiftly, his eyes watching a large bouncer heading over from the main doorway. Ellie put her drink down and rushed after Wayne.

She took Loshie's hand and pulled to move her away towards the door. Loshie resisted, and they both looked towards the action. Luke and the other man were of similar size and build and were goading each other, with the occasional push to the chest. Wayne grabbed his brother's wrist, before he could push the man again, hard enough that he pulled Luke sideways away from his aggressor. Luke resisted, but at Wayne's command, 'We're leaving,' he allowed himself to be pulled towards the door.

The bouncer made a show of watching that they continued to the exit, and that the other man remained where he was. The man who had been squaring up to Luke was smiling and joking with his friends, pointing at the departing Smiths.

Outside, Wayne apologised to the girls. 'I'm so sorry we ruined the evening. I'm going to take Luke home. Will you two be OK to take a taxi?' He had not let go of Luke's arm, and the younger brother stared fixedly at the pavement.

Ellie replied quickly, but she was confused about what had just happened. 'Sure. Of course we can. Look there's taxis just here.'

Loshie stepped forward and rose up on to her tiptoes in order to kiss Luke on the cheek. 'Thank you.' He looked at her and smiled.

Wayne and Ellie looked at each other, and she mouthed silently, 'I'll call you.'

He turned his brother around and they walked away along Western Road. The moon was a thin crescent visible just above the city buildings ahead of Wayne and Luke.

The city's streetlighting had been switched off at midnight, ever since rocketing energy prices had caused Brighton council to take drastic action. Even the LEDs they had recently installed to reduce energy use were still too expensive.

Ellie watched Loshie gazing at Luke's back as he diminished into the incomplete darkness. The storm had blown itself away as quickly as it had come in, and the sky had a few tiny clouds scattering across it, like insects on the surface of a pond. A few of the brightest stars were visible now but, even with no streetlights, the city's remaining light pollution meant there were never more than a few visible.

'What happened?'

Loshie did not turn away from staring after him. 'He passed the final test, Ellie. He definitely is the man I want.'

'What do you mean? What test?'

'I told him about that weirdo touching me on the dance floor, and Luke just went off it to protect me.'

'That guy touched you up? God, men are creeps.'

'Well, he sort of brushed past me, but Luke was instant. As soon as I told him, he shoved the guy away, stood between him and me and shouted at him. He was all ready to batter him. My hero.'

'Right.' Ellie watched Loshie staring wistfully into the shadows. 'Come on then, I'll walk you home.' The club was barely 200 metres from Loshie's place.

Ellie was unsure quite what it was about Luke's reaction to Loshie's accusation that her friend found so enthralling. If not for Wayne, a fight might have started, and the evening would have been a total disaster. She didn't want to imagine who else on the dance floor might have gotten involved, and what injuries anyone might have ended up with. It was all too horrible to think about. He was the real hero of Loshie's birthday.

The Times of Malthus
Thursday 27 July 2023
Not long after Loshie's birthday.

Luke and Loshie's relationship became intense much faster than the other two. Ellie knew that she was always slower with men than Loshie. Deliberately so. She often wondered if Loshie still tried to rebel against her traditional upbringing by being keen to get straight into bed with a new man.

The intensity with Luke was different though. It wasn't just sex; their relationship became serious at a pace that Ellie considered unreasonable. How could Loshie know she loved the man after only a few weeks?

Ellie decided this question was probably more a reflection on her own reticence. She was certain that she wanted to find her soul mate, and that couldn't be determined at the drop of a hat. Or his trousers. She became increasingly mad at herself: she was constantly reining back, refusing to believe she was falling in love with Wayne.

However, she knew deep down that the moment he had bodychecked her had been the proverbial Cupid's arrow. He filled her thoughts all the time and could do no wrong in her eyes. Everything he said and did matched up with her idea of a perfect man. *And, God, he's good looking. So why is there still a distance between us?*

Ellie sensed a similar aloofness from Wayne, in direct contrast to Luke, the same way she felt herself in contrast to Loshie. This merely served to increase Ellie's desire. To slow things down, she positively declined some of Wayne's offers of dates, whilst Loshie stepped up how often she met with Luke.

In the end, Ellie could stand her inner conflict no more, and asked Wayne directly. 'I feel like you're holding back from me a bit. I've been trying to take things slow. I want to be sure that what I feel for you is actually right, and that you feel the same. Tell me what you're thinking?'

Wayne gripped the aquamarine promenade railings with both hands, staring at the sea. He paused for what seemed like an eternity before responding. In fact, it was less than five seconds of silence. 'Ellie, I'm crazy about you. But you're right, I haven't been pushing things. I've got to tell you something and I don't think you'll like it. Or me, maybe, after you hear it.'

Ellie stepped back from him half a pace, thoughts whirling through her head. *There's someone else? Has he got kids? Can't be, we were at school together. But that was five years ago, that doesn't prove anything. Criminal? No way, not Wayne! What is it?*

She held one hand forward and put it on his. Her voice was soft. 'Just tell me. Please.'

'I've joined the Navy.'

Wayne helped out with the lifeboat at the station at Brighton Marina. Ellie knew this already. 'Do the lifeboats actually take people on full-time? Anyway, why would you think I wouldn't like that?'

'No, I mean the real Navy. The Royal Navy. I signed on about three weeks before we met, and I'm going to start basic training in October. Well, there's four days in Hampshire first to make sure you're right for them, and then I have to go to Cornwall for ten weeks. But after that, I'll be away at sea. I can't believe I've found such an awesome woman, just after signing up to a job that'll take me away from you most of the time.'

Ellie's heart was bursting. That was the moment she would always identify as when she fell completely head over heels, irretrievably, in love with him. As much for his sense of duty and commitment to service as for his desire to be with her.

Only in hindsight, though – at that instant, she railed wildly inside, lurching from one extreme thought to another.

Why wasn't he honest with me, if it was never going to be a long-term thing? Well, he's clearly not that bothered about us, or he wouldn't just leave. Wait, when did he say he'd signed up? Maybe it is just bad timing.

Ellie was looking at Wayne, but her eyes were slightly unfocused.

Yes, that must be it, he's been torn because he likes me just as much as I like him. And he never pushed sleeping together. That's so nice. God, he's actually lovely. No, Ellie, don't get sucked in! They're all the same. If he was so gentlemanly, why didn't he tell you before? He's obviously known for ages but kept it quiet to keep his options open. My mothers were right.

Stop! Listen to yourself! "My mothers were right." What the hell, Ellie?

She stared at him, eyes slightly squinting under a frown.

OK, calm down, let's talk this through. Find out when he signed up, and what it actually means... then hold your head high and walk away.

She turned and walked away several yards, before taking hold of the metal railings and studying the horizon herself. Ellie hadn't said a word since Wayne's bombshell, and after another few minutes, he approached slowly. She was rocking slightly and started at his touch on her back.

Ellie turned on him, without turning to look at him. 'Tell me the full story from start to finish. When did you sign up? What have you signed up for? What does it mean in practical terms? Why didn't you tell me before?'

Wayne retracted his hand from her back and leant sideways against the railings, so he was facing her as best he could, given Ellie's closed body language. Stuttering occasionally, pausing often, he answered all her questions slowly and carefully, apologising at every turn, and interleaving his apologies with statements of how strongly he felt for her.

She listened silently, and maintained her stiff, sceptical, almost contemptuous, body language throughout. When Wayne ran out of things to say, she remained silent, watching a container ship slide along the line where the blue sky met the steel sea. Once the ship became fully hidden by the Palace Pier, she turned her body a full ninety degrees, so they were facing each other.

'We'll make it work, Ellie, I'm certain we will. I desperately want to make it work – I've never felt this way about anyone before.'

She knew what she was going to say but held her silence. He didn't speak any further, and Ellie watched him squirming. It reminded her of their early conversation about fishing and killing the fish.

'Let's give it a try.' Ellie worried she was purring her words. She wanted to be calm and business-like, but she couldn't control the thoughts and feelings racing through her mind. 'It'll be exciting for both of us. The being apart will just mean we have to work harder. I reckon this will actually show us if we were meant to be together or not. If we don't survive it, then it was never meant to be.' Her voice cracked at the last sentence, and a few tears escaped her eyes.

There was no chance for Ellie to wipe her tears, or feel embarrassed about them, or even to assess what Wayne might be thinking. He swept her up in a bearhug and they swung around wildly. Wayne lost control of the spinning hug and had to keep turning faster and faster, in the hope that he would regain a solid footing and be able to bring her back down to ground safely. It didn't happen though. He caught a toe on an uneven paving slab, and they fell to the ground together. Ellie cried out in pain as her hip bone hit the floor first.

The pain shorted out her brain, so nothing else registered. She caught a fleeting vision of Wayne kneeling over her, holding a clammy hand and gibbering. 'Oh God, I'm so sorry! Are you alright? Where are you hurt?'

Ellie lay still, letting everything wash over her, ignoring all bar the pain in her pelvis. Her eyes filled with tears, and she grit her teeth. It took several minutes for the pain to subside enough to regain control of her consciousness.

He knelt beside her, constantly apologising. She could see he wanted to help in some way but was unsure about actually touching her. Ellie's eye caught sight of his roller skate, which had one wheel still spinning freely. It mesmerised her and distracted from the pain.

A crowd had gathered around the two of them, and several others were asking her how she was and where it hurt and so on. Wayne was desperately telling them not to call for an ambulance as it hadn't been a hard fall. And in any case, he'd take her to hospital if that turned out to be necessary. With the state of the ambulances, it would take hours to attend such an injury, if they came at all.

Ellie raised herself up a little, and Wayne helped her to sit.

'Are you alright, dear? You really should go to hospital after a turn like that.' An older woman was bent over so her face was close to Ellie's.

In the background, Ellie heard somebody say, 'It's OK, she's sitting up. Looks like she'll be alright.'

She turned her head in several directions, looking at all the faces staring down at her. 'My boyfriend's going to be a sailor in the Navy.'

The crowd wandered away as Wayne helped her up to stand and hold the railings for support.

The old woman called a parting shot as she descended the stairs towards the beach. 'Hospital, my girl. You never know what hidden damage you may have done.' She muttered on, but her words were increasingly lost.

They sat on a bench for another ten minutes, after which they got up and Ellie gingerly limped along hanging on to Wayne's arm. 'Did you call me your "boyfriend"?' His tone was teasing, although she could tell that he was also asking a serious question.

'No, not you. My other boyfriend is also joining up. Better watch out for him, or he'll punch your lights out – he's very jealous.'

'Seems like you haven't done yourself any serious damage. Although I think the phrase "*other* boyfriend" means you are calling me "boyfriend".' They tottered on towards home, smiling.

Wednesday 25 December 2024
Wayne's been more than a year in the Navy.

On Christmas Day, as she and Loshie stepped up the Smith's driveway towards the front door of the two brothers' house, Ellie worried that she should be with Jude and Roisin to celebrate. This would be the first time she had missed Roisin's legendary spiced faux-beef in a decade. The last time had been when her mother returned to Cookstown to help her family look after an elderly aunt who had fallen seriously ill.

Loshie smiled at Ellie and rang the doorbell – an enigmatic, Mona Lisa type smile. Jack and Diane Smith's terraced house in Kemptown was a few streets up from Brighton Marina. The area had been partly gentrified over recent years, but the Smiths lived in the same house that Jack's father had bought from the council, as soon as Margaret Thatcher first made council houses available for sale.

'In you come.' Diane bustled them inside with hugs and Merry Christmases all round. The two girlfriends presented the wine and gifts that they had. Ellie felt a slight trepidation. Beyond the worry of her mothers and Matthias feeling left alone on such a family occasion, Wayne was away on the new HMS Wellington in the Caribbean. This left Ellie as a bit of a spare wheel.

The Smiths had welcomed both women into their family whole-heartedly, but Christmas could always produce stress that didn't need to be there. Wayne's grandmother was deaf as a post, and his father, Jack, would most likely tease her mercilessly for most of the day. Grannie was never upset by her son's mockery, but it made Ellie feel uncomfortable. She wished Wayne were by her side.

As they entered the living room, Jack tentatively released the video-calling camera he had attached to the side of the giant television screen. It quivered precariously but held. 'I've got this working OK now, I think. Should be all set for our call with sailor boy at four o'clock. It's not designed to be loud enough for Mum though. No way I can turn up the volume enough for her.' He waved a hand towards Grannie in her green velveteen armchair.

Attentive to the action in the room, she was straining to hear anything. She uttered a muted greeting toward Ellie and started fiddling with the controls on her hearing aids. 'I'll get us all a drink. Diane, is that wine open yet?' Jack moved past them and out of the living room.

He was substituted by Luke. Ellie heard father and son squeeze past each other in the hallway and she went to sit down by Grannie, as Luke and Loshie embraced and kissed. Loshie would not be suffering from any concerns about being away from her family on Christmas Day. She referred to her parents as "a lapsed Buddhist and a lapsed Muslim", but always followed up with, "and even they wouldn't know who was which!"

They celebrated Christmas just as fervently as the rest of Brighton's population, but Loshie had been adamant about spending the day with Luke and his family. She had not appeared even to consider it a question. After eighteen months of dating Luke, it was the obvious scenario for Loshie's Christmas 2024.

Luke released her from his giant hug and Loshie's feet landed back on the ground. The two sat on the sofa, squeezing in next to Ellie, and Jack returned with a tray full of wine glasses. 'Di, come on, we'll make a toast!'

A clattering sound in the kitchen was followed by smaller noises. Everybody took a glass from the tray, and he was left shaking his head slightly, feigning impatience at waiting for his wife to join them. Luke leaned over the end of the sofa arm and pressed a button on an old hi fi system which burst out Christmas music. He turned it down to a quieter level,

Diane came in and took up her red wine. 'What shall we say?'

Jack put the tray down, flourished his own glass and spoke. 'Here's to a brilliant family Christmas with those who could be here and with those who couldn't be here.'

Everybody raised their drink and took a swig. In her head, Ellie repeated the toast, *Those who couldn't be here.*

Diane shot back out to the kitchen, and Jack took the final armchair.

Throughout the morning and the huge lunch, they all drank more than Ellie. Luke and his father were raucous, but everybody enjoyed the boisterous fun.

Christmas dinner at the Smiths had been decreasing in scale over several years. Across the country, wages were depressed in real terms, and food prices had skyrocketed. Jude had written an article about the relative costs of Christmas over the years, and the food and drink bill was the worst part. The global Food Price Index had gone over 200 for the first time this year.

Diane had still put on a good meal for their gathering, but they all reminisced about groaning tables and the old impossibility of cooking all the food in just one morning in just one kitchen.

Luke had provided the main element of the meal by fishing at the Marina. Even that had taken him a week of evening rod sessions, after his shifts at the factory. The sea too was offering less reward for more labour. He mused aloud at the table, wondering how well Wayne would be eating on board the warship.

Loshie had arrived that morning with her vegetarian contribution of a Tupperware of spiced rice, and Ellie had brought salad vegetables from Matthias' greenhouse. It was a cold Christmas in Brighton, with snowflakes even fluttering in the air. Matthias could not afford to heat the greenhouse throughout the winter, despite an arsenal of solar panels on his roof, but he had maintained it till yuletide and only turned off the heaters on Christmas Eve. Ellie smiled at the memory of the Swede, without a trace of irony, espousing the importance of a Christmas salad.

Grannie was insistent on the family traditions in the Smith household. After the King's speech, they had settled in to watch a repeat of the movie *No Time to Die*, with the plan to pause it when Wayne came online.

Loshie stepped up in front of the room and pulled Luke up off the sofa to face them all too. Jack twisted his head side to side to try and view the screen, but his wife pressed the remote controller and it paused, barely minutes after the start.

'We've got a bit of an announcement. Tell them, Luke.' Loshie was beaming.

The Times of Malthus

They both held a glass of wine. 'Erm, right, yeah. We're engaged. We decided this morning that we should get married.'

Diane clapped her hands together and Jack raised his wine glass.

Grannie leant forwards. 'What? What did he say?'

'They're getting married, Jean!' Diane all but shouted the news and waved her hand to indicate the affianced.

Loshie raised her glass to the room, and everyone else followed suit and then took a drink.

'Did he give you a ring?' Grannie asked. 'Let me see.' She strained forward to look at Loshie's hands without having to lever herself out of the armchair.

'Er no, Grannie. It was a bit of a sudden decision this morning.' Luke spoke to his grandmother and blushed. 'We'll go out in the sales and find a nice one.'

'I had to sell mine after your granddad was killed.'

'This calls for another bottle.' Jack made to get up.

'We've all got full glasses already, Jack. Sit back and listen to their engagement story. Everybody loves a good engagement story.'

Luke looked at Loshie. She smiled and leaned into him.

'You're not pregnant, are you?'

'Jack!'

'No, I'm not!' Loshie's voice was almost a shriek.

Luke put his arm around her and pulled her in tight. 'It wouldn't matter if she was, Dad. I want to marry this beauty either way.'

Ellie hadn't spoken at all, and Loshie caught her eye. She wanted to say something suitable, but she more wanted to take Loshie to one side and find out what the story was, girlfriend to girlfriend.

Leaning forward attentively, she smiled, and reiterated Diane's request. 'Yes, tell us the engagement story. Were you on one knee, Luke, or is that too old-fashioned?'

Luke was a bit flustered. 'Well, like I say, I didn't have a ring, so going down on one knee wouldn't really have worked.'

Loshie jumped in. 'It was a joint decision.' She looked up

into his face. 'We agreed we've been together long enough to know we want to spend the rest of our lives together.'

Diane smiled. 'Oh, how lovely. We're so pleased for you. Do you have an idea about a wedding date, or is it one step at a time?'

Luke looked down at Loshie. She turned and addressed the room again. 'We haven't planned that exactly. But we won't be one of those couples who get engaged and then are just engaged for years. We'll be getting married sometime soon.'

Ellie asked, 'Have you told your parents?'

Loshie gave a little shake of her head with a slight grimace. 'You know they're very …' She paused. '… traditional – I need to tell them in person. And we only decided this morning, so I'll talk to them when I go home this evening.'

'*We'll* talk to them,' Luke added and gave her another squeeze. Loshie smiled up at him. 'And I can't wait to tell Wayne. Part of the decision on a date will be when he can get back here to be my best man.' He pulled his phone out of his pocket. 'He should be online in about half an hour. Let's sit down and let everyone get back to Bond.' They squashed onto the middle of the sofa, between Ellie and Diane at the two ends. The TV screeched back into motion as James Bond resumed a car chase.

Ellie leaned into Loshie's ear. 'Where are you two going to live?' She was slightly put out that her best friend hadn't talked to her about getting engaged beforehand.

'That's another thing we haven't worked out. Well, we haven't even had time to think that we should think about it. The morning's been such a whirlwind.'

Ellie's brain ticked back through the events of the morning. Loshie had been very diligent in helping Diane. In the kitchen, Ellie had wondered twice whether she herself should offer more help. Loshie seemed to be everywhere doing everything. However, that meant Loshie and Luke hadn't spent much time together, especially not time alone where he could propose. Or more likely where Loshie could propose. She watched her friend, glowing whilst watching the movie.

At four o'clock, they put Bond on hold again and set the

videocall going. The TV loudspeaker shouted at them, 'We're on!'

An unknown sailor stepped back from filling the screen and moved out of sight. The foredeck of a large grey ship appeared in view, and Wayne, in sunglasses, shorts and a Hawaiian shirt, roller skated from the far side right up to the screen. 'Merry Christmas, family!'

A chorus of Christmas greetings was returned.

'How's it all going, son? You look like you've got a much better Christmas going on than we have.'

Diane spoke before Wayne could. 'We've got snow! And ice overnight. Your dad couldn't get the car up the street earlier.'

Taking off the sunglasses forced Wayne to shield his eyes with a hand. 'It is pretty nice here, but hot and sunny just seems a bit wrong. I'd much rather be there with you lot, cosy inside whilst it's all wintry outside.'

'Bloody freezing,' Grannie shouted. 'This one won't turn on the heating. Not even on Christmas when it's below zero outside!'

Jack retorted, 'You know it's too expensive, mum. We put that fire on in your room.'

Diane spoke quietly to her husband. 'She's teasing, Jack. Don't worry about it.'

'Well …'.

'I probably shouldn't tell you then that it's a steady twenty-four degrees here. And glorious sunshine.' He over-acted turning his face up to bask in the sunshine.

'We got engaged!' Loshie was almost as loud as Grannie.

'What?' Wayne cupped a hand round his ear but was grinning.

Luke took the bait. 'Loshie and I: we're going to get married.'

'Great news, bro. I'm so pleased for you. Hey, show me the ring, L!'

Luke continued, 'We just decided this morning, so I didn't have time to get her a ring. We'll go out in the sales and find a nice one tomorrow.'

'What did they give you for Christmas Dinner there, son?'

The conversation continued for a few minutes about the

Christmas rituals in the Smith household and aboard a Royal Navy ship moored in the Caribbean, until Wayne asked for a bit of privacy. 'Do you think Ellie and I could have a few minutes to chat just the two of us. I'm on duty for most of the rest of the day so I don't think we'll be able to call later.'

Jack leapt out of his chair and marshalled the rest of the family out of the room. Ellie had not spoken at all on the call before then.

'Did you know about this?'

'Merry Christmas to you too!'

Ellie blushed. 'Sorry. I love you, and I really miss you. And I hope you're surviving Christmas in the Caribbean! But this whole thing has got me a bit rattled. Loshie didn't say anything to me before they announced it to the whole family. Did you know about it?'

'You make it all sound a bit sinister. I didn't know it was going to happen today. Or at all for certain. Luke has told me before how great Loshie is and how he's so pleased he hit the jackpot in finding her. So, I mean, I think I probably expected it. Is there a problem?'

Ellie blushed again and shook her head. 'No, no, I don't know. Like I said, maybe they just took me by surprise a bit. Maybe deep down I'm a bit envious. For some reason, I guess I always imagined the older brother would naturally go first.'

Wayne cocked his head to one side. 'Oh, no, sorry, I'm not expecting you to propose too. I'm definitely not ready to say "yes" yet, so don't worry.'

'What do you mean worry? Why do you think getting married would worry me?'

'I meant don't worry, I don't want you to feel any pressure to propose. I want it to be something we talk about and agree on together. You know I don't really hold with any of the traditional guff around a ring and one knee and stuff. Although actually, it sounds like Luke and Loshie did it exactly my way, so maybe I'm… I don't know what it is. I want them to be happy, but I really want them to make a good decision and to know they're gonna last for good. Do you think Luke loves her enough for it to be forever?'

Wayne frowned at the question. 'Definitely yes. He's absolutely besotted. Isn't Loshie?'

This time, Ellie frowned. 'Um. He's all she talks about. I mean we've had girly chats about calling herself Loshie Smith, and how she has to keep defending him to her parents, which she does, erm, robustly. She defends him to the hilt. But there's just something nagging in the back of my head. I don't know if it's me, or if there is something.'

'Have you talked to her about it?'

'Well, no, maybe that's it. They dropped it on us an hour ago, and she and I have had no time together. Family Bond movie ever since. She is glowing. I'll talk to her later, I'm sure that'll confirm that she's totally committed, and I'm just being a jealous cow!'

'It does open up a chance for me to talk to you about our future.'

'Woah, hold on!' Ellie was smiling at him. 'Did you hear me say I'm not ready to say "yes"?'

He laughed. 'Yes, yes. Don't worry, I haven't got a ring box in my pocket. But I do want to come home to you. I think we're doing really well with the long-distance relationship.'

'We are, we definitely are.' She was intrigued: Wayne's Navy contract had nearly another two years to run. Had he managed to get some leave?

'I'm going to transfer to the coastguard and that'll let me join the station in Shoreham.'

Ellie's stomach gave a little flip. She hadn't seen Wayne in person since the previous Christmas, and Shoreham was literally the next town. They'd be able to live together. 'Can you do that? How soon does a transfer go through?'

'Oh, sorry, hang on. I can't get out of the Navy any quicker than the minimum three-year stint. But I mean I'm going to quit at that point and come home. But it's really easy to get a job in the coastguard if you've just left the Navy. That's how most coasties come to be in the job. And if I apply far enough in advance, I should be able to make sure I get Shoreham.'

Ellie's face fell and the elation drained from her. She thought it would have been better if he'd said nothing. 'Oh, I thought you meant soon.' She felt a stabbing pain in her hip. The fall on the promenade eighteen months earlier had only ever been a badly bruised pelvis, but it still pained her from time to time. Ellie assumed it was a psychosomatic pain that only appeared when she and Wayne were having some sort of stress.

'Sorry, I meant I've decided I'm not going to be Navy for life. I miss home too much. I miss you too much.'

'What about leave? Will you be able to come home soon, just for a holiday?'

The visage on screen nodded vigorously. 'Yep. Our patrol out here finishes in a month and the next deployment is to take the boat back to Portsmouth for maintenance.'

'I thought she was brand new?'

'Yeah, it's a thing about checking how everything went on this first trip. That's why we've had such an easy mission. We're really just showing her off around the place a bit and checking everything works. The captain has to provide a snagging list when we get back. There's not much I've heard that's wrong though, but we'll have to be in port for at least a month, and that definitely means shore leave.'

Ellie clapped her hands together. 'I can't wait. That'll be a good time for us to talk about our future together, won't it? Still not angling for a ring, but I'm thinking about where to live, and money's really tight for everything these days.'

'Of course. A bit before Easter, we should be home. I'd love to make plans with you then. Although, let's not forget I'm still two more years in the Navy though, so don't buy a house just yet!'

'Buy a house? Oh, you're funny. What is the pay like for the coastguard, though? You've currently got one of the few jobs where people actually make enough to live on. Mostly because you've got no outgoings. Maybe I should join up too and we should put in a request to be on the same ship. That's the only way we'll be able to afford to live together.'

Wayne took her a bit too seriously. 'Yeah, that's not how the

The Times of Malthus

Navy works. You can't just say "Oh, my girlfriend and I want to live together – can we both be on the same shift together please." Do you think you'd really want to do the Navy?'

'I was joking.' She smiled at him, and this time, Wayne blushed.

'You tease!' His riposte was one of their private jokes, and she laughed out loud.

Serious again, Wayne asked, 'We are good, aren't we? Luke and Loshie haven't made you worry about us, have they?'

Ellie felt her eyes welling up, and she nodded. 'We're good. I love you, Wayne.'

'I love you too.'

'To be honest, I think their little announcement has made me more worried about them than about us.'

Miles M Hudson

In 2025, a TikTok video for Hong Kong IT Inc's new smartphone, the Armulet, broke the record for the highest number of views of any TikTok advert.

Over a background music score of *Also Sprach Zarathustra* by Richard Strauss, the following spoken commentary narrated demonstrations of the new device:

- Responds to your voice, and only yours
- Responds to gesture commands in the 3D-projected, colour holoscreen
- All functions take place in the holoscreen in front of you
- KineBattery recharges from the movements of your body
- A.I. HoloHelper assistant built in
- No buttons to press; no screen tapping; no tiny icons
- No plugging in
- Wear all day in complete comfort
- Strap your Armulet on, and forget it's even there

The ad finished with on screen captions:

The phone you don't need to hold… or look at!
HKIT's Armulet™

Wearable sleeves available in a huge range of styles and colours. (Pictured: The Gladiator)

The Times of Malthus
Saturday 3 July 2027
Wayne and Ellie have been together four years.

Wayne had changed out of his coastguard dress uniform, and he and Ellie wore the shorts and flip-flops that were required in a heatwave of more than thirty degrees.

Their wedding had been a low-key affair. That was their way, but also, struggles with money meant that hardly anybody had a lavish wedding anymore. Barring the very wealthy, who had moved more and more towards prince and princess themed ceremonies in fancy castles. Nobody would buy the photos of Ellie and Wayne's wedding for a glossy social media spread, so they went with what they could afford.

The two had foregone any evening event and put everything into a ceremony and lunch for forty friends and family. Even that was only possible as Wayne's boss had offered the coastguard station's training hall as a venue.

He had only been stationed there for eight weeks, but the offer to use the hall had been something of a welcoming present. Wayne came from the Navy with excellent references, and his new boss had wanted to make sure he didn't leave.

The coastguard was under heavy pressure from the government. Immigrants were not welcome, and the ones trying to cross the channel were to be intercepted and returned forcibly to France. This was an increasingly stressful job for the coastguard's sailors, and it was becoming correspondingly difficult to recruit people to do it. Competent and experienced people were increasingly rare applicants given that public sector pay had been dropping in real terms for more than a decade.

Both sets of parents had offered to prepare the meal in the canteen kitchen, but Wayne and Ellie had adamantly refused. They wanted their family, and all guests, to have an actual party and not be stressed about creating the event. So, the majority of the costs went on outside caterers, and it had all gone exactly as the bride and groom had hoped. They had arrived very much in love with each other and, without any attempt to do so, had shown this love to all who attended.

A tear rolled down Loshie's cheek as she watched her dearest friend confidently say her vows. They had always been inseparable, but to see Ellie publicly declare her love for her husband's brother, seemed to tie them even closer together. They were more than just friends now, they were family.

There were no expensive white lace gowns or bridesmaids wearing over-sized satin dresses, but Ellie looked effortlessly stunning in the simple linen dress she had bought second-hand. Her dark sapphire eyes shone intently at Wayne, who was unable to stop grinning. He couldn't have looked prouder, in his pristine uniform, staring back at the girl he loved. The service was equally simple and understated but finished with warm cheers from the well-wishers, as Ellie and Wayne locked in a tender embrace as they were declared man and wife.

In the evening, they had chosen to have time to themselves to stroll the promenade. It was the place where they had first met, years after leaving school. As they reached the staircase Ellie had rushed up that lunchtime, Wayne gently shoulder-checked her in reminiscence of their first encounter. Ellie did a full twirl, threw her arms around him and they kissed.

'I love you, Ellie Smith.'

'Young love – isn't it pathetic?'

'What?'

Ellie grinned and kissed him again. 'Sorry, that's just something Loshie and I used to say to each other.' Ellie's Armulet bleeped and vibrated. She looked, gasped, and held up the screen for Wayne to see. 'That's something else we used to say to each other all the time. I can't believe she was thinking about that at the same time as me.'

The screen showed a written message: *Girlworld is at peace.* The text disappeared and was replaced by a photo of Luke and Loshie and Ellie and Wayne from the wedding. All smiles, all hugging each other.

She spun again, palms down on the front of her shorts as if they were a skirt that might float up whirling dervish style. Wayne smiled at her, leaning against the railing of the promenade. The place was busy with weekend tourists, but Wayne and Ellie were very much in their own world. The only thing in focus in his field of vision was Ellie. She was twirling just for him.

To conclude the first day of the rest of their lives, bride and groom walked hand in hand towards the setting sun, meandering back in the direction of the coastguard station.

They had no money for a holiday, but, in any case, Wayne's work was not allowing time off at that point. Even for a honeymoon. Ellie had reassured Wayne that the day had been just perfect, and they needed the money. There was a lot of overtime as the cross-Channel migrant influx had ramped up year on year to a level the politicians kept referring to as an "Invasion".

On the streets, a lot of people referred to it as the "African Invasion", but in reality, the desperate came from all over Asia as well. The poor were getting poorer all over the world. Natural disasters combined with the amplification of inequality in all societies meant that everywhere many people were hungry.

Britain had a legacy reputation abroad as a safe haven of decency and opportunity. The coastguard was swamped. Despite the political claims of increased resources being made available by government, it was simply a case of numbers. The small boats leaving Europe to cross the sea outnumbered British government vessels by twenty, some days up to fifty, to one. Even Royal Navy support meant that the quantity of interceptions was but a drop in the ocean.

The pressure for Wayne and his colleagues to solve the problem was utterly misdirected and caused significant stress, even beyond the difficulty and the heart-rending nature of the job itself. The consequent staff absence and overtime shifts meant that everyone involved was exhausted and the vicious circle continued.

Ellie had written an opinion piece in *The Guardian*, under Jude's by-line, likening the situation within the coastguard to the staffing disasters that had befallen the health care system, the prison service and the police in recent years. In the article, she predicted that schools would be next.

Jack picked up the newlyweds from Hove seafront and drove

them back to Jude and Roisin's. Ellie's bedroom was to become their marital home. She looked out at the vibrant streets of her hometown and wondered how long a thriving, positive community could keep a place alive in the face of economic depression. But for now, she basked in the happiness of the day, reliving every moment and wondered what life would hold in store for her and Wayne.

Just before their first wedding anniversary, in a move that beggared the belief of those within the local system, a cost-saving restructure meant the Shoreham coastguard boat was to be redeployed to Hartlepool. Shoreham had only had a boat for three years – it had been part of a previous claim by government that they were tackling the Invasion.

Wayne's duties changed to land-based assistance – helping with casualty transfers from the beaches, assisting the RNLI boat as it brought people ashore. He called the role "Baywatch in uniforms", but most of the time was spent acting essentially as a security guard, in support of the Border Force, when a lot of migrants were captured at once. In less than two months of not going to sea, Wayne had had enough.

They took an anniversary stroll along their stretch of the promenade and sat on a bench to look at the waves. The weather was as hot as it had been on their wedding day, and the sounds and smells brought the happiness of that day back to both of them.

'I love you, Ellie Smith.'

Squeezing his hand Ellie, smiled and stared at her husband who was focussed intently on the water.

Eventually he turned to her and said, 'I can't take it anymore. I'm going to join the lifeboats.'

The RNLI would be a volunteer position, at least initially. The organisation had very few paid staff, and it would probably be years before he had been in long enough to be able to apply for one of those. Wayne had wrestled with the decision ever since the coastguard boat was taken away. He and Ellie couldn't afford for him not to be earning. His father should be able to get Wayne back onto the factory floor, but it would have to be a zero hours contract, so there was no guarantee of any money.

To Wayne's surprise, she was elated. 'That's a brilliant idea! You haven't been happy for… well actually, I reckon much longer than just the last two months. You need to be on the water. This is a great chance – will they take you on straight away?' She was bright and smiling and held his hand up in both of hers.

Wayne's felt his shoulders lift. 'Oh god, I thought you'd be mad, or at least worried, about the money. You know the lifeboat's voluntary?'

She smiled and nodded. 'I'd eat grass if I knew it would be better for your mental health than the last two months.'

He laughed. 'I hope it won't come to that. I can always get a few shifts at the factory, it's just not regular. And there's no pension on that. Shit, I hadn't thought about the pension.'

'Stop.' She paused for the silence to sink in. 'We're years from pension worries. The world could end before then.'

He chuckled. 'Probably next week, at the rate things are going!'

'Anyway, your pension is another thing that is just insignificant compared to how unhappy you've been recently. Get on that lifeboat and get the saltwater in your hair again. Besides, that's more directly helping people. The coastguard hasn't really been about helping people for years.'

Wayne took on a serious tone. 'Well, hang on. The clue is in the name: they're supposed to be guarding our coast.'

'Whatever that means exactly. But you're already referring to it as "they", I'm so pleased. Let's get an ice-cream to celebrate.'

'I don't know that we can afford one now.'

'Oh, cheer up, mopey! It's our anniversary, and we're celebrating your new job. If we can't spend a tenner now, when can we?'

He stood up, pulled Ellie up to standing and kissed her. 'What did I do to deserve you? I feel lucky every single day.'

She twirled away and blew him a kiss. 'Come on then!'

Miles M Hudson

Sunday 1 October 2028
The day before the Bitness Revelations begin.

'I'm gonna need my boot socks,' Wayne called down to Ellie from their little room in Jude and Roisin's house.

She called back up from working on her laptop at the dining table. 'I washed them yesterday, and it's so humid nothing is drying. They're probably still wet – have a look on the drying rack and see.'

'I can't find the drying rack.'

'I'm looking at it – it's down here.'

Ellie was happy that Jude and Roisin were next door at Matthias's for supper. She knew that either or both of them would roll their eyes at Wayne's apparent helplessness. In her mind, Ellie heard Jude's standard sarcastic refrain: 'Did his mother always do everything for him?'

She heard her own typical reply: 'You know he was in the Navy for several years and was commended for his personal organisation on the ship?'

Wayne burst in and started squeezing thick socks. At each one he recoiled in mock horror at its wetness. 'I'm gonna come back with frostbite you realise?'

Wearing only T-shirt and knickers, Ellie twisted in her seat to look out of the kitchen window at the darkening skies, fecund with bulging clouds. 'If you come back with frostbite, we'll have a great article for the science news guy at the paper. "Brighton man loses toes to nanoclimate frostbite!"'

Wayne didn't look up from bending over to test the socks on the bottom rail of the rack. 'Trench foot then. I hate wet socks.'

'Isn't it hot enough that you could wear some thin ones?'

Wayne stood up empty-handed and frowned. 'You know they'll make the boots rub my feet.'

'What about two pairs of thin socks then? Besides, you haven't had a call up – are you sure you'll need to go out tonight?'

A loud gust of wind interrupted the conversation, and Wayne pointed towards the window. 'Oh yeah. There's migrant boats every day, and that storm is gonna be treacherous for the lifeboat, let alone their dinghies.'

'Well, if you wait until you actually get the call, then maybe your socks will have dried by then.'

He put his hands on his hips. 'I told you, I'm going out to see Luke now, so I get a chance before any call comes in.' The wind blew hard again, and this time it came with the start of the rain. 'Although, I'm not sure I'll get over there before the call comes.'

'How's he going? I had a really weird text from Loshie earlier. I think it's just baby brain, but I definitely think she's gonna need some support.'

'You speak to her every day, don't you?'

'I was really meaning support from Luke. I'm a bit worried that she could be ripe for postnatal depression. Make sure you tell him to give her a bit of extra attention. With all his shifts at the factory, and a new baby to look after, it's all too easy to forget about mum.'

'Don't worry, I won't forget about you as soon as Wayne Junior is born.'

Ellie was caught completely off guard. She had expected that they would want to have children at some point, but they had never directly discussed it. She shook her head to clear the confusion and told herself, *You're happy with the idea of motherhood. Where's the shock here, after his brother has a baby three days ago?*

To Wayne, she replied, 'One baby at a time. Make sure you support Luke, and that he knows to support Loshie. She claims that Maggi is an absolute dream to look after, and I suspect she's protesting too much.'

'Why don't you come along too? You can put your mind at ease and have a bit of a girls' chat support group thing too.' After a pause, he added, 'Might put you in the mood for making a baby too.' Wayne stepped around the table heading towards Ellie.

'Back in your box, Caveman! I've got a deadline. I'll be at this till midnight, probably.'

Wayne stopped, twirled away and blew her a kiss, mocking Ellie's own quirks.

She returned to the issue of Luke and Loshie's new baby blues. 'How is Luke, though? He's such a softie that I always assume he's happy and coping well. Has he said anything to you?'

'He's fine. You're right that she definitely wears the trousers there, but he's a trooper. He can cope with work, and Maggi, and any abuse from Loshie.'

'Don't use the word "abuse". She's overbearing and high strung sometimes but save that word for when it's really appropriate.'

'Um, okay. I mean of course she's not abusive. I was just meaning, um, yeah, overbearing I guess is the right word. But she's always been like that, it's nothing to do with Maggi.'

'What I'm asking is, how is that extra burden taking its toll on him? Is Luke OK?'

'Don't use the word "burden" – she's a joy, a delight.'

Ellie held up her hands in surrender. 'Of course, but you know what I'm getting at. Is he really a trooper, inwardly I mean? I'm just a bit worried about them. I want it all to be a joy and a delight, and if a little bit of support from us helps them go down that path and not a less good one, then let's do that.'

Wayne smiled, a little, confused smile. He stepped back next to her, bent over and kissed her cheek with a sort of half hug, as best he could manage with her sitting at the table. 'I'm pretty sure my brother's OK, but I'll go over, have a beer with him, coo over his daughter, and see how he's doing. See how they're both doing.' Wayne added, 'I can't wait till it's Luke coming over here for a beer and to check I'm doing OK with a new baby.'

She leaned her head over on to his arm and smiled weakly.

'You're keen on *having* children, aren't you?' he asked, standing back upright. 'I always just assumed you were. Please tell me you are. I never even considered you might not be.'

'I am. Not yet, but I'm looking forward to a family life with you.' She was talking through a smile. 'We're going to have to talk about names though, Wayne Junior is never going to happen.'

'Well, I get that, if it's a girl. But when we have a boy, I assume I'll be in charge of naming my son and heir.'

The Times of Malthus

Ellie tried to hit his arm, but Wayne had moved just out of reach. He grinned.

She pointed at the door. 'Your roller hockey socks are in the bottom drawer if they'll work in your boots.'

He scampered out. Ellie's face became serious. She turned her face to look at the laptop screen but wasn't focused on the words. They had a fun relationship. She enjoyed their banter, and they were able to inject humour into every discussion. She wondered if it was too much; if they never held a serious conversation, did he ever take anything seriously? Ellie shook her head to chase away the doubts. For all his light-heartedness, her husband was the most dutiful and responsible man she had ever met. She knew that the things they agreed were agreed. When he determined a course of action, he followed through, and she loved that reliability.

Ellie looked over the laptop screen into space and engaged in something of a Socratic dialogue with herself:

Who's going to earn the money if I'm off on maternity leave? I don't even have a real job that pays maternity.

Hey, you can still work exactly the same as you are now. You don't go to work, and half the time they don't even know you've written it, if it's for Mum's by-line.

Yeah, I get that I don't need to worry about being able to access the work, but, quite apart from actually finding the time to write, how will I concentrate? I won't get enough sleep for years.

Wayne will help a lot. He can juggle his work around and volunteer less on the lifeboats.

That's not really an option though, is it? His time is already completely filled, and he couldn't turn down a lifeboat call if they needed him. I wouldn't want him to either.

Everybody makes it work. It is work, but what would you do? Not have children?

Ellie sighed and stood up to make a cup of tea.

Miles M Hudson

Book 2

The Times of Malthus

The Times of Malthus

The Bitness Manifesto was originally posted in 2027 on a hacker website hosted in Guinea-Bissau. The reposting below hit global social media in late 2028, twenty-four hours prior to their infodump:

We Are Bitness

We are a globally distributed and disparate collective of information warriors. We seek to publish only truth and to discredit those who empower and enrich themselves at the expense of others, using lies, deceit and misinformation.

Our motto is: **There will be no secrets.**

Wikileaks tried to show you the truth. Snowden tried to show you the truth. The Panama Papers tried to show you the truth. The Pandora Papers tried to show you the truth. Bilpadean tried to show you the truth. None of it seemed enough to stir you into action to right those wrongs.

So, for the last ten years, we have been hacking from the bottom to the top. Any organisation with influence over more than a million people, we've hacked into their practices. Some are open about their exploitation of others. Some are not. But we have the tools to expose the truth to you. Most are corrupt, venal in one way or another. All are exploitative.

We investigated national governments, regional governments, municipal governments, local councils, multinational corporations, big companies, small companies, state companies, private companies, religious organisations, charitable organisations, armies, supranational organisations, drug cartels, the mafia, sports' governing bodies, manufacturers of medical devices, fast food outlets, shipping fleets, telecoms organisations, the list goes on and on and on and on and on…

THEY ALL EXPLOIT YOU

They often cheat, steal, lie and even kill to enable their exploitation, and they usually try to hide what they're doing. We will expose it all to you, the people of Earth. We do not believe the current way of living is right, but we do believe that you should be able to decide whether or not to accept it.

The Bitness Revelations will shine a light on the corruption – you do with the truth what you will.

After fifteen days of information releases, amounting to nearly a petabyte of data, in October 2028, the Bitness website and social media were updated with the following text:

The Bitness Revelations have now shown you the staggering scale of exploitation of human by fellow human.

It so astounded and enraged us that we extended our investigations to look at smaller organisations. We discovered that there is a tipping point. If an organisation has influence over fewer than 10,000 people, it will operate in a much more benign way. We found very few instances of unfair advantage in such small population influence groups. If they preside influence over more than 10,000 people…

THEY WILL EXPLOIT YOU

The Times of Malthus
Sunday 8 October 2028
Days after the Bitness Revelations begin.

A three-dimensional rotary dial telephone floated in the air in front of the ornamental fireplace in Jude and Roisin's lounge room. It shook as it blared out a ringing sound.

'Turn it down a bit, can you?' Roisin's question was really an instruction.

Ellie answered, 'It's just the ringer that's loud, it'll be quieter when they're talking.' She waved a finger downwards near the Armulet strapped to her forearm, and the ringing quietened. The phone disappeared, and a life size projected image of Loshie appeared. She was sitting on Jack and Diane's sofa, and Maggi lay in a baby bed on the coffee table beside her knees.

Loshie shouted away from the visible scene, 'We've started the call.'

'Coming,' came the muted reply from Diane, out of the projection space, probably in her kitchen. Jack and Diane walked in and stood beside the sofa, all four of them projected to appear in the other family's lounge as if they were there too.

Sitting beside Ellie, Wayne asked, 'Where's Luke?'

Their father answered his son, 'He's at the factory. The riots that have kicked off in town have got the owners scared – they're wanting everything shored up in case trouble comes to Kemptown.'

'Batten down the hatches, eh? Seems a bit much though – the protests are against government stuff. I mean, I know they were just rioting in Churchill Square last night, but a printworks in a mostly residential area? Surely that's not going to be a target, is it?' He looked to Ellie sitting beside him for confirmation.

'Everywhere's a target,' Loshie interjected. 'It's absolutely disgusting what's been going on! And I don't mean the rioting. No wonder we've all been finding life so tough these days – it's just robbery. Every organisation robbing us blind.'

Wayne was none the wiser. 'Our factory isn't stealing from people. It's just a business. People working hard to make stuff that other people need to make their businesses successful.'

Loshie seemed to be on a soapbox, and Jude and Roisin and Matthias all nodded in unison at most of the things she ranted. 'All business is contributing to the problems. Every one of them tries to minimise costs and maximise profits, without any concern for the welfare of the people. If anything, they're worse. At least all the corruption in government institutions is actually considered to be illegal.'

Matthias chimed in, 'All property is theft.'

Ellie squeezed her husband's thigh. 'But also, once a mob gets going, there's not a huge amount of reasoned consideration for the targets. I reckon it's a good idea to lock up the factory tight and see how many days these protests go on.'

Luke clattered into the image and gave everyone a wave. He was out of breath, but the conversation paused for him to contribute. 'Bloody hell, it's kicking off out there.'

Jack looked worried and asked about the factory security.

'Well, we boarded up all the windows and doors, so just gotta hope that people don't think of it as a bad place that needs wrecking. We took the sign down too, so hopefully for people who don't know this area, it'll just look derelict already. What's it like round Hove? It's absolutely mad at this end of town. Any signs, benches, bins, everything. If it's too small to help build a barricade, they throw it at the police or through a shop window. And if they can't move it, they set fire to it. I mean there's hundreds of people out there.'

Wayne replied, 'Oh my god, really? Near Mum and Dad's house?'

'Well, not in our street, but just round the corner they're attacking the hospital. I mean, a hospital for God's sake. You've got people smashing the place up at one end, and then they're going into A&E at the other when they hurt themselves in the rioting. It's nuts.'

Jude said, 'I wrote a piece, what, three years ago, saying that the healthcare privatisation would end in disaster. I didn't quite mean "Tear down the hospitals!" but I'm not at all surprised that they're a target. Private healthcare is one of the most pernicious capitalist enterprises there is. It really is exploitation of the little people. Have you read what Bitness found out about Sussex Hospitals?'

'No, what?' Diane was agog.

'Well, it's not really anything special for our area – all the healthcare companies operate in the same way, but basically, they're taking money from the taxpayer through the government subsidies, then charging patients as well – all publicly known stuff so far – but Bitness found that they were defrauding at both ends massively, and then also buying in second-hand equipment from the Far East, stuff that's not considered safe by our medical standards. A lot of it stuff that was rejected by the Chinese health system as substandard. I mean, "Tear down the hospitals!" maybe isn't such a bad incitement.'

Loshie said, 'You're right. We need a fundamental reset. It's obscene how the rich just take everything, and people nowadays physically can't work enough to make enough to feed their families. I'm with the rioters myself.'

Luke looked at his wife but said nothing. Wayne recognised the expression as the same as when they had been young, and Luke had told his big brother about failing a test in some school class.

Ellie thought her mother was being a bit smug, as Jude continued, 'This is exactly the stuff we've been trying to write about for the last twenty years. But nobody took us seriously. It's like everybody looked at the canary, dead down the mine, and sort of shrugged and mumbled, "Oh, that's a bit of a shame," without taking on board what it was telling them.'

Roisin followed up. 'Well, bear in mind not many people really read *The Guardian*.'

Jude countered, 'They do read it. They just don't act on it.'

'Not really. We've got a loyal readership who are all on board with doing the right thing. But the masses who are out there rioting right now – they're watching *Prison of Love* and getting their news from the Metaverse. It's the uber rich controllers of the big media who've been putting the scales on everyone's eyes for years, adding layers and layers of scales with pretty pictures painted on the insides. It's archetypal distraction propaganda.'

'Thank heaven that Bitness have removed the scales from everyone's eyes,' Loshie added.

Wayne said, 'Ironic really, that they all got the news of the Bitness Revelations so quickly via the Metaverse.'

Jack joined in, 'Yeah, I love that when there was bad shit that included them, Meta didn't have enough capacity to take down the billions of posts and videos about it.'

'I'm not surprised – there's so much of it. Everyday there's more, and not just one big story, hundreds, including stuff about every local area. I mean we all knew the big politicians are corrupt, but it's everywhere.'

'I'm glad it's gone down. Permanently I hope.' Loshie sounded the most bitter of them all. She shifted on the sofa, moving the baby to rest on her other arm.

Maggi chose that moment to start crying, and Luke bent down and picked her up into a jiggling hug. Loshie looked up at the two of them, but her face didn't soften: her conviction was clear.

Ellie changed the direction of their family conversation. 'How has Maggi been? She was very good just now, and she's quietened down immediately.'

Loshie was silent, so Luke responded. 'She's been OK. Like you'd expect a baby to be, I suppose. Mum and Dad have helped enormously when we've both had to go to work. I mean they've had to work too, but we've all sort of banded together and worked out our shifts so at least one person is always here for her.'

Roisin asked, 'How does that work with feeding her? I mean if you're at work, Loshie.'

Loshie shrugged. 'She's on formula milk anyway, so it doesn't make any difference. Anybody can make that up.'

Ellie gave her mother a hard look. Everyone knew that Loshie had declined to breastfeed Maggi, and the more they had tried to encourage her, the more she had insisted that it wasn't for her. She seemed to flit around a range of reasons for feeding with formula milk, and everybody wanted to try and support her as much as possible. The fact that the formula milk was incredibly expensive made things very difficult for the entire Smith family household.

Loshie's decision, on environmental grounds, to use cloth nappies that could be washed and reused had helped a little with the costs, but that in itself had made it more difficult for everyone to argue with Loshie about breastfeeding. With Maggi at ten days old, they presumed she had now passed the stage where they would be able to change her mind. Loshie wasn't the sort of person to whom you put that kind of question.

Maggi cried again, and Luke disappeared from view to go and change her nappy.

Roisin Keane, writing in *The Guardian* website of 9 October 2028, published an opinion piece with the following text:

All Governments Corrupt?

In just a week, the Bitness Revelations have provided conclusive evidence of what cynics of all political persuasions have been saying for years. But now the evidence is meticulously detailed and irrefutable.

It is truly damning.

From straightforward embezzlement and bribery to systemically enshrined exploitation, there is no area of moral decrepitude that governments have failed to abuse. Moreover, it is endemic to all governments, at all levels, in every nation. Something inherent in the fabric of governance makes man exploit his fellow man.

The old adage said, 'Power corrupts.' Now we have proof – corruption is within the very nature of society.

So, what do we do about it?

People are already protesting outside Parliament. The right to do so, and for those protests to enable change from the government, has been part of our democracy since its inception. However, Bitness has exposed that this can only be a veneer, glossing over the shabby framework on which society is built.

The Bitness research demonstrates beyond all doubt that we don't just need root and branch change – we need to scorch the forest to the ground and begin again with a fundamentally different landscape. The problem is one of large-scale influence. Without the checks and balances provided by knowing your leaders

The Times of Malthus

personally, they will always lose their humanity and, usually unknowingly, engage in the exploitation of their fellow citizens. We need to dismantle the whole of society and separate everyone into village-sized groups. These groups will need to be self-sufficient, so there can be no large-scale influence.

Is it even possible? How do you dismantle an entire society, and all its international, interlinked systems? How do you empower self-sufficiency in every community?

The first mental reset we must all accept is to recognise that a whole new order will initially cause hardship. We will all need to endure a sudden lack of modern comforts. This very newspaper has too much influence to be able to value and support all those over whom it has influence, which is a much wider group than merely the readership.

Could you do without your daily national newspaper? If you want to reshape a better world, we're going to have to. How did I get this past my editor, who is responsible to the shareholders in the end? Surely advocating the end of my employer is no way to succeed? The writing is on the wall. The very notion of distant shareholders dictating the actions of a company is the exact issue Bitness have revealed. Those whose actions can influence you must be in front of you. You should know them. They should have to look you in the eye and say what they want to say or do what they want to do.

However, that movement into small communities will, of necessity, break the supply chains for not just big things like cars but everyday comforts like chocolate. Unless your village can grow and process the ingredients to make chocolate, you won't be able to get it. 'She's mad!' I hear you cry. 'No chocolate?!'

This can be positive. To understand the way forward, you have to go back and think about how humankind has grown and lived for the vast majority of its history. Small village groups, your tribe, your clan, your family, survived for millennia on only what they could hunt, gather or grow. The idea that chicken comes ready cooked in a bucket is such a new concept that your grandparents may remember the time before it. Most of the foundation of your life is from this generation. Forget my grandparents, I can remember the time before the internet. Younger readers may not realise that there was a time, barely before they were born, when there were no electronic devices and communications were mostly done by *actually talking to each other*.

Before I am carted away ranting and screaming, let me point out that this new world order will be better than all the mod cons we've developed in the last couple of centuries. In recent times, we've been hit with a pandemic of poor mental health. This is a part of the human psyche, and we'll always have mental health issues to deal with in our community. However, the scale of problems in the last ten or twenty years has been a direct result of large-scale influences. The very fact that the term 'influencers' rose to prominence in the last ten years should have been a dead canary in the mine for us.

I said this would be positive: when you live in a small community, and you know your neighbours – especially if some of them are your kin – there's a natural tendency to support the community, to talk to and help your neighbours. That is exactly the low-level support the human mind was designed to receive daily, but we've been losing ourselves in anonymity. That low level support is real, and we gain comfort from those real interactions. Again, when you're talking to your neighbour face to face, you both gain empathy, and that is an elixir to our mental health.

Steel yourself for a very different daily existence. Your food will be repetitive, and it will be hard work to get it. You and your neighbours and family will strive together and laugh together. The satisfaction of that work will be better than all the money you could get paid for it, and the idea of money will seem trivial and annoying. Stop trying to find better elsewhere and look to the joys and delights that already surround you.

We must try. Every human must be valued and treated equally. If that valuing and decent treatment can only be ensured within a small local community, so be it. We must not settle for less.

Get out there and change the world. Make your village your whole world.

Miles M Hudson

Monday 9 October 2028
The immediate aftermath of the Bitness Revelations.

As the air filled with the sound of protestors shouting 'Smash the State! Smash the State!', Ellie marched along, with her mothers by her side, and her Armulet projected an image of Wayne directly in front of her. Although he was walking forwards, Ellie's projection of him created the illusion that he was in fact moving backwards, as she and the column of protesters progressed through the streets.

'Shouldn't you be working?' he asked.

'This is much more important. Ellie waved her hand dismissively in the general direction of everywhere around her. Newspapers aren't long for this world, mark my words. Where are you off to?'

Wayne frowned in puzzlement but ignored her rhetoric. 'That's why I'm ringing. There's two migrant boats in trouble – we've gotta go out and help them.'

'Be safe.'

'I'll be fine – it's you I'm worried about. Don't get caught up in anything crazy. There's no telling what a mob will end up doing, especially if the police come out heavy-handed.'

'Half the people in this protest are police. They get paid as badly as anyone else. And worse, they have to protect the people doing the exploiting and enforce their will, and always at a danger to themselves. The police are some of the most riled up people here.'

'Well, just be careful, please.'

'Love you!' She had to shout to make sure Wayne heard, but it wasn't a suitable cry for a protest march against inequality and corruption. Luckily, her shout was lost in the cacophony. Wayne teased her by signing off with a pirouette, and his projection vanished.

Jude started up a shout of "Thanks to all those who serve!", which was taken up by the crowd for nearly two minutes. The march was disjointed and often heated. Anything along Western Road that represented the State or big business was smashed, even benevolent things like litter bins. For every destructive act, it seemed like the marchers had a rallying cry to justify it. People held objections to everything. The Bitness Revelations had exposed exploitation in just about all things.

"Clean up your own litter, McDonald's!"

"Stop making packaging!"

Jude had to lean in and shout across Ellie so the others could hear her. 'This is not like other protests. There's an edge to this. I don't like it.'

'There's fire in their bellies this time, you mean,' Roisin shouted, her expression gleeful as she surveyed the crowd. 'Not surprising when there's been hunger in their bellies for so long. This is it, Jude. The revolution is here. For years, we've been moaning and complaining that nobody gets off their arse to actually make the changes that need to be made. Well, here it is.'

'Smashing up road signs isn't the change that needs to be made,' Jude shouted back, looking increasingly worried. Her hand gripped Ellie's ever more tightly. This lot aren't looking to make positive changes in society.'

'God, yes they are, Mum!' Ellie shouted, partly to be heard, but mostly in frustration at Jude. 'We've been building up to this for years. Every week, you've been writing about some new injustice or exploitation, for as long as I can remember.' She waved her hand back and forth to indicate both her parents. 'Now, all of that has finally come home to a head. But it isn't going to be fixed with just some small adjustments in life. The change that needs to come isn't going to be new legislation in Parliament. The change needs to be fundamental. Back to the land, no more big organisations, start again from scratch.'

'People can't do that.' Jude shook her head, but Roisin was nodding.

Ellie continued, 'Of course they can't, that's why the system has been able to grind them down for so long. I told you this in my first week at King's, and I told you again it in my first week back here after uni. Have you actually been listening to what you've been writing all these years?'

Roisin took up the challenge. 'I was listening. If we want a real human future, we're going to have to take such radical steps. We need to stop capitalism in its tracks. If that means you don't get to have video games anymore, people will have to live without them.'

Jude shook her head. 'But they won't. That's always been the problem. It's easy to show them what's shit in life. In fact, you don't really need to show them, they already know. What's hard to do is make them believe in some unknown future where they don't get KFC and watching football. Somehow, somebody needs to lead them into that promised land. Not just tell them about it, actually step forward and lead them to it. Otherwise, this is all going to end badly.'

The march had continued along Western Road and finished up outside Churchill Square, Brighton's main shopping centre. All the big-name stores had outlets inside or near the centre, and the crowd filled the streets, the square outside, the main indoor shopping concourse, and most side streets for several blocks. As Ellie had told Wayne, only a handful of police were there in uniform, and they were shouting anarchist slogans the loudest.

A man and a woman were lifted up onto the roof of a coffee shack and they addressed the crowd with a megaphone. The wind was gusty and short little clouds, like racing cars, whizzed across the sky, appearing from behind Churchill Square and shooting over the ringleaders' heads to disappear in the direction of the Jubilee Clock Tower outside Boots.

The man rallied the mob with invective against the rich and their exploitation of pretty much everyone. The woman turned these rallying cries into calls for action. Generally, she was inciting violent and destructive action.

The shopping centre security guards, meantime, were attempting to empty the place and lock the doors, even though it was the middle of the afternoon. The guards' hearts weren't really in their work. They agreed with the outrage of the mob.

The Times of Malthus

Nonetheless, the uniforms and their orders to repel the intruders and try to secure the centre turned into a flashpoint for the assembled masses.

With the mob's fervour at fever pitch, the woman on the coffee kiosk shouted instructions to different areas of the crowd, directing their wrath against the businesses near them. Those inside Churchill Square were told to smash the place and take all the goods and dump them in the street for the poorest to have.

There was a brief hesitancy, until the first rubbish bin was thrown at a shop window. It bounced off harmlessly, but it was like a starting pistol. Benches were raised aloft, and they did smash the huge glass panels. Doors were ripped off hinges.

In some stores, people simply filled their own pockets, but in most places, an order emerged from the chaos. Human chains spontaneously formed, and the consumer goods were passed out all the way to form a long pile lining Western Road.

Two security guards had not been quick enough to slip through the keypad-locked security doors into the bowels of the shopping centre. They were lifted up and passed overhead, like crowd surfing rock stars, to the square outside the main doors. Both shouted that they had to feed their families, and this was the only work they could get, and the crowd was sympathetic. Once they had been stripped of their uniforms, the men were left alone to leave the area. Coffee kiosk woman even told them to help themselves to some new clothes from the newly set up bank of goods for the poor.

Jude, Roisin and Ellie watched from the periphery of the action. Ellie got pulled into a human chain that snaked too close for her to avoid helping out. Mothers and daughter were all unsure of whether this lawlessness was in fact something they agreed with. Jude pointed out that these were radical steps and asked if they were the ones Roisin had envisaged. She had no answer. Ellie shouted to them to help and be part of the change they'd been campaigning for all their lives. They demurred, still unsure if this was in fact what they had meant in all their newspaper columns about redressing the inequalities in society.

Western Road was blocked by sheer numbers of people, and

the woman instructed them to continue to destroy all paraphernalia of government and big business, everything, from any remaining road signs, to the pay public toilets, to the bronze-coloured double-decker buses. Those bus drivers who had chosen to wait, in the expectation of being able to continue on their way when the crowd eventually dispersed, were politely asked to vacate their vehicle, before it was ceremoniously smashed up and set on fire.

The entire frontage of Marks and Spencer was scraped off by another bus, used as a bulldozer. Santander Bank was the focus of the most violent attacks. Again, the staff were told to leave, and a variety of makeshift demolition tools were employed to attempt to knock the place down. The bank's alarm started to sound after a Sky TV installer's van was commandeered to ram the big double doorway. No police responded to the siren's call.

Within the crowd, less than a quarter of the participants chose to try and loot goods for themselves. The majority feeling was very much to hurt the big businesses and organisations of the state that had propped up the capitalist system and destroyed so many lives over the years, and that Bitness had exposed as doing so consciously and deliberately.

People got hurt in the melee, but only accidentally. The megaphone told the mob that the lowly people working for these organisations in Brighton were not to blame and no violence against them would rebalance things. Indeed, many of them joined in the rioting. Another bank's manager refused to leave his branch and was killed, when the building was rammed and most of the frontage collapsed.

Jude and Roisin threw themselves into acting as medical support for the injured. The emergency services' phone number was constantly engaged, and no emergency services arrived at any stage. Even if they had attempted to attend, the roads were blocked by the thronging crowds, barricades of destroyed shop fittings, and vehicles on fire.

Ellie continued to support the directed activities, where she considered that the actions would benefit the poor. She couldn't see that setting a bus ablaze was going to help a single mother feed her kids, but making piles of children's clothes, shoes, and toys for them to take away would clearly benefit those in need.

Early October 2028 was sunny and twenty-five degrees. With the addition of fires that were often out of control, and a mass of several thousand people, Ellie was hot and sweaty for most of the afternoon. A little after five o'clock, she went into the Churchill Square food court and helped herself to a bottle of water. She walked over to a table where the chairs remained for sitting, did a full twirl and sat down to rest.

She tried to call Wayne, but her Armulet couldn't connect. The network was functioning well – she was able to watch a vlog broadcast from Loshie who was at a riot at Westminster, protesting the government directly – but Wayne was probably busy with the migrant boats. They were likely to be overloaded and unseaworthy. Most were, and the challenge for the RNLI was that their own boat was often too small to rescue everyone aboard a larger, sinking boat. They carried spare inflatable life-rafts and often had to make several trips to bring to shore all the scared migrants. That brought problems of its own. Often aggressive young men on the boats would not accept that the lifeboat would rescue the sick, injured, elderly, infirm, pregnant and youngest first. Language barriers always stood in the way of explaining this simply and reassuringly to the frightened men, many of whom could not swim. Wayne had recounted several instances where he had literally had to punch people back off the lifeboat to make the point clear.

Instead, Ellie called Jude and Roisin to come and join her for a break. They compared notes, excited and enthralled at the events unfolding around them.

'This is like nothing I've seen before.'

'Like nothing there's been before. I've seen bad actors hijack protests before to make anarchist statements, but that's not what's happening here. I don't know who those two are that are leading things, but they're working everything the right way,' Jude said.

Rosin agreed, 'Yes, I've never seen anarchists include keeping everyone safe as part of their rhetoric. And these aren't just criminal rioters – most people are collecting the stuff to share out just like that woman said to do. It's bizarre.'

Ellie said, 'It's what should have come out of the Bitness Revelations. This is a perfect rebalancing.'

'I wouldn't call it "perfect" – we've tended to a lot of people who've been injured. I can't imagine that nobody's been killed.'

Roisin nodded. 'They have, you're right. But making such a great change in society can only come with some sacrifices. Think how many people have died from the poverty the system entrenched. We're breaking out of those chains. We've got to think about it as saving lives.'

Ellie and Jude looked around the smashed shopping centre silently. They didn't argue.

Jude asked, 'Did you say Loshie was in London?'

'Uh-huh.'

'Well, who's looking after Maggi? She hasn't taken her to the riot, has she?'

'Don't be stupid, Mum, of course she hasn't. Maggi is at home with Diane.'

'Oh my god, on her own? We should go and look after them. I can't imagine being at home alone with a granddaughter and all this going on outside.'

'I messaged ten minutes ago – they're OK. Jack and Luke are out protecting the factory, but Diane reckons she's OK at home. She says the street's busy with people running backwards and forwards, but they're not smashing up little terraced houses. She's locked herself in and barricaded the doors but isn't really worried.'

The Times of Malthus
Friday 13 October 2028
Nearly a fortnight after the start of the Bitness Revelations.

Ellie watched Jude and Roisin as they worked with pen and paper at their kitchen table. Their laptops were closed up in front of them, power leads sat on top, wound up neatly, like ropes on the deck of a ship. They were scrawling quickly, and the letters were poorly formed. Both wrote feverishly as if channelling the words through some sort of automatic writing.

Matthias buzzed around making soup and sandwiches for lunch. He had used vegetables from the greenhouse and had finished the last of the breadmaking flour from Jude's cupboard. They didn't stop for a meal break. Like a worker bee, Matthias placed the food within arm's reach and cleared away dead cups of tea. The women were not queen bees though, they were working like drones themselves.

Since the Bitness Revelations had finished dumping information thirteen days previously, Jude and Roisin had worked furiously, reporting on all the reaction and protests against the governments and corporations. Ellie had been brought up to work hard, but this was unlike anything she had seen in all her life. She worried that her mothers had gotten themselves caught up in a cycle of reporting the news that was no longer useful.

For as long as Ellie could remember, they had investigated politicians and businessmen accused of operating illegally or immorally. Jude and Roisin always backed the common people against being ground down by the unstoppable machines of capitalism.

By their actions, they had shown their daughter that this was a mission, a duty, the charge of the righteous, and to shirk the responsibility was to betray humanity. The sheer scale of the illegal and immoral activities revealed by Bitness, though, was beyond the scope of what two journalists from Brighton could ever manage to report on. Even if they considered reporting on the responses of the outraged public in Brighton alone, the local protests and riots were being mirrored in every city and every country around the world. It would have taken an army of journalists to fulfil the news cycle with professional reporting.

'Mum. Mum! Will you stop so we can all have some lunch together. Give yourselves a break so we can talk about what you've found out. Stop!'

Roisin flourished a full stop, put her pen down and gave Ellie an obsequious smile. Jude continued in a trance-like movement of her pen, continuously flowing, producing a slightly wiggly line on her notepad, which everyone assumed she could comprehend to read back. Roisin looked at Ellie and then leant over and clasped her wife's hand. It kept moving as if possessed, but Jude was smiling to them all, theatrically sending up their non-stop work.

Matthias seemed pleased to be able to sit and talk with them, rather than simply to watch and feed them. Ellie grabbed a small apple from the wooden tub on the floor, dipped it in a rinsing bowl and crunched a bite of her lunch.

Matthias said, 'It's good to stop for lunch – you need to keep your strength up.'

Jude yawned and put her hand to her forehead. When she opened her eyes again, she replied 'I know how nice it is to eat together, but I really don't have time for a break. I've got ten articles lined up to write this afternoon-evening. I mean none of it is brilliantly written, but so much is going on, it's unreal. It's like we wrote in slow motion until Bitness, and now we're delivering what was possible, but we never tried for before. Of course, I guess with the power cut it's slowing down the actual process, but I definitely feel like I'm producing ten times the copy I could a month ago.'

Ellie scowled. 'Why are you doing this?'

'What do you mean?'

'All this…' she gestured towards the pens and notepads and piles of blank paper ready to be scrawled on. 'How is this going to help? We've passed a point of no return. The world is changing so utterly, your arguments and posturing are going to be irrelevant within hours if not days. You're wasting your time.'

Matthias hated any kind of conflict, and he leapt in to try and distract everyone from arguing. 'How can you submit your articles when there's no power?'

Roisin replied with a smile, 'You are old school, Matty. You're right that our laptops have run out of battery, but our Armulets run on kinetic charging.'

Matthias muttered, 'Course they do,' and nodded.

Roisin continued, 'Write the article text out long hand. Once you're happy with it, dictate it to the Armulet, and the infonetwork seems to still be operational, so the newspaper website is still available to get the news out to the public.'

Matthias wanted to have something useful to contribute. 'Ah, well, that's because the infonetwork is a distributed system.' He continued on as if everyone must know what that meant. 'The integration of the internet with mobile phone communications made it even more difficult to break now, than even just a few years ago. And whilst the power system is sort of distributed, it relies on far fewer crucial parts. The big power stations mostly. If they're all out, then the handful of solar and wind farms will stick some electricity into the grid, but it's never going to be enough.'

'Wait, how are the infonetwork servers still going then?'

'I don't know for sure, but I'd guess those that are still on have all got local renewables recharging their battery backups. Like the PV cells we've got that heat the water and the greenhouse. Or they're in other countries where the power is still on.'

'Nowhere still has its power grid running properly –'

'Hold on, have we still got electricity from your solar cells?' Roisin pulled her laptop towards her and uncoiled the power cable.

'Of course, like I say, it's wired into the water heating, and we run the hot water pipes through the greenhouse.'

Ellie butted in, 'You know it's twenty-two degrees outside.'

Matthias nodded. 'Of course, how do you think we got these peppers and tomatoes to grow?'

Roisin waved her hand dismissively. 'No, I mean could we use that electricity to power the laptops?'

Matthias tipped his head to one side in thought. 'Yes, probably. It takes so much electricity to heat the water, that we've always used the national grid for the sockets. I only ever installed the solar cells for the greenhouse really. They're on totally separate circuits, but I guess if the grid is out, then it should be possible to wire our cells to the sockets.'

Ellie butted in again, but more usefully this time. 'Isn't there a socket in the greenhouse that is already connected to those cells? I thought you added that separately when you put up the solar cells, no?'

Matthias pointed at Ellie like she was the winner in a television game show. 'Yes, you're right! Give me those laptops, ladies, Matthias to the rescue.'

Jude and Roisin handed over the machines and their wires and Matthias disappeared out through the door connecting their kitchen to his adjoining home. Ellie's mothers looked at each other with exaggerated, but silent, questioning shrugs, as if to say, 'How could he not have thought of that before?'

Ellie continued to interrogate her mothers' working practices. 'Didn't rioters destroy *The Guardian* offices on Wednesday? Why are you still working?'

Jude laughed. '*The Guardian* is not its offices. Like the infonetwork, we're distributed. Roisin and I write here, post online, the paper is helping the world through information, as we've always done.

To the uninformed, we're just another corporation, another way for media moguls to make a bunch of illicit money. It's not surprising that they trashed the offices. But we're still supporting the common people by disseminating the truth. Our reporting has been totally supportive of Bitness – I suspect none of those rioters ever actually read our articles.'

Roisin countered that being supportive of Bitness was not necessarily the same as not corrupt, or indeed the same as being positively equitable. The discussion then wandered around some of the events they'd been writing about and the difficulty of keeping pace with the events locally, nationally and internationally.

Jude seemed oblivious to Ellie's scepticism about the value of going on with reporting the news. She asked her daughter, 'Do you think you could help us with writing some of these articles? Your copy is always so clear and concise, I reckon you could rattle through a lot of this stuff.' She pointed at the research notebook in front of her.

Ellie looked aghast. Her mother had clearly not taken in a word of her worries.

Jude misinterpreted this further and tried to play on their struggle to keep up with the work. 'There's so much destruction on so many fronts, it seems impossible to keep up with it all. And there's so many human-interest pieces you could do to support the basic reporting. Poverty was everywhere before Bitness, and now so many workplaces have been destroyed that people are having to steal to eat. Everyday folk are looting, rioting and fighting each other for the spoils. You could do such a good piece about the turnaround in a person who is now willing to rob from a shop just to eat.'

Ellie's face turned to deeper confusion. Was her mother so naive about all the events around her? 'Stop and think slowly for a minute. Please. Everything you're saying is looking at the last two weeks through the lens of how life was before. Bitness has changed everything. We are heading for a totally new way of living, a totally new society.'

'That's what I mean, this is a real chance to change things.'

'No, Jude. You've missed the degree of change that is going on here.'

Roisin watched the other two. Her head bobbed occasionally up and down in agreement, but she said nothing.

Ellie continued, 'You will not be getting paid for writing these articles.'

Jude frowned.

'You will never be getting paid by *The Guardian* again. I'd be surprised if we even continue to use money.'

Her mother's eye twitched slightly.

Ellie carried on, 'Am I getting through? There's no electricity. They've attacked all the shops – we were there on Monday. That wasn't just a riot – they cleared out all the shops.

And that happened everywhere. Don't think the shops will be sending new stuff. Don't think they'll be advertising on *The Guardian* website. You must think differently about everything.'

Jude whispered, 'But what will life be like then? How are we going to make society fair, like we want?'

Roisin reached out and held her hand on the tabletop.

The Times of Malthus

In mid-October 2028, vlogger 'LOLoshie' posted this ArmuletLive broadcast:

Loshie stands in front of a protesting crowd, with hands clasped in front of her, and speaks directly to camera:

'I'm still outside the Houses of Parliament with the protest group Take Back Everything. From the Bitness infodump, we know that our fears about the corruption by the rich and powerful were only the tip of the iceberg of truth.

We're here to tell them, "Enough is enough," and level things up properly.'

Loshie turns to chant in synch with the protest group, shouts aimed at the main building of the British government.

'Take it back! Take it all back! Take Back Everything! What you have is ours! It's all ours! Give back everything! We're here to take it back! Take Back Everything!'

She pans her Armulet camera further along the side of the Palace of Westminster. The lunchtime light is an unusual orange pall. Another group of protesters have knocked down a stretch of iron railings with a bulldozer. They surge into the lawned space beside the main Parliament building. Take Back Everything break into more raucous individual shouts, some berating the other mob, some cheering them on.
Loshie turns back to the 3D recording focus point. Her Armulet projects a blue face in the air – an imaginary interlocutor for her to speak to, as if in direct conversation with her social media followers. Her hands are again clasped in front: King's College media-trained sincerity.

'You can see the scale of the rage that has been released by the Bitness Revelations.'

Around Loshie, thirty to forty colleagues from Take Back Everything are live streaming their own polemics and documentaries.
The more aggressive second mob have started throwing stones, railing spikes, and litter bins through the buildings leaded windows. Dressed in an incongruous mixture of all black combat clothing and England football shirts, they make much less effort to record and broadcast thoughts and ideas. This group is predominantly male, and actively attempts to break into the secured, but externally unguarded, building.
No police or soldiers are visible outside, but, from within, a tinny voice is broadcast all around. The disembodied voice threatens that violence will be met with equal force.
Jeering, cheering, the mob urge their bulldozer forward to break down a huge double gateway door.
Loshie croaks into her live feed:

'Oh my god, they're attacking! Yes! Look! Look, this is it!'

She directs the Armulet camera towards the scene of men armed with random, found weaponry, as they surge into the building. Hundreds funnel into the giant doorway.
Loshie's shouts get ever higher pitched but are lost among the screams of thousands around her.

'Go on! Take it back for us! Take it back for Maggi! Take Back Everything!'

The Times of Malthus

Automatic gunfire bursts out from inside the seat of government, around a hundred shots and then they stop. For a moment, silence holds everything still.

'Bastards! Kill them!'

Loshie's is one shout among hundreds. Masses of bodies surge towards the breach point in the long side of the building. Loshie runs to join in and is carried along with them, often lifted clear of the ground in the crush of the crowd. The ubiquity of Armulets, along with their AI processing, means that her ArmuletLive uses video feeds from all nearby Armulets to record the entire scene, placing Loshie centre stage at all times. The video cuts and pans, shifting to get the best view of Loshie, even when her own arm is held down in the crush.

'Where are they? Kill the fascists! If they're not with us, they're against us! Bully boys of the elites! Look, there's one, grab him!'

Loshie is held high in the crush of bodies squeezing through the gateway. For the first time in her life, she can see over the crowd and catches sight of an armed policeman in combat uniform. Held aloft, she cannot see the floor where bodies are crushed under the feet of the marauders. She is not alone in baying for the blood of the army unit left to protect parliament. Nobody is perturbed from their course by the sight of the dead and injured in the main lobby. If anything, it spurs them on – driven by the deaths of unknown comrades.
The militarised police unit have barricaded machine gun positions at the tops of two parallel staircases. They mow down attackers, as

they are pushed up the stairs by the inevitable force of the thousands pushing behind them. A bullet hits the wall beside Loshie's head and breaks the spell.

'Oh my god, stop, let me down! No, STOP!'

Her cries are lost in the noise and confusion, and the surging mob does not slow at all. Those at the front of the columns, halfway up the stairs towards the machine gun positions, look terrified. They try to turn but the crowd behind, pushing all the way from outside the building, cannot see or hear their predicament.
Another volley of bullets cuts down half a dozen and the next row continue being pushed ever closer. The noise of shots heard outside merely serves to anger the rioters more and push harder on the back of the crowd.
Loshie manages to clamber over the heads and shoulders of those holding her up. Just before they start to ascend the staircase, she leaps up into an alcove set in the wall and clings on to a marble statue of a Victorian politician. There is space to cower behind the statue, safe from the shoving masses, and probably from direct hit by machine gun fire.
After a moment to check herself for injury and assess her new vantage point, Loshie starts to document this interior battle.

'My god, we knew they wouldn't give up their filth easily, but they're killing people.'

Another volley rings out and several young men in football shirts scream and fall in front of their mates. Loshie holds up her left hand, so the Armulet strapped to her forearm has a clear view, and she points at the fallen.

The Times of Malthus

'No! Stop! Oh my god, my god. Please stop!'

The melee is loud. Nobody turns or reacts to Loshie's shouts. The machine gunners appear to have run out of ammunition, and the upper floor is reached. Several combat policemen are thrown over the railing to fall to the floor of the main lobby. Those who have breached the fortified positions are so enraged, and high with the adrenaline of the fight, that they simply throw their enemies over without any thought. The bodies land on protesters in the hall below. With their armour, they hurt several of those they land on, and none of the police is killed by the fall. They do not last long at the feet of the mob though.
Loshie pans the video broadcast to the top of the staircase beside her. An old security guard has been dragged from an office further along the upper corridor. He is pushed to his knees at the top of the stairs. A young woman screams incoherently in his face and then smashes the back of his head with a metal pipe. The old man slumps forward and his body slips headfirst down the stairs until it meets the corpses of those that fell on their way up.

'Oh no.'

Loshie bangs her fists together, one on top of the other, the gesture that tells her Armulet to stop broadcasting.

Tuesday 17 October 2028
Still only just post-Bitness.

An unusual windstorm had engulfed Europe. Rust-coloured sand, blown all the way from the Sahara skittered past Wayne and Ellie, as they ran along Kings Road, past the Palace Pier and on to Brighton Marina. The sun was a dim disk behind the uniformly orange sky. A powerful wind had been blowing straight and continuously for three days. It was mostly at their backs though, so they made quick and easy progress on the three-mile sprint to try and protect the lifeboat.

As they came to the marina, it was clear that it had been a major target for rioters. The fancy yachts, restaurants and casino had always smacked of wealth and privilege. Putting a cheap concrete supermarket at one end, rather than genuinely levelling up the area, had simply exacerbated the impression of inequality. All the major structures were on fire.

The lifeboat station was perched on one end of a quay that was dedicated to eating, drinking and being merry. With the three restaurants and the cinema all blazing, it was impossible to pass them on foot to get round to the lifeboat station and see what state it was in. Most of the boats in the harbour were also either on fire or scuttled. The flames on the highest buildings reached up to merge with the orange sky.

Ellie was astounded that any size of mob could have achieved so much destruction in just the few days since the final Bitness Revelations had triggered unprecedented social unrest. She followed Wayne, wrapped up in her own thoughts. *This isn't social unrest. This has been going on all over the country. This is revolution. God, what's going to happen?*

They ran back past the Asda supermarket and along the west harbour arm from where they could see across a small expanse of water to the lifeboat station. It appeared shuttered and sound, but the flames from the burning buildings nearby played intense heat on Ellie's face. She had to crouch down behind the harbour arm's walkway wall to block it out. Even if the RNLI building was OK for now, she didn't imagine it could last long; it was only a few years old, mostly made from plastic siding. The lifeboat was not moored up next to the building.

Wayne sat next to her and called his boss on his Armulet. He set the video to display on the wrist screen only in order to avoid attracting undue attention. She appeared in what he recognised as the bridge of their small lifeboat. 'Are you OK?'

'We are, but the only way to save the boat was to leave the station and hide out on the water. It's a nightmare with this wind though. We'll run out of charge soon if we have to keep battling it like this. But the reports from all the other stations are that the same thing is going on everywhere. I can't take her to another station as they're all overrun with riots. Even with the solar cells on here, we're having to run the motors faster than it can charge.'

'Especially with the sun so obscured at the moment, I bet. What about France? Have you got enough charge left to get there?'

'Maybe if we head more to the east, so we're not going straight into the wind. But the ports there are reporting similar rioting. In fact, most of them are off the radio. There are those forts in the Solent, but I expect they'll be occupied. What's the situation there now, Wayne? Would it be safe to come back?'

'Not to the marina – everything is so up in flames that you won't even get close to the quayside. There's no real crowd though. I think whatever mob set everything alight must have moved on. The people who are around are either just watching the fires or looting Asda. Not sure there's another landing that would be any safer either.'

He continued, 'Um, not a great solution, but if you only need to stop for a few hours to recharge and stay out of the way till it all dies down, what about the old Sovereign Lighthouse?'

'You think? It's in a right state these days. I can't imagine it's safe.'

'Mary, the entire marina is on fire. I think tying up to a crumbling concrete pile for a day is likely to be a lot safer. Besides, it's got those old solar cells on it, they might still be good for a connection. How are you set for food and water?'

'That'll not be a problem – we've got the emergency rations. They'd last probably a week with only two of us. I'll see if we can get to it. It's not so far that we couldn't go on and try somewhere further up the coast if it's actually fallen down now.'

There was nothing Ellie and Wayne could do to help anything or anyone at the marina. The fire was too intense to approach any part of it.

The harbour arm was a dead end of concrete piles snaking out into the water. They needed to get off the arm in case the end of the bowling alley building collapsed onto it and blocked their exit.

They ran along it towards the shore but were soon beaten back by the heat. Even without falling on to the walkway, the burning bowling alley was now effectively blocking their way back. Its flames climbed twice as high as when they had run out there.

Nobody else was out on the long series of linked concrete cylinders that formed the harbour wall. People were running around in many directions within the marina complex, weaving through slightly cooler spaces trying to find their own safe passage out of the area.

It might have been possible to wait at the end of the concrete wall until the fire died back enough to allow an escape, but they had no idea how long that might be. The only alternative was to jump off into the sea about five yards below. Wayne knew the waters were deep enough as long as they jumped away from the wall far enough to avoid any waves knocking them straight back against it. Neither felt that this was a problem, but Ellie was uncertain if she was up to swimming the 200 yards or so back to the beach.

There was no alternative, so they clambered down onto the sloping concrete cylinder that was as close to the beach as the heat would allow. Hand in hand, they ran a few steps and leapt as far forward as they could.

The entry to the water slowed them up quickly, and Ellie's feet gently touched the bottom. She bent down and pushed powerfully with her legs, to try and move a bit further from the wall. The wind was blowing hard and constant from the southwest, so was likely to drag them towards the wall before it took them to beach. The waves were not large, but it was choppy, and she worried that any exertion of battling to avoid colliding with the wall would sap the energy she needed to make the swim.

Wayne was close beside her. 'We'll be able to tell our kids: "The day of the apocalypse came, and we went swimming."' His grin was large and infectious.

Sea spray flew into Ellie's face and open mouth, and she coughed and spluttered. She wasn't in danger; it was just annoying. She gave Wayne a little punch on the arm, and they set off towards the sandy strip at the beach.

It took much longer than Ellie wanted it to, and once there, she had to lie on the sand for several minutes to recover. The temperature was in the mid-twenties, and the wind blew her dry in the time it took to get her breath back. The blowing sand filled her hair, and the sticky salt on her skin made every movement feel unpleasant.

From up on the main coast road, Ellie and Wayne looked back down at the conflagration. Even from a couple of hundred yards away, the heat was strong. It was lucky that the marina complex was well separated from other areas by a cliff running along behind it. It looked like it would all burn to the ground – or to the sea – but shouldn't affect anything else. The eastern edge of Brighton was a way up and back from the top of the cliff.

'I'm not sure how I feel about all this,' Ellie said.

'What do you mean?'

'Well, look at all that destruction. I mean it's completely senseless. Even if we overturn the entire structure of society, like people want, like my mum wrote about, what will we be left with for the new society?'

'Yeah, I agree. I mean, we're here to save the lifeboat, and Luke's been out to protect the factory, so hopefully some good stuff will be saved.'

'Well, but…' Ellie wasn't quite sure what she believed in at that moment. Nor how to express it to her husband, for whom duty came naturally and without question. 'I'm not sure I think the factory should be saved. If we're going to change the world, we're going to have to learn to completely rethink what's important. But that doesn't mean I think everything should be destroyed. People need to be able to live.'

'Gotta break a few eggs to make an omelette.'

'Exactly, but when you break the eggshell open, you still get the good food part, which is what makes the omelette. We need to leave some stuff to build a better society with.' She waved her hand down to the marina. 'Total destruction isn't going to be to anyone's benefit.'

Wayne pointed out to Ellie that the fundamental structure was mostly concrete or other stone. He reckoned the buildings and probably any boats would be destroyed, but the actual harbour skeleton ought to survive.

'I suppose you're right.'

'I may be right, but it's not the way to make progress. I mean, think how many people will have been killed in all that. People lived in all those houses and flats and on some of the boats. I can't believe they all got out safely. This isn't the way to make the world a better place. Killing all the rich people won't make life suddenly better.'

Ellie nodded and stared down at the numerous fires of the marina.

As they turned away to walk up to Jack and Diane's nearby house, similar spires of smoke could be seen climbing from many parts of the town. The smoke columns all curved over in the wind like wheat stalks. Kemptown, fortunately, did not look to be contributing much to the pall of smoke.

The Times of Malthus
Tuesday 17 October 2028
The same time as Brighton Marina burned.

'Bloody hell, Mother, what are you doing still working there?' Loshie was walking up Little Preston Street from her house, to go and find her mother.

She was talking out loud to herself, but nobody took any notice. There was far too much craziness on the streets to worry about a young woman who might also be a bit crazy. 'Working in a shop that won't exist in another week. Not just this Boots branch, Boots the company. There'll be no more shops at all soon. Why would you stay in there and put yourself in danger?'

There were few cars on the streets, and those few flew past on screeching tyres, ignoring traffic lights and signs. Some were abandoned in the middle of the road, smashed up and sometimes burned out. She saw one with blackened corpses sitting inside it. A lot of people had died in the riots, but so far, most bodies had been carried home by family and friends.

Street furniture had been damaged or fully destroyed. The wind gusted, blowing orange sand into piles in the urban corners. At times, Loshie pulled up the collar of her shirt to cover her mouth from the dust.

She walked further along Western Road, past the ransacked Churchill Square and the burnt-out Santander Bank. At the top turn, Loshie saw a mob gathered around a large store on the corner of North Street and West Street. Boots occupied a prominent location opposite the Jubilee Clock Tower.

Every one of the clock's faces had been smashed with thrown bricks and stones, but the tower itself remained standing. It had been erected to celebrate Queen Victoria's golden jubilee and the British public were unclear on the monarchy's complicity in the corruption that Bitness had uncovered.

The fact that a monarchy, by nature, was expected to be rich and powerful and have its fingers in every pie meant that the royal family didn't feature much in the information dumps for the United Kingdom. In many countries, they had been exposed as kleptocratic, but in Britain they were seemingly wealthy, as expected, but somehow viewed as being at arm's length from capitalism's endemic corruption. They hadn't escaped the rioting and looting entirely – the State as a whole was the problem – but Victoria's Jubilee Clock Tower had not been much of a red rag to the bullish crowds over the previous week.

Most of Boots' windows were boarded with wooden sheets that were quickly ripped off by the rioters attempting to gain access. The chemist's shop had opened as normal on most days, but the manager had been able to mobilise the staff to close it in minutes when events in the surrounding streets were out of control. She and the staff were united in their desire to support the local populace that needed medicine, and this goodwill had kept the store out of the firing line, for the most part, up to this point.

Now, two weeks since the Bitness Revelations, the population at large had run out of most medicines and were intent on getting whatever stock was behind Boots' locked doors. The tide had turned, and the manager had been minutes too late on the uptake. A dozen staff members remained, locked inside, and the mob was at both the entrances. A rumour had spread locally that the pharmacy had received a delivery the previous night.

A street sign was passed forward and used as a battering ram, but the doors were incredibly strong. The glass was thickened and, from the way it cracked without breaking, must have had several thick laminations. The locking mechanism on the sliding doors included long steel pillars that dropped into place at the edges, so no sliding was possible. It was as if head office had prepared the store against possible assault.

Loshie shouted a repeated refrain that her mother worked in the store, and she knew they had not had any deliveries for a week. Despite this, and despite her small size, she was unable to squeeze through the tightly packed bodies of the crowd. She got within about ten metres of each of the entrances, but in both cases, the only way to progress any closer was to get in the way of flailing sledgehammers or the run of the battering ram.

She again raised her Armulet to try and call her mother, but she did not answer. Neither did Loshie's father – she assumed they must be talking to each other. *This must be the longest conversation they've had since they came to this country.*

After more than forty minutes of unsuccessful smashing with a variety of heavy objects, a fire axe appeared at the front. This was enough to damage the door frame sufficiently that a glass panel could be levered out whole, albeit cracked like a spider's web.

The crowd surged. Loshie wasn't sure what medications all these people could need. The space to enter was a metre square, and the crowd was surging from behind, against a tiny bottleneck. Loshie squeezed her way between close-packed bodies. By the time she slipped through the bottom half of the holed door herself, she could see flames inside the building.

'Mother!' She ran up the shampoo aisle, searching, but the shelves were too high for her to really scan the entire space.

The tiny size of the available ingress point meant that the shop itself was empty in comparison to the crush outside. She saw several men pulling over the pharmacy counter in order to swarm in behind, to access the medicines storeroom.

Flames were up the advertising posters hanging down one wall, and a number of sets of shelves were ablaze. Several loud bangs were accompanied by cans of deodorant spray flying into the air. One shot over Loshie's head across the tops of the shelving on either side of her. She instinctively ducked but was naturally safer than the taller people ransacking the place.

Loshie had been into the staffroom a couple of times before to meet her mother at the end of a shift, and she headed towards the staircase, where a staff door led off the landing to more storerooms. The heat from the fire was pushing everyone in that direction, but ascending the stairs, Loshie felt hot smoke choking her lungs. She dropped to her knees and climbed the side of the staircase.

At the top, she reached up to open the staff corridor door, but the handle burnt her fingers. Loshie gasped at the pain, and at the realisation that there must be fire behind this door too.

She stood briefly to look through the small security window

and could see smoke filling the space behind the door. She could make out a figure lying on the floor – it was not her mother – and then she saw flames surge out of the staffroom at the side, filling the hallway behind the little window. Again, she ducked instinctively, but she was saved by the door.

Crawling back down the stairs, she could see the remaining people in the shop unable to flee the fire, as the crowd outside constantly pushed more people in through the gap of the missing door panel.

From a rack of face masks, she put several on at once. The scene was devastating – people succumbing to the heat and the smoke, and unable to escape against an endless stream of new victims being forced in from outside. No message of danger seemed to be able to get out past the portal they had made to breach Boots' defences. Loshie felt lucky that she had not found her mother.

Still, neither Mother nor Father answered her Armulet call.

The screams and flames reminded her of the Colombo nightclub fire from 2027. The three of them had sat around her laptop at home, tuned to BBC News for nearly thirty-six hours straight, watching the eyewitness reports. They talked of the scenes inside the place: the crush, the flames, the smoke, the bodies, the screams, the terrible smell of burning flesh. All these things came to Loshie's senses as she crouched looking around, desperate to see her mother running towards her.

She remembered one of the Sri Lankan victim stories – a young barmaid who had escaped the fire by climbing out of the toilet windows. In an instant, Loshie was up and running towards the worst part of the blaze.

Entering a cosmetics aisle, where trails of molten lipstick were running down the shelves, she dropped back to the ground. A spectrum of flesh and blood colours dripped onto the floor by her fists as she moved on hands and knees as fast as possible. There was so much debris that she had to slide forward with each movement in order to clear away what she might not see.

At the end of the aisle, she could feel the heat surging across in front of her, carried along the main walkway at the side of the store. She took a deep breath, sucking in through the masks, steeled against the burning in her windpipe and hurled herself through the gap in the wall opposite.

She was into the corridor with the customer toilets and a cupboard of cleaning supplies. The walls around her were solid and it was noticeably cooler than the big open space of the main shopping area. Loshie knew that the toilets had small, frosted glass windows. She had no idea where they might come out, but was certain she had seen daylight through them, when using the toilets in times gone by.

Her memory was correct. At the back of one cubicle was a small windowsill and two glass panes, one fixed and, above it, one that opened. The opening one, already propped open, was barely thirty centimetres square – she would never be able to squeeze through. Even a baby wouldn't have been able to escape through it. However, the solid pane was twice as high. If it hadn't any glass in it, she might be able to get out.

Loshie pulled and kicked at the toilet seat and finally managed to break it off. She whacked the glass with it but only managed to get a splintered piece of the seat plastic in her hand. The injury wasn't terrible, and she hit the window another few times until it shattered.

The broken shards were easy to knock out from the frame pretty quickly, but it was very difficult to sweep all the tiny pieces off the windowsill. She kicked open the toilet paper roll holder and wrapped both hands in a thick padding of toilet paper. After using her paper-wrapped fists to clear the sill of debris, she threw away the wadded paper and wrapped fresh strips around her hands.

Air rushed in through the open window, sucked in by the heat. She stood on the toilet and leaned her head through the window into the narrow alleyway. The air felt wonderfully cool on her face, and there were no people.

Loshie reached up and grabbed the metal frame of the propped open window. With a guttural shout to summon all her strength, she lifted herself up and partway through. She got one knee onto the windowsill and paused for a moment, half in and half out. The drop to the floor of the alleyway was over two metres, and if she was going to squeeze all the way out, she was going to have to let go of the window's metal frame. She froze, stuck, scared and befuddled about how to continue.

There was a loud, noisy cracking sound as the door to the women's toilets caught fire on the outside. Without realising what she was doing, Loshie launched herself through the gap whilst holding fast onto the top bar. She had no idea how it had happened, but the next moment she was hanging, as if from a monkey bar, outside the building. She let go and dropped, crumpling into a heap on the concrete below.

Loshie knew her mother had been inside the building and, lying in the foetal position on the ground outside the toilet window, it hit her that Mother must be dead. Her eyes were already streaming from the smoke, but her grief added to the tears.

She staggered to her feet and lurched along the narrow alley. Turning the corner into the service yard, Loshie saw a small crowd still trying to break through the roller shutters at the back of the store.

'It's on fire,' she croaked. 'It's all on fire. Everything's gone. Everyone's dead.' Nobody paid her any attention, and they carried on hitting the shutters with a piece of metal drainpipe.

Crying all the way, she walked on past them and broke into a run. It took less than five minutes to run back home. Loshie had no idea how she was going to tell her father about Mother. She was struggling to imagine how she would carry on without her, but Father had nobody else. Loshie did not consider herself as a possible support structure for her dad. They had never been close enough for it to occur to her.

When she arrived at the entrance to the family workshop, something was wrong. The double doors for the garage entrance were locked shut. The single entrance door next to the car entrance was also locked up tight. She had a key for both, but in both cases, the lock was fixed shut from the inside, the key slid in but could not turn. She could see through the slight gap between them that the fortress bar that went across the back of the vehicle access doors was in place. She banged her fists on the huge wooden doors. She kicked and banged on the pedestrian doorway. Loshie wailed for her father to open up.

The street was deserted – everyone who might be on this little road was either locked up at home, or out roaming with the mobs. From above, Loshie heard a crack, and a large shard of window glass fell from their kitchen window and smashed on the pavement right beside her. She ran across the street and looked up. Black smoke trailed out of the cracked window. Their house was on fire too.

'Father! Father! What's happening? Get out of there!'

She tried him on the Armulet again, and it still did not connect the call. She looked him up on the Family App and it showed his location as being inside. The location mapping was precise, and she reckoned it showed he was in her parents' bedroom. She clicked on the Health tab. Father's heart rate was zero. The app had a flashing red warning symbol.

'Oh, no, no, please God, no!'

She clicked on Mother and saw the same red warning sign.

Loshie slumped to the ground in the gutter of the little street and stared at the Armulet's flashing symbol.

Miles M Hudson

Thursday 16 November 2028
Six weeks after the Bitness infodump.

The wind still blew strongly up the Hove street on which Ellie's mothers rented half of Matthias' big old house. All surfaces were covered with a fine layer of orange-brown Saharan sand. Additional local sand and dust, but mostly litter, chased up the street around the parked cars and into smashed windows.

The smell of rotting corpses was strong in the gusts. Outside their walled front garden, people caught up in fighting for food, and finally killed for it, lay unregarded in the street. In the initial days of rioting, families had carried their dead away, but the numbers had become so great that most newly deceased had nobody to collect them, or nobody with enough strength to do so safely.

The heat of autumn had not helped either, as decomposition progressed apace at twenty-five degrees. Whenever they left the house, they took Matthias' only surviving dog with them, but it was all they could do to keep her from sniffing the bodies.

Ellie and Matthias weaved around a potted palm tree, holding a large wooden board between them. They had boarded up the back window in Jude and Roisin's kitchen and carried this board to fix it up over Matthias' lounge window. Ellie's long, blonde hair danced around her head in the gusts.

'We're lucky I kept this place fairly private anyway. The hedge all around the back is basically impenetrable. But it's going to be pretty grim having the downstairs in darkness all the time.'

Ellie replied, 'It's also lucky the neighbours have left town so you could pinch these fencing panels to board up the windows. But I can't believe we're having to protect ourselves against fellow humans, against fellow Brightonians.'

'It does seem like the world's gone mad, doesn't it?'

'Well, to be fair, it has. I mean Mum would say it's come to its senses, but this is all just so unreal. Protests I expected, even rioting, and that always brings looting, but the violence has gone to extremes. I mean look at us, we're boarding up the house!'

The Times of Malthus

Matthias nodded and said nothing further.

The two had, by this sixth window boarding, come to a good system of working together. He would hold the fence panel up as steady as he could whilst Ellie nailed the boards into the window frames. Matthias had managed a big shed and two greenhouses for years. He had plenty of tools and, they were hopeful, enough nails to finish boarding all the downstairs windows. He had regularly complained in the past about the way DIY stores would only sell packs of fifty nails when he needed just a few. His various over-purchases had come good though, as Ellie could attest by the blister on her palm from the hammer.

'Selsey, shift, will you!' Ellie tried to ease the dog aside, so she could reach the highest point to apply a nail.

Matthias' pet was keen to help, which meant being underfoot most of the time.

'Lägg av, Selsey, your mother would never have been in the way all the time, like this.' He chided the animal who looked at him without moving. 'I sometimes wonder if you really are Primrose's offspring, or some sort of litter changeling.'

To maintain the fence panel in position for Ellie, Matthias was unable to move at all and could only try to cajole his dog from a distance. She was panting and staring at him, triangle ears pointing straight up.

Under the hot sunshine, Matthias had sweat dribbling into his eyes and looked like he was becoming unsteady. Ellie scooted around behind him, grabbing the space she needed before Selsey could move between her legs again. She hammered quickly and efficiently.

'There you go. Those two should hold it enough to put the rest in.'

Matthias eased back his hold, and the panel hung across the window like an ungainly bouncer. Ellie continued nailing each strip of wood near its ends. Each hammer blow sent a shiver through Matthias as he thought of the wonderful wooden window frames he'd cared for, for so many years.

They stepped back to admire the battened hatch, and Selsey sat on her haunches looking up at the humans. She had a thick, orange-brown coat, and her wet tongue lolled out, panting heavily.

'Why is she called Selsey?'

'I name all my dogs after places, you know that.'

'Yeah, so what happened in Selsey?'

'This one's first walk was on the beach there.'

Ellie paused, thinking. 'Two questions. Firstly, does that mean you didn't name her for weeks, until you went on that first walk? And her mother was called Primrose – that's not a place.'

'Ah, yes. I was at Selsey beach on my own when musing about dog names and decided I'd call her Selsey. So, when the time came for her first walk, away from the house, we took a special trip there.'

'And her mother?'

'I got her from a rescue shelter at Primrose Hill in London.'

Selsey had lain down in the shade of the front garden hedge and did not get up as the two walked away to collect the next fence panel for the other front window.

Matthias asked about Wayne. 'How's your better half managing through all this? With the Army dissolving, does the coastguard still function?'

'He's been on the lifeboats for over a year!'

'Of course, sorry, it's all ships at sea to me. I should know better though; Sweden has the same double organisations doing similar work.'

'It's not really that similar. He moved to the RNLI in order to help people more than police them. The coastguard hasn't had a positive job to do for years now. Bloody Tories.'

Matthias held out both hands, palms down. 'It's OK, they're finally out now. The people have removed them by force.'

'I know, but it makes me so mad. How did it have to come to this?' She waved her hand up at the fence panel nailed across the window.' Selsey gave a little bark of agreement. 'Did nobody at Bitness wonder what would happen if they sparked off a revolution? You know they're calling it the Times of Malthus?'

'Yes indeed. War, famine, pestilence, and death all around. But what about Wayne? He hasn't been home for a couple of days.

Has the boat survived? Is anybody at sea to be saved?'

'Sorry, yes. Actually, he's having a relatively normal time of it. The lifeboat has electric motors, solar charged, and we saved it from the major rioting. They're taking it in turns to live on the boat so they can take it out of the marina if trouble flares up again, but since the whole place burnt down, there's nothing to attract people down there.

'But with no food coming in, a lot of people are taking their crappy little boats out fishing. He's picked up so many people just in the last couple of days – they've either run out of fuel or can't row themselves anymore. He says they've even had fights on the lifeboat between guys they've rescued who're trying to steal each other's fish. It's lucky the weather's been calm, he says they've had to tow people back, in their boats on occasion, so they don't carry on fighting. Even then, he's had to restrain some people so the others can get away along the docks. I'm worried he's gonna get hurt himself, but he says he wants to keep helping people. He thinks it's the way to show everybody that we're on the same side and need to help each other.'

'We send 'em home, and they come right back again. Carl, hunger is a powerful thing.'

'What?'

'Bruce Springs– never mind.' Matthias waved a dismissive hand, more to himself than to Ellie. 'When will he be able to come back here?'

'His turn on their rota finishes at six tonight. He reckons he's caught some fish to bring home. Even Loshie's eating fish now.' Matthias looked at her wide-eyed, and Ellie nodded in agreement with his surprise.

'Is he still getting news through the lifeboat's government connections? I think that's why I was thinking of the coastguard.'

The infonetwork was still functioning via Armulet connectivity. The kinetic batteries that powered Armulets were recharged by the wearer's movements. However, real news had become rare. Mostly, all they had to go on were vlog postings by random members of the public. These always told harrowing individual case studies of lost husbands, wives, children, brothers and destroyed property, mostly their shops. It was nigh on impossible to get an overall picture of events across the country, or the world, without spending hours trying to piece together snippets from all of these vox pop stories. And sourcing their own food and water, rather than watching vloggers, was taking up most of most people's time.

Ellie nodded briefly. 'He says somebody in Whitehall is still broadcasting on the government frequencies, but they keep acting like it's just a bit of a tough time and things will be back to normal soon.

'There's definitely no real transport going anywhere. Except for the odd electric car where they've got enough solar panels to recharge them. There's no fuel reserves left and, like you said, government run organisations have disbanded. Never really with any decision on that; the police and soldiers and, well, everybody, just stopped showing up. Most likely out searching for food, the same as everyone else. He says the broadcaster referred to it as "temporary staff shortages".

'But then they talk about places abroad, saying that all the oil refineries are on fire, and governments have given up or been overthrown all over the place.' She paused, and they stood in silence. 'How is it that it took less than a month for everyone to run out of food?'

'Indeed. So many people distracted with all mod cons and lost touch with the real fundaments of life. I just hope we can keep the greenhouse protected.'

'I think we just need to keep it secret. Boots had no medicines left, but they killed Loshie's mother anyway. If a mob gets an idea, there's no stopping it.'

Matthias said nothing and looked at the nailed-up fence panel.

The Times of Malthus
Thursday 21 December 2028
Three months into the Times of Malthus.

Ellie shuffled like a zombie, guided by Wayne along the Kings Road promenade. They both had rucksacks on and carried large plastic bags tied up at the handles with tape, so they would cut into the fingers a bit less.

Human corpses lay occasionally at the side of the road. Some looked like they had been knocked down by vehicles, some lay in pools of blood from weapon injuries, and all looked emaciated. They wandered past the place where they had first fallen for each other, five years earlier.

'Matthias' window boarding must have made them think that we had stuff to steal.'

Wayne thought better of pointing out that they had actually had food to steal. He tried to distract her with talk of their need to find safe shelter. 'Come on, we need to secure one of these spaces before dark.'

It had been Ellie's idea that the cavernous lockups underneath the promenade, which opened on to the beach, had good potential to be made into small, fortress-like shelters. Each one was under an arch supporting the street above and had a single access point at the front. Their rear and sides were simply the bedrock of the shore, lined with brick. They were fifty yards from the water's edge, so there was potential for Wayne to fish for their food.

The town at large no longer had any electricity or gas supply, the food supply chain had been non-existent for the last two months or more, and the water supply was intermittent, dependent on whether a particular place was gravity fed from underground reservoirs. If rioters could access utilities, they had been destroyed; if a utility needed power, it no longer functioned.

Wayne bumped the large Ikea bag he carried in his left hand against a canvas holdall that Ellie had grabbed from her mothers' house, when they had to leave with five minutes' notice. They had managed to fly under the radar of bandits for nearly three months, as any occasional thief was deterred either by the boarded-up windows, or by Selsey. She had been a placid, friendly dog hitherto but, since the Times of Malthus had started, the large Akita had taken on a wolf-like guard dog role with some relish.

Their house had been one of the few with any electricity, although the battery power provided by the solar panels was weak, essentially limited to some night-time lighting and keeping the laptops charged.

With the dog protecting the greenhouse at nights, and Matthias nurturing it in the days, they had been able to maintain a bare food supply. There had been no rain for three weeks, and many people were starving and very thirsty. In places, small groups had banded together for mutual safety and to share labour and resources. However, the supply of all necessities was so low compared to Brighton's population, that even well-meaning groups such as these suffered internal fights over food and water.

Selsey followed Wayne and Ellie down the concrete staircase to beach level. She was prone to eating bits off the corpses in the streets, and this provided her with more sustenance than the humans were getting. They tried to shoo her away from the body of a young boy at the bottom. In such a weakened state, many people were falling to diseases from the decaying bodies. Ellie knew they all had to avoid them as much as possible.

The poor boy Selsey had been sniffing could only have been ten years old, and the sight of him made Ellie's stomach convulse. It was only the lack of any recent meal that meant Ellie could not vomit.

The two of them had their hands full with the possessions they had grabbed in a hurry to leave the besieged house and could barely influence Selsey. She was good at avoiding the long dead who were rotten enough that she would get ill, and Ellie feared she would soon stop bothering to try and keep Selsey away from the human bodies.

In a dark moment, Ellie had wondered how long it would before they joined the dog. She feared how far those without the luxury of a greenhouse might already have been forced to go in order to stay alive.

The Times of Malthus

They knew this stretch of foreshore well, and as they walked around the Art Deco building that had housed Café on the Beach, Ellie pointed at the abandoned gift shop in the next archway. It was a single unit with solid walls close in. The entire space inside was about the size of a squash court, but, with a low ceiling and no lights working, it had the feeling of a dank cave.

'This looks perfect,' Wayne said.

Ellie looked around carefully, nodding, but she was not really there. In her mind's eye, she was still watching Jude and Roisin's house on fire. She was still listening to the screams as Jude engaged an intruder with a knife. Ellie shuddered. Her mother's final shrieks had been both war cry and death howl combined.

Wayne put his bags down and took the two from Ellie's hands. Selsey lay on the paving outside, panting. At the end of December, it was nearly twenty degrees. Inside, the beach hut was nicely cool though.

The place smelled of sea spray, and the ceiling was dripping in the back corner. The opposite rear corner had a boxed-in toilet room and there was a small sink. The plumbing did not have any water coming in, but the drips from the ceiling tasted fresh.

He took the handle of the front door, which was hanging on only its bottom hinge. The door swung wildly with the single pivot point, and he stepped outside to look along the several adjacent business fronts. There were a couple of bodies being picked at by gulls, but nobody else alive was visible as far as could be seen all along the length of the crazy golf course, right up to the next staircase descending from the prom. Selsey turned her head to follow his movements, as he took a few steps out to get a better view along the line of archway huts, but she did not get up.

'I'm going to see if I can find a replacement door,' he called back in to his wife. She was still elsewhere, staring blankly at a collection of Brighton tea towels, hanging on a metal display frame on the wall. 'Ellie.'

She turned towards him but appeared vacant.

He pointed at the hanging door. 'We need to secure this place right now. Can you help me?'

'Yep.' Ellie came to and stepped into the setting sunlight.

She shook her head, as if to dismiss the endlessly repeating images of her childhood home in flames. The vision would never leave her, but she was able to push it aside enough to help Wayne.

'The Atlanta has massive, thick doors.' She pointed along past the crazy golf course and the paddling pool. The Atlanta bar was not visible from where they stood. It was hidden behind the next protruding café block. 'I figured they were just grand for show, but I reckon one of them will cover this entrance perfectly.'

Litter blew around them, following the curved walls of the tourist attractions. As they reached the Atlanta, Ellie's confidence was proven right. The bar had been decorated with two large doors, thick solid wood, with iron fixings painted black. They would not have looked out of place on a medieval fortress.

Removing the right-hand door took some doing, but the bar had been abandoned in a hurry and Wayne found a number of tools in a storeroom. The most difficult part was transporting the door back to their hut. They used a trolley that had ferried beer barrels down the large slope from the road above. It was too small to carry the door, so Ellie tried to keep it balanced atop the trolley cage, and Wayne put his back into pushing the whole lot along the paved lower promenade.

When they arrived back to Selsey on guard, it was immediately clear that the door was far too large for the entrance. It would make a superb stronghold but installing it would not be possible in the half hour they had left whilst the sun sank into the Hove skyline. Neither of them could remember when the street lighting had last been on.

Ellie returned to the pub and brought back the long beam of wood that acted as the securing bar behind the doors. She reckoned it had also just been for show, but it would do the job they needed now. As a temporary fix, they pulled the door up against the smaller doorway. It was absolutely solid. The interior was black. The door completely covered the entrance.

'Armulet torchlight on.' At Wayne's command, his Armulet shone a beam forward over his left hand, so they could see to work. They jammed the wooden drawbar into the iron hook on the door and against the inside wall on either side of the entrance.

'Armulet lamplight on,' Ellie said and hers produced a warm glow that illuminated the room.

They started to shift the old shop fittings and furniture around to make the space useful. There was an ancient armchair in the back, opposite the toilet corner. It had been upholstered in thick cream cotton, which was covered in a thin layer of salt and sand. Ellie banged the saggy seat cushion a couple of times and coughed at the dust it raised. Everything they moved produced a similar pall of dust.

Wayne put his arm around her shoulder and held his other hand up as a Stop symbol. 'Let's just make enough space to sleep, and tomorrow we can take everything outside and give it a good clean, as well as inside here.'

Ellie turned to hug him fully. She looked into his face, and it appeared blue, shadowy with the light from their Armulets. He looked like somebody telling a ghost story at a campfire.

'Although we will also have to try and find food. I want us to be able to know where to forage always – we mustn't get caught out having to find food, when we're too hungry to fight.'

Ellie nodded, and then said, 'What's the fishing like at this part of the beach? That should be a good way to keep ourselves up to strength.'

'By the groynes is good, but it's a bit visible and exposed. I'm thinking it might be safer to go up the beach a bit and under the pier. And that's actually better fishing anyway.'

Ellie nodded again, extracted herself from his embrace and moved over to the toilet cubicle. She twisted her arm, so the light played into the mop bucket sat by the toilet. She took out the dry mop and moved the bucket so that it caught the drips from the ceiling. It made a repeated and surprisingly loud noise every second or so.

She collected two of the tea towels from the rack and put one into the bucket, so it softened the noise. She used the other to dry up the rivulet that ran along the floor from where the bucket now stood all the way forward to the doorway.

Wayne was moving his head back and forth to examine the

source of the drips in the stone ceiling, and the neighbouring walls and plumbing pipes. The drips landed right between the pedestal sink and the toilet bowl. He suggested that they should easily be able to set up a guttering system to collect the water, and the two of them both tasted some of it again. If it didn't make them ill, having a source of fresh water would make their new home a thousand times better than they had thought.

Wayne reckoned that the water was probably coming from a leak in the rainwater sewer system. They were at the bottom of the middle of a very large hill that gave Brightonians a great sea view from much of the town. He speculated that the Victorians would have simply routed the rainwater sewers to discharge to the sea. Ellie was sceptical, given the previous three weeks of zero rain, but she shrugged her shoulders and started to unpack some sleeping gear.

As they sat on sleeping bags on the floor of the dry side of the room, Ellie talked more about finding food. 'We don't want people to see us coming in and out of here. Do you think there's some way we can set up some sort of surveillance system outside so that we know if anybody's out there before opening up the door?' She shuddered at the memory of being woken by a gang breaking through the boarding she and Matthias had installed on their lounge window.

'Not without power. If we could find one, a Bluetooth camera could feed to our Armulets and could be pretty discreetly hidden in the brickwork of the café, or the promenade staircase, so it overlooks this area. But unless we can keep supplying it with batteries, we might as well not bother.'

'Did the factory have any sort of stores that might include batteries, and might still be there?'

Wayne thought for a moment, rocking his head from side to side, as if considering all the options. 'You know what, they had exactly the sort of cameras I'm talking about, mounted along the fencing, and there were some that had battery backups in case burglars cut the power.'

Ellie chuckled. 'Was a sign printing factory really likely to be a target for that kind of burglary? Surely that's only in the movies?'

Wayne smiled. 'I don't know. You're probably right, but the guy in charge of security bought them for that, so maybe he just got upsold by some security salesman. It doesn't matter, though, it means we can get a camera. Actually, I'll probably get two, so we can look in both directions across the front.'

'What about the batteries though?'

'Yeah. There were a couple of boxes in the store. I don't know how long they'll last, but it's a start. I'm sure we can find some shop or warehouse with a load more. They're likely to be something that a lot of people have looted, but so many people have died, that there should be tons not being used. We've just got to find them.'

Tears were rolling down Ellie's face. She was staring over Wayne's shoulder, no longer in the under-arch gift shop. She mumbled, 'So many people have died.'

Wayne leant forward but sitting on the floor made it a bit awkward to hug her. He chose to speak rather than try to get his arms around her. 'I think that's a decent plan for security. We'll need more than just fish to eat though.' Her eyes were blank. 'Ellie.' He touched her leg. 'Ellie!'

'Sorry, what?' She focussed on him.

'We'll need to find food beyond just fish. Any ideas?'

She stared at the wall beyond him again, but Wayne could tell she was mulling over the food problem, rather than reliving the attack that killed her parents.

'Um, well, in the pretty short term, we'll need some fresh veg, or even fruit. Actually, what's the possibility for harvesting some seaweed?' Wayne looked surprised, but Ellie pressed on. 'Or indeed any plants from the sea. We'll have to look up what's edible. Or in fact what's nutritious, but that stuff will keep growing, and I imagine few people will be collecting it to eat.'

Wayne stared at her, as overawed by Ellie's brains as the first day he'd ever spoken to her at school. He nodded. 'Yeah, brilliant. There's a lot of seaweed, seagrass and all sorts in the marina. I don't know what you can eat, but you're right, I bet some of it is really nutritious. And the infonetwork is still on, so we should be able to research the things we pick.'

'How is it that the infonetwork is still on?'

'Oh shit!' Wayne started tapping on his Armulet screen, strapped along the back of his forearm.

'What?'

'Make sure your locator's off. We can't have someone track us here through our Armulets.'

She put her hand across his device's screen. 'You made us turn the locators off weeks ago, don't you remember?'

Wayne's shoulders relaxed. 'Sorry, yes, of course. I'm exhausted.'

She moved her hand to hold his.

Straight back to business, Wayne answered her question. 'The mobile phone tower transmitters have solar panels with rechargeable batteries – the system will probably still be functional long after the last person with an Armulet dies.' He had been staring at his wrist device and looked up suddenly to her face, panicked that he might have set off another memory of the assault on their home, barely sixteen hours previously.

She was looking straight into his face with a calm smile. 'But what about the info servers, they're not on the towers.'

Wayne paused, stymied by the question. 'Hmm. No, I don't know. It is working.' He tapped a few icons to see the search engine function as expected. 'I guess probably some pages will come back with errors if their servers aren't powered anymore, but there's a lot of data farms around the world that held back-ups of everything. I don't know how they were powered, but it's still going for now.' He pointed at the little screen.

'I could grow some veg. I helped Matthias enough that I know what I'm doing with it. We just need to find a safe place with sun and water, where nobody will find what we're growing to steal it all.'

At the name of the kindly old Swede, Wayne's eyes also filled with tears. She clasped his hand, and they sat in silence for a minute or two.

The Times of Malthus

'Maybe a rooftop somewhere? We could go up the i360 Tower and look around for somewhere nearby that would work.' He waved his hand up towards the ceiling. The tourist tower stood vertically up from the promenade very close by.

She smiled. 'Well, that'll cover sunshine, but we'd need water. And soil too. Know any rooftops like that?'

He shrugged. 'We can but look.'

'I know, sorry, it is a good idea.' After a slight pause, she had another idea. 'Hey, I tell you where there are a lot of plant containers we could try using. The Holiday Inn right above us has flats above the hotel floors. They've all got balconies, and I know some of the balconies have window boxes. We may be able to collect rainwater on the building's roof, and those apartments will be pretty obscure for somebody randomly searching for food.'

'Great idea. Lot of work to do in the morning then. We should get some sleep.'

'We should call Loshie and Luke at your parents and tell them we're alright.' Wayne nodded and tapped his Armulet screen to place the video call.

Miles M Hudson
Monday 1 April 2030
After eighteen months of the Times of Malthus.

Ellie and Loshie were bent over a large vegetable patch growing from salvaged seeds, in a box made of old bits of wooden boats, bound together with a lorry's canvas ratchet strap.

April Fools' Day, and the sun was beating down on them on the roof of Brighton's abandoned, seafront Holiday Inn. The concrete was smooth and white, and they both wore sunglasses against the glare. The heat shimmered up from under their feet.

Selsey lounged in the shade of the stairway housing, panting, and toddler Maggi tottered about the dog, occasionally poking at her under the guise of an attempt to stroke her. Ellie, eight months pregnant, also tottered slightly. She was not showing very large with the pregnancy – food was too scarce to properly eat for two – but she was definitely feeling the heat. The two women nurtured the plants carefully. They rationed what was pulled up each day to feed their husbands, themselves and Maggi.

The families had rigged up an efficient rainwater collection system that drained the entire roof into a barrel on the floor below the fifteenth storey rooftop. The container garden also had a neat watering system that took water poured in at one end and spread it into the base of the soil beneath the plants. Ellie had designed this to minimise losses from evaporation. Rainfall was wildly changeable. There could be weeks with no rain, and then days when it poured. They kept several barrels ready down below, and when water was pouring from the sky, they would work throughout the storm to shift the collecting pipe from barrel to barrel as each filled up.

Ellie stood upright with several carrots in her hand and adjusted the floppy sunhat she wore. She wobbled slightly and closed her eyes.

Loshie took Ellie by the arm. 'Come and rest over here.' She helped Ellie over to a wingback armchair in the shade beside Selsey. It had only been three days since the last downpour, but the chair was bone dry. Ellie sat and wiped her face with the cloth bag she carried the vegetables in.

'I daren't think how hot it's going to get this summer. Do you remember when we were so pleased if a summer day hit thirty degrees?'

Loshie sat on the ground, cradling eighteen-month-old Maggi. She took off her sunglasses and nodded. 'Days of ice cream and bikinis on the beach. Hard to believe it was barely more than ten years ago when the seasons were normal.'

Ellie nodded too and put a hand to her stomach. She looked across the rooftop, over the raised edge to where the i360 Tower climbed above them. It was one of the few taller buildings in Brighton, and they could see Luke waving to them across the hundred yards of empty air in between. The glass observation pod had been in the highest position when the electricity last went off, so the tourist attraction gave them a good lookout tower to watch for Essex Raiders boats coming along the coast. The members of the Brighton Defence Force that could manage the climb up the internal spiral staircase took it in turns to stand sentinel for several hours at a time.

The pod was like a greenhouse, and even with all the upper vents open, Luke had often complained that the heat was more likely to kill him than one of the raiders. Sitting at the threshold of the stairway provided shade and produced a wonderful, cooling draft that rose up the central column. However, sitting at that point meant that the lookouts could only see north towards the city. They had to walk a short lap of the pod's interior to see the full sweep of potential approaches. Ellie remembered Wayne complaining that many of the volunteers who took a turn on duty up there never ventured out of the stairwell. She wondered if her brother-in-law might be one of those less committed guards. He was waving to them from the very front, face pressed against the window with his broad smile visible even at a hundred yards. The women waved back, and Maggi joined in when she spotted her father across the high gap. Luke disappeared from view. Ellie assumed he would need a few minutes in the shaded stairway.

Loshie leaned her head back against the cool wall behind her and inhaled the salty air deeply. She was still focussed on the i360's observation pod. 'Did they try breaking some of the windows in that thing? It'd be just awful if somebody fell ill in the heat. It must be like a pressure cooker in there.'

'Wayne reckons the glass is absolutely unbreakable. He says they even had somebody shoot at it. They're on the lookout for some suitable tools to remove a glass panel, but without electricity, he's not sure they'll ever manage it.'

'Solar cells not powerful enough?'

'I guess not. I've only been up there once, since we moved to the beach lock up, and it wasn't a very hot day.' She laughed. 'I couldn't really see what all the fuss was about.'

'Oh god, Ellie, just look over there. You can't imagine how hot it must be in there. I hope Luke's alright.'

'I'm sure he's fine – he's done sentry rota loads of times.'

'Well, we're sat in the shade, and I feel just drained by the heat.'

'Why don't you call him and check?' Ellie pointed at her own Armulet.

'I can't be bothered. Like you say, he's used to it, and I'm just not in the mood.'

'Mad dogs and Englishmen. We need to be more careful to be on the roof only at the beginning or the end of the day.'

'Well, I reckon we've collected enough for today. Shall we head back down?'

Ellie looked all around at the empty blue sky. She pushed herself up from the chair and passed the cloth parcel of carrots to Loshie who added them to a canvas bag of vegetables she had collected. 'I'm going to finish repairing that netting. Give me ten minutes and we'll go down. We'll need to check in on the ninth-floor balcony planters too, but that should just be a quick check.'

Loshie gave a resigned nod and let Maggi bumble after Ellie.

The interior of the hotel was cooler than the roof, but the air was still and oppressive. Loshie struggled to manage Maggi safely down the stairs. She was too heavy for Loshie to carry her, and she needed considerable marshalling to walk down the concrete stairway without incident. Ellie carried the canvas bag to help, but

The Times of Malthus

Loshie spent most of the descent complaining.

'Maggi is so much hard work. In this heat, I really don't know if I can keep bringing her up to the roof with you. I'm going to fall, or she will. Especially with Selsey pushing past us without knowing how dangerous it is.' She shooed the dog ahead of them. Selsey stopped and gave her an inquiring look.

'Maybe if we retime our visits up to the roof away from the heat of the day, that'll work for Luke or Wayne to look after her back home. Or Jack and Diane maybe? It is a long way for her to walk, I agree.'

'I can't leave her with other people. They're all so busy with everything that needs to be done.'

Ellie mopped the sweat from her brow. Even in the cooler stairwell, it was still hot. She gripped the handrail. 'OK, well let's get down and see how the ninth floor's doing.' She raised the canvas bag of veg and waved it towards downstairs.

The door of flat 9F was half open. Ellie paused to peer in from the corridor. 'You shut this last time, didn't you?'

'No, you were last out – it was your job,' Loshie snapped. 'I remember I went ahead with Maggi, and we met you in the lobby.'

'Yes, that's what I thought. I'm certain I shut it. I'm really quite anal about making it look like nothing special.'

They had no keys for any of the rooms or flats in the building, but about half of them were unlocked. In most cases when they had broken into locked flats, the occupants had died inside. Old people too scared to leave, or perhaps too frail, and their carers had just stopped coming. Wayne and Ellie had made some pretty grisly finds in some of the flats. She had wanted to stop breaking down doors – the smell was the worst thing – but every so often, a flat had been left unoccupied and had foodstuffs in cupboards. A lot of them had a lot of wine. Expensive holiday or retirement flats on Brighton's seafront attracted a certain echelon of Londoner.

It was common for raiders, or sometimes just the hungry, to search through the building to try and find food or anything else useful. The Smiths relied on using balconies on the higher floors to grow food, in the hope that nobody would work their way up that far. They also worked to make the place look utterly derelict to avoid half-hearted searchers from heading in too far.

Flat 10F had an open balcony which collected rainwater, and Wayne and Ellie had rigged up a pipe down from it to water the two containers of salad vegetables on 9F's enclosed balcony. It acted as a decent greenhouse and most things had flourished.

Sourcing seeds and cuttings had been the hardest part. In the first year of the Times of Malthus, every wild and garden plant had been eaten by the starving masses. It hadn't been enough to save the majority of people, and Ellie had often compared the results in Brighton's parks and gardens to the aftermath of a locust swarm. They had managed to escape her mothers' house with a backpack full of Matthias' most successful greenhouse food plants and a few of his packets of seeds.

'I don't like this, Ellie. The raiding parties have been getting much more frequent, and we definitely left this door shut, right?'

Ellie nodded and silently held her finger to her mouth. She moved it to her ear as a sign to listen in through the door.

Childish giggles echoed through the corridor behind them. Ellie whipped her head around to see Maggi and Selsey running circles around each other next to a set of fire doors. Beyond the fire doors, she could see an elevator lobby and, next to it, the stairwell.

Loshie took immediate action, stepping over to the fire doors as quietly as she could and scooping Maggi up in her arms. Then she shouldered the fire doors open and stepped through into the lobby beyond.

Ellie followed close behind, afraid if there was anyone inside the flat, they might have heard the little girl's laughter. Grabbing hold of Selsey by the scruff of her neck, she dragged the dog through the fire doors and crouched down next to Loshie in the elevator lobby, just out of sight of the flat door. Loshie had one hand over Maggi's mouth.

Ellie's knuckles whitened where they gripped Selsey. Moving cautiously, she peered back through the fire doors to see if there were any signs of movement from within the flat. They waited in silence, to see if anything would happen. There was no noise from the flat, or anywhere else.

Ellie signalled to Loshie to stay put, and she edged back along the corridor, holding back the eager dog. Selsey made no noise either, but she sniffed close at the door opening. Still no sound emerged from flat 9F. She covered her bulging belly with one hand and followed Selsey inside.

The flat was much as the last time she had seen it, but the plant containers had been completely stripped bare. Nothing but the soil was left in them. She sat on the edge of the first wooden planting box and stared through the balcony window out to sea along the Hove coast. She didn't cry, although her heart was telling her she should. The lost food represented about a quarter of their growing supplies. Alongside her and Wayne, she felt responsible for providing fresh vegetables for Luke, Loshie and Maggi, as well as Jack and Diane. They hadn't lost everything, but this would stretch already meagre supplies too thin.

She tried to call Wayne; he didn't reply. Ellie knew that he would be fishing, either at the marina, or under the Palace Pier. Both spots had good phone service, but for the occasional blind spot.

I wonder if we should better barricade the roof. But then it would look really obvious that something good is hidden there.

Miles M Hudson

Sunday 5 May 2030

The second summer of the Times of Malthus is heating up.

'I'm really scared.'

Wayne stopped hammering for a moment and turned to look down at his groaning wife. She had been in labour for most of the day, but they had prepared well. Despite how little food Ellie had been able to get hold of over the eighteen months since the Bitness Revelations, her gravidity had proceeded exactly as their research had suggested it should.

Pregnancy tests were one thing that had not been completely looted, so they had known at an early stage. She would be tired and very weak after giving birth, but she was a strong woman, who had enjoyed excellent nutrition in her youth.

At this stage, Ellie lay on their mattress on the floor. She was propped up by an array of cushions taken from the old VIP area of the Atlanta bar. The comfortable situation was contradicted by her appearance: shaking, she looked up at him with eyes he'd never seen before. The terror in those eyes sent a shiver down his own spine.

Wayne put down his hammer and went to sit on the floor beside her. As he took her hand, it was shaking too. He put his arm around her and pulled her close into his chest. They held each other tightly for several minutes without speaking.

Finally, she raised her head, took in a deep breath, and then shouted in pain. Her face went red with the exertion of a contraction and Wayne was unsure how tightly to try and maintain the embrace.

Her scream subsided. 'Argh. God, Wayne, I'm gonna die here.'

'You're not going to die.' His voice was firm, more command than reassurance. Internally, he knew he couldn't guarantee anything during her labour. With no medicines or pain relief available anymore, they had chosen to seal themselves away in their beach bunker and fight together for Ellie and Baby Smith to survive.

The Times of Malthus

'Owwwww! Yes, I am!' Ellie was crying with the pain. Wayne was starting to panic inside and struggled to maintain the calm expression that he felt she needed to be able to cling on to. He wanted to be a tower of strength to help her through but knew all the risks. At least in theory.

He was particularly aware of the incredible difference between the birth of his first child and that of his brother's, not even two years earlier. Loshie had been in a sterile hospital ward, with medical professionals surrounding her, and all the gas and air she could suck down.

The infonetwork had been clear that many mothers and many babies died during an unaided childbirth, and there were any number of other complications that they needed to be ready for, many of which needed a doctor to be able to diagnose properly, let alone treat.

Neither Ellie nor Wayne was religious, but they had agreed that, having made the best possible preparations under the circumstances, all they could do was hope and pray. Wayne felt he was ready to leap into action as best he could, but they had both been caught out by the reality of the intense pain Ellie was suffering.

The contractions started to subside, her grip on his hand a little looser now, and he lowered her gently down to rest, promising as he did so that he wouldn't forget all the different scenarios they'd talked about, the many things they might have to deal with.

She kissed Wayne, and they talked through all the solutions that he was ready to jump in and administer, depending on what might go awry as the labour progressed. The conversation was a distraction and a balm for Ellie. She could see from his panicked expression that Wayne was floundering, his despair at what to do or what not to do as plain as day in his knotted brows and drained complexion. It wasn't like he'd done this before. Or like either of them had ever expected to do it all alone.

She shooed him back to finalising the temporary fortifications. The last nail went in easily, and he put the hammer on the floor by the door that he'd just barricaded shut. If the Essex

Raiders set the door on fire, they'd need to be able to remove the planks quickly to escape.

As far as they knew, nobody else was aware that they lived in the under-promenade archway home. Selsey could generally be relied upon to follow instructions to be silent. She seemed to have learned, as well as her humans had, the occasions when it was more prudent to remain hiding in silence, as opposed to those when the best course of action was to charge straight at an enemy, screaming like some crazed berserker.

Wayne sat next to Ellie, half lying on the floor. He held her hand and felt a tight squeeze as she puffed her breathing loudly. 'That's it. We're completely sealed in; a week's food in that fridge, and three jerrycans of water in case the drip dries up for some reason.'

Ellie forced a smile between noisy exhalations. 'You think the fridge will run OK off the solar panels?'

Wayne split a broad grin. 'Surprise birth present! I managed to rig up a Tesla Powerwall in the next-door shop. It's connected to those cells on the café roof, and then also into here through the wall.'

'What? You're a superstar! How did you drill through the wall though?'

'I didn't – there's that gap up by where the water comes in. We don't need very thick wires to run a fridge and some lights, but the Powerwall will keep it all running uniformly. I'm afraid the fridge will add to the heat in here, but we can have iced drinks.'

'No way! I can't remember the last time I had ice. Is it ready now?'

Wayne paused and listened. Neither of the two reading lamps were on. 'The fridge isn't going yet – I think the batteries will need a long, slow charge to kick them into action.'

'Oh. You think it will actually work at all?'

'It's brand new – I found it still in its packaging in a garage up at the fancy end of Hove. Looked like they were preparing to install it just when the Times kicked off. I don't think I'd have been able to connect it up right, but the instruction book was there, still plastic wrapped. So, it should all work well – it even had all the new wires we needed – but it needs to charge up to a certain minimum before it'll work at all, and I don't know how great the solar cells we're using are.'

'Owwwww!' She squeezed his hand again in the gloom.

'Are you OK?'

'No, I'm not OK. Owwwww! It's like you're stabbing me with a big bloody knife. Ow, Wayne, make it stop!'

He stared at her silhouette against the sliver of light coming through a millimetre gap between the door and its frame at the entrance. Selsey joined in with a howl. This made Ellie try to hold in her screams. She sucked breath in and out.

Her voice was strained at best, squealing at worst. 'Quiet, Selsey! Stop her, Wayne.'

He looked over and then back at Ellie and moved over to try and comfort the dog. Stroking through thick fur, he said, 'I hope she doesn't go stir crazy, cooped up in here for a whole week.'

'I hadn't thought of that – I'm more worried she'll cook in this heat.'

'I don't know. I reckon if we're keeping the hot air out, the cool stone walls will actually make it alright in here.' He continued, hoping the conversation would distract her from the contraction pain, 'We're definitely OK for enough water for her, but I don't expect the meals are going to be very interesting. For her or us.'

'Surprise birth present!' Ellie laughed, albeit weakly. 'Look in the top drawer.'

'I won't be able to see anything.'

'You know what I mean.' She sounded put out that her surprise was losing impetus. 'Feel around in that top drawer!'

He stepped carefully across to the white chest of thin drawers that the old gift shop had used to hold ribbon, fancy paper and tape to wrap gifts. He pushed his hand around in the small clothes that lived there now and came out with two food bars. He recognised the shape and could hear the old wrappers crinkling.

'What are they?'

'I found a box of old protein bars. They're nuts and caramel and raisins and stuff.'

'And you reckon still edible?'

'I don't know if it was a bit over optimistic given the heat we live through now, but their best before date is end of May 2030.'

'Awesome, right on time. You want one now?'

'I'm not sure I could keep it down. You have one and give me a bite. The rest of the box is in the bottom of the potato bucket. There's about twenty bars in there.'

'You're the superstar, you know that?'

They lay together for several hours, as Ellie's contractions got closer together and more painful. Wayne struggled to endure her pain. He desperately wanted to help, but there was nothing he could do directly. They had researched the mechanics of giving birth, but information videos in an Armulet projection could never fully convey the reality of the pain Ellie had to deal with.

Towards midnight, Ellie asked Wayne to read her some news from his Armulet to take her mind off the labour. Since the Times of Malthus had destroyed the news organisations, along with all other organisations, any new information on the infonetwork was generally unreliable. Most of the time, it was some sort of scam to get people to go somewhere and then rob them. As time had gone by, even these fake news stories of safe havens had died out, as people no longer had anything worth stealing. With the massive loss of life to starvation, plenty of consumer goods were left in warehouses and shops all around the country. Foodstuffs and medicines though were so rare that people would sometimes kill for them.

'Look up something from the BBC on the baby's birthday ten years ago. Actually, no, 2020 was Covid pandemic time, that'll be shit news. How about fifteen years ago today?'

Wayne moved his fingers in a way the Armulet understood and worked through various menus on its news app. 'Oh, wow. Lucky baby is going to be born on the sixth of May: seventh of May 2015 was the day the Tories won the election on their own and dumped the LibDems.'

'Oh, God, yes, I remember. Shit, that was a dark day. Do you think it's too much to say that the Times of Malthus actually started then?'

Wayne laughed. 'Yes, I think that probably is too much.'

'See if you can find something nicer, please. What about something actually on the sixth?'

'Erm, it's pretty much all election news stories. Ed Miliband says blah blah. Oh, here you go. From the Belfast Telegraph: "new 3D X-ray scans detect 40% more cancer tumours".'

'Lovely. Swap out the end of civilisation for a reminder that cancer will take us all in the end, even if we avoid the Essex Raiders and find enough food to stay alive.'

'Yeah, you're right. I suppose that X-ray machine won't be in use anymore. Was good news at the time, but I'm not sure what old news would stand up as good news nowadays.'

Ellie leaned her head into Wayne's shoulder. 'We're making our own good news today.' She closed her eyes and screamed, her tight grip on Wayne's hand cutting off its supply of blood.

A pile of Holiday Inn towels, covered in blood and mucus, lay in the front corner of their lock up. Selsey had jumped up at the first cries of the new baby. Now swaddled in the final clean towel, the tiny infant gawped at Selsey's beige fluffball of a face. The newborn had no intent behind her facial expression, but, as all new parents do, Ellie ascribed thoughts to it. She was pleased to imagine her daughter as already curious about the world. She had forgotten the research they had previously done that her baby's eyes could not really focus yet. By the light of a candle, saved for a special occasion, Ellie lay in Wayne's arms on the cushions, and the dog stood between his feet peering at the new little friend.

Ellie asked, 'Have we done the right thing? Is it really fair to bring Clara into this hellhole of a world?'

'Clara? Whatever happened to calling her Jackie? I really do want to name her after my father.'

Ellie smiled and shook her head. 'Sorry, girls go after my mother's mother, boys can go after your dad. That's just the way it is.' Ellie started to cry. 'I wish my mothers could see her.'

Wayne hugged Ellie tighter and stroked the baby's cheek.

'Look at her. There's no way we can have done the wrong thing. Humanity has to keep on going.'

'To what end though? What good is having humanity scrabble to survive, fighting each other, and stealing from each other?'

Wayne stared at Ellie in the gloom. 'Wow, what have you done with my bright, vibrant Ellie?'

'People have always wished for no more wars – we just got lucky to grow up here. Imagine if we'd been in Afghanistan or Syria, this is all we'd have ever known.'

Ellie sounded tetchy. 'That's exactly my point. I wish we could find a community that is free from all this danger. It's exactly because I've known a stable, prosperous life that I want it for Clara. I know we can have that.'

'We'll come through all this.' Wayne motioned his arm around at the room. 'People will come through this. The population will settle down to farming what they need to eat, and it'll be Clara's generation who do it – the ones who don't know they should be expecting video games and online shopping for shoes.'

'There isn't time for video games or shopping. There isn't even time enough to find enough food.'

'Exactly. What we can do is teach her to share her food with other people, not fight them for theirs.'

Ellie smirked. 'Oh, you old romantic. Anyone would think you didn't drive that speedboat out at nights to fight Essex Raiders with a knife.'

Wayne shrugged his shoulders. 'Well, we'll need to teach her to defend herself and her community, but that her first thought should always be, "How can I help these people?" until she finds out that they can't be helped.'

'But who will she play with? Where's her roller hockey team? We need a stable community to live in now. You can't nurture that kind of generosity of spirit in an environment where you're suspicious of everyone all the time.'

'Well, Maggi's not even two years older than her. And we do

have a community. There's Luke, and our family, and the Brighton Defence Force is protecting others like us. So between us that's, what, maybe a hundred people? That's a community, Ellie. That's the village to raise our child.'

'The village to raise our child? They didn't even have time enough to help us with her birth. Everyone's hunkered down in their own little space, just trying to survive.'

'Humanity has lived like this before and survived. We'll come through it. Our community will get back to a closer way of living – more like a genuine village. People are still reeling with the shock of the Times of Malthus.'

Ellie remained silent, but her body language gave away that she was unconvinced.

Miles M Hudson

Sunday 14 July 2030
Clara is almost ten weeks old.

Wayne bounded up the wide staircase to the entrance doors of Brighton's old Holiday Inn and ran through the lobby. In the midday heat, the stuffy foyer choked his heavy breathing. Outside on the Kings Road, the adjacent sea had cooled the air enough to breathe, but the hotel reception area seemed airless as he raced onwards, not even taking a moment to look over his shoulder.

Luke had stayed outside with comrades from the Brighton Defence Force, taking on a boat full of Essex Raiders in hand-to-hand fighting on the beach. He had urged Wayne to get inside and get Ellie and Loshie and the children into the safe room.

The Raiders were there to plunder food, so if they found some, hopefully they would leave. If they came across the women gardening, they would attempt to steal the food and that would most likely involve attacking anybody in their way.

The best outcome would be for Luke and the others to send them packing, but a second boat had arrived, and these new bandits ignored the battle and ran straight up the beach to look for food stores.

The hotel's lifts had been without power for nearly two years. Wayne was used to taking the stairs. Where the lobby had been still and stifling, the stairwell was cool. He took the steps two and three at a time and knew exactly which floor to make for.

He hoped the searching would keep the Raiders busy on a floor-by-floor approach. The Brightonians moved the vegetable-growing boxes regularly, and randomly, in order to try and avoid theft. With six flats on every floor above the hotel, and the possibility of garden boxes on each balcony, it would take them some time to get up to Eleven, where Ellie and Loshie were watering on the shaded north side of the building. The current garden balcony faced away from the sea, towards the city, so the women would not have seen the action down on the shingle.

Wayne ran the whole eleven flights but was unable to speak by the time he burst into 11D. Ellie guessed immediately what was happening and grabbed up her things. Baby Clara was already in a sling across Ellie's front, and she shouted to Loshie and Maggi to come immediately. They all rushed back into the stairwell and could hear shouting at the bottom. Men instructing each other about which floors to head to and which flats had provided bounty in the past.

The two families ran down four floors. They had a safe room built into one of the flats on Six, and the access point was in 7B. Wayne stepped down an extra half flight as the women carried Clara and Maggi onto the landing towards 7B.

Selsey joined Wayne, barking for all she was worth, but it did not stop two of the Raiders bounding up towards them, screaming like banshees. They were dressed all in camouflage pattern clothing. It didn't match in any specific, uniform way but formed a theme that all the Essex Raiders held to in their dress. Their camouflage served no function in urban raids and was intended to exude a military strength.

The Brightonians who repelled these bandits had seen enough raids to know that their weaponry was generally not military grade though. Guns were extraordinarily rare, and knives, axes or machetes were the weapons of choice.

In any case, the stairwell offered no space to wield any large weapon. Wayne hurled a fire extinguisher down at them and leapt after it to punch the first one as soon as he raised his face after avoiding the extinguisher. Wayne's single blow knocked the man back into the other, and they both staggered down a few steps. Before they could regain themselves, Wayne and Selsey ran back up to the seventh floor and along into the flat.

In the main lounge room of the flat, a hole three metres in diameter had been broken through the concrete floor. Wayne dropped himself through it and landed with a thud on a slab of wood laid down on top of the floor immediately below the hole. A plank ramp allowed Selsey to run down into 6B as well.

Ellie knocked Selsey's ramp away, and it fell with a crash. She grabbed Wayne's hand and pulled him towards the hallway of the downstairs flat. The entrance door was barricaded with the rubble from the hole that the Smith brothers had smashed in its ceiling. Even if the Raiders found which flat they were in, they could not get at them through its front door.

From above, the screaming attackers could be heard charging into 7B. Wayne had not even attempted to close that front door. They were in a battle frenzy. Without stopping to think, the big ginger man Wayne had punched leapt down through the hole. As he did so, Ellie and Loshie pulled the wooden slab away, to reveal that a second hole had been cut in that floor as well, opening a double drop down into flat 5B. The crunch as the man's leg broke could be heard clearly.

His colleague seemed unfazed. He hung down by his hands from the edge of the upper hole, attempting to swing and land on the remaining middle floor where the Brighton residents were gathered. As he swung forwards and let go to fly into the room, Loshie grabbed his legs and, with a heave, pivoted him back down the second hole as well. The second man landed headfirst on the carpeted concrete below with a sickening crunch. Ellie saw blood and brains splatter out from his contorted body and wrapped Maggi up in a smothering embrace before she could see the worst of it.

From 6B's balcony, they could see the battle on the beach. Several bodies lay still or moving slightly, with half a dozen men and women actively walking around checking on the state of the injuries. Wayne saw Luke had a slight limp but seemed to be actively involved in the post-combat assessment. One Essex Raiders' boat was still at the water's edge, so with the Brighton Defence Force in charge of the beach, the battle appeared to have been won.

Wayne came back into the lounge room of the flat to find Ellie sat on the sofa, breastfeeding Clara. Selsey stood looking through the hole, watching what the enemies might do. One was dead, whilst the other moaned occasionally but could not move anywhere. Loshie was standing at the edge, holding Maggi's hand, pointing down through the hole, and telling her two-year-old daughter that this was what happened to bad people.

The Times of Malthus

After exiting down through the second hole, and dragging the surviving Raider down the stairs, Wayne rejoined his BDF colleagues, and they ran through what had been gained and lost in this battle. A new and powerful rigid inflatable boat with a top of the range electric motor and long-range battery was now theirs. One BDF fighter had been killed. Another had been bludgeoned with an iron bar to the spine. They were unsure if she would survive it: she would likely be paralysed if she did.

The raiding party of six had suffered three deaths, the ginger man captured with a broken leg, and two others captured with minor wounds. Any follow-up from the Essex Raiders would need a new boat, and new personnel strong enough to take on a battle with the fear of not knowing what had happened to their comrades.

The local community now had three prisoners to deal with. Balancing the needs for justice and mercy with the blood-boiling anger of direct combat was a confusing and difficult task. The 300 or so surviving residents of Brighton tried to put together some sort of new judiciary. Kangaroo courts were springing up all over the country.

The official recorded minutes from the first Brighton Seafront Kangaroo Court, circulated by Armulet to the nearly 300 population that lived near the beachfront, contained the following text:

Date: 14 July 2030
Minutes recorded by Gary Palmer, fisherman.

Declaration of Authority:
We have survived the Times of Malthus for nearly two years, working together in defence, the growing of foodstuffs, and the search for other resources. We have come together as a matter of survival, with everyone helping everyone, regardless of actual family connections.

Our community is now stable and in need of a judicial system. We all lost friends or relatives as a result of the hoarding by the rich elites before the Times. Our new system of government must be utterly democratic. Every person should be involved in decision making.

Our community court will be officially named The Kangaroo. This is not mob justice though; everyone in the community will decide the judgments and sentencing, so there can be no corruption in our court.

Brighton Seafront Kangaroo Proceedings
Location: Beachfront amphitheatre, Kings Road, Brighton
Start time: 8pm
Present: 179 members of the Brighton community (see accompanying register)
An attached video file began with a list of names of those

'Attending Via Armulet'. It then showed the audience of the amphitheatre, with each person's name flashing up above their heads as the camera panned past them. Most were standing in the audience area of the amphitheatre, including Loshie Smith and Maggi Smith.

Ellie Smith and Wayne Smith watched the proceedings from the promenade above, shaded by a large purple golf umbrella. Ellie Smith held up the hand of the baby slung across her chest to wave it at the camera. The video's AI labelled the baby by name too: Clara Smith.

In places, those Attending Via Armulet were also visible on the video, as they were 3D-projected into a space beside relatives or friends.

The video concluded by covering the stage, where the participants' names were also annotated with roles held: several as 'jailer', three labelled 'prisoner', and finally, the 'Kangaroo Leader'.

Minutes:

The Kangaroo held a minute's silence for Anthony Jalpar, BDF fighter, killed this afternoon by the marauding Essex Raiders. There was applause to thank Kathy Lucan, BDF fighter, injured this afternoon by the marauding Essex Raiders. The Kangaroo Leader expressed the community's hopes that she will recover fully.

The Kangaroo Leader described the battle of this afternoon: he explained how the three prisoners had come along the coast to steal the food from our gardens, and in doing so had killed our comrade, Anthony Jalpar, and Kathy Lucan could also die soon from her injuries.

There was a brief pause to proceedings as the crowd tried to get at the prisoners. The community members were justifiably incensed, but our jailers protected their charges and held some members of the audience back from mounting the stage.

Our Kangaroo Leader then asked: 'Guilty or not guilty?'

The community responded en masse, 'GUILTY!'

Our Kangaroo Leader asked: 'What is the sentence then?'

As one voice, Brighton cried: 'DEATH!'

Sentence was passed by the Kangaroo Leader: 'Take them away! Off the pier!'

The Essex Raiders were taken from the stage and into the old seaside's mini land train. This prisoner transport's bell rang all along the front to announce the condemned men.

Our Kangaroo Leader lit Jalpar's funeral pyre.

The crowd became solemn and respectful and many cried at the loss of their friend.

By the time the pyre burnt down to a small residual fire, the land train had passed up the ramp to the Kings Road, and then onto and along the Palace Pier.

Our leader threw a heavy blanket over the pyre and turned everyone's attention to the end of the pier.

The Kangaroo Leader held up his Armulet, in videocall to Luke Smith, jailer, and the crowd repeated, 'DEATH!'

The prisoners were thrown off the end of the pier, with heavy blocks tied to their feet.

Justice was done.

The Times of Malthus
Friday 30 August 2030
For the four months of Clara's life, the temperature had fallen below thirty degrees on only six days.

'What are we going to do?' Wayne asked.

Clara lay in the small cot, wrapped in wet blankets. The temperature was unbearable again, and even in the relative cool of their beach hut home, they worried about her overheating. The baby was clearly undernourished, and they couldn't be sure if she was actually ill, or simply weak from lack of food and hot from the excessive August temperatures.

Food was in seriously short supply. With no rain for months, it was hard to grow anything. They were lucky that the subterranean stream of water that arrived in the top corner of their arch space had continued, albeit down to mere drips again. It was barely enough for their own drinking needs, so did not help much to water vegetables.

They had stored a lot of water in the barrels in the Holiday Inn, but even that was running low. The garden crops they managed to nurture often provided less nutrition than they might, as Ellie had to pick them before they were ready, when there was nothing else to eat.

The fish in the sea seemed sparser too. Wayne was managing to catch about one fish every other day. It was too hot to stand in the sunshine, and the catch from under the piers was diminished. Moreover, it was too dangerous to fish alone, so he could only go when Luke or his father were available to join. This was quite often though, as everyone needed to try and catch as much food as possible. Nobody was thriving.

'We're going to survive. And so is our daughter.' Ellie was unshakeable. She was determined that neither war nor famine, nor indeed pestilence, would defeat her and those she loved.

Fish meant they were not dead already. Living by the sea offered food sources that those inland probably didn't even imagine, but the minimal amount they could harvest from it was still a recipe for malnourishment. What could be safely foraged was becoming less certain too. Brighton's littoral shellfish had died off significantly with rising water temperatures, and those that persisted harboured excessive quantities of dangerous bacteria. The edible seaweeds were highly nutritious, but they no longer grew very close to shore.

Nappies remained plentifully available from the abandoned supermarkets of Brighton. In the two years since the Bitness Revelations rioting began, the number of babies born had been very few. People were significantly pre-occupied with their own survival. Those who were keen to have children had mostly chosen to wait out the dangerous times. They all hoped that soon the communities they lived in would stabilise and become safe enough for a pregnant mother or a new-born child to live well.

Ellie and Wayne had gone against this grain. Ellie felt tough enough to beat any circumstances, and she was convinced that Wayne was a capable support in that fight. Clara's nappy filled with a greeny-brown liquid, and she was pale and clammy.

Wayne took the filthy package away to throw in the sea. There was no functional sewage system other than the sea. The toilet in the archway beach hut emptied straight into the water, via a long pipe, installed in the 19th Century, that went out as far as the end of the piers. It couldn't cope with any detritus though, so they took used nappies and threw them off the breakwater on the side where the currents should carry everything away. The process grated on both Wayne and Ellie, but they agreed that they had to remove any source of disease. They reconciled themselves slightly with the fact that the population was now so low that direct dumping of sewage in the oceans was something Mother Earth could now cope with. Eight billion had been too many for that. A minuscule fraction of eight billion, Gaia could manage.

Ellie did her best to encourage Clara to take a little liquid regularly, but the poor thing was sickly, listless. She clutched her to her breast and felt the baby's feverish sweat against her own skin.

Luke shouted for Wayne, his voice resounding around their little home from outside. He had been on watch up the i360 Tower, and she could hear his big feet pounding alongside the dry, concrete paddling pool outside.

Returning along the beach, her husband shouted back to his brother, and Ellie clearly heard Luke tell of an incoming attack boat. Daytime attacks were becoming more frequent, and that smacked of desperation. The hunger in the pirates' bellies had become so strong that nowadays it overtook any careful planning and forced them to come surging along the coast at any time.

Luke could have called from the top of the tower via Armulet, but, as it was right next to their home, he had probably decided to just collect Wayne in person.

Ellie stood in the doorway and could see along a sweep of the shingle beach. Even with her sunglasses on, she had to hold a hand up to shade her eyes. Heat reflected from the pavement of the beachfront area, and the cool of their beach hut at her back felt wonderful.

To the right, the i360 tower and the Upside-down House tourist attraction blocked the view west. In the other direction, she could see the stones and the water's edge for nearly three quarters of a mile up to the Palace Pier.

Wayne arrived back from nappy disposal, and Luke appeared down the stairs from the promenade. A charcoal grey boat had landed on the beach in the distance by the pier and several figures were buzzing about dragging the boat out of the water.

'What did you see?' Wayne asked his brother.

'Definitely Essex Raiders – they're all wearing camo gear.'

Wayne opened his mouth to speak but was cut off by Luke's Armulet ringing. He waved at his wrist and Loshie appeared in projection in front of them.

'Come quick, Luke! The Raiders are heading up towards the house.'

'What? Where are you now? Are they in our street?'

'They're on Madeira Drive, but they're heading our way. I'm scared, Luke.' Loshie's image crouched down suddenly, and she could be seen to be peering around something not in the shot.

'Get inside the house! We'll be there really soon.'

Loshie turned and started running and the feed cut out.

The brothers checked they had their knives and grabbed their bikes.

As he raced away, Wayne turned back in the saddle and shouted, 'Lock this place up tight. I'll be back when it's all quiet out here.'

'Be safe!' She turned away quickly, so Wayne wouldn't see the anguish on her face. He was repeatedly heading out to fight, and she already had a sick child to worry about. What was wrong with their daughter?

As soon as Wayne had departed, Ellie placed Clara back in her cradle. Using a gardener's plant mister, she sprayed a little water on the baby's blankets and head.

Selsey was alert at the door, excited by all the action and shouting. Ellie sent her back to bed. The dog was well trained – she moved quickly and remained silent.

The big wooden door from the Atlanta was still troublesome to manhandle, but since it had been mounted properly on giant hinges, Ellie could manage it alone. She hefted up the drawbar with both hands and slotted it centrally in the iron mounting hooks. The thick heavy bar had seemed like overkill, but now she felt safe from attack inside a fortress of their own making.

As far as they knew, the Essex Raiders were still unaware anyone was living in the space beneath the archway. They knew bandits had passed by and looked at the place, but with the solid door, and no obvious human activity, they had always moved on without attempting to break in. Once a place was known to have been used by Brightonians, the Raiders would return again and again, and the archway gift shop would never be safe. Concealment was paramount to their security. She often stared in wonder at Clara and Selsey, amazed by their silence at the critical moments.

To increase the safety factor, they had hung a heavy theatre curtain across the middle of the living space. It was so thick and heavy and black that Wayne reckoned she could use her Armulet behind it and still be invisible to someone from outside peering through the door frame crack. She had never dared to try.

The Times of Malthus

Some time later, when Clara had fallen asleep in her cradle, Ellie started at the sound of a sudden, loud banging reverberating around the cavern-like space. Somebody was thumping on the wooden door with a large solid object. As muffled as it was by the heavy curtain blocking her and Clara from direct view of the door, the sound of the knocking was enough to make her almost gasp with fright.

Ellie thought of Donne's tolling bell. The sound was actually low and woody, not gong-like, but she still felt a deep sense of the loss of humanity. Who might this person have been just two years earlier?

She peeped around the curtain. A vertical sliver of light came through the hinge gap of the door. This light was blocked up to about a foot from the top. Still holding her breath, she turned to see Selsey watching, and beside her, Clara in the cradle, her eyes wide and seeming to shine in the darkness.

The banging stopped. Ellie realised she was in pitch darkness behind the curtain. Her visions of the dog and her daughter had been in her mind.

The banging restarted. It did not seem aggressive, not attempting to knock the door down. It seemed just intimidatory. An attempt to scare any occupants out. The three of them remained silent. Ellie gripped the edge of the curtain and realised how badly her hand was trembling.

She heard shouts and the sounds of running feet. Soon she heard the voices receding further down the beachfront. Her best guess was that they had run off past the Café on the Beach and away beside the crazy golf course.

Wayne had passed on much of his military training to her. They were wary of the subterfuges of war. She did not make any attempt to move the curtain or open the door. Instead, Ellie fed Clara and stroked Selsey. She could hear the dog panting again and knew that Selsey had been just as careful to avoid discovery as her humans had been. Ellie ventured enough light to fill her water bowl and drank from the same bottle herself. Just the dimmest glow came from her Armulet screen but, in the blackness, it was blinding.

After forty minutes or so, she began to whisper to Clara. The regular hours spent in silent blackness offered Ellie much time to think. Once, when Ellie had explained her solo security scenario, Loshie had commented to her, 'That's a lot of soul searching.'

Her friend lived with Luke's parents in Kemptown, and there was always somebody else to share what their grandparents would have called the Blitz spirit. Ellie had only her own thoughts – her own demons and angels – to converse with. She always loved time alone to muse, and Loshie's comment had, if truth be told, been a succour to Ellie.

She wouldn't go as far as to say she liked the attacks but, surprisingly, she felt safe and at peace. If she had been in the house with the extended family, there would have been more access points to defend, and more people to be responsible for. Uppermost in her logic, though, was that there would be more people to fail in their role and endanger Clara as a result. Much as she loved the Smiths, they would be added links in the chain, and the weakest link would not then be known. If Ellie was the only protector, then she alone was in control of any failure.

Ellie worried that for all her willingness to fight to save Clara from attack, straightforward disease would be the most likely thing to take their daughter. She encouraged Clara to suck a little more milk, but the infant was incoherent. Dim as it was, Ellie's eyes had adjusted well enough she could see that Clara's were closed in sleep, and her head lolled. The new mother bit her lip to keep from panicking. She put her ear to the girl's tiny chest and could hear her heart beating – it was the best doctoring Ellie had. The infonetwork provided no specifics about what these symptoms might indicate. Once again, against her preference, Ellie was forced to pray for the illness to be beaten. She whispered encouragements to Clara's immune system.

A fist banged on the door twice, followed by a kick. Again, two fists and the foot. Ellie's heart raced and her chest tightened.

Two fists and a kick. Two fists and a kick. It went on several times before she heard Wayne sing out, 'Buddy, you're a boy, make a big noise playing on the streets, gonna be a big man someday.' It was their passcode, so she would know he was alone. Ellie scrambled to open the heavy door, and they hugged and kissed.

She was shocked to see he limped as he entered, blood streaked across his shirt.

'Not mine,' he said quickly, seeing the direction she was looking.

A thousand questions came to her mind, but instead she stepped up close to him, drawing him into another embrace, careful as she did so not to get the blood on herself.

'Was it bad?'

'For him,' he said, 'not so much for me.' He sighed. 'I liked this shirt. But I'll never get this blood out.'

'Plenty more where it came from,' said Ellie, stepping back now. More clothes in abandoned shops than any of them would ever need.

Wednesday 25 September 2030
Two years since Bitness started its Revelations.

Wayne and Ellie were sitting around a campfire they had made on the beach, when a sound like a clanging hand bell suddenly issued from his Armulet: the group alarm for the Brighton Defence Force to head to the Marina to intercept an arriving boat.

'Shit. The sentry on watch up i360 Tower must have seen a light moving in the darkness.' Wayne looked up to the tower, the pod glinting but barely visible in the scant starlight.

'Don't they usually maintain complete blackout to evade detection?'

Wayne turned to look east along the beach. 'The moon set at, what, around five-thirty? The coastline's so dark now, they'll need navigation all along the journey from Clacton or Southend.' The complete darkness made it a perfect evening to spot that light from the tower.

Ellie checked her Armulet. 'Eight o'clock's a bit early for a night raid, isn't it?'

'I'm not sure there's much planning to their attacks. I'd better go and find out.'

She kicked and pushed pebbles over their fire, and Wayne shoved the last piece of fish into his mouth. They both ran back to the beach hut. Wayne pulled on his black boots – he was already wearing black combat trousers and T-shirt. He manhandled an electric scooter into readiness, and she grabbed his arm and planted a kiss on a cheek.

Ellie passed over his black backpack, and Wayne trundled off into the night. Once he'd reached the top of the concrete ramp, she saw another scooter approach his, its lights blazing against the darkened promenade, and knew it must be the watchman from the i360 Tower.

Inside, Ellie hushed Selsey into her bed and put Clara into her cot. She hung the blackout curtain and switched on a solar rechargeable nightlight.

At the doorway, she looked out to sea. The world was dark,

and the Milky Way was bright. A thousand stars pricked the blackout curtain above. As Ellie stared out past the Palace Pier, the Milky Way lay horizontally above the water. She wondered how she could have spent so much time on this same beach in her younger years never knowing of the cosmic wonders hidden from them all by Brighton's lights. All that had changed, now all the power grids everywhere were down, seemingly forever.

Touching the thick wooden door they had brought from the Atlanta reminded her of the noise and light that filled the area ten years ago. She wore a thin dress, just like she might have on those summer nights to flirt with the tourist boys. Drink would have flowed like water. Today, water barely flowed at all. The darkness all around blotted out the destruction and dereliction of her hometown. She could picture drunks staggering in pools of light that spilt from the bars.

The white water of breaking waves caught Ellie's eye. The beach out front of the Atlanta had a relatively shallow gradient, and the water's edge was probably fifty feet closer than it had been in their teenage years.

She remembered midnight swimming with Loshie. A smile played on Ellie's face. *I must chat with Loshie. It's been too long since we remembered the old days.*

After ten minutes, she saw two boats surge into view, on exit from the marina. They had powerful searchlights mounted on their bows that lit up the sea before them. As Ellie watched, they zigzagged in separate hunting patterns, aiming to intercept or scare away the incomers.

She hoped they had not rushed out in haste, leaving Brighton undefended against those Raiders who had already made landfall. The dark was the enemy's friend, but it could also be Ellie's defence.

After heaving the door closed and barring it, she extinguished the nightlight. It was necessary to trail her fingers along the wall to guide herself to retire behind the thick curtain.

Clara gurgled sleepily when Ellie lifted her into her arms. She had worked hard in the sunshine on the roof of the Holiday Inn all that hot September day, and once she was settled in the cream armchair, mother and daughter fell asleep together.

Ellie woke some hours later to Selsey licking her leg. 'What's up, girl? Do you need a pee? Me too.' She put Clara back in the crib and stood stretching her arms high. Looking around the theatre curtain, the door frame's thin gap was letting brilliant morning light illuminate the front half of the beach hut. Clara's nappy smelt, but Ellie decided to head down to the sea to relieve herself first.

She hadn't had an all clear from Wayne though and she tried to videocall him. No answer.

Worry stabbed at her, and she searched for him using her Armulet's locator: Wayne was still at sea and, for all she knew, in the midst of a battle.

She tried texting instead of calling but got no immediate response.

Didn't he say the boat battery charge would only last eight hours at a go?

She scowled, worry digging its claws ever deeper.

Ellie called Luke.

He didn't pick up, but she heard a shout through the door. 'I'm outside, Ellie.'

She heaved the door open, and saw Luke, only ten yards away, walking towards her. Despite the bright sun, he wore a black beanie on his head. All his clothes were black. The same look as Wayne had worn the night before.

Blinking in the bright sunlight, she nearly missed that Luke's face was bruised and his eyes were very red. As soon as she spotted the injuries, she couldn't stop looking at them. She saw that the redness around his eyes included tears. Her breath caught and her fists closed involuntarily.

Selsey pushed past her legs and headed towards the beach toilet area. Ellie's own toilet needs were forgotten.

His voice cracked as he stuttered, 'He's gone, Ellie.' Luke hugged his sister-in-law. He gripped her tightly like a bear but even when he released the hug, she still couldn't breathe.

Her legs gave way, and Luke helped her to sit down on the

low wall around the paddling pool area.

Ellie was stunned. She sat in silence.

When she finally spoke, her voice was pleading. 'What happened? I need to know, Luke. Don't spare me anything, I have to know what happened.'

Luke struggled to articulate; his brain fogged with grief as much as Ellie's. She was also gripped with fear for the future. Wayne had been the block, keeping the desperation of the Times of Malthus from infecting her. She would now have to protect Clara without him.

Ellie squeezed Luke's hand and, over fifteen minutes, interrogated out of him the events of the night, after which she sent him home to be with Loshie, Maggi, and Jack and Diane.

Selsey returned and they went back into the beach hut together. Ellie's sobs made Clara stare. Her mother was always so purposeful and calm. The girl had never seen her devastated. She was about to join in with the crying, when Ellie sucked in a big breath and blew it out in a loud exhalation, eyes closed. This changed the atmosphere and Clara paused, curious.

'I need to tell you the most important story of your life.' Tears free-flowed down Ellie's face for the next ten minutes as she set forth a family history that would be retold over and over down the years.

'Your father was the bravest man who ever lived. He defended our country and Brighton throughout his whole life. And he gave his life to keep us safe.' Her voice cracked, and Ellie lost herself to grief. Selsey's ears flattened, and she whined, confused and frightened, as Ellie slid slowly to her knees.

Do this now, she told herself. *But not after*.

After, she alone would take care of Clara. For now, she could grieve, and so she gave herself over to it, to the one thing she had feared the most and which now, she realised, as if in a moment of perfect clarity, had been inevitable.

Clara did join in crying. Eventually, Selsey wailed too, a plaintive howl. The dog's cry brought Ellie back into the room. She smiled weakly and patted her head. Clara was confused again and paused crying. Ellie turned her smile to the girl. She kissed her on the forehead, breathed in deeply through her nose, and wiped her Armulet strap across her own cheeks.

She continued with the story. 'Wayne was the leader of a squad in the Brighton Defence Force. The boat squad all dressed completely in black. Not a specific uniform, just black clothes, except for the hat. The six of them would all wear identical ribbed, fisherman's hats.

'One on the boat carried a handgun, but they were out at night and accurate shooting at sea is almost impossible, even in the daytime. Wayne never used the gun. He believed the Raiders were just hungry people, like us, and he fought them back but didn't want to kill anybody. To keep them away from our home, there was often hand-to-hand fighting on board the small boats. There were a lot of close-quarter shootings, and stabbings, but most deaths occurred when people were knocked unconscious and overboard.'

Ellie stopped and wept again. Her chest felt compressed like she was in a vice. She thought she would keel over with the empty feeling in her stomach.

'Your father had been stabbed and kicked overboard and they couldn't go looking for him till it became light this morning. Uncle Luke and all the BDF searched since the sun came up, but they couldn't find him.'

She held up her Armulet to show the small screen, rather than project and fill the room with confirmation of the death. Clara looked at it, and when Ellie tapped the Health tab for Wayne, the red warning triangle flashed up and the nightmare was confirmed.

'See, that red means he's no longer with us.'

Luke had told Ellie he would stay and look after them until at least the next day. 'As long as you need,' he had said.

She had so wished that she could accept and would not be alone with Clara. Ellie found herself shuddering, face sodden with tears The baby could not understand her grief and would be distressed by her mother in this state. Luke's presence would be such a comfort, such a distraction, and such a help with Clara.

His hunched shoulders, and catatonic staring at the ground,

had told her he could not stay. Ellie knew Luke needed to be with his parents and with his own family. She could tell the man was as destroyed as she was and that every moment away from the rest of the Smiths would tear him apart even more.

She had hugged Luke and promised they would visit later in the day. Her brother-in-law had staggered away up the promenade, his world upside-down. She had almost fainted onto the concrete wall outside their under-arch house.

Ellie was determined to tell three-month-old Clara her father's story. The fear of forgetting any detail drove her to repeat everything again and again.

'Shot in the thigh, Wayne continued to repel boarding members of the Essex Raiders militia. Despite a broken leg, he knocked the first and largest Essexman back into his dinghy, with a single knockout punch square on the nose.

'The big man was immediately replaced by two screaming women who leapt up on either side of Wayne. One had long and wild black hair and waved both arms around with a short knife in each fist. The old man in Wayne's squad crouched in the middle of their boat and shot her through the side within a second of boarding. She slumped to the floor gurgling, the mess of hair dangling over the side.

'The other woman was tiny – both short and petite – but she was lightning quick. She wore a black and green patterned, lycra bodysuit, and a wide, black plastic belt highlighted the tininess of her waist. She also carried a blade in each hand, bound in place by studded dog collars wrapped around each palm. Almost too fast to see, she had sliced across Wayne's forearm even before her partner hit the deck.'

Ellie fell silent, staring out of the open door. Her eyes squinted slightly, and the story paused for nearly a minute. Behind the squint, her eyes flicked left and right, up and down. When they stopped still again, the legend continued.

'The knifewoman left Wayne briefly, bouncing down into the centre of the vessel to slice the old man's neck arteries, and leapt straight back up. Wayne turned as fast as his damaged leg would allow, but she had already stabbed his left side. He crumpled under the pain and attempted to roll onto his back to be in a position to protect against her raining knife blows. Like a lizard's tongue, her right hand repeatedly flicked out and back again. Wayne struggled to follow the speed of movement but felt each one with a new spike of pain in another part of his body.

'The remaining members of his squad, including your Uncle Luke, were each involved in a fight of their own. Nobody could intervene to help. Still alive, and bleeding hard from his side, the harpy rolled your father to the edge of the deck. She stood up and gave him a vicious kick to send his brave body into the black water.

'Luke had wrestled his attacker overboard, and he picked up the gun. He pointed it at the little woman and fired, but the boat was wobbling, and he missed. She leapt down onto their attack boat, which sped away into the night. They left Brighton, two alive out of six who had arrived, but on our boat only Luke was still alive. The old man was the only one still on the boat with him, and he died very quickly. Your uncle radioed for help, but he was out in the only boat with any charge left.

'They went out at dawn, three boats ready again by then, but they couldn't find any bodies. None at all. After seven hours in the water, the currents probably took them all away somewhere. Your father loved the sea his whole life. He would be happy to be buried out there.'

She lifted Clara and hugged her tight. 'We loved him very much.' Clara gurgled and patted her mother's face. Ellie smiled, and then immediately sobbed again. 'What have you done, Wayne? Why did you have to go out there? What will I do without you?'

As soon as she had called out to him, Ellie cursed herself. Her mind was whirling. *He saved us all, many times. Don't be so selfish. We'd have died last year if not for him. Clara will take his spirit into the future.* She looked at the baby's face and smiled, saw the love of her life in it. 'You will go on to do great things – you'll defend people and save them, just like your father did. And we'll love him forever.'

The Times of Malthus

She stood up and carried Clara out to the beach. Together, they looked out at the silver sea. It was choppy in the gentle breeze. The shape of the little white horses on the waves reminded Ellie of Wayne's goatee beard, and she pointed this out to their daughter. Clara gurgled in cheerful response, with a big smile on her face.

Ellie was exhausted. She just wanted to lie on the bed next to Clara and hold her daughter tight and safe. She leant against the wall as she moved back inside the big wooden door and heaved the drawbar into place to lock them and Selsey inside. The three lay together for hours, crying and occasionally managing to fall to sleep. She often saw Wayne's round, slightly chubby, face in Clara's. Each time the vision appeared, Ellie smiled and cried at the same time.

Ellie created a monument to Wayne on their beach. A giant cairn of beach pebbles, under which she buried everything of his that would not be of use to her and Clara in the future. They never found his body, so all his worldly goods acted as the substance of her husband. She kissed each item and placed it in the centre of a circle of the biggest stones she could move. Steadily getting smaller, she added more and more stones into a grand cone. It was taller than Wayne himself had been, and the base was as wide as his spare fishing rod was long.

Ellie kept his best rod. She would get Luke to teach her and would try and catch food for the two of them. The cairn took three weeks to build, and everyone still alive in Brighton contributed to it. Some just added a nice-looking pebble from the same beach, some brought a special stone from their own place, and a few of his closest friends and family brought a special object to incorporate into the memorial.

Luke made the wooden plaque naming his brother with the dates of his life. He used a hot piece of metal to brand the letters into a large piece of driftwood. On the back, he wrote, 'From the sea to the sea, now he skates with Davy Jones.' Ellie wasn't sure why it meant something, but Luke was so earnest that she embraced the epitaph and would say it every day as she stopped by the cairn.

In the days after Wayne's death, Loshie repeatedly insisted that Ellie and Clara should move in with them, but Ellie was adamant they must stay in the old gift shop. 'We've survived this long, and our fortress will keep us safe in the future.'

Loshie stared at her. 'You're on your own now. You can't possibly get food for both of you and defend yourselves. The BDF has no more volunteers – I'm not going to let Luke out with just the three or four they've got left. We need to stay together. Safety in numbers.'

'Jack and Diane's place can't feed two more mouths, and we're just making one place more attractive to the Raiders. Better you guys keep it all quiet there, so nobody finds you.'

Loshie stared again, frowning. She shook her head and got up. Maggi was in the dog bed with Selsey, and Loshie pulled her away and headed for the door.

'We'll keep calling each other every night. I don't think the infonetwork is going off, if it's lasted this long. And you're only a mile away – let's keep meeting up in the hotel and work together on growing food. We can definitely help each other there.'

Loshie shrugged her shoulders as she dragged Maggi towards the brightness of the doorway and out onto the cracked paved area that had once been for diners of the Café on the Beach.

The Times of Malthus
Wednesday 31 January 2035
Ten years since the launch of the Armulet.

The video clip showed an Asian man speaking loudly in English. Ellie's Armulet imposed the image against Brighton Beach, and she watched through dark sunglasses. He held himself very still as he stared towards any viewer of his ArmuletLive broadcast. Loshie had forwarded the short clip taken in Hong Kong on 5 January 2035, for her friend to watch.

Ellie sat under a shade umbrella on the shingle. She leant back against a groyne at the side of the beach, below their lockup. Four-year-old Clara was trying to pile stones into a tower, but they were rounded from millions of years of grinding by the waves. More than three in a stack was proving very difficult to balance.

The recorded Asian man was shouting about how his organisation had returned to the destroyed Armulet company headquarters building. It had been ransacked in the early days after the Bitness Revelations, with over one hundred executives executed by the rioting mob, most of them thrown out of windows on the higher floors of the tower.

The destruction of the water pipe network in the building had flooded the lowest eight basement floors. They had been inaccessible for seven years as the impermeable bedrock into which the basements were dug had held the water like an abandoned quarry.

The man was now in the defunct building's twelfth basement floor underground. Only two further floors remained flooded at this point, after a small earthquake had cracked and fissured the solid rock. The room was one giant server hall – the carcasses of old computers standing in rows like soldiers on parade. As he spoke, unnecessarily loudly, the man waved his arms around to indicate the servers as the focus of his story.

'These secret basements were never open to most employees. They were the centre of Armulet Inc's clandestine research and development operations.' He spoke like an old-fashioned television news reporter. Ellie remembered how Roisin had often structured her sentences in this way, even in family conversations. The memory brought her joy rather than pain.

She recognised the embroidered badge on his shirt as being from a renowned group called the Hong Kong Pirates. They had secured large areas of the main island of the old city as a safe haven for the population that had survived the initial rioting and starvation there. They were known for ruthless violence, as a means to repel anyone who would endanger their small community. Having destroyed the bridges and tunnels that connected them to the mainland, the Pirates maintained vigilance over their island's shores in the same way that Wayne and the Brighton Defence Force had protected the area of town centred on the Palace Pier from seaborne bandits.

'Now the floodwaters have subsided, we have been able to search through the old records that survived. Those were the ones protected in plastic sacks, as most of them were held on paper to avoid hackers finding out what they were doing here. The technological advances were quite amazing, and nobody discovered these secrets before.'

He waved the viewer across as he walked to a nearby office to the side of the main hall. The conference table inside had numerous large papers spread across it. Some were booklet form reports, and some appeared to be blueprints or circuit diagrams. The person filming did not take their Armulet too close to the papers but turned again to the commentating Pirate.

'Built into every Armulet – and we have tested ours to see if this functionality is actually in there – is technology to sense your brainwaves. They developed a system that was sensitive enough to pick up the tiny magnetic fields generated by the electric currents of your nerve impulses. This was put into a testing phase with a machine learning experimental suite, which, we believe, is in one of the lower basements, still flooded. The outcomes of this research led to development of the software that interprets the signals from your optic nerve and displays what you are seeing on a screen. Like a video camera feed, but from your eyes. And it is on all the time.'

The Times of Malthus

Ellie paused the projection playback and squinted into the horizon. 'Be gentle with Selsey, Clara. Don't pull on her.'

Ostensibly, she was checking that Clara was OK, but in her mind, she played through what she had just heard. *Interception of brain signals that show you what I'm seeing. So, no need for a camera on the device. Is that the point?*

The Pirate leapt back into life. 'Same thing with your ears. Whatever you hear can be transmitted by your Armulet to somewhere else. Everything you see or hear is recorded by your Armulet, and it always has been since they were first produced before the Times of Malthus began.

What was not switched on back then was the transmission of those recordings elsewhere. The technology has just sat on all our wrists for ten years, waiting to be found. Here, we have found the instructions for opening that up.' He picked up a comb-bound paper book from the conference table and waved it towards the viewer.

Ellie tipped her head on one side. *It seems like amazing technology, but why has Loshie forwarded this to me?*

'On Hong Kong Island, we have instructed the cell towers on the island to gather the feeds and send them to our little computer centre. We have enough solar cells on one tower block to power enough computers to operate the surveillance system as Armulet Inc intended. The title on the cover of the instruction manual said, *Enabling Audiopt Surveillance Feeds*.

Ellie frowned.

'Now I can watch what anybody I choose is looking at and listening to.' He held up his own Armulet and made it project at the end of the small office. The scene that appeared showed two other men talking and laughing on a deserted street corner on some Hong Kong street. A third, female voice could also be heard.

'This is what my wife is seeing and hearing right now. She is with friends down by Victoria Harbour. These "audiopts" are the perfect surveillance system. We can monitor what raiders are seeing as they approach, so we know exactly where they are. We have been using it for three months now to protect Hong Kong Island. It has changed the atmosphere completely – our enemies do not even try to raid our community anymore. We all feel safe here.'

The man switched off his wife's conversation with friends, and he sat down in a casual pose. 'This is a breakthrough for mankind. Everybody should feel as safe as we do. So, today, we are publishing this instruction manual on the infonetwork. Any community can implement it via cell towers in your control. You will need a central server to collect and broadcast the feeds.'

Ellie mused, 'That won't work. The raiders would just leave their Armulets at home.'

The video Loshie had forwarded was weeks old. When she clicked on the link in the video player, the infonetwork jumped to showing a page with the instruction manual he had held. The page also summarised what he had just told her, and a lot more information. One of the FAQs asked *Can't people avoid the surveillance by not wearing their Armulet?* She clicked to read this paragraph.

Her objection was cast aside. The claim was that other Armulets and even the cell towers themselves all joined in the surveillance, so it was almost impossible to effectively avoid the audiopts system. Reading through it all, the only requirement that might pose difficulty was the central computer hub to relay all the feeds.

Most places in the world had plenty of photovoltaic cells for the size of the population remaining. The usual problem was not access to equipment, but a safe enough environment to install it and have it remain functional. Ellie figured this would be the easiest approach for bandits to avoid detection – they'd need to destroy the cell towers or the central computer or both. The FAQs suggested that several computer hubs could be set up in separate locations to ameliorate this problem. Moreover, the computers did not need to be attended to; they were just a relay system. As long as they remained powered up, they could serve to surveil a locality, even if hidden in a stronghold.

Ellie's mind was whirling so much that it took Selsey nudging her leg for Clara's cries of pain to cut through her mental focus on Brighton's security needs and possibilities. Clara had tumbled down a bank of shingle where the stones slid easily. The grazes did not appear serious, but for a four-year-old it was like the end of the world. 'If only you knew,' Ellie said.

Miles M Hudson

Sunday 6 May 2040
Wayne has been dead for nearly ten years.

'I know, Mummy, "studded dog collars used to strap a knife into each hand".' Clara beamed at her mother.

Ellie smiled. It was her tenth birthday, and her daughter knew the story by heart.

'Your dad would have loved to see you grow to be such a big girl.' Clara was barely four feet tall, and she was skinny. Her hair was long and blonde, her features small. Cousin Maggi was no taller, but Loshie was a full foot shorter than Ellie. Early years of malnourishment had beaten back Ellie and Wayne's strong genes to make Clara diminutive and prone to sickness. Her smile, though, was bigger than anyone's in Brighton.

Together, mother and daughter stood looking past the cairn memorial, out to sea, and chanted, 'From the sea to the sea, now he skates with Davy Jones.' The cairn had an extra bulge of stones where they had buried Selsey five years after Wayne. The old Akita had lived longer than Ellie could ever have hoped and provided unfailing support through the initial grief after Wayne's death.

She had left a legacy too. A year after Clara's birth, Selsey had hidden herself away behind the dumpsters of the old King Alfred Leisure Centre to have a litter of four puppies. Only one survived longer than a week, and, following Matthias' long-standing approach, Ellie named the puppy King Alfred.

The dog nuzzled and licked Clara, offering another birthday greeting. King Alfred was much more tactile than Selsey had been but was otherwise barely distinguishable from her mother.

'Maggi's coming today, isn't she?'

'Yes, she is. Mummy and Loshie need to go and do some gardening. Will you help us?'

'Up on the roof? Yes, please! Yes, please!' Clara skipped in a circle on the dry paddling pool, singing about going up on the roof.

Clara was always cheerful and much more infantile than her years. Most people had taken on a dour stoicism under the weight of the Times of Malthus. She had never known anything else, and her mother had always cherished and encouraged Clara's approach: that life was still for fun and laughter, skipping and singing.

Loshie stood at the top of the steps from the promenade above and called down to Ellie. 'I remember when you used to be like that.' She waved towards the skipping Clara and then gazed beyond. She looked out to sea towards the little clouds scooting across the sky. This birthday was warm, in Brighton – twenty-seven degrees – but the wind gave some relief. Loshie held onto the handrail and paused, her expression contemplative.

Maggi bundled down the stairs in front of her mother and ran over to present a birthday gift to her friend. Clara sat on the low wall around the old paddling pool and tore open the padded envelope that had been used as gift wrapping. She cooed at the sight of several pieces of roast rabbit meat, dusted in curry spices. Maggi stood in front of her, eyes rooted on the treats. Without a second thought, Clara shared them with her friend, and the two sat in silence slowly chewing and staring at the ground.

'You shouldn't have wasted your own food,' Ellie protested, as Loshie joined her by the old tourist pool.

She nodded and agreed, 'I'm pretty sure that must be the last rabbit in Brighton. Jack sometimes disappears off and returns with an animal. But he reckons the urban environment is killing all the animals.'

Ellie looked along the front, her eyebrows knitted. She scanned the bushes growing out of cracks in the concrete, and the full-blown trees twisting up in the i360 Tower compound, their tops just visible above the edge of the promenade overhang. They were young trees, and no match for the column's height, but in the last ten years Ellie had seen nature reclaiming what she had previously considered would be artificial forever. 'What do you mean? We see more animals around the place than ever before. Still not many, but they're getting a foothold.'

Loshie shook her head. 'No, Jack reckons they're all aged or sick and this place will be completely dead in a year. The drought is killing the plants, and so the whole ecosystem is gonna die.'

Ellie looked back at the trees and bushes and nodded at how sparse and brown they looked.

Loshie continued, 'I listened to that old song by The Animals the other day: *We gotta get out of this place*.' She sang a couple of lines of the song that her mother had loved and played regularly in their flat above the garage. 'It's true though, Ellie. If we don't leave Brighton now, we'll all be dead in a year too.'

Ellie shot Loshie a look and turned back to see if the children had heard. The girls were on their feet, arms stretched out for balance as they followed one another along the narrow upper ledge of the wall where they had been sitting. They were oblivious to the parents' conversation.

'Shh! Don't talk like that.'

'Somebody needs to be realistic here,' Loshie insisted. 'The hotel's run out of water, so it won't be long before the veg goes the way of that rabbit. And then we'll be next.' She reached out to touch her shoulder. 'Ellie, we need to leave Brighton. I hate the idea, but I've got to do what's best for Maggi.'

Ellie's throat tightened at the thought of leaving so many of her memories behind 'What does Luke say about it? And Jack and Diane?'

'They agree. We've got so many mouths to feed, and food has gone from scarce to non-existent.'

Ellie stared at Loshie and then looked past the girls to Wayne's memorial.

'It's what he would want you to do, Ellie. He'd want you both to live.' Loshie paused and then launched a new idea. 'Have you heard about Hereford?'

'What do you mean? Of course I've heard of Hereford.'

'No, I mean the safe community there. Apparently, they've implemented the audiopt surveillance system now, and so there's nobody stealing the food. And it rains regularly. Wales always got the most rain in the country, so it's now about the only place.'

'Hereford's not in Wales.' Ellie's reaction was a knee-jerk gainsaying of Loshie's information.

'No, but it's in the catchment area for all that water. They

The Times of Malthus

have a little community, so the rich fields all around the town can easily supply the veg they need, and it's surrounded by countryside where the animals are thriving, not like here.'

Loshie waved at her Armulet, and it threw up a projection of a map of the south of England. It had a route marked on it with animated bicycles rolling along the line in various places.

'Here, look. If we get some electric bikes together, we can make it there in just a couple of days.' Loshie stared up at the promenade by the road. She sighed, 'If only we had enough solar panels rigged up to charge an electric car.'

Ellie raised her left arm a little. 'Show information about Hereford.' A second projection appeared in the air beside Loshie's map. It showed an encyclopaedia entry for the cathedral city of Hereford. It was clear that the entry had not been updated since before the Times of Malthus. 'Show latest news about Hereford.' Below the encyclopaedia entry, several more results appeared. None was more recent than Clara's seventh birthday. That most recent one cited the weather in Hereford – it had been much the same as the weather they now sat in on her tenth birthday.

The next article was four years old. It appeared to be a blog entry by a person in Gloucester, written in the style of a newspaper article. The headline was 'Cirencester residents resurrect old GCHQ computers,' and it went on to explain how a farming collective in Cirencester had managed to get the audiopt surveillance up and running, and it was working successfully as a security measure against banditry. The story included the throwaway line, "…just like Hereford."

'There's nothing about Hereford. What makes you think it's this Shangri-La?'

'Of course they're not going to advertise it on the infonetwork. They'd be snowed under with people going there.'

'So how did you hear about it? And what exactly did you hear?'

'I met this guy up by the station a couple of days ago. A traveller bloke. I told him about the warehouse with camping products in it, and in return he told me all about when he passed through Hereford. He was there only two weeks ago, Ellie, and they've got more food than they can eat.'

'Wait. You told some stranger about us? How do you know he wasn't a Raider?'

Loshie countered, 'No. I told him about that warehouse way up past the station, on the edge of town. Completely the opposite direction from here, and I didn't tell him anything about us. We just had a general chat about how hard it is to find food. And he told me a bit about his travels.'

'And you're sure he didn't follow you back here?'

'No, look, it wasn't like that at all. He appeared round a corner behind me – could easily have attacked me, but he didn't. And he wasn't wearing camouflage clothing.' She paused. 'And he had a rucksack full of food. And I mean fresh veg and stuff. Not things he could have stolen from here. Stuff he got from Hereford.'

'So why didn't he stay there?'

'I asked exactly that. It's not his way. He says he's been walking the country since the Great Fire of Birmingham ten years ago. Reckons he couldn't settle down now, even if he found the best place in the country. He showed me a turnip he'd been given in Hereford. They have a box in the market square where people put their spare veg for others to take away to eat. For free. No bartering, no working for it. They just give you food.'

Ellie gave a frowning, sceptical look, but their discussions were interrupted as the girls wandered back.

'I'm hot, Mama,' Maggi whined.

Loshie put her hand around Maggi's head and pulled her in against her hip. Maggi's arms wrapped around her mother's waist. 'Come on then, let's go up to the hotel. It'll be cooler in there and you two can stay inside while we look at the plants.'

Ellie held out her hand to Clara, and the four of them headed up the steps to cross to the Holiday Inn. King Alfred followed panting, but easily beat them across the road to the shade of the lobby.

Wispy, brown plants grew up from the carpets in the lobby, leaning against the glass frontage. The healthiest ones grew through the occasional broken window or on the threshold of the missing front doors. As they passed through the lobby to the staircase near the back, fewer plants had made inroads into growing inside. Some evidence of animal activity, mostly seagulls, dirtied the old furnishings, but it was all past activity. Loshie's dire forecast looked to have come true, in this building at least. As if to say, "I told you so," they had to pass a maggot-infested bird carcass just outside the stairwell door.

The balconies they visited to tend to growing boxes for vegetables all showed the same pattern. Utterly desiccated soil held brown strands of dead plants. Other plants trying to gain a foothold in carpets, or the corners of open balconies, were faring little better. They had used all the rainwater caught over winter, and this year, no torrential storms had yet come to refill the baths and barrels they'd dragged on to the roof. Even when they did fill, the intense heat dried these water stores in a matter of days.

Wayne's carefully designed plumbing system to carry the water in and down to barrels inside the hotel had finally failed when Clara was eight. For all her best efforts, Ellie could not find the pipes that were leaking, and could not find where the water was ending up after leaking. It was as if it ran down from the roof and evaporated in the pipes before not coming out in the four flats Wayne had set up for water storage.

They came back down empty-handed, and Ellie worried that their growing boxes might never produce any food again. She was pleased that Clara had had a few pieces of rabbit that morning. Her own stomach ached from hunger. When they got back to the beach hut under the promenade, Ellie produced the only other food they would eat the rest of that day.

'Where did you get that?' Loshie demanded.

'I found a basement apartment near Matthias's house that had never been broken into. This is the last of what was in there, which wasn't much, but I saved this for Clara's birthday.' She opened the tin that had been manufactured thirteen years earlier and tipped out a beige looking lump into a bowl. Wayne's Powerwall installation had stopped working a week earlier, so she could not microwave it as the instructions suggested.

They kept a fire burning most of the time in an old, concrete litter bin by the Café on the Beach, so she roasted the brown mess in a saucepan with a lid. The sauce was sticky, but the non-stick technology of the pan worked perfectly.

As the four of them shared the birthday treat, Loshie poked at it and stuck her tongue out in disgust. Ellie thought that, although the colour was very definitely odd for chocolate sponge pudding, the taste of the thick sauce mixed with the crumbly sponge was delicious. The flavour and textures in her mouth transported Ellie back to a birthday celebration of her own, with Matthias and her mothers smiling and laughing around the dining table.

As soon as the food was finished, Loshie urged Maggi to get ready to go home. 'Think about Hereford. We'll be leaving in a few days probably. It's only two days away – why not come with us? You can always come back if it's not as good as that man told me.'

The Times of Malthus
Tuesday 8 May 2040
Two days after Clara's 10th birthday.

Ellie woke to hear banging on the solid wooden door of the beach hut. King Alfred was alert on the threshold but did not seem aggressive or perturbed by the knocking, which became a desperate pounding. Clara sat up, rubbing her eyes. A faint light found its way through the thin gap at the hinge side of the door. Ellie estimated it was probably just about dawn outside. With their sleepy eyes adapted to the dark, Clara and King Alfred could see when she held her forefinger to her lips, instructing them to remain silent. Both were flawlessly obedient. Both knew that noise at the wrong time could be fatal. In a bandit attack, the only safe option was for the raiders never to know you were there.

A muted voice hissed through the hinge gap, 'Ellie, it's us. Let us in, quick!'

At Loshie's voice, Ellie bounded to the door and heaved the drawbar up and away. Loshie immediately bundled Maggi inside, and Ellie saw Luke behind them.

He was facing away from the door, watching up the beach towards the Palace Pier. Ellie reached out and gently pulled his large backpack. Without turning from scanning for danger, he allowed himself to be guided backwards and inside. He helped Ellie put the drawbar straight back and set the backpack down against the door.

Ellie waved at her Armulet to provide a dim glowing light. Loshie's face was tear-streaked, and she looked exhausted. Luke looked worried, scared even. Ellie could make out a significant bruise on Luke's right cheekbone, which extended across to his ear. His knuckles were dripping with blood. She grabbed a Souvenir From Brighton tea towel and wrapped it round both his hands. King Alfred nosed Maggi's little chest, and the fear in her face relented slightly.

'What's going on?'

Loshie's voice was frenetic. She answered fast, with no intakes of breath. 'Jack and Diane are dead. The Essex Raiders came in the night. They knew our house and burst in, setting the place on fire. We only just escaped over the back fence, and we had to run all over town for hours to lose them.' She looked urgently to Luke. 'They weren't behind us, were they?'

He shook his head. 'I'm pretty sure we lost them. We had to keep moving through buildings and hiding and then moving on, so they wouldn't be able to find this place. We got separated for a while, but that probably helped us to shake them off.'

'What happened to your hands?'

'Mum and Dad fought them in the lounge, so we could escape. But they were all round the front of the house. The only way we could get out was to break down the boardings on the kitchen window and get into the garden. Dad had put that stuff up so well that I had to punch through it with my fists. Didn't feel anything at the time. Adrenaline, I guess.' He winced and looked at his knuckles. 'Now I'm thinking about them, it's really painful.'

Ellie waved them to sit down – there was the cream armchair, which Luke took, and Loshie and Maggi sat on the edge of the mattress they used as the bed. 'I'm so sorry, Luke. I can't believe it. Jack and Diane.' She shook her head.

Loshie responded, 'And the house. There's nowhere for us to live now.'

Luke put tea towel wrapped fists up to his mouth and drew in a significant breath. He was clearly trying to avoid sobbing. Ellie knelt down by the chair and put her hand on his knee. She tried to embrace him, but his position deep in the chair made it awkward, and he didn't move to engage in the hug.

Ellie leaned back on her haunches to look across to Loshie. Luke remained unresponsive. 'Stay with us. For now, at least. Until it's safe. The store next door has some spare bedding we can bring in.'

'Yes, we will. Maggi, we're going to stay with Clara and Ellie for a few days. That'll be nice, won't it?'

Maggi looked up at her mother but was as unresponsive as her father. Ellie wondered how much of the fight and the danger the little girl had witnessed. She had spent her entire twelve-year

The Times of Malthus

lifespan in the Times of Malthus, so Ellie assumed that she had witnessed all possible horrors.

She squinted at the girl, trying to see into her thoughts, and wondered about the death screams Diane might have made, or the blood spattered up the walls from an axe in Jack's chest. Ellie realised with a shock that she too had become desensitised to the horrors. *How can you picture such things?*

Luke lowered his hands and looked Ellie straight in the eye. 'Thank you, Ellie, but we can't endanger the three of you.'

She gently slapped his knee. 'Nonsense. What do you think Wayne would have said if he were here? There's no way I'm not giving shelter to family.'

Loshie and Luke argued about whether they should stay. Luke was mindful of the lack of food that every family faced. Loshie felt they needed the security of numbers. More eyes to watch out, more hands to fight if it came to that, and a guard dog.

King Alfred was the clinching argument. Luke nodded and told Ellie he would make sure he caught enough fish for all of them, including the big dog. She knew he would try his damnedest, even if the English Channel no longer submitted to his will when it came to providing fish. She mused that Wayne had always been the more successful angler of the two Smith brothers.

Bandit raids rarely lasted more than a few hours now. The Essex Raiders had a decade's experience. They knew the sweet spot, in terms of time enough to find as much food as possible, traded off against the danger that the community they were attacking regrouped and cut off their return to the fast boats they used. Occasionally raiders came from other locations, but the Essex Raiders had established an organised system of banditry. Wayne had sometimes referred to them as 'the Clacton Vikings'.

Most places ran out of food quickly after the supply chains failed, and urban populations were far less able to supplant the food deliveries with farming, hunting and gathering. Town and city populations had suffered the Malthusian checks of war, famine, pestilence and death as an almost total wipe-out.

Brighton was one of the few scattered places where people had managed to harvest enough to survive the initial hard times and settle into a tough life of scrabbling for daily food. Mostly, this was down to the bounty of the sea, which inlanders could not access.

The Brighton Defence Force, before it had been disbanded due to low numbers, had been adept at watching for the landing of the boats and ambushing the pirates as they reached the top of the beach. At the same time, another BDF squad would arrive in their own boat to take out the raiders' getaway driver and commandeer their boat.

The community in Brighton had become more splintered and suffered greater losses without the defence force. Fortunately, the Essex Raiders were clearly having their own struggles at home, as the raids had reduced in frequency to perhaps only once every couple of months.

Luke looked shattered: exhausted by the physical fight and hours long night-time chase, but he had also had to process his parents' deaths, without any downtime to stop and do so.

He inhaled deeply and stood up. 'I'm certain they'll have gone now. They never stay more than a few hours these days. I'm gonna go and get us some food. Do you have some fishing gear?'

Ellie pointed at the overhead rack above the door where she kept the rods and lines. Luke knew the rack well. He had helped Wayne install it. Ellie stood up next to him. 'Are you sure you're ready to go out there? Maybe have a few hours' sleep and go this afternoon when you're more with it.' She pointed at the bed where Clara and Maggi and Loshie looked up at him.

'No. I'm gonna get out there whilst I've still got some of that adrenaline in my veins. Besides, dawn is the best time for fishing. I'll come back for a siesta when the fish disappear off for theirs.'

Loshie told her husband. 'Good. You go on then, and we'll organise the extra bed on the floor in here. Make sure you bring back lots though – Maggi is starving.' The young girl looked up wide-eyed at mention of her name, and Luke smiled at her.

He reached up and took down two rods, the best reels and beach tripods. The marina was the best spot for being sure to catch something, but it was too exposed. If he went out on the harbour wall arms, he would be stuck in a dead end should anybody decide to mug him. He would be able to escape by jumping in the sea and swimming for the beach, but he would lose all their fishing gear. In the current famine, that was more dangerous than the possibility of catching nothing by casting his lines from the water's edge on the beach.

Luke opened the giant door slowly, peering through the opening. He picked up the net and bucket, manoeuvred the rods through and headed west along the beachfront.

Ellie secured the door quickly behind him. Loshie had tucked the two girls into bed, despite the sweltering temperature in the close room. Maggi protested, but Loshie shushed her. Clara lay smiling.

'They're exhausted, the poor things,' Loshie breathed to Ellie.

The girls didn't look especially tired, but Ellie figured she should let it go, as it was probably Loshie that was truly exhausted. 'Maybe you should have a sleep too? I'll keep watch for Luke coming back and in case there are any Raiders left in town.'

Loshie gripped Ellie's upper arm. Her voice was a whisper. 'We can't stay here. We will all die if we stay in Brighton.' She had an intensity in her expression that worried Ellie.

'I'm not sure I believe that it's any safer anywhere else. Here we know the geography, we know where food will grow, where to forage, there are fish to catch, and we have a strong, safe house to live in.' She waved her hand to indicate the beach hut, and paused with it pointing into the far corner of the ceiling where the water dripped in. 'With its own water supply. That's not something you get everywhere.'

'You do in Hereford. There's a river that runs through the middle of the town. The river Wye. It's never dried up since the start of the Times. Ellie, we must go there.'

'I'm really not sure about leaving. And for some hope of a better place. We've got no sure-fire information, just some story you heard from an old drifter. What does Luke say about going?'

'He's – well, don't worry about Luke. I'll make him see what's best for us. There's nothing left for us here. As soon as we get bikes sorted out and put together a little food parcel for the journey, we'll go. You really should come with us, Ellie. You'll be sitting ducks if it's just you and Clara.'

Ellie stared past Loshie into a shadow by the chest of drawers. She imagined herself and Clara alone on the seafront, down at the tideline looking for whelks, whilst keeping one eye out for approaching boats, then pottering back to the beach hut to nibble at the miserable meal they had gathered.

The daydream frightened Ellie. The future looked to be tougher than even the last ten-year nightmare had been. Her fingers tightened into fists. The thought of leaving Brighton frightened her even more. Leaving all of her memories, and the safety of the place that they knew, filled her with dread.

There was something else though: a gnawing, nagging something in Ellie's chest. Loshie sounded as if she might do anything to make Hereford happen.

Ellie turned and looked to the bright rectangle of the doorway. The vista went straight out to Wayne's cairn. *What would he have told you to do?*

Ellie felt a shock, like she'd been punched in the sternum. Nothing had hit her – it was her thought question: it was the first time she had used the past tense when thinking about Wayne. For ten years, she had constantly imagined him at her side and had always thought of him as present. She sat down to avoid falling, put a hand to her chest, and breathed deeply.

'Are you OK?' Loshie stepped over to the mattress on the floor and bent down to her friend.

Ellie managed a nod and said, 'Let me think about it. You know I'm sceptical about Hereford, but you're right that it's becoming more and more difficult to live here.'

'Difficult?' Loshie stared at her in disbelief. 'It's completely impossible. No food, hardly any water, and the constant raids by bastards.'

She accepted that her reasons to stay didn't stand up to practical scrutiny, but Ellie could not accept Hereford as a positive, certain solution. *Would we survive trying to find food as we travel across the country?*

'OK,' she agreed, sounding exasperated. 'Let's talk more about it when Luke gets back. We'll decide all together.'

Loshie looked towards the door and nodded. A long, slow nod. 'Sure.' She paused and her mood seemed to lift. 'Right, I reckon my adrenaline is still going strong too. So, if you watch the girls, I'll go out and see if I can search out some veg. We haven't tried the north side balconies for weeks, have we?'

Ellie shrugged. She was getting exhausted now. 'Sure. Um, no, yeah, try that.'

Loshie was already at the door, pushing the drawbar up over her head, like a weightlifter. She leaned the bar up against the door frame, looked back at Maggi and rushed out pushing the door shut again immediately. Ellie could hear her flip flops slapping the pavement as she ran off toward the steps up to the hotel.

Twelve hours later, darkness was falling, and Ellie had to turn on her Armulet glowlight again. It did not surprise her that Luke might still be trying in vain to catch a meal, but she worried at how long Loshie had been gone. Ellie felt she could check every growbox on every balcony in the entire hotel in less time than Loshie had been gone. Neither of them had answered Armulet messages all day. Ellie did not want to videocall them, in case they were in hiding again.

They had all watched several old movies and put wet flannels on their foreheads when the heat of the day had become too much. The three had stayed locked inside the entire day. Ellie had only briefly reopened the door to allow King Alfred a quick trip out to empty her bladder. Maggi suffered separation anxiety from her mother, and Ellie was running out of ideas for keeping her distracted.

There was the tiniest knock at the door, and Ellie let Loshie in quickly and efficiently. She entered with a basket of vegetables, more than Ellie had seen in one place in over a year. Nothing fancy, but they all looked healthy and fresh. She passed the basket to Ellie and, without a word, went straight to give Maggi a long, tight hug.

'This is incredible. Where did you get it all?'

'I raided all the secret little places I know. I figured a big sort of Last Supper would be a good plan. I won't need to be able to go back to those places once we leave, so we might as well harvest it all.' Loshie pulled on the hem of her clean, white shirt. 'And, um, I picked myself up these new clothes too.'

Ellie frowned. 'Did you see Luke at all? He's not answered any messages I sent.'

Loshie's voice was defensive. 'No. Is he not here?'

Ellie gave an expression of confusion, a look that said, "Are you mad?" Out loud, she answered, 'No, I wondered if you had visited him fishing. Did he catch anything?'

'How should I know? I haven't seen him since he left this morning.'

Ellie shook her head slightly. 'OK, well, if you're not worried, maybe you could look after the girls now. I'll get a cooking fire going outside. Maybe the three of you could peel the veg and cut it up?' Her question was directed more at the children – this might be a new way to keep them busy. They dutifully got up and collected knives and chopping boards.

King Alfred exited with Ellie. Their fire had gone out, but even after twelve years, the DIY store on the edge of town had some remaining stock of gas barbecue lighters in the back warehouse. Every so often they took a trip there and carried back what they could. Paper was another commodity that was readily available from all the abandoned houses. The nearest Ellie knew of was now three streets back from the front, but it would take decades to burn all Brighton's paper. She restarted the fire with some scrunched up art stock and piled on a couple of big, old books.

The dog reappeared after having wandered off and gave a sharp little bark. She stood at the edge of the shingle, with an alert body posture. King Alfred didn't say much, but Ellie knew all the different types of bark. This short one meant, 'I've found something. Look, I'll show you.'

Checking on the progress of the burning books, Ellie added a broken piece of table leg and reckoned the fire would survive untended for a few minutes. 'Come on then, what is it?'

King Alfred led Ellie along the front past two breakwaters to the third stretch of shingle from their home. In the bright moonlight, she could immediately see what the dog had found. The two fishing rods were set up in their tripods at the water's edge. As she followed down towards them, she saw a body lying, prone, between the two upright rods.

'Luke!' Ellie called out but muted it as best she could. The threat of raiders was still high in her mind. He didn't stir at her words. When she arrived next to him, she saw, to her horror, a knife protruding from the side of his chest. A kitchen knife, a large one, maybe a carving knife.

Ellie squatted down next to him, feeling for the moment numb, and knowing in her heart that he was dead, and there was nothing anyone could do for him. She put her hand on Luke's forehead. He lay flat on his back, with a large pool of blood on the stones beside his waist where the knife handle stuck out. Luke's eyes were open and stared sightlessly up at the thin clouds darting across the sky.

Miles M Hudson

Friday 18 May 2040
Shortly after Luke's death.

Four days later, Luke was still on the beach where he had died, now covered in a mound of stones, just like his big brother.

Ellie and Loshie had been unable to move Luke's body. He was too heavy to carry, even with both women working together.

Before the Times, Ellie had gone through a phase of lifting weights at the gym. She had built and toned her body to a peak of strength and fitness. At age forty, after more than ten years of insufficient nourishment, she was a shadow of that young weightlifter.

Loshie had never been athletic and could offer little in the efforts to transport her dead husband away from the lapping waves. Their little trolley wasn't big enough for him and, in any case, it wouldn't move across the shingle.

Distress at his death and at their new circumstances triggered arguments between the two women. Loshie wanted to build a funeral pyre where he lay, but Ellie was scared it would act like a beacon for bandits. They had argued back and forth, achieving no conclusions, until the horror was visited on Ellie's daughter.

After it had lain for a day in the sun, Clara found the body. They tried to watch the girls at all times – an attack could occur at any moment. Maggi and Clara had not been told about Luke, and they frolicked on the beachfront as they always did.

At one point, Clara had slipped her mother's surveillance and wandered along to the next section of beach, a place she had known well her entire life. For all the bad times she had lived through, the sight of her uncle's swollen, fly-infested and bird-picked corpse had shocked the ten-year old.

The mothers immediately began working to build Luke a funerary cairn, but it was too late. Clara stopped talking that day and did not emerge from the mute zombie-like state for the next week.

The sea came up close to where Luke lay, so building the cairn was intermittent. As it grew in size, the waves at high tide lapped on the stones and they sometimes shifted. The smell was terrible, it often brought tears to their eyes. Loshie and Ellie persevered and after four days, the cairn impressed them all: even larger than Wayne's.

Loshie had fashioned a piece of driftwood branded with an epitaph in the same style as the one Luke had made for his brother. Ellie didn't really understand how it related to Luke, but Loshie said it was traditional Sri Lankan:

Impermanent alas are formations, subject to rise and fall.
Having arisen, they cease; their subsiding is bliss.

The wooden signboard took Loshie an entire day to make. It looked good, and she was very pleased with it.

The four Smith women held a funeral service of sorts for him, and Loshie seemed almost enthusiastic that the rising tides might eventually destroy the cairn, in line with her inscription. She pointed at the handful of iron pilings that were all that remained of what had once been Brighton's West Pier.

Ellie was confused about what to make of this idea: did Loshie really want the memorial to disappear? Clara distracted her from asking Loshie what she meant. Still mute, her daughter pointed along the beach. They all saw the boat landing a half-mile away near the still-intact Palace Pier. The mothers took their daughters' hands, and they all ran as fast as they could back to the brick arch lock-up.

'They must have seen us!' Loshie's voice was a wail as they crossed from the shingle onto the cracked concrete of the beachfront area.

'Let's get in there. It's the only safe place we have,' Ellie replied.

They shoved the door closed and heaved the drawbar across the back of it.

In less than ten minutes, the noise of clomping feet and shouting men came right along in front of their entrance.

Ellie covered Clara's mouth. It was an instinctive response.

She had momentarily forgotten the girl had stopped speaking. The shouting outside continued, as men discussed where to search and how to get into places.

'It's our only chance – we've to to get away from this place, or we'll all be dead in a month.'

'Shhh. They'll hear us.' Ellie took her hand off Clara's mouth and put it over Loshie's instead.

King Alfred continued barking intermittently.

Through the sliver of a gap where the solid oak door met the door frame, Ellie could make out a human silhouette wavering back and forth. Further along the coast, the sun was approaching the horizon, and it lit a fine, yellow line vertically up the wall. The thug outside moved around, blacking out parts of the streak of light in different places at different moments.

The heat was stifling, and Ellie could feel sweat from Loshie's face trickling over her fingers. Loshie shook her head away from Ellie's hand and hissed, 'Exactly! They'll kill us and probably eat us. If not today, then tomorrow, or next week.'

Ellie leant sideways and whispered straight into Loshie's ear. 'If you don't shut up, it *will* be today.'

The lumbering figure put his head right to the gap. The women froze and clutched hands back over the mouths of their daughters. Ellie closed her eyes and held her breath.

King Alfred charged the door, now growling. The shadow jerked back, probably only able to make out a pair of red eyes hurling themselves towards the door. Angry dog pheromones were bound to have permeated the man's nose. Ellie smiled at the thought that the Essex Raider was probably just as grateful for the thick doors as she and Loshie were, in that instant. The brute moved out of view, but they could hear little over King Alfred's ongoing barks and growls.

'Hush, girl.' She whispered. Ellie wanted to gain as much intelligence about the raiding party as they could without being seen, heard, or discovered.

'Lucky they left their dog locked in – sounds right vicious.' The drawling accent from a few miles around the coast was easy for Ellie to differentiate from the more trill Brighton voices she'd grown up with. *Definitely Essex Raiders.*

'That means there'll be food in there though,' the deep voices continued.

'Well, I'm not about to open the door and let that dog at us.'

On cue, King Alfred began barking again.

Another, similar male voice shouted down from the promenade above, 'Get up here! We found the motherlode in the hotel up here.'

Ellie saw Loshie's head turn to her, just visible in the light that eked in around the door frame. Ellie mouthed, 'Did we leave something up there?' Loshie shrugged.

'Where we found the veg growing on the balconies before?' the nearby voice asked upwards.

The other voice laughed, 'Yeah, they never learn. On the roof this time. Almost literally manna from heaven.'

The discussion continued at an ever-decreasing volume as the men wandered away. Ellie hugged Clara's skinny body close to her and kissed the top of her daughter's head. King Alfred's barking reduced in tempo until she appeared uncertain as to whether to continue it at all, giving a yap every several seconds.

Loshie touched her Armulet, and the device glowed gently on her forearm illuminating the whole archway lock-up interior. She looked Ellie straight in the eye. 'We cannot stay here. Hereford is only a couple of days away. It's safe there. The girls will be able to play in the woods, and there's more food than people to eat it.'

'So you keep saying, but I'm really not sure it actually exists. I mean–'

'You don't think Hereford exists?' Loshie's interruption was sardonic. 'The place they used to make all the cider. You know, the capital of Herefordshire.' Her voice squeaked a little at the end.

'Of course, Hereford was there. We don't know anything about what it's like now. What I'm saying is I'm not sure about this Shangri-La safe haven you say is there.'

'I told you; I met a man who was there only two weeks ago.'

Ellie nodded. She couldn't bring herself to tell her friend that she thought she had become fixated on an idea, a hope, something that would probably destroy them.

In the cool of that night, several hours later, Ellie and Loshie went up to assess what had been taken from the roof of the Holiday Inn. The growing boxes where they had nurtured vegetables for the last ten years were destroyed. The roof was spread with dry soil that appeared to have been deliberately cleared out through smashed holes in the sides of the wooden boxes.

'Why would anyone do this?' Loshie wailed.

'Hmm.' Ellie examined one of the boxes closely using her Armulet torch. 'We didn't reckon there was anything harvestable in these yesterday, did we.'

'No. Why would you smash them up. That must have been such hot work, just to be destructive.'

'You heard that guy though, didn't you. He reckoned they'd found loads of food up here.'

'Maybe some of the seedlings had taken under the surface. This clear-out of the soil was to find all the tiny baby carrots and potatoes.'

'There weren't any potatoes, but yeah, that could be it. But I'm just wondering…'. She quickly turned, scanning the rooftop as well as the vague moonlight would allow. 'Turn your light off! Now!' Ellie moved next to Loshie and whispered to her. 'It's a trap.'

They skulked over to the low wall that edged the roof and could see a light on in an inflatable boat that had landed along the beach by the pier. It had been hidden from view along the seafront by being pulled up behind a burnt-out wreck that had failed to get away from the attacks back in 2028. From their vantage point it was clear that the raiders had not left as expected.

'Ellie, we left the girls on their own.' She turned in a rush to head for the stairwell, but Ellie grabbed her arm.

'Wait! We need to be careful here. Let's go down the fire escape.'

Loshie looked alarmed. The service ladder went over the side of the building and down four floors to the giant balcony of the hotel's best suite. The ladder was hard to see clearly in the dark, but they had never tried climbing it before. The bolts to the wall had been crumbling with rust for years.

A clanking noise came from the stairwell across the roof, and Ellie was up and over the little wall in a second. Loshie's fear of the rickety, old ladder left just as quickly, and they descended as fast as possible. The half-moon lit up a large square of slate tiling and sun-bleached patio furniture.

Looking back up, a head appeared over the wall. The man was only held up for a second stowing his axe into his belt, but its length caused him trouble coming down the ladder. The swinging handle kept catching in the ladder rungs as he lowered each step.

Ellie pulled the sliding door open to the master bedroom and turned back for Loshie. In the shadow by the fire escape, Loshie's dark skin obscured her features. Ellie could see bright, white eyes gazing upwards, as Loshie gripped the ladder and shook it hard trying to rip it away from the wall.

'Stop it, Loshie! Let's go!'

Her friend ignored Ellie's call and finally managed to cause the ladder to fall. The raider landed hard, falling at least ten yards. As he groaned, Loshie pulled at the axe. With a strength that surprised Ellie, Loshie unleashed a full circle axe swing, up and straight down into the man's torso. He screamed and thrashed but quickly stopped moving and fell silent.

'Hey!' Another voice was shouting from above, but he couldn't chase them down as the ladder was gone. His head disappeared back over the parapet, and they heard his footsteps running across the roof.

'Loshie, come on!' The axe was left sticking out of the raider's body, like a carrying handle, and the women ran through the bedroom and hallway and into the corridor. The suite had its own express lift and an emergency set of stairs beside that lift shaft. Ellie had only been down them once before but grabbed Loshie's hand and dragged her into a pell-mell descent down a tight winding concrete staircase.

At one point, Ellie tripped, losing her balance, and Loshie

crashed into her, both women landing in a tangled heap on a turn in the steps. They were not hurt – the stairs turned a right angle every five steps, so their fall was only a small distance.

Less than a minute later, they emerged into the dark of the basement car park. The exit ramp was less than ten yards down Little Preston Street from the car repair workshop. Loshie had only been back once since the fire, and Luke had had to break down the door. The fire had destroyed everything. Her father's charred remains had been sat in his armchair, upstairs, clutching a photo frame. The few inches of the frame that survived had been enough for Loshie to know it was her parents' wedding picture.

Ellie and Loshie glided through the shadows and in through the broken wooden door. They remained only just inside the threshold, ready to run if they were discovered. They were twitching to get back to the beach hut and make sure Clara and Maggi were safe, but it was a dilemma. Might they lead pursuers to the safe place that hadn't actually been found? Was it safer to go there and fight any attackers, or safer to keep their trackers chasing ghosts, and away from the beach?

Ellie took Loshie's hand and whispered, 'OK, that's it, let's leave Brighton.'

The Times of Malthus

Miles M Hudson

Book 3

The Journey

The Times of Malthus
Friday 25 May 2040
Twelve years into the Times of Malthus.

It took a week to source four electric bikes and get them fully charged up. Finding bikes was easy, getting good sizes for mothers and daughters was a little trickier, but getting all four functional posed the real problem.

The Powerwall storage battery had given up. The solar panels were still working but getting the electricity to the right voltage and into the bike batteries took some serious work. All the information needed to build the circuits was available in how-to videos on the infonetwork but searching through abandoned houses and shops to find what they needed was a long, hot job.

Regardless, Loshie was energised. Leaving Brighton and heading for a new life in Hereford had shifted from being just a journey to being called 'The Journey'. The prospect of The Journey clearly excited her. Ellie reckoned she had not seen her friend so driven on any project since they had revised for their A-Level exams.

After four days of sourcing parts and winding bits of wire together, they had a system that would charge the e-bikes' batteries. The weather fortunately remained sunny and high twenties throughout May 2040 – but they couldn't hurry things. The charging process had a limited speed, so they just had to wait.

During the charging of the second child's bike, as they sat outside the beach hut watching the girls climb on the crazy golf windmill, Ellie asked, 'How are we going to recharge the bikes when they run out?'

'They work like normal bikes too – you don't have to use the battery.'

Ellie rolled her eyes theatrically. 'You know how heavy they are. There's no way a person could cycle them with zero electric assistance. You remember when we cycled the Hebrides in that uni summer holiday, and your battery ran out on the second day? That ride is burned into my brain. We are not going through that again.'

A long silence followed, as they both mulled over how far

they might get before running into battery troubles. Ellie followed up, 'All that gubbins to make the solar cells charge the batteries is going to be too much to take with us. It's so heavy, and we're going to need to travel as light as possible anyway.'

Loshie nodded and gestured at her Armulet, bringing up a projection of bike shops that had existed in the South Downs area, Surrey and Hampshire, in 2028. 'These places will all have had bike chargers. I reckon the best plan will be to stop at every one en route and get a charge any time we can. Or maybe we should just take several batteries and dump each one as it runs out of charge, what do you think?'

'Those batteries are really heavy. We could never manage that, especially with the girls' bikes to carry them for too.'

'No, you're right, but do you think we'll easily find power outlets already connected to solar cells?'

Ellie shook her head. 'Carrying all the transformer cables and boxes would be as bad as trying to carry a load of spare batteries already charged up.'

Loshie shrugged. 'I'm pretty sure those bike shop chargers were set up with outside sockets and solar power. That was kind of the point, I think – to give the bikers the freedom of the outdoors. And they must have had big storage batteries so the bikers could quickly get a recharge.'

'But didn't you have to pay to use them? How will we get the machine to deliver the electricity without bank cards?'

'No. I went to one once and the charger was free, but they had a café for you to sit and wait in whilst you got the recharge, so they made their money back through the café.'

Ellie asked, 'Are you sure? How much time will all these stops add on? And we don't know if any of these places are safe. We know Brighton well. We know where is uninhabited and where to avoid, but we're talking here about heading out into basically a new, unknown country. I'd really prefer not to meet anyone at all on the way.'

'Yes, I agree. But think how few people there are left. We'll have to be pretty unlucky to meet people. I'm guessing that towns big enough for bike shops are less likely to be inhabited. Don't you think anyone out there will be living in the countryside where it's easier to grow food?'

'I suppose.' Ellie became distracted by the thought of living off the land. She gazed into the air, wondering about how well food may be growing in the less urban areas outside town. Her stomach cramped a little with hunger, as she imagined pulling up fresh vegetables in the corner of a muddy field.

Finally, Ellie came back to the conversation. 'I worry this is going to take us weeks. What will we do for food then? If it was going to take us the two days you said, we can carry enough from here. Well, assuming we can find enough and don't get attacked again before we leave.'

Ellie stood up and stepped over to the charging battery to see how many of its ten green LEDs were now lit. Three lit and seven still flashing red. 'This is so slow. She looked up at the sun and the solar panels on the café roof.

'Any bike shops we go to are going to be inside towns or villages. We should be able to find food. Those little places were abandoned much faster than Brighton, and they suffered less looting because the population was less dense.'

Ellie blinked in surprise. 'Really?'

'I'm sure we'll find food one way or another.' To Loshie there seemed no problem with the plan: nothing that might make them think twice about heading straight off.

'Talking of food, I'd better go fishing, or we'll starve before we're even ready to leave. You OK to watch the girls?'

Loshie was fiddling around on her Armulet screen and didn't respond. Ellie stared, as her sister-in-law continued to ignore her. She was dismayed and confused but had learnt recently to avoid aggravating her.

She worried about whether Loshie was more set on The Journey just because of her grief and upset, rather than for the rational reasons she used to argue for it. A darkness seemed to have consumed Loshie, and Ellie thought the death of Luke must have really shaken the poor woman.

Untangling the fishing tackle went slowly as Ellie was

distracted by her thoughts. *Is this all just some sort of attempt to escape her demons? Are we just going to be heading into a dead-end wilderness?* One of the hooks was bent so much it would be useless. *Then again, how could it be any worse than trying to stay alive here.* She shook her head.

She knew that they both felt the weight of fear of their situation. There was always danger, every day, but if the other was to die, one mother would be left to feed and defend both the girls. The task was hard enough already. Even the idea that, were something to happen to Loshie, she might then have to continue on alone as carer and provider for both girls filled Ellie with dread.

But she *had* to go on. How else could she protect Clara?

As Ellie gathered together the fishing equipment, it struck her as odd that the rods had not been stolen by Luke's attacker. She thought back to the image of his body and all the undisturbed gear. It was as if he had known his killer.

Three days later, as the two women breakfasted at a corroded table and chairs set up outside the archway beach hut they now called home, along with their two daughters, it felt as if they were the last people in Brighton.

Their four bikes stood in a line by the old Art Deco café wall, with full panniers at the rear wheels, plus a backpack for each adult. They had been up the hill to the top of town to get new clothes from the old Asda warehouse.

It seemed to Ellie that the sun shone down with such intensity that it alone might be enough to further fracture the already cracked paving slabs. Sunglasses had become so necessary as to appear like an evolutionary addition to the human form.

The flapping shade umbrella was not long for this world, and Ellie felt like they had timed their departure perfectly. They ate some of the fish Ellie had caught and some crackers from Asda's staff room cupboards. The shop had been stripped bare within a few months of the Bitness Revelations, but seemingly nobody had thought to look in the staff break room. An open box had long ago been eaten by vermin but seeing two unopened boxes had felt to the two women like finding treasure.

Ellie drank the last drops of water from her Palace Pier tin mug, stood up and attached it to the pannier strap on her bike. They left their other cups and plates discarded on the table and wheeled the bikes up the ramp to the promenade.

Gazing in the direction of the spot where she had first met Wayne in the company of his brother, Ellie turned her bike towards the west, pausing only to look down at his cairn. She scanned the beach in front of the only home their family had ever known. *Sleep well, my love*.

Clara said, 'From the sea to the sea, now he skates with Davy Jones'. Mother and daughter briefly hugged as best they could reach whilst balancing their fully laden bikes.

'The Journey begins!' Loshie announced.

They trundled gently along, and Ellie looked out to the handful of remaining West Pier piles, twisted and rusting above the bright, blue water. A whale spout attracted her attention briefly, but no person was visible anywhere. King Alfred trotted along beside the bike convoy, and they all took it easy, the electric motors mostly switched off, drinking in the desiccated final views of a deserted city.

The coast road was flat and straight and took them past the old water-skiing park and on to Shoreham. That initial seven-mile stretch was barely an hour's cycling, even with their restraint in the use of the electric motors. Loshie, who had taken up a point position a few dozen yards ahead of the rest of them, mused that they would be in Hereford even sooner than expected.

However, the road turned inland and then sharply uphill. The sun continued to burn down, and the temperature rose quickly. Away from the cooling sea, the land was even more parched than Brighton itself. Fields of early poppies, collapsing back to the soil, lined the A283. It was a wide road, and the surface was still mostly in good condition.

Loshie had the navigation for The Journey all mapped out, but she knew nothing of the route's details. Information about such things as passable roads and current populations had not been updated during the Times.

Reaching the top of that first long hill took several sweaty and exhausting hours. They stopped for a rest and water in the shadow of the broken-down Shoreham lime works. It had been closed since well before the Times of Malthus and had long been in decline, much of it overgrown.

As they passed an old row of abandoned miners' cottages, Ellie pointed to the hulking outline of Lancing College rising out of the distant hills. It dominated the horizon and had occupied many an hour of their teenage conversations about the wrongs of private school education. It must surely by now, she thought, have been long abandoned.

Although bikes had been a good way to get around post-Bitness Brighton, none of them were used to long-distance cycling. By mid-afternoon, Maggi and Clara were moaning about their aching backsides and thighs. Ellie felt the same pain but also wondered if they were simply exhausted. She checked the battery charge levels, and all were lower than they would have liked. Maggi's was particularly worrying. Worse still, they had already used up all their water.

They stopped at a stream on the edge of Pulborough. The water tasted delicious, and they decided to stop for the night. The shade they sat in was at the end of a garden with an idyllic-looking cottage at its far end. They could see, however, that it was locked up with strong and new looking padlocks.

'I'm not so sure about staying here,' said Ellie, once Loshie returned from reconnoitring the property. 'It looks like it's still occupied, don't you think?'

'I don't know,' said Loshie. 'I didn't see any signs of life but making sure means taking too much of a risk when we've got two kids in tow. But I saw a shed up the back there, and it all looks overgrown. We can hide the bikes behind the shed, and it's far enough from the house that, even if there is someone in there, if we're quiet, we'll be OK.' She glanced over at Maggi, biting her lip in a familiar expression of concern. 'I don't think Maggi can ride any more today.'

Working as quietly as they could, they set up inside the shed, with just enough room for all five of them to lie down inside. There was a lock on the door, which still had its key in it, so they felt secure enough.

Once darkness fell, Loshie and Ellie raided a well-tended vegetable garden beyond the stream. They tried to make the veg patch look just as it had before they arrived, and they took care not to take more than about a quarter of the produce there. A fire would give away their position, so they were forced to dine on raw, uncooked vegetables. A haul of raspberries they saved for last went down much better.

During the night, it rained heavily. The shed roof kept them dry, but the sound kept Ellie awake. They planned to leave at first light and stop for breakfast along the way. It had been stupid, Ellie now realised, to steal the vegetables and then stay on site for the night.

The bikes were dripping wet, but the panniers were waterproof, and another hot day loomed anyway. By the time she and the girls packed their water bottles away, while Loshie checked which route they had to take, King Alfred had managed to catch herself a rabbit for her breakfast.

'Who's that man?' Clara asked her mother shyly, pointing through bushes to the back of the cottage. Ellie and Loshie exchanged a look of alarm.

Dropping down low and tugging Clara back from the bushes, Ellie peered through the leaves to see the man whom her daughter had seen. A second man emerged, from the same door in the cottage as the first man, carrying a spade. The first carried an axe.

Miles M Hudson

Saturday 26 May 2040
The second day of The Journey.

Ellie hissed, 'We've got to go, Loshie. Bad guys coming out of the house.' They all wheeled their bikes as fast as they could manage up an overgrown bank directly away from the cottage, keeping the shed between them and it as much as possible.

They reached a track in the woods behind that led left to rejoin the tarmac road away from the cottage. Ellie turned to look back as the others pedalled away, sliding a little in the mud.

She saw the bigger man, the one with the axe, standing staring after her and the others as they fled. Clearly, they hadn't hidden themselves as well as they thought they had.

He raised his axe just then, and shouted something guttural, but she couldn't make out his words. The meaning was clear enough, however: *don't come back.*

Even at six in the morning, it was too hot to chase ebikes whilst carrying a big axe. The overnight rain had cleared the air, but it had also cleared the clouds, so the temperature was rising as rapidly as the sun.

On the proper road once again, they made good progress for half an hour, into the pretty village of Petworth. The old stone buildings, many with Sussex flint in the walls, looked frozen in time. The entire village looked abandoned, but it could have been abandoned in the 1930s as easily as the 2030s. The window and door frames were all painted in a bright sunshine yellow colour, and the high-quality paint was doing a formidable job of resisting the elements. They saw only a few places that had cracked or peeling paint.

The mothers felt safe enough to sit at a picnic bench in the market square and organise some breakfast. They felt like there wasn't time to build a fire. Nor could they be certain the village truly was abandoned. Without a fire though, the vegetables were a chore to eat.

The bike party had passed a stream on the way into the village, so all four had paused to fill their bottles again. It made their bikes heavier, but the scarcity of water sources made it unavoidable, especially in the summer sun. Maggi's battery was down to twenty-five per cent – they would have to find a charge point soon.

With hills and the heat, they made slow progress along the little roads, heading north over the South Downs. This part of The Journey was unspectacular – a lot of roads with banked edges and some scraggly overhanging trees to offer bits and pieces of shade. Ellie struggled to see very far, other than along the road in front of them, but the shade was an absolute boon.

The night's rain on the plentiful foliage had made the earlier landscape seem like the traditional, rolling, green fields of England. As they climbed up and over the South Downs, they discovered the country's interior had become arid and the vegetation parched. In several places, the trees were blackened and broken – inescapable signs of forest fires.

About an hour out of Petworth, two men on horseback appeared, coming towards them along the road. Ellie and her travelling companions stopped their bikes and moved to the side of the road, where they could stay hidden initially, amidst the bushes there, and try to figure out what to do.

The high banks on the sides of the road had them hemmed in. Loshie was panicked. Her voice was urgent. 'Quick, turn around! We need to get out of here.'

Ellie put her hand out and caught Loshie's forearm. Inside, her stomach was jumping with anxiety, but she could sense that Loshie was about to lose control. She looked her friend in the eyes trying to exude calm.

'If they want to catch us, those horses can easily outrun Clara's bike. We're already caught. Let's go forward. If they're also unsure what to do, an air of confidence from us might just do the trick to keep them from trying anything.'

Loshie pulled a knife from her pannier.

Ellie hissed, 'Put that away! If they're not going to cause us trouble anyway, you pulling a knife on them will definitely start trouble.'

Ellie continued with instructions for the girls. 'We're going to go straight past these horsemen. Everybody needs to stick one behind the other. I'll go first, then Clara, Maggi, and then Loshie will be at the back.' She made direct eye contact with Loshie again, this time with a commanding look and a little nod.

The groups passed each other awkwardly. They gave friendly greetings, but the horses were agitated by King Alfred's presence. Ellie stopped and grabbed her by the big hair at the scruff of her neck. She knew that King Alfred's demeanour was friendly and unthreatening, but the horses did not know it. The men did not stop; they urged the horses quickly past the dog.

The women waited and watched them trot away, Loshie's hand in her pannier holding the knife all the while. More than once, each man turned to look at the bike party. Ellie did not speak but she thought to herself, *What is this world now, where strangers rush past each other, scared to even just pass the time of day?*

In Haslemere, at an old petrol station, they clutched each other with relief when they discovered a charging point for the bikes that was still functional. The station was boarded up, but at one end of the forecourt, they found a tyre pump and a bunch of tools on long chains. The solar panels mounted high on the south-facing wall were still connected, and the whole place looked like it had suffered little in the way of riot damage.

Ellie frowned. *Was it mad to stay in Brighton all these years? Did these rural places simply not suffer the craziness?* She plugged Maggi's bike in, and the LEDs flashed to show that they were receiving juice.

'This is way too open.' Loshie was looking around, checking for strangers and dangers in all directions. 'And it's going to take us hours to charge all four bikes, with just the one charge point.'

'Maybe we can wait in there,' said Ellie, pointing up and across the street to Haslemere Methodist Church. 'We're probably going to have to stay all night, but that looks like a decent hiding place. The little tower will mean we can see all around and watch for visitors.'

The modern brick building had glass doors with a triangular arch shape. The glass was framed in forest green, matching the building's name sign, which had the same triangle shape as the doors. The main gable above the doors held a large, simple wooden cross, and there was a three-storey tower attached directly to the side of the main church building. Many small windows, maybe two-foot square, were also framed in the green metal. Like the petrol station, the church seemed to have suffered little damage over the years.

Loshie removed Maggi's panniers, laid the bike down, and then dragged a wooden bench over it. She said, 'That'll keep it invisible from a distance. As long as nothing looks out of place, hopefully nobody that lives round here will come snooping during the night.'

They dropped Clara through the church's broken window and passed all the panniers through. Skinnier women and girls might be able to squeeze through the broken window, but anyone larger would not. The main doors were locked and the only other entrance – a fire exit – could not be opened from the outside.

Loshie and Ellie wheeled the other three bikes into the bushes that had overgrown the house next to the church.

'Where's Maggi?' Ellie could not see her friend's daughter but assumed she would know where Maggi was.

Loshie whirled around and ran to the church window. She stuck her head through and almost shouted at Clara, who was just feet inside. 'Is Maggi in there?'

Clara shook her head, her face locked in fear.

Loshie ran back across to the petrol station and looked behind the bench. Only the bike lay there.

Ellie chased after. She could see the panic welling up inside Loshie. The four of them were utterly vulnerable. Anyone wishing to do them harm easily could.

But we haven't seen anyone. There's no sign of people at all. Where did they come from? How could they grab Maggi from under our noses?

Loshie told her Armulet, 'Find Maggi', but before it could respond, she heard Maggi calling out, her voice faint and barely audible over the wind.

'Mama.' The voice was almost too quiet to hear, but Loshie

caught it.

She followed the sound to the door to the mechanic's garage. Old boarding was being pushed outwards, Maggi's dark little fingers clutching around the edge of the wood.

The two women tugged hurriedly at the largest plank. The old and rusted nails holding them together loosened enough that Maggi could force a large enough gap to get back out again.

The girl was jumping from foot to foot, excited as anything. 'There's food in there, Mama.'

'What do you mean, food?'

She held up a small, rectangular tin of tuna. 'Packets and tins and boxes. Like we sometimes find in Brighton.' Maggi beamed.

The gusting wind brought another shout to their ears. It was indistinct but definitely a human voice. They crouched and spun around, scanning for people. Nobody was directly visible.

Ellie said, 'Let's get inside the church. We're sitting ducks out here.'

The adults ushered Maggi back across the road, but she was starving.

'Mama, let me go back in! I'll get us all lots of food. There's shelves with tons of stuff in there.'

Loshie pushed her daughter on towards the church. 'Soon. We must go and hide for a while.'

'But I'm hungry, Mama!'

Ellie tried to quiet them all down: 'We'll get inside and eat this tuna, and then we'll come back later when it's dark, so nobody can see we're in there. OK?'

Maggi glared but was silent.

They all clambered in through the church window, taking care with the broken glass at the frame's right-hand side. They broke the protruding glass bits off as quietly as possible, hoping the noise would not attract somebody's attention.

King Alfred could not get inside, and she wouldn't listen to the instructions to stay outside away from the window. In the end, Ellie clambered back out and ran the dog up to the next house and tied her in the bushes by the hidden bikes.

The Times of Malthus

Loshie kept watch, looking up and down the street from the edge of the tower's top window. Maggi described convenience snack foods that had been popular in the 2020s, the staple sales of petrol station shops. Without completely destroying the wooden boarding, only Clara and Maggi would be small enough to squeeze through the entrance hole.

Ellie and Loshie were worried about what dangers might lurk unseen inside the sealed building but agreed that humans were unlikely to be one of those dangers. They decided that they would hole up in the church until all the bikes were recharged, and then attempt to harvest some of the foodstuffs from the shop just before heading out of town.

Ellie also reminded them of the problem that the food was years old. Each item would need to be vetted in order to check on whether it would be safe to eat. Crisps and biscuits were unlikely to be viable, but some provisions could still be reasonably low risk.

The mothers took guesses at the exact foodstuffs that might be hidden inside. They raked their memories for petrol station shop commodities, discussing Coca-Cola, along with wine and tinned foods, like tuna or baked beans, possibly even honey.

It was a small station and Ellie took care to manage expectations. Maggi was unable to offer any detailed clues about what she had seen. She had never known the shiny consumer world of her parents' generation and didn't recognise logos or branding, or even pictures of processed foodstuffs.

The bikes' recharge timing meant that they would probably be on course to raid the shop in the small hours of the morning. The village would be shrouded in darkness, but it was still not wise to hang around in the open too long.

They planned for the girls to clamber through the little gap and then pass out everything they could find. Loshie and Ellie would then pass it as fit for consumption, as well as being actual food, as opposed to, say, engine oil or bleach.

Once they had retrieved as much as they and the panniers could carry, the plan was to make haste and leave town as fast as possible. A more careful assessment of what they had gathered would come when they stopped for a break some way away.

'Imagine the breakfast we're going to have!' Loshie was not listening to Ellie's entreaties to manage expectations. 'I told you, Ellie, this trip is going to change our lives. We've been out of Brighton for two days, and we've already found streams with water and an Aladdin's cave of food.'

'We don't know anything yet. What Maggi saw sounds promising, but this is a small petrol station. For all we know, they may only have sold car accessories.'

'Every petrol station sold Coke. And that's one thing that simply doesn't go off.'

'I'm not so sure about that. Everything goes off eventually – even tinned food.'

'No, it doesn't, that's the point of tinned food.'

Ellie held up her hand in an apologetic, yet quietening, gesture. She feared that falling out with Loshie would be worse for morale than finding nothing to eat in the shop.

After a hot day's cycling, everyone was ready to sleep. The big, brick church building was pleasantly cool, and they were able to make beds from bean bags scattered around the children's Sunday School classroom area. Loshie volunteered to continue with the first sentry duty.

When Ellie woke in the middle of the night, Maggi and Clara were sleeping like she remembered Matthias would do in a hammock in his garden. She had sometimes watched across the fence out of her bedroom window, and she smiled now, as Clara's snoring whistled slightly, just as she remembered Matthias' had.

Ellie sat bolt upright, her heart beating loud and hard.
Where's Loshie?

Rain was hammering the street outside, and Ellie realised that the cool night had not been a result of the church's construction, but a storm coming in. The building creaked and groaned in the wind, and Ellie could hear rainwater landing on the interior floor several yards behind her.

She looked down from the tower window, as the wind howled in the street, and saw, to her vast relief, Loshie on the forecourt swapping which bike was attached to the charger. Loshie paid no attention to the weather and worked resolutely. Ellie was impressed at how carefully her friend hid the fully charged bike before heading back across the road to rejoin them inside the church.

'That's the last one connected up now.' said Loshie with a grin, once she had climbed back in through the window and up the tower.

'Are they still charging, even in the dark?'

'Yes. There must be a battery storage unit inside somewhere connected to the solar cells.' Loshie joked about the storm, 'Unless the full moonlight is bright enough for the solar cells.

'I guess this is why there's water in the streams – do you think they have more rain inland than we got in Brighton?'

Ellie mused, 'Dunno, maybe. Maybe that's why our dripping pipe in the beach hut never dried up. Water worked its way from here down to the sea. I can see that water evaporated from the sea might be pushed inland before the hills cause it to fall. I think that's how that works generally, isn't it? You're probably right.'

Ellie was pleased to be able to compliment Loshie on a good idea. She had found her best friend's intellect dimming in the last few years. *This whole trip has really made Loshie buzz. She's so much more her old self.*

Miles M Hudson
Sunday 27 May 2040
Three days into The Journey.

The cycling party wobbled their way out of Haslemere, loaded to the gunnels with tins of sardines, beans, a can of Coke each, and a lot of bottled water. They had decided to gamble with one packet of pasta but didn't want to waste too much carrying space in case it wasn't edible. They also discarded tinned soup as it was too heavy for the amount of food inside – mostly just water. The Cokes were to be their one treat, if the drinks turned out unspoiled. A decent amount of food would likely be extravagance enough anyway.

The road seemed to be sweating with the remains of the storm, as the summer heat picked up again. The sun had not yet risen, but the full moon had not set completely, and the pre-dawn light was plenty to navigate their exit from Haslemere.

In eighteen hours, they had not seen a single person. Despite the extreme weight they were carrying, everyone was in buoyant mood. The bikes were fully charged, and Loshie had mapped out a short route to the next bike shop charging station. She led the group, and they headed in the direction of Farnham.

Less than one hundred yards from the church, the road curved to the right, and Loshie stopped. Before Ellie could catch up to her, Loshie had U-turned and turned the girls around too.

'There's half a dozen men on quad bikes at the junction up ahead.'

Pausing to squint in the half-light, Ellie saw the danger. A hundred yards or so further up the road, she saw several stationary quad bikes with riders, some dismounted. The men did not appear to have noticed either Loshie or Ellie.

Swinging her bike round, she set off behind Loshie and the girls. They pedalled frantically and took the first turning on the left after the petrol station. Loshie led them through residential streets, right and left and right and right again, trying to outfox anyone who might be following. King Alfred trotted ahead of the cyclists. After five minutes, they paused to give the girls a brief rest and decide on a new route.

Loshie pointed at a street sign. 'Look, Farnham Lane. That'll take us to Farnham and the next charge point. Let's get going immediately so that we're definitely clear of those guys back there.' She glanced around. 'Are you okay, Maggi?'

Her daughter nodded and put one foot on a pedal in readiness.

Passing huge, expensive-looking houses, half-hidden behind fences and security gates, they rode up the incline of Farnham Lane for a couple of miles. They saw no sign of inhabitants.

Ellie stared at each one as they struggled slowly up the hill. *I wonder if their gates and walls saved them from Bitness-inspired retributions or just made it that much easier to find them.*

The hill above the Hindhead Tunnel was the steepest they had seen yet. The tarmac road ended at a house, and the track that continued beyond was muddy and overgrown. Armulet mapping software hadn't been updated in a long time, so they had anticipated that sometimes it would take them somewhere unhelpful.

The gradient was too much for their electric bikes to handle, so they got off to push. They had not travelled far enough from the petrol station to risk stopping yet. The adults had overburdened themselves with much more weight than Maggi and Loshie, but even so, the bikes would have been too heavy for this hill even without the extra pannier payloads.

'Loshie, can we go a different way around?' Ellie begged between gasps. 'This is futile, and it surely can't be the only way to go, up and over what must be the steepest hill in Surrey.'

By now, exhausted, they had all stopped, and Loshie finally laid her bike down. It had no stand, and even laying it down on the ground required considerable effort that left her red-faced and exhausted.

'It's way longer if we go round,' she said, chest heaving as she pointed up through the trees. 'Look, you see that bank up there. That's the top of the hill. I reckon the best bet is if we carry the panniers up to the top there, and then we can bring the bikes separately. It can't be more than fifty metres. Might take a few trips, but we're in the shade, and it really will be much quicker than going back down and around.'

Ellie reckoned the place Loshie had pointed to probably wasn't even forty yards, so she agreed to Loshie's plan, again impressed at her dynamism. She really reminded Ellie of the student activist she had known twenty years earlier.

Carrying everything up to the top of Gibbet Hill took longer than anticipated. The luggage was no great difficulty, but, even unladen, the bikes were unwieldy and difficult to get moving. Despite being less than four miles from Haslemere, they were all exhausted. Their clothes stank from being continually soaked through with sweat, but the summer smells of vegetation were stronger, and considerably more pleasant.

The dense woodland gave them a sense of added security, and the shade here was cooler than on the trail, so they breakfasted on Esso shop tinned stew. They drank much of their supply of water, but kept some aside for King Alfred, who lay panting in the grass as they ate. After sustenance, and with a downhill stretch in the offing, the group were back on a high.

The laden bikes were still heavy, and the trail was muddy, albeit drying rapidly. As they descended the steep bankside, everybody picked up a little too much speed. It was exhilarating and reckless but, after the almost unendurable stress of the upward journey, it felt wonderful. They felt the wind in their faces, and Maggi squealed with delight at her lack of control.

The track through the woods terminated at a wide path around the Devil's Punchbowl. In its former existence, the path had been the old A3 road from London to Portsmouth, which had circled the high slopes of the steep-sided valley. After the Hindhead Tunnel had been cut through the hills, the old road's tarmac had been ripped up, and the whole area given over to leisure walking.

The mothers were ahead of the children and, as they swerved past the last trees to emerge onto the former road, Ellie turned hard left to stop on the flat. Loshie tried the same manoeuvre, but her speed was too great. Before she could brake, she had gone flying over the edge and down the steep, wooded slope on the other side.

As soon as she realised what had happened, Ellie threw

herself off her own bike and let it fall behind her. Running to the verge, she looked down the hill in time to see Loshie's bike go crashing into a tree with enough force that Loshie was flung free, tumbling to a halt amidst a tangle of bushes a few yards further downslope.

Loshie made no sound during the crash, but Ellie watched her fly through the air and knew she would be hurt. She turned quickly, as Clara and Maggi emerged from the first slope, also at speed. Ellie fielded them like a rugby player, managing to knock each one back to stop on the level ground.

'Wait here,' she told them urgently. 'Look after my bike and do not move.' She stared hard at each girl in turn. 'Loshie went down this side, and I need to go and help her back up.'

At that, Ellie heard a cry of anguished pain, which at least told her Loshie was still alive and not dead of a broken neck.

Maggi heard the cry and shouted, 'Mum!'

With a shocked expression, she made to get off her bike, but fell in haste and ended up underneath the frame. She wriggled and struggled until Ellie helped her free and then hugged her tightly.

Maggi was in tears. She tried to wriggle free. 'Mum!'

'Don't worry, I'll get her. Please stay here so we know where everybody is. It's easy to get lost in these woods. Don't worry, I'll bring her back up.'

Another cry of anguish.

'I'm coming, Loshie, just hang on. I'm seconds away.' Ellie had noted carefully the route of Loshie's fall and, although the going was treacherous, she made her way down carefully and safely. The bike lay with the saddle lower down the hill than the wheels but looked intact.

Loshie was twisting from side to side, facing downhill and punching the ground on either side of her. Ellie thought she looked like a toddler having a tantrum. She had removed her backpack and thrown it to one side of her writhing.

Using the most soothing voice she could, whilst breathing heavily in the heat, Ellie sat beside her friend and put a hand on her shoulder. 'I'm here, Loshie. Try and sit still. You're going to be OK.'

The thrashing continued briefly and then stopped. Ellie could see blood all around Loshie's right ankle, but leaf litter had become stuck in the blood so she couldn't see how bad it was. One short, blue sock was matted with leaves and tiny twigs and dark, red blood spilled past the sock and down over her black gym shoe.

'I've broken my leg, Ellie,' Loshie hissed, her face a mask of pain. It kills.' She slapped the ground on either side with the palms of both hands.

'OK, just take a breath, and let's get you sitting up. Keep your weight off the leg, and I'll have a look at it in just a moment.'

'Mama…?' Maggi's voice called down from above.

'Tell her to stay up there,' Ellie said sharply. 'Tell her you're alright, and we'll be up in a minute.'

Loshie whined, 'I'm not alright.'

'I know, but tell her – we don't need to scare her, and we do not want her coming down this hill and falling and getting hurt too. Tell her!'

Her face pale with shock, Loshie tipped her head back to look upslope and called out to her daughter. 'It's OK, darling, Mama's OK. Just wait with Clara and Alfie, and we'll be up in a minute. My bike's a bit damaged, so we might take a while to get it back up to you, but just wait there.'

There was silence from the girls above.

'Ow. Fuck! Ellie, I need pain-killers now.' She punched the ground.

'Sorry, sorry,' said Ellie.

She went below Loshie and gently cupped her right calf and foot. Loshie grimaced in anticipation. She was breathing in short, noisy gasps.

'OK, I'm going to move your leg in little bits, and we'll see what the damage is.'

Ellie remembered a time she had rushed over to Wayne when he had fallen while skating on the promenade. He had been moving at quite a lick, and the skin on his knees was shredded. He had been embarrassed by her ministrations and shooed her away, claiming it was part of the deal for roller hockey players. When she pointed over to Luke's knee pads, Wayne had simply asked her to let him get on and skated away, blood trickling down his shins and staining his skates.

She lifted Loshie's leg slightly to a moan of complaint. She gave a gentle twist of the foot, and Loshie seemed not to notice. *This isn't broken.* 'You're going to be OK. This isn't as bad as it may feel. I am going to need to get a look at where this blood is coming from before we try moving you though. Lie back down, and I'll wipe away the leaves and stuff, so I can see this injury. Actually, lie back and rest a bit – I'm going to get a cloth from your panniers. Two seconds.'

'The best one is in my pack.' Loshie grunted, her voice stiff with pain. 'Look in the side pocket with the little dangling penguin on the zip.'

Ellie found a suitable facecloth and a bottle of water. 'OK, a bit of water first, and then I'll wipe it clean. Grit your teeth.' She took off the shoe and sock and raised the injured foot to rest on her own knee. Elevation and stability, as she'd been taught long before in a first aid class.

Loshie did as she was told and remained quiet throughout the cleaning. Ellie discovered a deep gash starting at the ankle bone and slicing up the inside of the leg about four inches. She guessed that the force of the crash had smashed her leg against the pedal.

'OK, I need to get some compression on this. where's your first aid kit?'

'What first aid kit?'

'I gave you a little green wash bag with some bits and pieces in it, to pack for you and Maggi.'

'Oh.' There was a long pause. 'I didn't think it was worth taking up space for and left it behind.'

'Jesus, Loshie. You really did have this idea that we were going on a country bike ride to the Garden of Eden.'

'Sorry.' She paused again. 'Have you got one?'

'Of course I have. One for me and Clara. There's not much in either of them.' She sat on her haunches, looked at the bloody ankle and then at Loshie. 'Right, shit, you're gonna have to wait here while I go and get it. Keep your foot as high as possible to try and reduce the bleeding.' She propped Loshie's leg up on her backpack.

Ten minutes later, Ellie returned with a green canvas pouch. She pulled out a long, white bandage. It was not wrapped and had been used several times over the years living under Brighton promenade.

'I've got nothing to stitch that up with,' she warned Loshie. 'I just hope this bandage can go tight enough to close the wound a bit, without cutting off the circulation. But infection is the worst danger.'

She had another bottle to swirl water all over the cut again but stopped before opening the container. The bleeding looked to have stopped. Despite the depth of the gash, it looked like the blood had clotted well.

Rather than potentially wash off the clots and restart the bleeding, Ellie chose to go straight for dressing it. Making sure not to let anything else touch the wound, she wrapped the bandage around the leg and ankle and under Loshie's heel to support it and help keep the bandage in position. The finish looked neat and sound.

'You're gonna have to keep this on all the time to stop the bandage slipping. She held up a new, long sock and gently slid it up her friend's foot and leg.

Loshie could not stand. 'Ow, ow! Ow, ow, ow, ow!' She tipped her head back onto the leaf litter. 'This pain is going to make me pass out, Ellie.' Her voice raised even further. 'Fuck!'

The first aid kit held one strip of ibuprofen tablets; a treasure Ellie had guarded for years. She looked at the pain and distress in Loshie's face.

Exhaling loudly, Ellie asked herself, *Well, I suppose this is it. What are you saving these for, if not for something like this?*

Concerned that clambering up the steep incline was exactly the sort of action on the injured leg that would stop any healing, and maybe even open the wound up more, she looked around them.

'Right, you see that slight bump over there?' Loshie followed

Ellie's pointing finger but said nothing. 'It's about the flattest space around here. I say we camp there for a day and see how you are then.'

Loshie remained silent. 'Let's get you over there now, before I bring the girls down. OK?'

Loshie nodded weakly, her eyes were half closed.

Don't you pass out on me now!

'I'll lift and support your leg, you drag yourself back on your bum. Can you do that? It's only about ten yards.' Ellie raised her voice. 'Loshie!'

'Mmmh?'

'I've got your leg supported safely. You drag yourself back over to that flat bit. Come on, we need to move now!'

Loshie shuffled, with numerous cries of "Ow!", but they made it to the makeshift campsite location.

Ellie dragged the backpack across and then went to bring Loshie's bike to her as well. There was a big dent on the fat strut that held the battery, but the wheels looked OK, and the bike moved straight. She took off the panniers and laid it down, making sure everything was in reach. Loshie slid one of the panniers under her head as a pillow and closed her eyes, passing out from the pain.

Ellie propped the other woman's right leg up on the backpack again. She took a long look at Loshie, silent and unmoving, and then trudged back uphill again to bring the girls down.

Miles M Hudson

Monday 28 May 2040
The Journey is paused in the Devil's Punchbowl.

Loshie slept for most of the day, having spent the previous night awake, monitoring the bikes recharging and swapping them over when needed and then maintaining sentry watch in between. King Alfred slept the entire day beside Loshie. It was a chance for Ellie and the girls to enjoy a leisurely day lying in the sultry shade of multiple large trees: a brief, if unexpected, pause in The Journey.

The drought had most trees struggling to survive. Perhaps half of them were actually dead, but even those remained large and intact enough that the leafless branches still added to the shade canopy. The forest was seriously old growth. The topography funnelled any water falling within the scope of the wide hills down this narrow valley. Ellie figured that these trees probably had the best chance to survive of any for many miles around.

The sides of the Punchbowl were so steep that, through all of history, it was unlikely many people had passed where they sat. Ellie enjoyed a feeling of security in their obscurity. She had felt constantly on edge ever since they set off along the Kings Road in Brighton, but the feeling eased here.

A lack of buzzing insects caused her to wonder if Wayne's father had been right about the death of the ecosystems due to the warming climate. In Brighton, she had seen evidence of what he cautioned, and here too, the place should be alive with insects, but she saw none.

Fewer birds, too. Ellie wondered if they were also resting, in the extreme heat. Her Armulet said thirty-two degrees Celsius in the shade. Whatever mud the previous night's rainstorm had created had morphed back into desiccated, crumbling dirt.

This had been the climate for many years now: weeks of heat, occasionally broken by dramatic storms, but the rainwater quickly ran off the hard-baked soil and evaporated within a day. Even the winters, in the south of England at least, offered very little retained water for the ecosystems.

Maggi and Clara mostly read textstories or watched 3D

videostories projected above the brown grass bank. They seemed oblivious to Loshie's plight. Asleep, she wasn't reminding them of it, so all seemed peaceful.

Occasionally, the girls wandered downwards, exploring or playing. Ellie's Armulet always had their location showing. Even when the woods blocked her view, she knew they never went more than thirty yards away. Every time they clambered back up the hill to return to the camp, both girls complained about how hot and exhausted they were.

In combination with general boredom, the girls' exertions meant that the three of them went through most of the recently acquired food and drink delights. Everything appeared safely edible, but the tin of black olives had a flavour that Ellie found unpalatable. By nightfall, all that remained for Loshie was a Coke, two bottles of water, a tin of sardines, and the bulk of the olives.

Ellie took the time to teach Clara and Maggi how to build a fire and make it as safe as possible in such a combustible environment. The last thing they could afford to do would be to set fire to this wood. A fire amongst so many close-packed, tinder-dry trees would be huge and burn very fast. Ellie expected they would not escape if a nearby tree ignited.

Digging was hard work, but they created something of a hollow and cleared away as much try tinder as possible, keeping it aside to help start the fire. The hillside did not have many exposed rocks, but they managed to gather enough to make a reasonable fire pit. Amidst all their preparations, the two women had somehow managed to forget to bring a lighter or matches, but Maggi had triumphantly exited the petrol station with a big box of matches in her hand. The tree shade meant there would be no chance to create a fire using the lens that Ellie carried in a velveteen pouch.

Loshie woke just as the meal was cooked and ready. Mostly, they had roast vegetables from the garden by the shed where they had slept on their first night on the road, but they encouraged Loshie to eat her sardines and olives as well. Nobody wanted to admit to her that, whilst she slept, injured, they had quietly consumed the rest of the treasured luxuries.

The nearly full moon's silvery glow gave the sloping woodlands a magical appearance. Trees and the hillsides shimmered as if in a fairy tale. That night turned out to be Ellie's best sleep for a decade. The safe, empty countryside, a full belly, a warm and balmy night and clean forest air all combined to make the perfect conditions for slumber.

An apple each for breakfast, and they were keen to get on the road again.

'My leg is painful, but we need to get going again. I reckon if I strap it up a bit more, we'll be able to make some distance.'

'Are you sure? We all want to get to Hereford, but it's pretty safe hidden here, and we could be in trouble if you're not fit to run from strangers if we need to.'

'We've got to go, Ellie. We've already eaten most of the food we picked up in that petrol station. There's nothing to eat round here.'

The sound of singing attracted Ellie and Loshie's attention. Their daughters were dancing around each other singing, to a made-up tune, the refrain, 'We're going to Hereford, we're going to Herefood. Food, food here for everyone.'

Ellie shrugged. 'I guess that's the decision made. You sort your leg bandage out, and I'll get the bikes back up to the footpath up there.'

From back on the old A3, on the lip of the Devil's Punchbowl, their first hour – ten miles – was mostly downhill, so Loshie was able to cruise gently and carefully along. It was only when they had to work uphill again shortly after Bentley that she discovered the crash had damaged the bike more seriously than she thought.

The battery still seemed well charged, but the electric motor was not engaging – Ellie reckoned the wiring inside the damaged strut must have broken. The battery would not come off as the dented metal held it tightly in place. It was impossible to look inside to see if the problem was repairable.

Loshie moaned, 'I can't pedal. Riding is OK but pushing with this leg is agony.'

They had to swap bikes so Loshie could ride solely on electric boost. This meant Ellie had the full weight of Loshie's too-small bike to pedal.

Barely ten minutes had gone by, and Ellie called for them to stop. She was breathing hard. 'I just need a moment. It's so hard pedalling your bike – it's too small, so I can't extend my legs properly each time round.'

Loshie nodded sceptically. 'Well, you're in a better state than me. I definitely can't pedal at all.'

'Yeah, sure, like I said, just give me a minute to catch my breath.'

Clara presented her mother with a little tin of sweetcorn. 'Here you are, Mummy. You need this more than me.'

Ellie's heart melted as she leant forward to take the can. After peeling the metal lid back and tipping a mouthful down her throat, she passed the tin back to Clara. 'Have some yourself, and then share it with the others.'

The girl nodded and rolled forward to be next to Loshie and Maggi. Without a word, Maggi grabbed the tin and tipped it up to her mouth, before passing it over to her mother.

'God, you lot didn't leave much, did you?'

'That was Clara's. Don't be so ungrateful.'

'It was all of ours. Everything we find should be shared.'

Her comment had been framed so there was no arguing to be had with it. Ellie bowed her head.

Loshie continued. 'Right, shall we be getting on?' Without waiting for an answer, she trundled on, all electric, the foot of her bad leg not even on the pedal.

With memories of their Hebridean cycling holiday twenty years earlier, Ellie struggled on at the back for the next several hours. Going slowly, they managed to reach Basingstoke by mid-afternoon.

A derelict motel marked the edge of town. It looked like it would have been severely dilapidated even before any Bitness Revelations rioting. The building was extraordinarily ugly, but it was steadily being reclaimed by nature, which was acting to beautify it significantly. However, that vegetation was now also struggling in the long drought.

They stopped to take a break by the motel, and Ellie sat in the shade of the boarded-up front entranceway, dripping with sweat. Clara offered her mother her own bottle. There was little left in it, but Ellie sucked the water down faster than gravity could have poured it out. With that, they were all out of water. The day's route had taken them past any number of streams, rivers and ponds, and all had been dry. She leaned her head back and looked across to Loshie. She sat on a low wall next to the entrance terrace, examining her leg and grimacing in pain.

Clara and Maggi went exploring and, ten minutes later, wandered back from around the building, with King Alfred panting along behind them. The place was as desolate and abandoned as everywhere they had been since leaving Brighton. Despite this, Ellie's sense of unease returned, and with it the nagging sense that they were being watched.

'Maggi found another secret way in,' said Clara.'

Several of the buildings' windows were smashed and open, and at least one fire door at the eastern side had been kicked in.

'What do you mean? The hotel isn't shut up – look, we could all go in that door if we wanted to.'

'I know,' said Clara, her voice bright and unconcerned. One cheek was smudged with dirt and cobwebs from her exploring. 'But it's more fun to go in the secret way.'

Ellie and Loshie looked at each other. Loshie wobbled her head from side to side in a Sri Lankan gesture of agreement. 'Can't argue with that.'

Ellie smiled. 'You're right, girls. Come on, show us where it is.'

The rear entrance was also boarded up, but the sheets of plywood were held in place over the door with only a few nails, and Maggi had relatively little difficulty tearing one side loose. They wheeled all the bikes in and let the board flop closed behind them. Ellie was relieved at how quickly they had been able to find a place to hide out of sight so soon after arriving.

The Times of Malthus

The corridor inside the entrance was dark but opening several of the room doors and propping them open with a bike in each allowed light to filter from the bedroom windows through into it.

They explored the rooms along the first corridor. All had been broken into at some time years before, but most were as the hotel had left them. Beds and sheets and pillows were not much use to looters looking for something to eat.

Loshie sprawled on a big bed and groaned at the pain in her ankle. They agreed to spend the night there. Ellie would need to try and find some tools to see if the damaged bike could be fixed. Most importantly, they needed to find water.

'I found water, Mama.' Maggi was calling from a few rooms away. Ellie shot out and along the corridor.

'STOP!' As she charged into the other bedroom, Clara and Maggi were standing in the en suite bathroom, with the tap in the sink running. Ellie shut off the water.

She tried the shower, which also poured out water. Only cold, but it worked. 'Right, this is great, but it's old water. We can use it to wash – a shower will be really nice. But you must never drink this water. Even when you're having a shower. Do you understand?'

There was silence as the girls stared at her.

'Look, this water has probably been in a big, metal tank in the roof for years.' She waved her hand overhead. 'It could have any yucky stuff in it: algae, pigeon poo, maybe even dead rats.' She made a disgusted face.

Both children mimicked the expression of disgust, and Clara said, 'Ew.'

'Do you understand? Never drink any water from the taps in this place. It isn't safe to drink. Understand?'

'Yes, Mummy.'

'Maggi?'

'Yeees.'

'Good. OK, let's go and find some good drinking water. Sunglasses on!'

They left Loshie to rest and went searching through the neighbouring streets with an ageing blue Ikea shopping bag filled with empty plastic bottles, King Alfred trotting along beside them.

Ellie had looked at the map and had a plan. She hoped that Black Dam Ponds might have some water they could collect. The park was about a half-mile away and Ellie needed a leg stretch after being cramped on Loshie's too-small bike all day.

The first half of the walk through the urban outskirts of Basingstoke was hot and without shade. Ellie quickly regretted bringing Maggi and Clara, as the unknown route led them through narrow streets and close by many buildings. An ambush would be easy here.

She kept the group close together and encouraged King Alfred to be alert to strangers, more as a warning to the youngsters than as something the dog might understand.

Entering the woods at the end of the park changed the mood. It felt safer, out of sight, and the place was cool. They could already smell the watery ponds at the far end of the old recreation area. As they approached the long, narrow ponds, the water level was low, but at least there was some water. There was no way they could test if it was safe to drink, but Ellie liked the look of it.

King Alfred charged forward around the bankside, barking. From the other end of the water, perhaps fifty yards away, a scrawny man clambered up the steep banks, out of the pond, and ran off away from them. Ellie was so startled she didn't react, she just stood gawping.

The man quickly disappeared across the old A30, which skirted the woods, and into the trees on the other side. His figure quickly became little more than a shadow, as he passed out of sight through the tree trunks. King Alfred, who had run up to the side of the road on the far side of the pond, turned back to Ellie as if to ask what she should do.

Ellie looked all around them to gauge the danger level. *Are there any more of them? I knew I shouldn't have brought the kids.* She put her arms around Maggi and Clara and pushed them gently forward to descend down the near end bank of the pond to fill the water bottles.

'Get yourself a drink, Alfie.' She pointed to the pond and

The Times of Malthus

King Alfred bounded down and splashed them all with a full belly flop into the water. Ellie kept glancing around nervously, in case the man returned with friends. She hoped they could fill all their bottles and sneak away before anyone showed up.

She had cursed the hot walk, all the way from the old motel, but she was now glad that their hideout might not be immediately obvious if the locals came to these woods looking for them.

Being half a mile from the water supply was a good distance away. She wondered if they would be able to survive and leave town without another water resupply. She preferred the idea of searching for a river in the countryside. There was at least one person in Basingstoke and, unless you knew them, every single person they encountered had to be considered a danger.

They reconvened in the bedroom Loshie lay in. Her breath came in short, shallow gasps, the sheets beneath her dark with sweat, the room so musty and hot Ellie hardly dared draw breath. The thick duvet and pillows looked comfortable enough but were also extremely hot, even to lie on top of.

Her sock showed a yellowy-red stain oozing through. Loshie asked, 'Was the cat out there? Why wasn't she in here?' It made no sense, and she went back to panting. King Alfred lay under the little table and joined in the panting.

Ellie looked at Loshie and sent the girls out. 'Can you two go to all the rooms on the corridor and open all the windows, please? Let's get some ventilation in here.' She paused. 'Ah no, let's think about this.' She had knelt down near the door so their daughters would only look at her. Despite Loshie's moaning and noisy, quick breathing, the trick worked. 'We don't want anybody to know we're here in case they're bad people. Remember, strangers are dangerous. What are strangers?'

'Dangerous!' Maggi and Clara cried out in unison. It was a mantra their grandmother Diane had started, and the whole family had jumped on board with it to train the youngsters for survival.

'Good. So, if we don't want anybody to know we're here, we can't open the obvious windows. If you go along and turn right at the end there, then all the rooms on the right on that corridor are facing an inner courtyard sort of thing. Nobody will be able to see those windows from outside the hotel. Go and open the windows in all those bedrooms, please.' Clara and Maggi trooped out and down the corridor.

It was a struggle to hold Loshie still while Ellie took off her shoe and sock. The dressing was soaking in blood and pus. She pulled a pillowcase off and used Wayne's fishing knife to cut it into long bandage strips. She filled the old kettle from the adjacent room with the working taps and did her best to wash and redress Loshie's wound. Her friend was delirious but still felt the pain as Ellie tended to the wound. It smelt awful, but the colour didn't look as bad as Ellie had feared. It must be infected, but no infection was obviously visible inside the laceration.

Ellie dug a silver blister pack of eight pills out of the little, green first aid kit. Just like the precious pain killers, she had saved these antibiotics for years. She fully expected that they would be out of date and ineffectual, but Loshie was in a bad way. Pills that should have been thrown away a decade before were all Ellie had to try and help her friend. She was glad of the good night's sleep in the Devil's Punchbowl. She expected to get no sleep at all for at least the next night.

The Times of Malthus
Tuesday 29 May 2040
The fifth day out of Brighton.

Maggi's seeming radar for discovering things worked again, finding a cupboard full of clean towels. They enjoyed cold showers as the morning warmed up, drying off with the most luxurious towels the girls had ever used.

There was little food left, despite the recent gathering successes, but Clara managed to pick several handfuls of raspberries from the bushes growing around the perimeter of the motel car park.

King Alfred disappeared for an hour and returned with a dead kitten in her mouth. Ellie looked it over closely. The cat was freshly killed, and Ellie nodded in approval. 'Well done, girl.' She joked, 'I don't suppose there were any more?'

To her surprise, King Alfred left the cat there and strode back out towards the rear exit. Ellie followed and the dog led her to a spitting mother cat that snarled and hissed as they approached. In the hedge where she had her brood nesting, a couple of inquisitive kitten faces peered out.

Ellie looked into the mother's eyes and recognised anger and fear. *God, I bet I look like that half the time.*

As she reached forward to grab the tabby, it lashed out with claws and bit her sharply. Ellie held onto the biting head and stabbed it swiftly. She killed the remaining four kittens in quick succession. *What have we become? Killing kittens to survive. How can it be that it's kill these poor little innocents or starve to death?*

With blood all over her hands, she looked to the sky and let out an almost silent scream, muted to avoid alerting anyone nearby, a hiss of anger and fury mostly directed at herself and what she had become. In her mind, Ellie spoke to Clara. *'I hope you see it through to a better world than this one.'*

Holding the dead cats up by their hind legs, like some gamekeeper with a catch of rabbits, she gave a kitten to King Alfred to carry back for herself and took the others back to skin in the hotel kitchen. The sharp knives and spacious cutting tables made the job much easier than she had found it back in Brighton.

In a fire set in the hotel's kitchen sink, Ellie barbecued the cat family. She knew from the last ten years of scavenging for food that there's little meat on a cat. They would probably need to cook all the meat to make a sufficient meal.

This kitchen is awesome. I wonder how long we can stay here. Ellie's thoughts were about the ease of cooking, but it became clear that they would have to stay until Loshie recovered. Her fever was still high, and she remained somewhat confused, with little inclination towards, or understanding of, the idea of getting out of bed.

The good news was that, by morning, her wound was less malodorous and somewhat cleaner than on their arrival at the motel.

The motel provided a good supply of useful equipment, including a lot of clean linens for bathing and dressing Loshie's injury. The beds were comfortable, and the living spaces like the kitchen were very well equipped. Even so, Ellie couldn't help but worry about the man they had seen. *Is he one of many? Will he, or others here, be dangerous? Will they want us to leave, so we're not competing for food? Is there much available round here?*

In the end, Ellie's dialogue with herself petered out when she remembered Loshie's recovery. They would have to stay till she could move. The damaged bike was another problem to solve before they could leave.

Clara wandered into the kitchen. 'I'm hungry, Mummy.'

The reminder that the most urgent item on the to do list was always to find their next meal snapped Ellie out of her reverie. There was nothing left of the provisions discovered en route so far. They were back to a hand-to-mouth existence, and in a place they didn't know. Where food might grow, or animals might live, was knowledge they needed to gather quickly.

She handed her daughter a hotel bowl. 'Can you go and get us all some raspberries from just outside, please? Don't go far, make sure you can see the back door at all times. Got it?'

'Yes, Mummy.' Clara beamed a smile. 'Maggi, let's go and

get raspberries!'

Maggi appeared. She looked stony faced. 'I'm worried about Mama.'

Ellie wrapped the little girl in a big hug, getting a mouthful of her black, wiry hair. 'Of course, you are. We all are. She's sick, but she'll get better. She's a tough one, your Mama.' Maggi shuddered with a deep breath and pulled away. Ellie wiped a tear from her cheek. 'Will you go and help Clara gather some raspberries? There are some left out there aren't there?' Maggi nodded, and the two girls exited.

She checked on Loshie, whose condition remained unchanged. The dog lay panting on the floor by the bed. 'Alfie, you stay and look after the patient, till we get back.' The room was very hot, but there was no obvious way to improve the ventilation.

After stroking King Alfred for several minutes, Ellie left to join the raspberry pickers. The three of them ate all the remaining raspberries in the car park, after which she led them back to the ponds to collect more water.

The pondwater was still, and in the heat of the day, it looked murky. In the clear plastic bottles, it looked much better, and Ellie decided they would have to accept it. After filling all the bottles, they sat in the bushes at one end of the ponds. Ellie made a game of it, telling the girls they were trying to spot any strangers, but without being found themselves. She wanted to get an idea of how many people were around. The girls couldn't be left alone, and Loshie couldn't supervise them, so Ellie had to work out how to explore the local area and keep them safe. At ten and twelve years old, they were good at following orders and keeping themselves safe, but Ellie felt they were still not old enough to go off alone.

They played the game attentively for five minutes, and then started to drift. Here insect life was thriving, and Maggi and Clara happily lay hidden in the shade watching flies and beetles potter about. Occasional birds swooped down for a quick drink. The breeze rustled tree leaves – these trees still had enough water to survive. The sun passed overhead and moved twenty degrees across the sky.

Clara poked her mother awake. She pointed through the leaf

cover to a location halfway along the pond, where a middle-aged woman was collecting water.

Ellie whispered, 'OK, girls, when she moves away, we're going to follow. She mustn't know we're here, and we want to see where she lives and if there are any other people around here. Try to remember where you see any food growing along the way, so we can go back and get it later. Keep hidden as we move, and absolute silence.' She put a finger to her lips to emphasise the last point.

They crept backwards and out around the edge of the woods. Ellie was impressed at Maggi and Clara's ability to follow in secrecy. *God, I hope it isn't me that gives us away.*

The woman had brown hair, hanging down to her shoulders from under a wide-brimmed sun hat, and walked in the open, seemingly unconcerned that she might be seen.

She set off in the same direction the man had run away the day before, across the scrabbly tarmac surface of the A30 and around the next woodland. She crossed a wide, empty dual carriageway and entered woods on the other side. A driveway passed into a parting in the trees, with a sign that read 'Basingstoke Grand Hotel'.

Ellie held the girls back to keep hidden and then they ran quickly across and straight into the cover of the next copse. They paused, hiding behind tree trunks and trying to catch sight of the woman again. She was easily spotted striding through the woods towards a big square building.

This second hotel had a long frontage and a square attached annexe. Ellie pulled the girls down behind the bushes at the edge of the car park. The rusting carcasses of three ancient, petrol-powered cars stood crumbling in the final row of spaces, providing additional cover for the Smiths.

They moved forward, crouching low, one hiding behind each vehicle, with Ellie in the middle. She looked over the bonnet, through the front and back windscreens, and watched. The woman walked past the main entrance and on across the frontage to a door into the annexe. Ellie checked she had infonetwork connection and decided. *Now or never.*

She whispered left and right, 'Girls, you wait here. If you see anyone else arriving, send me an Armulet message. Just text, no sounds. I'll send you a grinner emoji back, so you know I got the message. If I don't reply, or you see more people coming, send the message again, but then you run back to Loshie and stay with her. Do not try and follow me inside that building, whatever happens. You understand?'

The girls nodded, wide-eyed. Everyone had been in dangerous situations with unknown bad people before, but they'd never seen their parents deliberately go looking for trouble.

'And if nobody comes,' Ellie continued, 'you wait one hour and no longer. If I don't come back out by then, stay silent and sneak away and back to Loshie. You understand?' They nodded again. 'Promise me!'

They crouched dumbstruck.

'Say it! I promise.'

Maggi answered, 'I promise.'

Clara stared at her mother. Her eyes were full, but no tears escaped. Ellie reached out across the gap between them and squeezed her daughter's hand. She squeezed again and Clara's voice was barely audible. She was hardly breathing, in or out. 'I promise.'

'Look at your Armulets – 1.25pm, right? So, what time will you leave here if I don't come back out?'

Maggi spoke in a hushed tone. '2.25pm,'

'Good. What I'm hoping is that these nice people will give us food. But we can't be sure they're as nice as they look, so we need contingency plans.'

'What's contingency plans?'

'Never mind. Stay here, sharp lookouts, right, like you're guards up the i360 Tower. Message me if you see anyone and go back to Loshie after an hour. Got it? You're my backup crew!' She gave them both a smile and a thumbs up. Maggi and Clara couldn't help themselves – they grinned and gave a thumbs up back.

Ellie turned and went away from the hotel and into the thicket behind. She emerged again fifty yards along the car park, following the treeline around its edge, and then she crept along the front of the end of the building. At the open entrance door, she peeked in and then slunk through to a dim interior corridor.

Her Armulet lit up and she dived into the nearest open door so as to avoid being spotted whilst reading the message. It was from Clara. *We saw the woman in a window just near where you went in. She's looking out to the car park.* Ellie sent an auto response that consisted only of a cartoonish smirking face.

She looked out of the window of the bedroom she had leapt into, over towards the three cars. Originally, yellow, red and a dirty silver colour, the vehicles were all dusty and rusty. They stood on flattened tyres and had the odd panel hanging loose. Maggi and Clara were not visible at all. *Well done, girls.*

Ellie passed along the corridor, listening at each door first, and then looking into any room where the door proved unlocked. Mounds of leaves had gathered in a few corners of the corridor. The long passageway window had a floor length curtain that was mostly intact, but one end was hanging loose, no longer connected to the rail hooks.

The air was hot and deathly still, and the whole place smelt of mildew. This annexe was a square with rooms looking out over the woods outside of the building, and on the other side, the corridor had windows facing an inner courtyard, much like the motel where Loshie was resting up.

Ellie took care to keep low in case somebody might see her across the yellowed grass enclosure. She came back out of the first room and nearly bumped into Clara standing in the corridor. She grabbed her, and Maggi who stood a pace behind, and bundled them all into the room she'd just cleared.

'What are you doing here?' Ellie hissed at them, her voice low and furious.

'We came to tell you about the lady.'

She shook Clara by the arm. 'What did you promise me?'

'But Mummy, she's just up the corridor. You're going to bump into her, and we don't know if she's a friend or a bastard.'

The Times of Malthus

Ellie stared at her daughter. She and Wayne had often referred to raiders as 'bastards' but she had never heard Clara say it. She realised that she had never heard Clara refer to bad people at all, using any vocabulary. In Ellie's mind, her daughter played her way through life with a beaming smile and had little direct experience of the terrible events of the Times, exempt in some way.

Ellie peeked out of the door along the corridor. 'OK, do you remember how many rooms along she is? How many windows along the building did you see her?'

'She's here.' Maggi was at the corridor window. She was pointing a stubby dark finger towards the glass and to the right.

'Get down!' Ellie whispered her shout again. Maggi responded by bending her knees to lower her head below the windowsill. Ellie and Clara crawled over, and Ellie peered over the sill. She saw the back of the woman cross the courtyard to enter another door at the end of the first corridor that Ellie had cleared.

'Right, you two stay close behind me. If we see anybody, we're going to keep out of sight, got it?'

This time she did not wait for an answer but led them along the corridor and out of the exit door into the little quadrangle in the centre of the hotel. As they got across the diagonal route to the second door, Ellie saw the woman through the security glass. She stood facing them and made the door lock with a loud click.

Ellie turned and made to run for the first door but stopped suddenly, as she saw the thin man from the pond the previous day emerging from it. Closer up, he appeared to be in his late forties and thin to the point of looking sick. He held a shotgun level from his shoulder, aimed straight at Ellie.

Without taking her eyes off the gun, she grabbed hold of the girls to get them behind her. They moved quickly. She felt small hands cling onto her trouser waistband at the back.

'What do you want?' Ellie croaked.

'What do we want? You followed us and broke in here. What do you want?'

Tuesday 29 May 2040
Moments later in Basingstoke's Grand Hotel.

'We mean no harm. I'm sorry, we're very hungry. Please don't hurt us.'

'Everybody's hungry, we've got nothing for you.'

'I'm really sorry. We'll leave right away.'

Although the man looked like he was getting on for fifty years old, the hard last decade may have aged him more than expected. He was shaking a little, perhaps from weakness and the weight of the shotgun. The woman had worked her way around the corridors and appeared behind him. She put a hand on his back, and he steadied. They stood, glaring.

'People aren't hungry in Hereford.'

'What?' he barked.

It was Maggi speaking. She leaned around Ellie's waist to talk to the man. 'That's where we're going. They have plenty of food for everyone.'

The man laughed loud. 'Who told you that?'

'My Mama. She's sick though, so we need to find some food to make her better so we can continue on our way to Hereford.'

'You don't look very sick,' the woman snapped.

Her voice was quiet. 'I'm not her mother, Loshie is.' Ellie wasn't sure how this information might turn the situation. 'She's my friend and she's resting with a fever, back out of town.'

The woman squinted. Everybody had removed their sunglasses inside, and the light in the yard was blinding. 'What's this about Hereford, though? How do you know it has food?'

'We've come from Brighton. Loshie met a traveller there who told her that Hereford has a safe and stable community, and their crops grow so well they all have enough to eat. Apparently, they've got that audiopt surveillance up and running, so they can protect themselves easily. We'll be on our way as soon as Loshie is better, but we don't want to steal anything from you.' Ellie could see the body language and facial expressions softening. The shotgun was no longer levelled directly at her.

The Times of Malthus

'You could come with us if you want to.' This time, Clara spoke.

Ellie shushed her and pushed her back behind. In thinking it through, this unexpected invitation struck Ellie as a brilliant idea. These people may have some food they might share, and they had a gun. If they were struggling to survive here, and friendly enough to join the party of four on The Journey, more eyes for security and more hands to gather food could only help. If they meant any harm, she reckoned the gun would already have been fired.

Ellie could picture cogs whirring in both their heads. She said, 'Look, you are very welcome to join us on our way to Hereford, but I'm sure you will need to discuss it. I'll come back tomorrow at noon, and you can say yes or no then. Either way, we'll be leaving town then.'

'Go on, then.' The man and his wife edged around the courtyard wall and waved the gun back towards the only open door to dismiss them. Ellie turned and shepherded Maggi and Clara away.

They tried to work their way back to their motel via a convoluted, different route. Ellie wasn't sure she needed to avoid the others following them, but they needed to search the area for food. New roads were always a risk though. The couple they'd met might not be the only folk living in Basingstoke, and others might not be so willing to listen and talk.

They found a few more berries – three different types – but it wouldn't sustain them for long. They did bring Loshie back plenty of water, and she needed it. They'd been gone several hours, and her bedroom was stifling in the mid-afternoon heat. The sheets were soaked. King Alfred disappeared out of the door as soon as the three got back. Ellie and the girls helped Loshie to move to the next bedroom. It was no cooler, but the sheets there were new.

Just after dark, the woman from the other hotel called softly in the corridor. 'Hello? It's me. We met earlier. You talked about Hereford.'

'What? Who's that?' Loshie was awake and coherent again. She was weak and tired, but she had broken the back of her fever. Ellie had already explained the events at the other hotel. She held up her hand as if to say, *Keep calm, it's OK*, and went out to meet the woman and brought her back into the room.

'Loshie, this is the lady I told you we met today.' She turned to the dark-haired woman. 'Sorry, my name's Ellie, and this is my friend Loshie. We are the mothers of the two girls you met earlier.' At that moment, Clara and Maggi were in the inner courtyard, lying under a big bush in the corner. Ellie pointed through the window at her daughter.

'I'm Charlotte – Charlie – and my husband is Alan.'

Loshie did not present a friendly demeanour. 'How did you find us in here?'

Charlie smiled. 'You're the first newcomers we've had in a year. Anything changes and we spot it. We knew you were here before you saw Alan at the ponds. We don't mind others coming here, but there isn't enough food if you start taking it. That's why we were so, um, wary, earlier.'

'We understand,' Ellie replied. She was sitting on the bed, next to Loshie lying full length, and pinched Loshie's leg behind her back, out of sight of the other woman. 'I'm sure we'd have been just the same if you'd come onto our patch in Brighton. Don't worry though, we'll be gone by tomorrow.'

Loshie would not be back to full health by then, but Ellie was confident they would be able to move on to at least the other side of town. Out of Charlie and Alan's hair at a minimum.

Charlie came straight to the point. 'We'd like to come with you.' As an afterthought, she added, 'Please.'

'That's great!' Ellie clapped her hands together, and then returned one behind herself to squeeze Loshie's good leg gently. She turned her head to focus on her friend. 'Isn't it, Loshie? More people travelling together, safety in numbers.' She sounded unconvincing, but Loshie said all the right things in agreement.

Ellie called the girls in and introduced them properly to their new travelling buddy. Clara smiled brightly and appeared genuinely excited at the prospect of new people in their lives. Maggi was positive, but a little more reticent. The two youngsters quickly lost interest in the adult conversation and ran back outside.

They talked about the route and what luggage the two new companions should bring. Charlie said she and Alan had no means of transport other than walking. Loshie and Ellie discussed the situation with their bikes. The need to find charging stations restricted the routing significantly, and the fact that one bike was not functioning properly made it actually more of a struggle than walking would be.

They finally decided they would leave the bikes and The Journey would be on foot from that point. They would need to reorganise what they carried. Ellie and Loshie would have only their backpack each, so some stuff in the panniers would have to be left behind. Maggi and Clara might be able to carry a pannier each, but they would be cumbersome, and the girls couldn't carry much weight anyway.

Charlie said, 'We have a whole range of backpacks. I'm sure we have some smaller ones that would be suitable for the girls. Why don't you come over tomorrow morning and we'll show you what we've got, and Clara and Maggi can each choose one they like.'

'Sure.' Loshie's contributions to the conversation were minimalist, but Ellie was glad to see her recuperating steadily. She felt Loshie was the right side of a recovery tipping point.

'That's very generous of you, Charlie. We'll bring the girls over in the morning, and we should be ready to leave by lunchtime, like we said before.'

When Charlie had gone, they discovered that she had left a cloth bag with food in it. There were four apples, a jar of blackberry jam, and a loaf of bread.

'Wait! Loshie, there's bread here. How the hell did she make that?'

Loshie already had her finger in the jar of jam. 'Wow, there's honey mixed into this. It's delicious.'

Ellie opened the bedroom window. 'Girls, get in here! We've got the most incredible meal!'

They ate everything very quickly.

An hour after dawn, they walked in the relative cool of the early morning over to the other hotel. Loshie came out with them. The evening meal had pepped her up, and she was keen enough to get back on the road that she wanted to prove to Ellie that she was fit for it again.

Loshie's ankle had scabbed over, and the blackness was diminishing. The red streaks that indicated infection were lessening too, and she took the last of the antibiotic pills. Her gait had something of a limp, but she claimed to Ellie that walking was actually much easier than cycling had been.

Charlie and Alan were in the midst of packing a backpack each, and they all discussed whose bits of equipment for various jobs were better. It would be useful to be able to carry only one of each item and share the load amongst all six of them.

The women introduced King Alfred, who immediately took to Charlie and Alan as if they had always been friends of the family.

Charlie provided a breakfast plate for everyone. Alan eyed them all disapprovingly, and his wife told him not to be so selfish. If they were all going to travel together, they would all have to share everything.

He confessed that the shotgun had no ammunition, but they agreed he should bring it. Britain had few guns, and it would be a strong deterrent should they run into people with bad intentions.

Ellie and Loshie took their daughters back to their own hotel to complete the packing with the children's new backpacks. Clara's was a novelty Star Wars pack, mostly red, whilst Maggi had chosen a small daypack in a camouflage pattern green. They had not asked where Charlie got them all, or indeed why she had so many, but the choice had been vast: perhaps thirty different rucksacks in every size and colour.

Whilst Ellie helped the girls pack and completed the job for the adults, Loshie went back out to the ponds to fill bottles with water. They had discussed at length the trade-off between carrying more weight and having more water stock. In the end, they agreed on Ellie and Loshie carrying four litres each, whilst Clara and Maggi would carry a one-litre bottle each. Finding water on the road was difficult, and would become more so, as they headed further into summer.

The Armulet map suggested the walk would take them about four days. Carrying packs in the intense heat, Ellie suspected it would likely take closer to one week. She wondered how circuitous the route would need to become in order to seek out water sources on the way.

New, different company, with additional equipment, and a good store of food to set them on their way, filled her with renewed hope. Ellie estimated that the provisions Charlie had shown her would last several days, if not the whole week's walking time. She admitted to herself that they would need more calories with the exertions of hiking with packs, but she was sure they would find supplementary foods en route.

Loshie returned, wet from sweating profusely. Her olive-green T-shirt was soaking. The water bottles were full, but she had struggled with the weight of carrying them all back. She sat and rested, whilst the packs were buckled up and laid out in a row, ready to go.

Ellie was finally excited for the future, after years of eking out a life for herself and Clara, with no clear purpose. Her mind kept oscillating from blissful optimism, about the life they would build in the haven of Hereford, to serious worry that there would be nothing there, no safe community nor any food.

They set off at noon to meet Charlie and Alan, which was perhaps foolish given the heat, but they planned to make only a short first leg to ensure that everyone was managing OK.

At the hotel, they wandered the corridors and looked in the rooms they had met them in earlier. There was no sign of either, but their backpacks were fully packed and tied up, set out in the hotel lobby, ready to roll.

'Charlie?' Ellie called out, trying to ignore the creeping dread that had arrived from out of nowhere. 'Hello?'

No answer.

Ellie wandered into the hotel restaurant, expecting that the two of them were laying out a grand lunch. She had the impression that Charlie at least was looking forward to having new friends as much as Ellie was.

'Alan? Charlie? Are you ready to go?'

No answer.

She moved back through the waiter's door into the kitchen area and stopped. Ellie's hand moved involuntarily to cover her mouth. Charlie and Alan were on the floor, dead. They had been attacked violently – there was blood everywhere, and both bodies had several large stab wounds all over the torso.

Her mouth moved to cry out, but no sound came.

The Times of Malthus
Wednesday 30 May 2040
After the Basingstoke murders.

Loshie came into the kitchen and stopped next to her friend. She looked back and forth between Ellie and the bodies. She looked stunned.

Loshie's voice was quiet. 'What the… Did you do this?'

Ellie stared at Loshie. 'How can you even ask that?'

Loshie sprang into action. She stuck her head back out through the waiter's door to the dining area. After a quick scan out there, she moved across the kitchen and knelt by the bodies. She made a show of putting her fingers to Charlie's wrist to check for a pulse, even though the blood and stab wounds made it clear that the couple were very much dead.

She looked back up at Ellie and commanded, 'You go and keep the girls out there. I'll see if there's any food left. I'll bet the bastard took it all.'

'What? What are you saying, Loshie? We can't just take their food and leave them like this.'

'Ellie, they're dead. And their killer's likely still nearby. We need to leave now. Go and get the girls ready to go. I'll see you in the lobby in one minute.' She stood and pushed Ellie back towards the swing door exit. 'Go!'

Clara and Maggi had perched themselves on high stools at the old bar and swung around in unison as Ellie rushed to the large reception area. She chivvied the girls to the door and hurried their three packs onto their backs.

Loshie came back in less than two minutes and shook her head at Ellie. She grabbed Charlie's loaded backpack in the lobby. 'We're just going to have to carry this between us.' She picked it up and held out a strap for Ellie to take. Ellie stared at her. 'There'll be a ton of food in here, Ellie. Come on, we gotta go now.'

They took a meandering circuit, skirting the edge of town, and finally got onto the old Kingsclere Road to head northwest out of Basingstoke. The road made for a long, uphill slog in the heat, where the few trees always seemed to be on the wrong side to provide any useful shade.

The landscape soon changed. The rain that fell just in from the coast did not seem to penetrate this far north. The soil appeared desiccated, and the grass and bushes were yellowed and dusty and dead. Streams, even rivers, were dry to the sandy bottoms. The dry air felt like it sucked the moisture out of everything.

They peaked the crest of the hill, and a thicket of brittle trees offered some shade for a rest. They were leafless, but in better times had grown close together. The sun's heat had been intense on the walking party, and they lay out exhausted. The drinking water was quickly depleted, over half of it gone already.

That morning, it took them over two hours to walk just five miles, and they wanted to get as far as possible from the dangers of Basingstoke before nightfall. Maggi projected an Armulet view of the next ten-mile stretch. It was predominantly downhill, and spirits lifted somewhat at the three-dimensional profile that showed easier hiking for the rest of the day. Clara and Maggi started singing a made-up song about walking downhill, and King Alfred joined in with the occasional bark. Her drooping jaw and lolling tongue gave the impression of a jolly smile.

Nobody mentioned Charlie and Alan. Back at the hotel, Ellie had reassured the girls that they would join later. She hoped the girls understood this to be a lie and had learnt over the years to avoid asking too many questions, when it was obvious that something bad had happened.

They wandered through once-classic English countryside, dehydrated by the new, unforgiving climate. Stands of skeletal trees dotted hills and fields turned brown by the drought. Farmhouses, and even whole villages stood derelict in the blazing sunshine. Lavender managed well with little water. Many of the fields were empurpled by it for the third time that year.

What they never spotted were any people. There were signs of a human presence in a few places, but it was difficult to tell if they were current or had been left behind years ago. The North Wessex Downs had become too dry to sustain life, and Loshie and

Ellie agreed that anyone who had not died would have left. They took a half-mile detour to Ewhurst Pond, but it too appeared to have been dry for years. The vegetation gathered around the watercourses was long dead.

'We must have gotten really lucky finding those ponds in Basingstoke,' Ellie said.

'They were well shaded.' Loshie paused and looked around. 'But actually, I reckon it's probably that this is all up a height, and that means the water has drained away downhill. Maybe it even all drains down to that Basingstoke pond.'

'I'll bet that's why people lived near it.' Ellie couldn't bring herself to say Alan and Charlie's names. 'I wonder if there were many other ponds that we never saw.'

'At least one, that's for sure. This has got to be much safer, up here.'

'Until we die of thirst.'

Loshie jiggled the rucksack they were carrying between them. 'The food we've collected here should have some water in it. I can't wait to open it up tonight. I bet there's more of those apples in here. And they must have packed some water of their own too.'

Ellie winced. She had lived through twelve years of the Times of Malthus, knew of the dangers – horrors – and of necessity. "Eat when you can," had been a mantra that Wayne had learned in the Navy, and Ellie understood the logic. She just could not get over the inhumanity of what had happened to the world. *"Six things to look for in the perfect yoga studio" – God, what were we thinking? Food and water to look for in the perfect yoga studio, more like.* She shook her head, and they trudged along in the dusty heat.

Kingsclere was equally dry. An empty swimming pool sat beside a long-evaporated pond to one side of the village. The riverbed looked like it had never felt the cool touch of water.

They moved on, their pace steadily decreasing, until dusk came, and they approached Greenham Common's old airfield. The bunkers that had held nuclear weapons in the 1980s loomed out of the gloaming. These giant shelters were low and sleek, but the straight lines showed them up as artificial landscape. As the five approached, the silos' details became visible: giant metal doorways with alcove entrances and a lot of concrete under the shaggy grass roofing.

'Hey Clara,' said Ellie. 'Your grandmothers came here when they were still younger than you. There was a big protest here. Lots of women set up a camp to tell everyone that they should stop using nuclear weapons. They were really bad, big guns that could kill thousands of people at once.'

'Millions,' Loshie chimed in.

Ellie nodded, but the enthusiasm to pass on Jude's story had evaporated, as she remembered her mother's bright grin under a crocheted beret. She had always mocked her mother's clothing, but the memory of that hat made her heart ache.

They made a camp at the threshold of one of the shelters. It was a deep space in the concrete pile, like a giant empty garage, and they had chosen one hidden by the architecture of the other surrounding bunkers. The common was open land, and while there were enough trees to collect firewood, the vegetation was sparse enough that they would need to use the relief of the bunker complex to hide their fire and campsite.

Ellie and Clara returned with arms full of sticks of varying sizes, chirping that they had enough for an excellent fire. They were greeted by the site of Loshie throwing clothes and shoes around the place. Charlie's backpack was empty, and its contents strewn all over the area.

'Nothing. Absolutely nothing.' Loshie almost screamed at Ellie, as she dropped the firewood in a pile away from Loshie's stomping around.

'Hey, what's the matter? What's going on?'

She kicked the rucksack. 'We carried this all bloody day, and there's not a single bit of food in it. No water, nothing. Just old clothes and shoes.' Ellie hugged Clara by her side, as her friend ranted.

'OK, but we have the food we brought.' She stepped slightly towards Loshie but stopped again at the next outburst.

'What were they planning – to eat all our food? I thought they had loads. They deserve to be dead.'

'Loshie!' Ellie shouted, and then there was silence. 'That's a terrible thing to say. I'm sure the killers stole the food. That will have been why they were there, why they did it.'

'Oh, and I suppose they took out the food and then neatly snapped the straps closed again, so we could pick it up and carry it away without any bother.'

'Look, I don't know, but let's just get on with cooking up what food we do have.' She gathered up the wood again and moved it to a spot at the edge of the shelter's giant entrance. The thick concrete made the bunker cool, even just a yard inside the threshold.

Loshie did not reply but started to throw Charlie's various items as far to the side as they would go. She sat down, leaning against the low wall at the edge of the shelter doorway, and examined her ankle injury. Maggi fussed over it, whilst Ellie and Clara built the fire at the other side.

They had eaten well at breakfast and had a few vegetables to cook for a meal. Hunger would not take them that night, but Ellie was worried about water. They drank half of the last litre and saved the rest for the morning. In thirty-two-degree heat, it was not enough, but it was some.

A skinny, wild cow wandered along the wide space between the two rows of bunkers. She was curious but wary, presumably looking for water too. Loshie perked up at the possibility of all the meat. They knew they should also drink the blood, but, looking at the animal, no one could bring themselves to imagine doing so.

They tried to approach from two different angles, Ellie distracting from the front, and Loshie sneaking up from behind. She had Wayne's knife raised, but they didn't have any exact plan about how to kill a cow. In the end, it made no difference. The animal was too wily for them. At every approach, it ran away ten yards. It was much sprightlier than either woman, and despite being scrawny, the big, moving bulk was patently dangerous. It finally got sick of them trying to catch it and ran off further and faster than they could follow.

Nobody slept very well. The previous night had been hot in

the hotel, but restful. This night, all four of them suffered a variety of insomnia-causing demons. Loshie's ankle was very sore after the long day's walk. Ellie could not get the images of their slain travel companions, stabbed in the kitchen, out of her head. Maggi moaned that it was too hot throughout the night, and Clara tossed and turned although she never opened her eyes or said anything.

The Times of Malthus

**Thursday 31 May 2040
A week into The Journey.**

They left very early, aiming to beat the heat of the day.

Passing the third bunker along, King Alfred wandered off inside the shelter. The giant metal doors were open enough to leave a gap of about two feet. 'Come on Alfie, we need to get on.' The dog didn't reappear at Ellie's call, so she went back to chivvy her along. 'Hey, what are you doing in here?'

The Akita sat away in the shadows, and it was more than an hour before dawn. Even with a bright moon outside, Ellie struggled at first to see a row of three human skeletons sitting on the floor, leaning back against the concrete wall. As soon as she made out the shapes, she could not stop seeing them, despite the dark light. On the floor at the farthest end were two dog skeletons. There were no clothes, and anything else that might have been there must also have been taken away by scavengers.

Ellie shivered. 'Come on, I know it's not very nice, but there's nothing to be done here. Let's go. She waved a hand, and the dog ran out. She looked at the five, long dead, and took a long look back outside to her companions.

Newbury proved to be another dry town. They followed the railway line west from the station, as it passed innumerable canals and ponds. They searched these for most of the morning but found not a drop of water. In vain, they continued to follow the empty channels, trenches and ponds northwest across the parched downs.

Ellie had become increasingly bewildered at how big rainstorms could be completely dried up again in such short timescales. *Where does all that water go?*

Turning more northerly, the route climbed. It was a long, shallow gradient, all the way up to the old M4 motorway just south of Swindon. The little B road had the occasional shade tree, but these provided barely any respite from the inescapable heat. Mostly, it was still brown fields that hadn't been farmed in more than a decade. The walls and hedges delineated them, as they had for hundreds of years, but the soil hadn't seen crops since Bitness unleashed their Revelations.

In one of her heat daydreams, Ellie wondered if this life was what Bitness had envisaged. *We were all so excited that change was finally happening. Surely nobody anticipated this? They couldn't have thought all this would be better than what we'd had, could they?*

It was too hot to complain, too hot to talk. They simply plodded on, one foot in front of the other, their hats and sunglasses scant protection from the furious light, for hour after hour. The pace slowed and slowed again, until the road reached the M4. They dropped down the embankment to sit in the shade of the bridge where their former road continued north over the motorway.

It had taken ten hours of walking from the cool bunker at Greenham Common to reach the swooning heat of the M4. The stone banking under the bridge felt cool against their backs, as they sprawled in a row. No campsite decision was made – they didn't discuss anything – they all simply fell asleep.

Ellie woke up, surprised that she was too cold to sleep. The clear skies, sequinned with stars, always filled her with wonder. Ellie knew, from long experience, that a lack of cloud made the temperature drop significantly overnight.

She put on a jumper, the only extra clothing she had brought, and turned over to try and sleep again. She looked along the line of bodies and felt reassured at their peaceful sleep. *How wonderful to be away from the brutality that lives in every place now.*

Hearing a sound like dripping or slurping, Ellie sat up. Looking up the stone bank, right where it met the underside of the bridge, which curved down to form a wall, she made out the silhouette of King Alfred licking the wall.

Ellie picked her way carefully up to look closely. 'What are you doing, girl? Has the heat sent you mad too?'

The moon was bright, but the shadows made everything unclear. She put her Armulet torch on to see if maybe the dog had found an ants nest or perhaps some salt deposit. The light reflected brightly from water trickling down the wall. The sight of it made her throat tickle.

Touching her fingers to the rivulet and up to her mouth, Ellie tasted delicious, pure water. She scanned the torch up the wall, the underside of the bridge over the motorway. The concrete had crumbled away in many big patches, exposing the steel reinforcement bars. She couldn't be certain, but Ellie speculated that the metal bars had gotten sufficiently cold overnight that they were condensing water from the air, and this then trickled down.

A small, muddy puddle had collected in a hollow in the concrete. As it had only just appeared, it should be reasonably potable. She figured that alerting the others to it would cause such a commotion that they wouldn't efficiently collect as much as possible. They would all wake up desperately thirsty, and the rising of the sun would evaporate the water fast. As magically as it had arrived, the puddle would disappear.

As quietly as possible, Ellie pulled the empty bottles from the rucksacks and used a spoon to try and fill them as fast as she could. She was so parched herself, that many of the early spoonfuls simply went into her own mouth. It took three times as long to fill the first bottle as it could have done.

'Hey, what's going on?' Loshie shouted.

Ellie turned to see her storming up the sloping stonework.

'What have you got there?' she demanded. 'Where did you get that water?' She grabbed the bottle. 'Tell me!'

They stood close together, and Ellie could see a maddened look on her friend's face.

'How much have you kept hidden from us?' Loshie didn't wait for an answer, she tipped the bottle and poured half of it down her throat.

Their daughters were now awake and looking up towards them. Ellie could not make out their expressions in the dim light. Loshie ran down to Maggi and passed her the bottle. 'What is it, Mama?'

'It's water. Drink it up, my darling.' Loshie pointed an accusatory finger at her lifelong best friend. 'That thief was trying to keep it from us.'

Ellie walked slowly down the bank, a hand extended as if to

say *Stop this!*

Loshie stared at her blankly, as if she'd never seen Ellie before, as if she were some stranger come to steal from them and then kill them.'

She said, 'No, no, we've found water. Up there.' She pointed back to where King Alfred had not paused in licking the wall since waking Ellie. 'Not much, and it'll evaporate fast if we don't collect it, but it's something. It's enough to keep us alive, this morning at least.'

She returned to the dirty puddle, picked up another empty bottle and started to fill it too. 'Come up here, Clara. Come and help me, please.'

Clara looked across at Loshie and Maggi and then back to her mother. 'Yes, Mummy.' Clara scurried up to her mother and sucked on the bottle as fervently as the others had.

The other two rushed up and crowded into the small spot. The scrabble to collect the liquid was exactly as Ellie had feared. Loshie tried to stick her bottle into the puddle, but it was only half an inch deep and would not fill. Maggi stuck her face down and started lapping the water like King Alfred. This meant nobody else could get near it. Loshie and her daughter took turns to slurp directly from the water surface.

Ellie tried to hold a bottle up to one trail of drips sliding down from a steel reinforcement bar, but it was desperately slow. In the end, she just stood and watched. They would not stop, or even listen to her entreaties to work to a more productive system.

Clara tried to lick the wall like the dog, but it was not effective, and she spat out crumbling concrete which just made her more thirsty.

By the time Loshie and Maggi stopped, the puddle was down to the mud, and the first rays of sunshine were spiking over the horizon like searchlights. They walked down again, slung on their backpacks and Loshie said, 'Right, are we going then?'

Ellie looked at the waterless puddle and then up at her friend. 'I guess we are.' She shook her head in disbelief, but Loshie missed it as she had already turned to head off along the middle lane of the motorway.

'Are you OK?' Ellie put her arm around Clara, who stood silently. They let the others make a hundred yards head start and then trudged after them.

There was no conversation between the two groups during the morning. The asphalt surface quickly heated up to an unbearable level, but the motorway was mostly cut down into the land, with steep sides that were no good for walking on.

In places, the once-grassy central strip made for better walking, but much of it was too pitted to be good underfoot. Often the metal crash barriers cut across it too, so they had to clamber over every few hundred yards. It took a sapping eight hours to make a little over eight miles.

The road started to rise towards another motorway junction at the southwest edge of Swindon. The light ahead was blinding. Ellie remembered stories of people in the throes of dying who headed towards a bright light. She wondered what lay ahead. As they climbed an exit road, they gained enough height that the reflected light was no longer straight into their eyes.

The bright reflection came from the shattered wreckage of a huge aircraft. Spread across the entirety of the motorway, it was surrounded by a halo of debris and the burned-out wrecks of cars and trucks that must have been unlucky enough to be in its way when the plane had crashed.

They scrambled down the shattered concrete of the exit road and found that inside the cracked body of the plane was even hotter than everywhere else. The blinding reflection and this intense heat made Ellie feel ill. She retired back outside, into the shade under the bridge forming part of this new junction, and passed out almost before she could lie down.

Ellie's fever dreams took her back to Brighton in her teens, but it was a Malthusian Brighton. She went dancing in the Atlanta, whilst seagulls pecked at bodies on the shingle just beyond the pools of light that spilled from the hedonist waterholes under the prom.

As she hugged Wayne's cairn, the stones rolled away to reveal the tomb was empty. Selsey barked from beneath the neighbouring cairn, but, as many rocks as she threw aside, she could never dig deep enough to reach the dog.

The slightest wetness moistened Ellie's lips, and she came to a vague consciousness. Loshie's face was very close to hers, and she was dabbing her mouth with a wet cloth. Ellie still lay in the shadow of the bridge, but it was night, and the shadow was from moonlight.

She instinctively licked her lips to gather the film of water. Loshie dabbed again, releasing a little more this time. Steadily, they increased the volume of water that Ellie received each time. Within a couple of minutes, she was able to lean up to receive the neck of a water bottle and swallow a whole mouthful.

'We've managed to get some more condensation from the metal of the plane. It's not much, but enough to bring you back. Ellie, I thought you were going to die.'

Clara knelt beside her mother, fanning her with a cardboard box lid. Behind Loshie, Maggi watched with a worried gaze.

'More.' Ellie indicated the bottle, and Loshie held it to her lips again.

'We need to go, Ellie. There's nothing here, the plane is empty. And we should move by the light of the moon, when it's a bit cooler, and rest in the heat of the day.'

Ellie gave a slight nod and tried to sit up. At first, she fell back, but Loshie and Clara managed to help her to sitting up. After another half pint of water – all they had collected while she hallucinated – Ellie was able to stand. She was unsteady, but also not fit to argue, discuss, or even think about Loshie's plan to get going again.

In only a few steps, Ellie had to lean against a bridge stanchion and retch. The water she had drunk came back out, and the spasms in her stomach caused her a bout of diarrhoea at the same time. Her digestive system had been so starved of content that there was very little quantity in her knickers, but the stomach pain was excruciating. She dropped to all fours, with her gut continuing to dry retch over and over. Ellie collapsed, lying flat out face down.

The Times of Malthus

Friday 1 June 2040
The Journey continues.

There were no dreams this time, but Ellie was unconscious for nearly a whole day. A huge crashing sound woke her at dusk. The sound came again, and she opened her eyes to see the hulk of the downed plane across a close-up view of the motorway road surface.

They had moved her a little way from where she fell, and cleaned her up, but Ellie felt groggy and weak. Clara came and sat beside her and offered a wet rag to suck a little water. A thunderclap rolled out across a sky turned grey, rousing her to awareness. After a much slower recovery than the day before, Ellie sat up and leaned against the bridge support pillar.

Loshie moved to be in her eyeline and pointed across the motorway behind Ellie.

'I'm certain I can see rain falling a few kilometres over there. It's just the other side of Swindon. I'm sure of it. Do you think you'll be able to move? We need to collect some of that water before tomorrow's heat dries it all up again. Are you OK to go, Ellie?'

Loshie was right, she knew. They should move. Ellie's body was less willing. However, with much help, and at a snail's pace, she was able to walk along the grey ribbon of the carriageway beneath the gibbous moon.

After a couple of miles, they clambered down across a field to follow a narrower road Loshie had chosen as the best route. They were back into farmland countryside, and the road passed between long-dead fields on either side. Everything became ghostlike and close in, trees menaced with leafless branches, and the wind blew hot along their route.

The thunderstorm had continued for nearly an hour, when the lightning flashes they were aiming for finally ceased, and the wind dropped again. Ellie struggled to maintain any pace at all, and they stopped to rest on the trailer of a decrepit tractor, abandoned in the middle of the little road. They had nothing at all to eat or drink, and they still had not reached a point where the storm had wet the ground.

Ellie felt a stab of pain in her belly, and she stared at the ground, willing the pain away. 'I don't think that thunder and lightning came with any rain. We must have walked five miles already and there's not a drop here.'

Loshie breathed out heavily through her nose. Ellie was in no state to make good decisions, but Loshie always wanted their route to be heading towards Hereford. She waved the route map into life in front of them and it showed they were going entirely the wrong way. 'What the hel…' Loshie sounded confused and angry.

She looked at the other three one after the other, as if accusing one after the other of misdirecting them.

They spent twenty minutes moving the map and looking back over their route, checking if the Armulet was functioning OK in other respects, and asking it to check again. Loshie looked up at the stars and at one point even got Maggi to check that the compass on her Armulet agreed with Loshie's. 'If the Earth's magnetic field has shifted, then the mapping software will be up the spout.'

Ellie didn't think the Armulet route mapper worked like that, but she was too weak to know if she knew anything, let alone to debate it with Loshie.

They agreed to sleep for a few hours in the hope that they could make better sense of things in the morning. The four of them lay underneath the tractor trailer and used their rucksacks for pillows.

The heat of the morning arrived immediately after sunrise, and Ellie felt no better. She could stand and put one foot in front of the other, but she knew she could do nothing more than follow what the others told her to do.

Maggi piped up. 'Mama, you'd set it to take us to *Hertford*, that's the problem.'

'Shit.' Loshie looked around the group, but there was no complaint. Hunger and thirst meant that nobody was compos mentis. 'I only re-set it back at the plane, so we haven't gone far wrong.'

She re-engaged the three-dimensional map projection, and it showed a route west to the M5, and then more north on the motorway, to cross the river Severn just north of Gloucester. Loshie had set the parameters to minimise hill climbing en route. 'OK, good. Right up here a little way and then we turn to Braydon.'

After only a quarter of a mile, the road forked with both separate routes continuing on in similar north-westerly directions. They ignored the slight left turning and followed the sign saying "Braydon Road".

The heat continued to drain any strength or will. Ellie meandered all over the narrow lane, and they had to stop and rest every hundred yards. King Alfred walked with her nose virtually dragging on the ground, legs as unsteady as the humans. *We aren't going to survive another day of this.*

'Loshie,' said Ellie, her throat now so parched, and her lips so cracked and dry, she struggled to form words. 'We need.' She swallowed hard. 'To find water. Or we'll die.' Ellie blamed her lips, but there was a suppressed worry that it was the hand of Death tapping on her shoulder already.

'Mummy, look at that lake up ahead. Look, it's full of water!'

They all peered past Clara, shading their eyes, even behind sunglasses. Ellie's immediate thought was that her daughter was also succumbing to delirium. They stared, and then looked at each other, and then back at the distant glare.

'That must be a mirage,' Loshie scoffed. 'You know what a mirage is, Clara?'

'No.' Her voice was quiet, muted.

Ellie croaked, 'Mirage or not, that's got to be a chance.'

Maggi brought up her own Armulet map projection. It was difficult to make out the projection in the bright sunshine, but they could all see a cluster of ponds and lakes a couple of miles ahead. The map was labelled Cotswold Water Park. Everybody looked into the distance again. The mirage shimmered brightly.

Loshie shook her head and answered, 'They must be dry. Surely there can't be that much water left in them?'

There was no more discussion. The map was switched off and they continued along the lane.

On arrival at the water park, they collapsed into the shallows and drank, and drank. The cooling liquid was glorious against their sun-dried skin and cracked lips. King Alfred was so dehydrated, stumbling, that Ellie and Clara had to hold her up in the water against the possibility of drowning. She drank greedily too, and quickly recovered. They wallowed and played for more than an hour, before crawling onto the grassy bank to loll in the glow of revival.

'Is this Hereford, Mummy?'

Ellie laughed. 'I'm afraid not. But it has saved our lives.'

'But there's water here. Why aren't these ponds dry like everywhere else?' Clara's face showed that she assumed her mother would know the answer.

Ellie felt overwhelmed. She was barely back to thinking straight, and she thought questions of hydrology and microclimate would probably have been beyond her when firing on all cylinders. She hazarded a stab at an answer. 'There must be some sort of special soil or underground reservoir that keeps it full.'

Clara's thoughts had already moved on. 'So, is there food here?'

No amount of water could make up for the absence of actual food. They were starving. 'I don't know. You see that sign over there?' Ellie pointed to a wooden shack with an openable hatch that currently hung closed.

'"Café"? Like the house next door to our beach hut?'

'Yes. Let's go and see if there's any food in there.'

Loshie called from the water, 'There won't be. You can see the door is hanging open.'

She was correct. The dilapidated shed had been ransacked, and, judging by the profusion of weeds and wildflowers growing within, had not been visited again for years. Ellie and Clara searched through the mildewed boxes and dead fridges, but there was nothing to eat.

Beside the café, a shipping container had been repurposed as a storage unit-cum-changing room for watersports. A rack held more than twenty wetsuits in varying sizes, and there were wooden boxes with lockable lids. All the padlock hasps had been forced open, but the contents remained – swimming goggles and snorkels, inflatable paddle boards, water polo balls, lifejackets, and several strings of floats for sectioning off portions of the pond. Leaning in a corner stood two small nets on bamboo poles, the sort of thing children might use for pond dipping.

'I wonder if there are any fish. Do you fancy fish for lunch?'

Clara was wide-eyed, unbelieving.

Managing expectations again, Ellie said, 'Sorry, you're right. We may not find anything, but let's go and see if we can catch something.'

There were trees around the park, which consisted of three small, interconnected lakes. Firewood lay all around, but Loshie insisted on breaking up and burning one of the wooden chests from inside the shipping container.

They feasted on barbecued frogs, for their first meal in nearly three days. The amphibians held little meat, but Ellie and Clara had managed to catch nine of them. Two each, and then Loshie tore the limbs off the last one and shared these out. Without any discussion, she gave Maggi the remaining body, and she wolfed it down.

King Alfred had disappeared during the fishing expedition. On her return, she lay down and went to sleep, without showing any interest in the cooking of the meal. The smell of the frogs burning was intense and must have been incredibly strong to a dog nose.

Loshie nodded. 'I'm surprised if she's still got the strength and speed to catch anything. I could see you two had no chance with the fish in there.'

Ellie agreed, 'Yeah, I definitely don't feel myself yet. I wonder if we can set up some sort of fish trap or find a net to catch them more easily.'

'Good luck with that.'

'I do think we should stay here awhile and get our strength back as much as possible.'

Loshie glared at her friend. 'We're not there yet. Hereford will be even better than this. We should push on.'

Ellie was calm, persistent. 'Sure. What I'm thinking is about how a few days here will actually get us there quicker.'

Loshie snorted. 'How do you figure that out?'

'Well. Think how slowly we walked the last stretches of road to get here. It took two days to walk what might have only taken a few hours at a normal pace.'

'I don't know, that first leg out of Basingstoke was a really long way.'

'OK, but think of that few miles on the M4, a whole day there. And we weren't in any fit state to protect ourselves from the heat, so it only got worse.' Ellie paused, but Loshie remained silent. 'So, I'm thinking if we can take on food and water properly here, build our strength back up – I'm still feeling quite ill – then we can make a good, fast, last push for Hereford. What is it, fifty miles still? I reckon at full strength we could manage that in two days. At yesterday's pace, we'll be dead before we get there.' She could see Loshie was listening, maybe even convinced. 'What do you think?'

'You are right, but how long are you thinking we stay here?'

'I don't know. How about we play it by ear and see how easy it is to find food here. And of course, we also need to find out how safe it is. If this is the only water for miles around, I'd expect lots of people to come here.' She paused and looked around at all that they could see. 'Or, shit! I wonder if anybody lives here. We should scout around the area and see if there're signs of anyone.'

Clara piped up. 'I saw two people at the edge of the pond over there.' She pointed around the side of the lake to a stand of trees right at the water's edge. Nobody was visible. 'But they're dead.'

'Oh. Are you sure?'

'I've seen plenty of dead people, Mummy. They were rotting. Like those people we found in that church in Brighton.'

'OK. Well, we'd all better have a bit of a look around and search for other people, living people.'

The Times of Malthus

They spent six days at the water park, sleeping on piles of wetsuits, eating more frogs, some mice, and finally trapping fish under an overhanging bank. Fewer berries grew there than Ellie thought likely, but they found some. The hot weather never abated, and it never rained. The ponds lay obviously lower than their maximum capacity but seemed to remain at the same level despite the heat.

No people ever appeared, and no large animals or birds seemed to visit the waterhole. Ellie caught herself wondering if the water was contaminated with something toxic. She put the fears away in the back of her mind and locked a mental door on them. If they did not drink this water, they would die anyway.

In planning the next stage of The Journey, they agreed to minimise the hill climbing over the Cotswolds, and set out due west towards the M5, which would then take them north and then northwest to Hereford. The moon had moved on to almost new moon phase, so they decided they could not walk at night and would operate during two sessions each day, with a long siesta.

The food supply was not great enough to build up provisions to carry away, but all the water bottles were filled. At dawn on 7 June 2040, they gave themselves quite a fanfare, hooting and singing as they set out again.

Miles M Hudson

Thursday 7 June 2040
The Smiths have been on the road for a fortnight.

Four miles before hitting the M5, they descended a winding road through pretty woodland into an equally pretty town: Dursley.

The sun was low in the sky, and the temperature seemed less deathly than previously. The light shone through trees that looked healthier than any they'd seen for a long time. The shadows lit up the landscape in glory, in what Ellie had once heard that photographers refer to as The Golden Hour.

Clara and Maggi sang a song about arriving at Hereford, and Ellie somewhat grumpily corrected them. 'Not yet, girls. Maybe tomorrow, but this is a different place.'

Dursley was abandoned. Through a few front windows, corpses – mostly skeletons – gave the impression of living in the stone-built homes. They sat on sofas seeming to watch TV or lay on kitchen floors as if they had just keeled over. The pretty, little church contained a congregation of skeletons, lined up in the pews as if they had all expired one Sunday, years before. Ellie looked up to the pulpit, half expecting to see a skeleton priest delivering a sermon. It was empty.

They set up for the night in the old police station. The place was free of bodies, and there were beds in the cells. They had no food to eat, banking on reaching Hereford the next day, so supper was half a litre of water each. They had not found any more water on their way to this town.

In the morning, they spotted an old orchard at the bottom of the wooded slope behind the police station. It was overgrown, but the plum trees were laden with ripe fruit. They gorged themselves on the sweet fruits and gathered as many as they could squeeze into the backpacks.

Clara and Maggi chased each other through the trees, smearing purple juice over each other's faces when they caught up. Their mothers sat happily together, eating one fruit after another. The adults played too, throwing the plum stones at a nearby tree to see who could hit it.

Ellie thought to herself how this was the first time Loshie had been happy and friendly since before they left Brighton. *Since before Luke was killed. I know how tough that can be.* She looked as her friend cheered a tree-hitting throw. Loshie's big grin displayed her normally bright white teeth, stained violet.

'Stop right there!'

Ellie's eyes jerked up to the sound of the voice. A group of men with rifles surrounded them. All the women had been so focussed on the fruit-picking and games that they had not seen the men until it was too late. There was no escape. These were well-fed, healthy men, with multiple guns, outnumbering them three to one.

Ellie leapt up and sprinted through the trees, towards her daughter. From behind a trunk, a large arm appeared horizontal in front of her and knocked Ellie flat on her back. She lay gasping, winded and disoriented. The man from behind the tree had rough stubble and big hands. He grabbed her collar and dragged her to her feet.

She could see Loshie had made it twenty yards away, but the orchard was fenced and so the bottleneck of exiting through the gap where a gate had once stood meant that Loshie was simply funnelled towards more men guarding that exit. She kicked one hard in the shins but was quickly bundled to the ground and subdued.

Clara and Maggi were dragged back to the point where Ellie stood, tightly gripped by her assailant. All three were then frogmarched down to the entrance gate were Loshie had also been lifted to standing. King Alfred barked loudly at the entire group from ten yards away. Nobody dared go closer to her, but she made no move either.

'Shut that dog up, Miss, or I will shoot it.'

He was talking to Loshie, who stood dumb. Ellie tried to shake herself free but was not released from the firm grips on her upper arms and wrists.

'She won't hurt you. Let me go to her, and I'll calm her down.'

The leader nodded to the guards, and they let go.

She stepped over to the barking dog, grabbed the scruff of her neck and shushed her. King Alfred was well-trained, and, despite the clear danger, she quietened down.

The men dragged them through woods, along well-trodden paths, up to the old golf club. Various poor-quality sheds and huts were scattered around a plateau that looked out and down to the first hole. They were taken straight into the main clubhouse building.

An emergency Kangaroo Court had been convened, and the four prisoners were thrust onto the floor of a slightly raised dining area. Their hands were tied with string, and they looked like some cheap Vaudeville act, about to entertain the golf club members with amateur escapology. King Alfred was locked into a cupboard in the hallway. Ellie was relieved to see some women present amongst the fifty or so townsfolk, including one acting as a guard at her immediate side.

The apparent bossman called them all to order and projected an image of Loshie picking plums. The video came with a soundtrack, and their gleeful chat about the fruit discovery was clear. Ellie stared. The footage looked like it had been taken by Maggi, filming her mother's antics.

She leaned down and whispered the question to Loshie's daughter. 'Did you make that video? It sounds like you're the one filming.'

Maggi looked stupefied. She shook her head but uttered no sound.

Years before, Ellie would have called the man's voice "posh". She imagined he might once have been the golf club president. 'I think the evidence we have seen here is clear. You are accused of stealing from our orchards. What do you have to say for yourselves?'

Loshie blurted out, 'We haven't stolen anything.'

Ellie put her hand out, took Loshie's and gave a little squeeze to silence her. 'We're so sorry. You're right, that video shows us collecting plums. We are terribly hungry – we haven't eaten in days. If we had known anybody was living here, we would never have taken your food. All we can do is apologise.'

The female guard slapped Ellie, to stop her talking. She complied immediately and bowed her head.

Unprompted and in unison, the crowd chanted, 'All strangers are danger,' several times.

The bossman proceeded to request the audience vote on the guilt or innocence of the party from Brighton. Many hands went up for each option, and he intoned that all those watching from home by Armulet should submit their votes too. Ellie looked around the room, but it wasn't obvious that anybody had an ArmuletLive video broadcast going.

The evidence was irrefutable, and they had not attempted to refute it. They were pronounced guilty, almost unanimously. Some of the men who had brought them in frogmarched them outside again and locked them in what had once been the pro shop of the golf club, to await sentencing. The minutes passed slowly.

Bizarrely, they were delivered a large plate of food to share after three hours in the hot, windowless building.

'What are they going to do to us, Mama?'

Loshie held her daughter close. 'I don't know, darling. We only took a few plums, so hopefully they won't hurt us.'

Clara had lost her smile, but she did not appear fearful.

Ellie shot Loshie a daggers look. 'You sent those thieves off the pier at our Kangaroo. What do you think they will do, here? Why should they spare us any more than we didn't spare those men?'

Loshie replied in hushed tones, arms around Maggi's head so she would not hear. 'They were killers. They didn't just steal a little food, they killed our friends.' She was right, but before Ellie could argue, the door unlocked.

Two women came in, and Loshie dropped to her knees. 'Please don't hurt us. My daughter is all I've got, and I'm all she's got.' She wailed and started sobbing.

The women cut the hand bindings. King Alfred was with them, wagging her tail and nosing Clara's skinny chest. 'We aren't going to hurt you. The Kangaroo has decreed that you must leave Dursley and never come back. We would have shared our food with you, but we cannot tolerate thieves in the village.' After a moment, she added, 'Sorry.'

'Oh, thank you, thank you.'

Ellie ignored Loshie's almost prostrate gushes and started quizzing the middle-aged, blonde woman who had spoken. 'How did you get that video footage of us? It looked like Maggi was filming it, but she says she didn't. And even if she had, how could you get hold of that from her Armulet?'

The woman was at the door, to lead them out, but she stopped and turned back. 'Have you heard of the audiopt system? We got it up and running about two years ago.'

'I saw the thing that the Hong Kong Pirates published. Loshie forwarded it to me, actually. Does it really work?'

'Perfectly. It took a few months for us to round up the locals who had been stealing food from people, but the audiopts made that easy. Once they knew they couldn't ever get away with anything, they stopped stealing and joined the community.'

The other woman said, 'Come on then, we've to escorts you to Stinchcombe bridge and makes sure you leave.'

They went out into the bright landscape. Hats and sunglasses went back on, and the six paused for a moment as their retinas had been washed out by the light. Even late afternoon sunshine was blinding in the cloudless June sky. Their backpacks waited for them, leaning against the pro shop wall.

The path down to Stinchcombe was a scar in the brown grass of what was once the eighteenth fairway, a hill down from the clubhouse towards the west. Ellie spotted the M5. Like a bigger scar across the sunburnt landscape, she thought the fairway path was a tendril, leading to a giant stalk in the distance.

'Can nobody evade the audiopt system then? What if you don't have your Armulet with you?'

'Other Armulets in the vicinity can pick up the nerve signals too. Plus, the infonetwork towers have the technology built in too. When the Armulet company invented it, they made sure it was foolproof.'

'But that's so much information. Armulets don't have that

much storage space, do they? There's no way they could record all the sights and sounds everybody nearby sees and hears. The storage would fill up in minutes, surely?'

'I don't know the technical details, but I know we had to set up some of the computers at the old GCHQ building in Cheltenham. Lots of villages have commandeered some of the old servers to do all the audiopt work for them.'

Ellie stumbled, her foot caught on a bramble stalk across the path. The path went through a fence of wooden posts, and they continued along a shaded narrow lane. It passed well-spaced houses.

'But that's still too much information. Even if the computers could handle it, who's going to watch it all so that you can actually catch criminals? I mean there'll just be a ton of irrelevant stuff on it as people walk around the town or watch a videostory or whatever.'

'Leave the poor woman alone, Ellie.' Loshie had perked up no end when she realised that they were simply going to be sent on their way, having been given a decent meal by the Dursley authorities, such as they were.

Ellie stopped speaking for nearly five minutes but could no longer hold in the questions bursting to get out. 'Sorry, I hope you don't mind me asking all this? It just seems unbelievable. I mean how did you all catch us in the orchard? Why was anybody watching our lives?'

The blonde woman smiled. 'It's not a problem. The whole thing can be pretty disturbing, especially if you're as old as me.' She looked pointedly at Ellie. 'Who would have thought, when we were growing up, that we would choose to put in place a system that monitors every second of our lives and publishes it online for anyone to view? There's software that monitors all the feeds, and it has algorithms to raise concerns. Then we have a couple of our community who work at the Doughnut – the GCHQ place. They look at all the feeds the software suggests, and they message us with reports about what might need acting on. The computer caught you in the orchard and raised a flag, and our friend sent it through to William. I don't think he ever told you his name. That's the man who ran the Kangaroo today; he's this year's Dursley mayor.'

'Wait, did you say, "anyone can view"?'

'This is it.' The second woman stopped and pointed in front to where the road went on a bridge over the motorway. 'We've to see you crosses that bridge, and to tells you that the Kangaroo won't be so generous in our sentencing if you returns to Dursley. Please stay west of the motorway. This side is all Dursley.'

Loshie questioned, 'We're going to walk north on the motorway. Is that alright? We're headed to Hereford, so we won't be back here again.'

'That's fine,' the blonde woman smiled. She turned to Ellie. 'I don't know what you think of the audiopts, but Hereford has had them for years. They were one of the first to set up the system.'

'Goodbye,' the terse woman dismissed them, and the two watched as the Brightonians descended to the motorway carriageway.

They saw the women turn and leave and then grouped in the shade under the bridge to discuss things.

'That's incredible. Those audiopts are just extraordinary.'

'Yes, look, that's what I've been on about. I told you Hereford was safe. We must just be on our best behaviour though, so they don't turn us away. Like these morons.' She waved up towards the golf club on the hill.

'I can't get my head around it. I mean the tech is mad enough in the first place but think about the ethics. Everything you see and hear published online for anyone to view.'

Loshie laughed. 'Yes, maybe we don't want to go to Hereford after all.'

Maggi was confused. 'Why aren't we going to Hereford, Mama? You said it was the best place.'

'I'm joking. Sorry, my love, of course we're going to Hereford.' The sun was at the horizon, and the blue sky was darkening and slipping towards purple. 'But there's virtually no moon tonight, so let's sleep here and head off at first light.'

Maggi tapped her Armulet several times and scowled.

The Times of Malthus

'Mama, this says it'll be quicker to walk two hours to a river and take a boat.'

'Show us.'

Maggi pulled up the routemapper projection which did indeed recommend heading to Sharpness docks and taking a boat upriver. 'It says if we catch the tide at eight in the morning, it'll get us up to here.' She waved at the map, which moved and zoomed to show a bend in the Severn several miles north of Sharpness. 'Look, it says in like half an hour. And then it's only eight hours walk from there. But if we walk up the motorway from here, then it's two days walk.'

Ellie shrugged. 'Good research, Maggi. Sounds better than all that walking. It should be cooler on the water. Do you think there'll be any boats there, though?'

Loshie's Armulet brought up a satellite image of the docks. It was from before the Times, but there was a marina with what looked like fifty or sixty boats. 'They can't all be sunk.'

'Do you remember Brighton Marina?'

'Yes, but they were the boats of rich people. These look tiny. I can't see people being incensed by the wealth of these and torching them all. Plus, we're in the countryside, there wouldn't have been enough population to even have a mob here.'

They decided to walk to the river before night fell properly, so they could sort out a boat and be ready for the morning tide. The clincher for this plan was the notion that the riverside would be cooler. The river Severn was so immense that they assumed it couldn't possibly have run dry. If it had, they'd walk across, and it would be a short cut.

Miles M Hudson

Friday 8 June 2040
One day's journey left to Hereford.

By the time they reached the docks at Sharpness, the air was thick and muggy. The river stank. The smell was overpowering, and, inviting as the cool water of the harbour appeared, only King Alfred took a dip.

The others lay down in the shade of bushes that had taken hold, breaking through paving slabs outside the shipyard office.

The water was undrinkably salty – at this point, the river estuary was almost at the sea.

The heat had not diminished, even hours after dark, and the fetid air made it almost impossible to sleep. Twice, Ellie got up from her camp mat and wandered around the docks, bored with her wakefulness.

It was dark with the moon absent, and, with no knowledge of the local population, she feared using her Armulet light. Even the dimmest glow would be like a bright beacon in the intense blackness.

Once her eyes got used to the dark, Ellie could move around slowly by the starlight but was still wary of falling in the harbour. The dark water was distinct from the marginally lighter grey of the concrete dockside, but the range of trip hazards there might be in an old loading dock numbered more than Ellie could count. She pictured each shadow being some new danger.

On her second round of the abandoned warehouses and boat sheds, Ellie walked further around to reach the adjacent pleasure boat marina. About thirty long thin wooden boats rocked gently in front of her. She froze at the sight of a light on one canalboat. She felt sweat running into her eyes and held her breathing as quiet and slow as she could.

Having crept forwards to investigate, Ellie found the boat lit but the only sound was the lapping of the water against the hull. *Are they asleep? But why is the light on?*

She waited a long time, before edging forward to try and sneak a look through the window to see what might be going on inside. The boat was empty. It looked like it had not been used for many years. Leaf litter and an old bird's nest on the floor of the galley convinced her nobody was using the little boat.

Looking around, she worked out that the light had been left switched on, and the solar cells covering the roof kept the batteries fully charged. This boat would be lit at all times.

She moved inside the next boat and surreptitiously shone her Armulet torch on the battery dial in the main cabin. It was also fully charged. *Well, we won't be out of power at least.*

The cupboards were bare, and, in most cases, their doors hung open, highlighting that they had been searched by scavengers probably many times before. No food was likely to be found on these boats.

Ellie's wanderings had been to try and alleviate insomnia. She was now excited that the boat plan was actually going to work. She had only been onto two of the boats, and they were definitely abandoned, and ready to sail.

At the first inkling of dawn light, the plan crashed back to Earth. The boats could not be moved onto the big river. The marina connected back out to the narrow Sharpness canal, but even if all the locks still worked, that would be slower than walking. At the front end, where the others remained sleeping under bushes by Sharpness shipyard, the harbour gates onto the Severn were huge. They looked like they'd need some mechanical system to open them.

She stood on top of the angled wooden gates that kept the river from the shipyard and wondered if they might have just wasted time on a long detour. The approaching new day was already amplifying the stifling heat. The humidity was suffocating. Ellie felt sweat rolling down her spine and worried about rehydration. If food and water continued to be scarce, lost time could be dangerous. Southwest, out along the Bristol Channel, the sky was dense with cloud.

As the light brightened, Ellie started to poke around inside the old tin buildings on the dockside. There was much paraphernalia of the business of loading and unloading ships, but nothing obviously useful, and certainly no food.

The marina and harbour both contained the same water as the river, too brackish to drink. *So, I've spent the whole night awake and found nothing. Once again, I'm going to be exhausted and hungry and thirsty. Brilliant.* If the humidity could only bring rain, they would survive a few more days.

Ellie stopped dead as she lifted a thin plastic sheet. It concealed a plastic-hulled boat, just like the ones the Essex Raiders attacked with. She could operate this boat, and it sat on a wheeled trailer, so they could get it over to the river.

'Have you found some food, Mummy?'

Clara stood in the doorway of the boat shed, a tiny silhouette against the dawn light outside, not much taller than the fluffy dog silhouette beside her. Ellie pulled the sheet completely clear and stepped over to her daughter. 'Not yet, but I have found us a super fast boat to get us upriver quickly. We'll be in Hereford really soon.'

Switching the electric motor connections to ON, to check on the battery power, Ellie's face fell. This boat was dead. Loshie and Maggi appeared at the threshold too, and Ellie explained all she had found. She finished with the idea that they might be able to transfer fully charged canalboat batteries into this boat, the one they could get into the river.

All four worked together to pack up their camp and then try to get the boat working. The big batteries were heavy, and the women suffered weakness from lack of food. To carry them 200 yards, from the pleasure boat marina around to the shipyard, took more than half an hour per battery. However, the engineering was simple. After searching out the right kind of spanner – the boat had its own toolbox – disconnecting and reconnecting the two marine batteries was easy. The plan worked, and the boat's propellers spun silently in the air atop the trailer.

Ellie's heart skipped at the thought they might make it to the destination she had thought was just a fantasy. She slid down the wall by the shed's big doorway to sit and breathed deeply. Despite Clara's hugging arm around her neck, Ellie felt she might pass out from the exertions. They had pushed themselves hard and fast to get the boat to work, but that had taken the last ounces of strength from her.

'Let's go then!' Loshie said. 'If we can roll this over to the river, we'll be in Hereford by sundown.' She was excited, bobbing from foot to foot.

Ellie didn't respond at first, tipping her head back where she sat against the wall. Then everything seemed to fade to black.

The next thing she knew, Loshie was leaning over her and shaking her, while Clara shrieked, her eyes wide and her face pale with worry and fear.

'Mummy, Mummy!' Ellie came round, with Loshie shaking her, and Clara yelping.

Ellie shook her head groggily. 'What's happened?'

Loshie had been bending over Ellie and stood upright again, placing a hand on her chest. 'Oh, God, I thought we'd lost you. I couldn't imagine how we'd get the boat in the water if something happened to you.'

Ellie felt woozy and couldn't understand what was being said to her. Clara's thin arms back around her neck were the only comfort she could make sense of, and she clung on to them.

They forced her to drink a little of the harbour water, but it made her feel sick. The ever-rising temperature did not help, but when they splashed water on her to cool her, Ellie felt a little more clear-headed. King Alfred licked her face occasionally, which pepped her up too. After thirty minutes, they helped her up and set about wheeling the boat outside.

The Armulet route advisor had suggested they should catch the tide from Sharpness at 8.09am. Ellie's sickness meant that it was forty minutes after that by the time they manhandled the metal framed trailer to the riverbank. The tide would be rushing up, albeit slightly less forcefully than if they had hit the 8.09am target time.

There was no slipway, but they did not need to save the trailer; they just needed to get the vessel in the water. If the trailer sank underneath, so be it. The sky darkened as if warning them that they would never manage it.

Facing the river, Clara and Maggi sat in the boat, clinging on to ropes and plastic handles, and Ellie and Loshie ran the trailer at the water's edge from ten yards away. A drop off the bank took it down and out of the mothers' hands, but the wheels stuck in the mud. They waded in to float the boat off the metal frame and, after a little push further out, they jumped in over the gunnel. The boat floated forward, and Loshie engaged the motors.

Ellie shouted over the rushing sound of the water, 'Woah, take it easy or we'll all fall out.'

Everyone gripped on tightly, and they laughed at the excitement of Loshie's initial burst of speed. Reaching the middle of the wide waterway, the incoming tide caught the little dinghy, and they shot upriver. Everyone still had a tight hold, but Loshie petrified them all. She refused to disengage the motors, despite the rushing Severn tide moving at a frightening pace on its own.

'Loshie, turn off the motors! Please! It's too dangerous, you'll kill us all!'

She ignored Ellie, and the boat bounced and leapt over the slightest waves. Each turn of just a few degrees sent their stomachs lurching. Only when Maggi started crying for her mother to slow down did Loshie rein back the throttle. She did not switch off the motors, but the new breakneck pace felt safer in comparison. King Alfred shrank down into the bottom alongside Clara. Maggi clung to her mother's leg.

The sky remained dark, and the mugginess felt crushing. Despite the increasing breeze, also pushing them faster upriver, the atmosphere seemed airless. Ellie sucked in breath, as if oxygen was running out.

Rain began falling, and they all looked to the sky in wonder. Maggi lay out a tarpaulin sheet from her backpack to try and catch as much drinking water as possible. Nobody waited for that though. They licked the giant, lumpy raindrops from the bottom of the boat almost as soon as they landed. With the splashing of salty river water into it, this was not refreshing. Clara sucked at her shirt, and Ellie tried to catch water in the Palace Pier tin mug she had carried all the way from Brighton.

A huge crack of thunder seemed to coincide exactly with a

flash of lighting that hit an old electricity pylon on the shore. They were in a dangerous position, the only large object on the river, and the storm had erupted directly overhead. The wind speed increased and began to swirl wildly. Gusts twisted the boat this way and that, churning the water into a roiling maelstrom.

The little dinghy rocketed upriver. Ellie pictured it as a combination of a log flume and a rollercoaster from the old theme parks. Loshie clung to the steering wheel, wrestling it around each bend of the river. These soon got much narrower, and by the time they scooted past a riverside pub at Epney, Ellie had grabbed onto the wheel too to try and help keep the dinghy from crashing into the banks.

The river narrowed, and the bends became tighter. The wind blew harder, and the gusts twisted more wildly. At times, Ellie felt like she and Loshie were pulling in different directions. They shouted at each other, but their voices were whipped away. Lightning and thunder continued to crash around them, as if the storm were chasing the boat upriver.

Ellie pulled at the throttle to slow them down more, but Loshie thrust her away. 'Get off! I'll outrun this storm, and we'll get to Hereford today.' Loshie's hair flew around her head, and her eyes blazed.

'No, Loshie, this is too dangerous. STOP!' As loud as Ellie could shout, the wild wind flung her words into the sky. King Alfred barked, but this sound was lost too.

Loshie kicked Ellie in the thigh to knock her down into the front of the boat. She landed on top of Clara, and they hugged each other with one arm each, whilst gripping handholds with the other. The two cowered down in the front, as Loshie sped faster around tighter bends. The boat skidded and skipped across the choppy surface, regularly lifting off and crashing down again.

They surged around such a tight bend that Loshie overcorrected the steering and the boat spun completely sideways to both the current and the wind. A wave crashed against the side of the hull, and its momentum, together with the wind, capsized the boat.

Ellie hit the water hard and went under. She could see only

darkness and felt like her lungs were empty. She was terrified her next breath might be all water. The maternal instinct kicked in, and Ellie strained her eyes to look around for Clara. The darkness was blurry.

When she surfaced, the angry dark skies continued to assault her senses. She inhaled hard through her open mouth. The water tasted fresh, not salty. She gulped a few mouthfuls down.

Ellie spun in the water, screaming out, 'Clara! Clara! Where are you?'

She heard a voice. There was no telling who it was, or what they were saying. She swam towards the upturned boat, the apparent source of the plaintive sound. Clinging to the rope at the prow, Ellie found her daughter. She gripped the rope too, and they held tightly on to each other. There was no sign of Loshie or Maggi or King Alfred. The water swirled and dragged around Ellie's legs, and she clung on tightly to the rope and to Clara, doing her very best to keep the girl's head above the water surface.

After what seemed like forever, the storm quietened a little. The rain continued, but the thunder and lightning were gone, and the wind dropped to a gusting breeze. The boat floated close to the shore, and Ellie's feet touched bottom. She could not release her grip on the rope – her fingers had become frozen, clenched like claws.

Clara began to move on her own and Ellie realised that she had reached her depth as well. She was so exhausted that she could not talk to Clara at all. For the second time that day, the world darkened and closed in, and Ellie passed out.

The Times of Malthus
Saturday 9 June 2040
The end of The Journey.

Ellie woke up with her head dangling down, about four feet above a smooth, brown surface sliding past her eyes. She felt sick as the bouncing kept banging her stomach on a hard surface. She was strapped down and could barely move.

The sound of Clara crying made Ellie turn her head to the side as much as possible. Beside her, a large rolled up blanket felt solid against her shoulder, and it obscured her view of anything else further forward. Looking the other way, she could see a rotating cartwheel dangerously close to her nose, but above that, next to her prone body, all their luggage was also strapped down.

'Hey! What's going on?'

'Mummy, where are you? I'm stuck.'

The cart pulled up to a standstill, and Ellie heard the sound of someone dismounting. Black cargo pants above work boots walked into her line of sight and then passed to the rear of the wagon.

'Hey! Who are you? Where are we?'

A young man's voice replied, 'Just a moment there. I'll untie you, hold on.'

The straps across Ellie's body loosened and she was able to move free and sit up. There were two fully wrapped rolls of blanket. They were clearly in the shape of people, two small bodies, wrapped up tight, including the whole head hidden in the material. Beyond these two shapes, Clara had also sat up and was crying. Ellie leapt down to the ground and moved along beside the cart to lift Clara down into a big hug.

She turned to see the driver standing at the rear, one hand still resting awkwardly on the strap fastening. 'My name's Tony.' He was tall and thin, with a straggly, dark beard and shaggy hair. 'Sorry, I didn't mean to scare you, but I didn't want you to roll off the back whilst we went along. I couldn't wake you, so I just had to tie you down.'

She couldn't process what the man was saying – Ellie's brain was whirling. From the front bench, where the cart driver would sit, King Alfred barked, as if to corroborate the man's story.

Her heart leapt at the sound of her dog. 'Alfie! You're alive.' She didn't have the strength to move forward towards her but beamed a smile at King Alfred.

Tony stepped around to the same side as Ellie. Still confused, she faltered backwards a step, clinging on to her daughter.

He stopped and held up one hand. 'It's OK, I won't hurt you. I'm sorry, your friends were dead already when I pulled you two out of the water.' Ellie's mind whirled again. *Dead already? Already when? Dead?*

He paused a moment, and then changed the palm held up to just be his forefinger. He waved his other hand at the Armulet, held on his forearm in a beautiful leather vambrace.

Off to the side, a video projection showed a rocky riverbank, with the boat Loshie had piloted, upside-down and caught in an eddy in the shallows. The point of view of the recording looked down at what were clearly the same black trousers as the mystery wagoner, knee deep in the water.

They watched as he carried Clara's limp body out and up to a grassy patch in an abandoned beer garden of the Severn Bore Inn. He lay her down and ran down to the water again to pull Ellie out of the river. She was also unconscious, and he kept calling out over the howling wind, to try and wake them. He felt their wrists and put his ear to their mouths.

'What are you showing us? What is this?'

He looked away from the moving images with a slight frown, which then vanished. 'Ah, sorry, where are you from? This is my audiopt recording from about an hour ago when I found you.'

Ellie's head was still fuzzy, and she shook it to try and clear out the cotton wool fog.

'Um, the audiopts?' he ventured. The man was about eighteen years old. 'Where you can see and hear what I saw and heard earlier. I'm wanting to show you that I'm not a danger, that I helped you.'

'OK.' Ellie understood but was non-committal. She wasn't

sure where they were being taken, or why she had been tied up.

'I'm sorry about your fricnds.'

'What do you mean?' So much confusing information was coming so fast, she had no idea what was real.

He again gestured at his Armulet with a practised movement, and the recording restarted from where he had paused the playback. The next time he had headed down from the pub garden to the boat, he had grabbed the rope at the front and tied it to a metal rail by the concrete steps down to the water. They watched his viewpoint as he lowered himself right down to the water surface and heaved up the boat to look underneath. It was almost completely dark underneath, but Maggi's head floated right up to him, clearly lifeless. They saw him drag her body out before dropping the boat back down.

Ellie's hand fluttered up to cover her heart, and she gasped. 'Oh, God, no.' She tried to deny the recording. 'This isn't real?' Her voice raised to a sharp command. 'Tell me it's not!'

Back up the steps, he had tried to resuscitate Maggi for more than ten minutes. At no point had she responded in any way, and Ellie felt suddenly sorry for the man who had struggled so heroically.

Clara cried at the images of the loss of her friend. In the projection, he proceeded to head back down to the water and found Loshie's body, also under the capsized boat. Ellie wailed and waved one hand towards the projection, in a clear gesture of denial, as if she could will it out of existence.

He had made no less effort to revive Loshie, but the outcome was the same. The two of them must have been trapped under the hard plastic boat, unable to shift it, or maybe had been knocked unconscious in the boat accident.

The playback disappeared, and she looked back to the man. He stroked his beard and said nothing. He waited silently while Ellie and Clara hugged and sobbed.

It felt to Ellie in that moment as if her entire world, everything she had ever known, had been washed away by the storm. Looking down at the top of her daughter's head, thoughts crashed around. *How will we survive now? How can we go on?*

Hereford was Loshie's dream – I don't even know if I want to go there now. How will I keep you safe?

Out loud, she demanded, 'Where are you taking us anyway?'

'Highnam. It's my Kangaroo, my village. It's just up the road here, we're literally only fifty metres from the Spokesperson's house.'

Ellie frowned again. 'But why?'

The man pulled his head back and stared at her. 'Because you need help. You nearly drowned, and it looks to me like neither of you have eaten for a while.'

'So why tie us up?'

He stared again, and then pointed to the luggage strapped on the flatbed of his cart. 'Like I said, to keep you safe. There's no sides on this thing. You were out cold, so I didn't want to lose anybody, or any of your bags, off the sides as we bumped up the track. The old A40 is pretty smooth from Minsterworth up to Highnam Court, but the turn off into the village is just a dirt track, and it's pretty bumpy at the moment.'

Ellie looked all around. The man had waved in various directions to support his comments, but all she could see was a bumpy, muddy track through thin woods. Up ahead, the trees looked to disappear, and she could make out a couple of houses across a large grass area. One of the two horses snorted in the heat, and King Alfred barked in agreement. Ellie gazed at King Alfred, who seemed perfectly at ease with the stranger. She contemplated Clara's snotty nose and made a decision.

'OK, come on then, let's go.' She looked the man in the eyes and followed up: 'And thank you.' They climbed up onto the wooden bench at the front and made King Alfred jump over to ride on the back.

The townsfolk of Highnam insisted that Ellie and Clara recuperate in their medical centre. The man they called 'Doctor' quickly gave them the all clear. All that he insisted upon was that they stay inside and eat and drink small amounts regularly. Ellie did not believe he was medically trained, but she did feel much better than she had in days.

The care and generosity of their hosts overwhelmed her. She found the constant attention and meal deliveries so out of synch with their previous lifestyle that she was unsettled all the time.

Visions of Loshie came to Ellie often, sometimes the dead body from the audiopt projection, sometimes the angry Loshie from under the motorway bridge and, very occasionally, the happy, bookish friend from years before. It was a real struggle to reconcile the happy girl Ellie had grown up with and the mercurial, troubled woman that had driven the boat so hard it killed her.

At Maggi and Loshie's deaths, Clara initially stopped talking again, just as when Wayne had died. However, the attention they received from all their visitors at the medical centre in Highnam was so kind that her beaming smile returned in just a few days.

King Alfred looked healthier too, and she was allowed to roam around outside. However, it was cooler inside, and she mostly stayed in Ellie and Clara's room.

Under doctor's orders, mother and daughter were stuck inside all the time. At first, Ellie feared this was a ruse, and they were actually prisoners. However, the visitors and food bearers were faultlessly kind, and Ellie could not maintain her belief that they were in danger. On the second night, she tested the front door of the building, and it was unlocked. They could leave should they wish to.

It became increasingly clear that the people of Highnam were not in the least concerned about strangers arriving in the village. They were genuinely concerned though for the Smith women and their struggles and loss on the river. The doctor suggested to Ellie that the villagers could not help but feel guilt at the deaths that had occurred to visitors on their river. She found this difficult to process, as the last decade in Brighton had been spent wary of all newcomers.

Tony, the bearded wagon driver visited them every day. He was the kindest of them all, and Ellie took an instant liking to him. He worked with his father, creating leatherwork items. Simple belts, Armulet straps, bags; their range was large, and every item was expertly made and beautiful. He gave Clara a delicate wristband, which she insisted on showing off to everyone she met, whether they had seen it before or not.

Loshie and Maggi were buried in the graveyard of the old church on the Highnam Court estate. With the excessive summer heat, the villagers did this almost immediately, whilst Ellie and Clara were in the first throes of recovery from their ordeal in the river Severn. Tony apologised that the town elders had insisted on burying them so quickly. He offered that they could organise a memorial service at the graveside.

Ellie was not sure she would have wanted to attend a funeral for them. She remembered the wild look in Loshie's eyes, as she careened the boat across the stormy waters. She felt that she had actually lost her friend years before, but Ellie still choked up when Tony played her the audiopt recording of the burial.

There was no kind of service during the interment, but those involved were very respectful and treated the small bodies of a lost mother and daughter with true dignity. She wondered if she felt more choked up at the loss of Loshie, or because of the wonderful people they had discovered in Highnam.

Tony taught Clara how to access the audiopt recordings on her Armulet, and one evening, Ellie watched it again with her, just the two of them.

'You remember your father's cairn of stones on the beach?'

'Of course I do, Mummy. Selsey's in there too.'

'Yes. We always like to look after people even after they die.'

'And dogs too.'

Ellie smiled. 'You're right, dogs too.' She called King Alfred over from the big dog bed she'd been given. Mother and daughter stroked her for a minute, all three hugging, and the humans buried their faces in her thick ginger fur.

'So, the video of the people putting Loshie and Maggi in the ground is their way of looking after them, now that they're gone. A lot of people in Brighton died with nobody to look after them afterwards. That's why there were so many bodies in the houses and in the streets.'

'I know, Mummy.' Clara sounded confused as to why her

mother would explain something so obvious.

'Good, but what I mean is that burying them was the best thing we could do for them here. And I'm glad the nice people here did it so carefully.' She paused watching her daughter's face. 'What do you think about losing Maggi and Loshie?'

The young girl thought for a moment before answering. 'We haven't lost them, have we? That place must be nearby – I saw Tony in the video. We can go and visit them, can't we?'

Ellie paused again. Nodding, she replied, 'Yes, of course we can, but you know that they're…'. Her throat seized up and wouldn't say the last word.

Clara had been staring at the paused projection of the gravediggers standing by the two fresh mounds, and she looked up at Ellie. 'Dead? Yes, I know.' The girl's voice was wistful, and a tear rolled down her cheek. 'Many people die, but we can still visit them.'

After a moment, she launched into a plan: 'When we go there, I'm going to tell Maggi all about Tony and my new bracelet.' Holding up her hand, she pulled the leather wristband to show off the thin strands again.

Clara studied her mother's face. 'I'll miss Maggi, but I'll still visit her and talk to her. She just can't talk back to me.' They squeezed each other's hand.

Ellie's cheeks poured with tears, but she smiled through them without speaking. Clara hugged her mother to comfort her, but she had missed the point. The source of Ellie's distress was the matter-of-fact approach that Clara took to death. The young girl had cried a little, but she cherished the happy times she and Maggi had had together, and her beaming smile continued to light up the room. Through the Times of Malthus, Clara had learnt to enjoy even the tiniest good moment.

When the doctor was satisfied that they had regained strength enough to be discharged, Tony took them for another short ride on the wagon. He pulled up in front of a boarded-up house in the woods.

It was at the top of an incline, with a long slope behind that fell away down to a stream. The L-shaped house had a fenced off garden in front and an overgrown patio in two parts. The long, folding glass doors had a large area of paving slabs outside, and then to the side, there was an ornamental paved area with sculpted slabs forming patterns. The remainder of the space they could see from the wagon was scrubby grass.

'Everyone has agreed that we'd like you to stay here. We can offer you everything that Hereford can, and we need good people like you to join our community. We'd like to offer you this house to live in. Of course, we'll help you clean it out and fix it up, so it will be lovely to live in.'

Ellie turned. Once again, she found herself staring at Tony, non-plussed. He was wise beyond his years, but she still marvelled at the idea that an entire village had left an eighteen-year-old to offer a free house to strangers.

Ellie's gaze shifted to Clara and King Alfred, who nosed through long grass around the trees just outside the old fence around the house. Clara picked some purple flowers and held them to King Alfred's nose for the dog to smell the bouquet. Ellie turned a full circle to take in the entire surroundings. Her mind circled around apparitions of Wayne, the beach hut, Jude and Roisin, the Palace Pier, Loshie and Maggi, with Clara and King Alfred scampering between them all.

The Times of Malthus
Sunday 11 November 2040
The Times of Malthus are over.

Blue sky over The Lake made for a delightful picnic scene in the grounds of Highnam Court. Ellie and Clara sat on a blanket on the grass and watched King Alfred chasing along the bank, barking at fish.

They had refurbished the old farmhouse into a lovely home. The community they had joined could easily have been the sort that Jude and Roisin would have espoused in a *Guardian* story about some novel commune.

It was a warm Sunday afternoon, but Ellie still insisted that Clara wear a thick jumper. Partly, it had been a present from Tony's mother, who was a whizz with the knitting needles. Mostly though, Clara's skinny frame was difficult to keep warm. She was regularly cold and suffered chills easily.

They had chosen to picnic by The Lake as a prelude to heading up into Highnam Court manor house for a special Kangaroo meeting. The town held a Kangaroo every Sunday, but they had been told this one was special.

The manor house's old orangery had been converted into a large conservatory café area years before, when the place was open to the public as a visitor attraction. This was the venue Highnam had chosen for its weekly Kangaroos, and the town Spokesperson brought them all to order.

He was an old man. Ellie figured he would have been grey and hunched long before the Bitness Revelations. 'Friends.' He held his short arms open in welcome to the assembled members of the community. 'Thank you for attending today, whether in person, or via Armulet. We are indeed on the cusp of something very special for our troubled world.'

The crowd seemed tense. Ellie sensed its desire to applaud, but nobody dared start it off. The Spokesperson deftly diffused the anxious atmosphere. 'Luckily, there is not too much for us to do except join in the momentous ideas coming from Jerusalem today. Let us all take pride in being a part of a new safer world.'

The audiopts surveillance system had become widely enough adopted that it was possible to propose a new global constitution. A peace conference hosted from Jerusalem aimed to bring the world's surviving communities together. The proposed constitution was to consist of five simple and deliberately vague tenets.

Bitness had taught the world that the only way to avoid corruption by those in power was to keep the population that they influenced small. To ensure this, the peace conference had, paradoxically, come up with a constitution for all Kangaroos across the planet to adopt.

The wizened, old Spokesperson waved a hand to engage a giant projection above his head, against the backdrop of most of one wall.

The people of Highnam sat in the folding chairs of the old orangery café and watched the ArmuletLive video call with just over 800 communities connected from around the entire planet. Clara sat on Ellie's knee, and she whispered in the girl's ear to explain what was happening.

There was to be no vote on the contents of the Covenants of Jerusalem. Either each community would sign up to them, or it wouldn't. However, the five rules had been drafted in such generalised language that signing up did not really hold that community to implementation in any specific way. They would just do their best to follow them in whatever way they interpreted as best for their own community.

1. Nothing will be hidden or secret.

Ellie whispered in Clara's ear, 'That's what the audiopt thing is. The Armulets and the infonetwork monitor what you see and hear, and they publish it so anyone can see. So, you can't hide anything. In the past, people did all sorts of secret business deals that stole money from other people.'

Clara nodded silently, but Ellie knew that the notions of both business and money were outside her scope of experience.

The Times of Malthus

2. Everyone will act for the benefit of all.

The young girl contributed herself after Covenant 2 was read aloud. 'That's what I do. I always try to help people.'

'Good. Now, everyone will always be out to help each other.'

'Not like Loshie.'

Ellie turned Clara so she could look in her face. 'Why do you say that?'

'She wasn't always nice.'

Ellie tried to pursue the questioning, but Clara offered no specifics, and she was staring up at the video projection, engrossed in the strange business of adopting a new system of government. Their discussions meant that Covenant 3 had passed, and they were now onto number four.

3. Actions will be judged by everyone.
4. Local population groups will be self-determining.

'So that means that meetings like this will decide what we'll do here in Highnam. Nobody from outside will tell us what to do, and we can make our own rules.'

'Can I make a rule?'

'Sure. Well, actually, only if the Kangaroo meeting agrees. Everyone in the village will have to vote on it to make sure we're all happy with your rule. That way it's fair and nobody is taking control unfairly.'

'My rule is that everybody must be nice to everyone else.'

'Ha, OK, I'm pretty sure we'll be able to get that one through the meeting. I mean that's pretty much Covenant 2, remember?'

'Oh, yeah!' Clara grinned at her own error.

5. No influence over more than 10,000 persons will be permitted.

'That means that any village or town can't be bigger than ten-thousand people. If you get too big, then some people don't know other people, and that often means they don't care so much about each other. If we limit the number of people in Highnam, we'll be able to make sure everybody is nice to everybody else.'

'Well, the audiopts will make sure anyway, won't they?'

'Um, yes, I suppose they will. I don't think they can keep track of that many people though, so we have to help by making sure everyone in our Kangaroo knows everyone else. Much harder to be mean to someone if you know them.'

As they walked back past the graveyard, Ellie smiled at the thought of lapsed Buddhist Loshie buried in a traditional Christian burial ground.

That morning, they had headed down to where the river Severn, much narrower up near Highnam, passed under the old A40 road bridge. Ellie and Clara had built a mini cairn in memory of Wayne, a replica of the one on Brighton beach, complete with the side bulge of stones for Selsey. From here, the river snaked down to the Severn estuary and out into the Irish Sea. That connected around the coastline to the waters where Wayne had been lost.

The adoption of the Covenants of Jerusalem by Highnam Kangaroo meant that they needed to formalise the surveillance monitoring of the audiopts. They agreed they would appoint two technicians and two sifters – monitors of the audiopt feeds. The surveillance system's computing power was based in a basement server hall of the old GCHQ building in Cheltenham called the Doughnut. The technicians would keep the computers functioning, and the sifters would watch video footage to keep track of crimes and misdemeanours in the village.

The townsfolk voted to support these four workers by supplying them with food and other materials, so they could work twelve-hour shifts to keep on top of the continuous recordings from all around Highnam. The audiopt instruction manual came with details of built-in algorithms that could pre-sift the audiopt feeds, so the work would be possible with just four members of the community at any given time.

They chose to establish these roles as annual appointments and voted in two of the five volunteers who had stepped forward to take on the jobs. Only two members of the population had any experience of fixing and programming computers and they were pressured into agreeing to go to the Doughnut as well.

A festival mood ran through the Kangaroo, celebrating a new constitution to live by and a strengthened commitment to the surveillance that would protect them all. A future without secrets had begun.

* * *

Read about the audiopt surveillance society we built, in *2089* and *The Mind's Eye* by Miles M Hudson.

* * *

Other novels by M M Hudson include *The Cricketer's Corpse* and *The Kidney Killer*.

* * *

Printed in Great Britain
by Amazon